Elemental Relics

Craig van den Heever

ELEMENTAL RELICS

BOOK ONE OF THE ELEMENTAL RELICS SAGA

CRAIG VAN DEN HEEVER

Thank you for stepping into the world of Elemental Relics
May the elements guide you, and may your story be just as powerful

TABLE OF CONTENTS

CHAPTER 1

The Beginning

Early morning mist cloaked the horizon of East County Grove, softening the contours of the landscape and dulling the once-vivid fragrance of springtime dandelions. The blossoms, vibrant and sweet mere weeks ago, had already surrendered to the relentless passage of time. Maximillion Haywood—known simply as Max to his friends and family—sat hunched on the edge of his bed, his right arm throbbing with a persistent, searing pain. Tears pricked at his eyes, and he clenched a damp dishcloth between his teeth, its threads soaked from the night before. Somehow, he had anticipated the agony to come. A subtle ache in his bicep had hinted at this unbearable torment, a forewarning that had haunted him in the darkness.

The pain erupted and vanished as abruptly as it had come, leaving no trace but a lingering confusion. It was as if a fiery current had surged through his arm, from shoulder to fingertips, only to disappear without explanation. The doctors at East County Medical Research Centre were baffled, their arsenal of tests—ultrasounds, IVPs, X-rays—yielding no answers. Theories ranged from increased blood flow to nerve-related issues, but none were definitive. Max had no interest in seeking out a neurosurgeon, brushing off his mother Charlotte's insistence on the matter. Despite their wealth, he doubted anyone could succeed where the research centre's advanced specialists had failed. At fourteen, nearing fifteen, Max wanted his autonomy respected. After all, he knew what it was like to lose someone. His father, Brad Haywood, had disappeared years ago, leaving his mother to carry the weight of grief alone.

The sudden swing of his bedroom door startled him, momentarily shifting his focus from the dull throb in his arm. He leapt to his feet, the luxurious king-sized bed behind him a stark reminder of his family's wealth. Positioned squarely in the centre of his meticulously decorated room, the bed was draped in silk sheets and flanked by solid oak furniture. Above it, a grand chandelier hung low, projecting delicate patterns across the room. The bedroom, much like the rest of the Haywood estate, was a testament to opulence—a museum of untouchable beauty. Housemaids and butlers navigated its halls with the cautious precision of tightrope walkers, ever mindful of Charlotte Haywood's unyielding expectations. Though strict, Charlotte's discipline was tempered by fairness, a balance Max knew well from his many scoldings for venturing into the bustling marketplace, a realm she dismissed as unworthy of their stature. Yet, her protectiveness was undeniable, a mother's fierce love cloaked in layers of propriety.

"Come here, my son," Charlotte's commanding voice called from the doorway. "Stand up straight."

Max obeyed, walking toward her as she surveyed him with a discerning gaze. "The pain has returned, hasn't it?" she asked, her tone sharper than he expected. She had a way of knowing, even when he tried to mask the extent of his discomfort. What began as an occasional tingle in his fingers had, over three relentless weeks, grown into a full-blown, inexplicable agony radiating through his arm.

What is happening to me? Max wondered as Charlotte fussed over his appearance, smoothing his light beige chinos and buttoning his white collared shirt. His polished shoes gleamed under the chandelier's light, but his rebellious streak stood defiant in the form of his spiked hair, streaked with bold red and black hues. Gone was the ash-blond of his childhood, abandoned years ago in favour of this statement of individuality. While Charlotte silently loathed the style, she tolerated it as a fleeting phase.

"Madam Haywood!" a voice boomed from down the hall. "The architect for the new conservatory is here to discuss the skylights and wood finishes you requested."

With a nod, Charlotte turned, her heels clicking purposefully against the polished floor as she descended the staircase to greet the architect. Max lingered, watching her disappear, then returned to his bed. From beneath the pillow, he pulled out a crumpled photograph—his father, Brad Haywood, staring back at him. The image was his only connection to the man his mother spoke of only in hushed tones, her grief too heavy to put into words. Despite years of pressing for answers, Max had found none, only whispered stories from the housemaids that painted Brad as a rebellious, aimless youth. Max, however, did not see himself as aimless. He had ambition, though not the kind his mother envisioned.

To Charlotte, success meant wealth, power, and influence. To Max, it meant love, family, and a peaceful life far from the suffocating expectations of East County Grove. He imagined himself in the western outskirts, building a life filled with adventure and purpose, always with Jocelyn Rivers by his side.

Jocelyn, a vision of effortless beauty, was Max's age. Her long, sculpted legs, toned frame, and flowing blonde hair that cascaded down her back were enough to turn heads wherever she went.

For Max, Jocelyn wasn't just beautiful; she was the embodiment of everything he wanted—a partner to share a life of meaning, far removed from the gilded cages of their respective homes.

Beneath her flawless exterior lay a tenacious spirit. Frequent illness had shadowed much of her childhood, often leaving her sidelined from school and social events. Despite this, Jocelyn possessed an unstoppable drive, achieving her goals with a blend of charm and persistence. Her parents, Tom and Mary Anne Rivers, were affluent yet distant, their constant business travels leaving Jocelyn in the care of Venice, the family's au pair.

Although Venice was helpful, she remained reserved and private, never divulging any details about her personal life to Jocelyn. This left Jocelyn feeling isolated, except when Max was around. Max's presence had a transformative effect on her— her spirits lifted, and her demeanour brightened as if he were her soulmate. The bond between Max and Jocelyn was undeniable; they were inseparable, sharing countless experiences together.

One sunny afternoon, Jocelyn informed Venice that she was heading out to see Max.

Without waiting for a response, she darted out the door, hurrying down the road to Max's house. On the second ring of the doorbell, Max appeared, his silhouette framed by the warm glow of sunlight. Jocelyn stood before him, the sun illuminating an almost angelic radiance around her. "Come on, Max," she said with a playful grin, leaning in for a quick peck on his cheek. Grabbing his hand, she tugged him outside, eager to spend the day basking in the sun and indulging in carefree adventures like any pair of spirited teenagers.

Their usual hangout was the central park, where they would lie on the soft grass, gazing at the drifting clouds and imagining their future. They dreamt of a life free from parental constraints, where they could make their own rules. Armed with sandwiches prepared by their housemaids, they would chat about anything and everything, though their conversations rarely veered into serious territory.

However, this day was different. Max lay beside Jocelyn, his heart pounding as he worked up the courage to share a thought that had been gnawing at him. Finally, he turned to her and said, "Run away with me. Let's leave everything behind and see where the road takes us." Jocelyn froze, her mind racing. While she had noticed Max's growing unhappiness over the past few months, his proposal shocked her. It felt selfish, as though he expected her to abandon her family, friends, and everything she knew in East County Grove.

"How could you even think of this?" she said, her voice trembling with anger as it bubbled to the surface. Her expression betrayed her disappointment, and Max immediately regretted his words. "Forget I said that," he pleaded. "It was a stupid idea. I wasn't thinking." But Jocelyn wasn't ready to let it go. She wanted to understand the root of Max's discontent.

Max avoided her probing gaze, focusing instead on a blade of grass. In his mind, he imagined himself as a ladybird, flying far away from the weight of his life. The only thing tethering him to this place was Jocelyn. To him, she was his anchor and his future. In his dreams, they would one day marry and raise two children—a boy and a girl, the perfect family.

His thoughts were interrupted by the sight of a group of teens at the far end of the park. They called themselves "the Renegades," a notorious clique known for their rebellious antics. Max had been warned to steer clear of them, but he couldn't help observing the group. The leader, Ross, was broad-shouldered and solidly built, he carried his strength with a quiet confidence, not showy, just undeniable. His short, dark hair was neatly kept, and his steady gaze seemed to weigh everyone it landed on. Max couldn't tell if he was more curious or cautious, but one thing was clear: Ross wasn't someone you ignored.

The other members included Jonas, a lanky boy with an awkward gait; the twins, Anastasia and Greer, who shared an almost eerie connection, often finishing each other's sentences; and Siobhan, a striking girl with fair skin and radiant auburn hair. Siobhan, adopted by Dr. Keith Rodgers, had a complicated past marked by the mysterious death of her adoptive mother.

Jocelyn's elbow jabbed Max, breaking his trance. "Max! Have you been listening?" she snapped, exasperated. Realising he had been daydreaming, Max scrambled to his feet as Jocelyn motioned for them to leave the park. As they walked back, Max couldn't shake the image of Siobhan and the Renegades from his mind.

Later that evening, Max's grandmother dropped by with an envelope of old photos. "I found these while clearing the garage—thought you might want them."

Max flipped through the pictures absently— until he saw one of his mother, smiling beside Dr. Rodgers. He had no idea they knew each other before he was born. When Charlotte entered the room, he confronted her about it. Charlotte brushed it off, insisting it was unimportant. Frustrated but unwilling to press further, Max let it go.

A few days later, Max ran into Siobhan at the local deli. After an awkward encounter involving a dropped sandwich, Max nervously asked if he could walk with her. Siobhan, intrigued but guarded, led him to the park. Their conversation revealed a shared curiosity about the past. When Max mentioned the photograph of their parents, Siobhan seemed genuinely surprised.

Before they could delve deeper, Jocelyn appeared, cutting the conversation short. Her disdain for Siobhan was palpable, but Max ignored her pointed remarks. Later that night, the phone rang. Siobhan's voice on the other end startled Max. "We need to finish our conversation," she insisted, suggesting they meet in person. Max agreed, sensing this was only the beginning of a larger mystery.

At the deli, Max approached Siobhan, his tone tense with curiosity and concern. "What is the meaning of all this? Why did you call me late last night and summon me here without explaining anything?"

Siobhan shifted uncomfortably, guilt flickering across her face. "I'm sorry, Max," she said, her voice low but sincere. "I was in my father's office and stumbled upon some notes about your condition. I overheard a conversation—it was vague, but they mentioned bugging a house. I don't know exactly who or what they were talking about, but I felt like you needed to know."

Max furrowed his brow, her words heavy with implication. He pondered the situation for a moment, then nodded, a sense of gratitude warming his guarded expression. "Thank you for telling me," he said, his voice softening. "Shall we investigate further?"

Siobhan's eyes narrowed with intrigue. "What do you have in mind?"

Max leaned in close, whispering a plan into her ear. With a shared resolve, they left for Siobhan's house to uncover more.

When they arrived, they found the place eerily quiet. Siobhan informed Max that her father, Dr. Keith Rodgers, was out and wouldn't be back for a couple of hours. Together, they crept upstairs to his study, a room Siobhan had been strictly forbidden from entering.

"It's locked," Max observed, trying the door.

Siobhan smirked. "Not a problem. I have a spare key." She retrieved it from a drawer and unlocked the door. The hinges groaned loudly, sending a shiver through the silent house.

Inside, Max's eyes roamed the room. The walls were lined with tall bookcases crammed with volumes, their spines whispering of subjects far beyond his understanding. "Has he really read all of these?" Max wondered aloud, his tone a mix of awe and scepticism.

Siobhan dismissed his musings with a wave of her hand and pointed to a thick file resting on the desk. "This is the one," she said.

Max opened it and found a collection of photos, drawings, and pages of text littered with medical jargon. His stomach tightened. "Doctor's scribbles," he muttered under his breath, unable to decipher the meaning. He set the file down and gave Siobhan a grateful nod.

Just as he turned to leave, his gaze snagged on another file—this one marked with Jocelyn's name. Intrigued, he reached for it, but a loud crash from downstairs froze him in place. The front door had slammed open.

Siobhan grabbed his hand. "Hide," she whispered urgently, pulling him under the massive oak desk.

The sound of footsteps and muffled voices grew louder, each one hammering Max's already racing heart. His arm throbbed with a sharp, searing pain, and he bit down on his lip to keep from crying out. Siobhan noticed his clenched jaw and the beads of sweat on his forehead, her worry deepening.

Dr. Keith Rodgers entered the study with another man, their conversation barely audible over Max's pounding heartbeat. The snippets he caught were alarming: "Time is running out... Charlotte mentioned increasing pain in his arm..."

Max's mind spiralled into chaos. His condition was deteriorating, and the urgency in their voices suggested they knew more than he did. The pain in his arm surged, almost unbearable now, but he held on, clenching his fists tightly to avoid making a sound.

The men didn't linger. They grabbed one file from the desk and left, their voices fading as they descended the stairs.

Max's vision blurred as the pain overwhelmed him. Then everything went black.

***

Max awoke to the sound of voices, disoriented and groggy. He was lying in an alleyway, surrounded by the Renegades. Ross, the leader, crouched beside him. "You're safe now," Ross said gruffly. "We had to get you out of there before they used you like some kind of lab rat."

Max struggled to make sense of the words. "What... What are you talking about?"

Siobhan interjected, her voice cutting through his haze. "You passed out. They left the study shortly after and headed to the research centre. We barely had time to get you out."

Max's patience wore thin. "Enough," he said, his voice firmer now. "What aren't you telling me? If it concerns me, I have a right to know."

Siobhan hesitated, then glanced at Ross, who gave a subtle nod. He gestured for the others to leave. "You two talk," Ross said simply.

After the group dispersed, Siobhan turned to Max, her face a mix of fear and quiet strength. She opened her mouth to speak, but the words caught in her throat. Finally, she took a deep breath and began.

"Max," Siobhan began carefully, her voice measured, "how much do you truly understand about what's happening to you?"

Max looked up at her, his bright blue eyes wide with confusion, as if searching for something familiar in her words. "What do you mean?" he asked, his voice tinged with the uncertainty of someone caught in a storm of thoughts.

Siobhan pressed on, her gaze unwavering. "Your condition—how much have you really been told? What exactly do you know about it?"

Max's eyes shifted, the uncertainty now mingling with a glimmer of the little knowledge he possessed. "I have too much blood flowing through my arm at an exaggerated rate," he said, as if repeating a diagnosis he'd been given. "The doctors call it Artbraderial Blood Disease," he explained, the words feeling disconnected from the reality Siobhan was trying to convey.

A visible frustration crossed Siobhan's features. Unable to contain herself, she slammed her fist into her open palm, the sharp sound of the impact echoing. "Disease!" she exclaimed, her voice rising with the intensity of her disbelief. "So that's the story they gave you? That you have a disease? Well, let me set the record straight..." Her words hung in the air, heavy with the weight of the truth she was about to reveal.

***

On the other side of town, at that very moment, Dr. Keith Rodgers sat hunched over confidential documents in his office, the soft hum of his desk lamp the only sound breaking the silence. The ringing of the office phone shattered his concentration, and he answered it after a couple of rings, his tone professional but strained with the urgency of the situation.

"Yes?"

"Mrs. Charlotte Haywood is here to see you, Dr. Rodgers," came the voice of his receptionist, clipped and to the point.

Dr. Rodgers nodded, as if she could see him, and replied quickly, "Let her in."

He placed the phone back in its cradle, straightened in his chair, and braced himself for the conversation that was about to unfold. Charlotte entered the office, her face marked with a troubled expression, her presence a contrast to the calm demeanour of Dr. Rodgers.

Her hair was pulled back into a high ponytail—an odd choice for someone of her age, perhaps a subtle attempt to cling to youth. Charlotte had always dressed younger than her years, a habit that had drawn whispers from neighbours who seemed eager to pass judgment on her ways. Despite the murmurs, Charlotte revelled in what she called the 'high life'—basking in the sun in Marrakech, cruising the Caribbean seas, sipping daiquiris on Algarve beaches. It was a life of excess, one she wore like a badge.

"You said it was important—what's happened?" Charlotte asked, her tone laced with concern, yet edged with an air of impatience.

Dr. Rodgers leaned back in his chair, his face growing serious, all traces of casual professionalism gone. "I believe our children have started communicating," he said, his words weighed down by their implications. "Max's file was left open on my desk. Someone has been poking around. We need to act swiftly."

Charlotte's expression turned grave as she absorbed the information, her mind racing to connect the dots. "So, what's our plan?" she asked, her voice now softer, the concern deepening.

Dr. Rodgers leaned forward, his voice lowering, firm with conviction. "We must make a decision soon. If we don't, I will take matters into my own hands. We can't afford any loose ends."

Charlotte sighed deeply, her lips pressing into a thin line. "It's too soon," she murmured, a faint tremor in her voice. "He's just a young boy."

Dr. Rodgers' eyes bored into hers, heavy with the weight of the situation. "I'll give you one week," he said firmly. "If you can't make a decision by then, I'll do what needs to be done."

Charlotte nodded, her jaw set, her thoughts swirling in the storm of their conversation. They both understood the gravity of the situation—this was no longer just about Max, but about everything they had carefully orchestrated. With a silent agreement, Charlotte left the office, leaving Dr. Rodgers to his thoughts and the documents that held their shared secrets.

***

"The so-called disease, this Artbraderial Blood disease, as it was coined, is a rare and almost unheard-of condition that has only been studied once before your case. What you possess, Max, is not a disease at all," Siobhan continued, her voice steady but full of awe. "On the contrary, it's quite remarkable."

She paused, as if to gather her thoughts. "Can you recall Ms. Granola teaching us about the different roles that blood cells play in the human body?" Siobhan's eyes locked with Max's, a strange sense of familiarity in her words. "She also explained how blood is divided into four distinct components:"

She ticked off the list on her fingers, her voice steady and knowledgeable.

- "White blood cells fight infection, like soldiers defending a fortress."
- "Red blood cells carry oxygen from your lungs to your tissues, like a constant stream of fresh air."
- "Platelets, their main function is to control bleeding, acting like repairmen rushing to seal a wound."
- "Plasma, the pale-yellow liquid part of our blood, serves as a transporter, aiding in the movement of water, nutrients, minerals, medications, and hormones to different parts of the body."

"It's intriguing," she said, her voice softening with a sense of wonder, "how these components work together to create the intricate system that keeps us functioning."

Max's mind was racing as he listened.

"The blood coursing through your veins," Siobhan continued, "flows at such an exaggerated speed that your white blood cells don't just fight off infections—they obliterate them entirely, leaving no trace of any infection ever being there. It's as if your body is constantly purging itself of any illness, a self-healing mechanism unlike any we've seen before."

Max's brows furrowed as he tried to process the information. "Typically," Siobhan went on, "an average person's red blood cells have a lifespan of about four months. Yours, though, exist for just four minutes, perpetually regenerating themselves. Your platelets are functioning in overdrive, and your plasma is in a constant state of activity, almost like a machine that never stops working."

Siobhan's voice softened, almost to a whisper. "Show me your scar," she requested.

Max, utterly perplexed, frowned. "What scar?" he asked, his confusion evident.

"Precisely," Siobhan retorted, her voice sharp but laced with urgency. "Don't you see?"

She took a step closer, her eyes searching his. "Scars are the result of fibrous tissue replacing normal skin following an injury. They form as part of the body's natural repair process after a wound occurs in the skin or other tissues. In essence, scarring is a normal part of the healing journey—nearly every wound results in some degree of scarring. But you," she said, her voice filled with awe, "you defy that norm. Your regenerative ability doesn't allow for scars. Instead, your tissue regrows exactly as it was before. Your blood holds the extraordinary potential for regeneration. It could be the very means to physically heal those who are unwell."

Max was left stunned, the weight of her words sinking in like a heavy stone. "This is truly remarkable," he thought initially, but confusion and frustration quickly clouded his mind. "Why has no one discussed this with me before?" he demanded, his voice rising with emotion. "Why was I kept in the dark? Why did no one tell me the truth?"

Siobhan hesitated, unsure of how to approach the rawness of his questions. "I wasn't sure how to explain it," she began gently. But before she could continue, Max's emotions overtook him.

"You've known all along and never said a word," he accused, his voice shaking with frustration. "Your father, my mother—none of them mentioned this. Why was I kept in the dark all this time?"

His barrage of questions poured out, desperate for answers. "And why am I experiencing this pain, specifically in my right arm?"

Siobhan's face grew serious, her tone sombre. "It will eventually spread, taking over your entire body."

Max's concern deepened; the idea of his body succumbing to whatever this was was overwhelming him. "Will the pain ever cease?" he asked, his voice barely above a whisper.

Siobhan's answer came with honesty but uncertainty, her voice soft. "I don't have that answer."

Frustrated and seeking clarity, Max pressed again, his voice raw with frustration. "But you haven't explained how you know all of this."

Siobhan hesitated, searching for the right words when suddenly, the Renegades arrived, interrupting the moment.

Max rose to his feet, the weight of urgency pressing him forward. The need to uncover answers and reclaim some semblance of control over his situation grew unbearable. With a quiet nod, he excused himself, explaining that he had to pursue the truth, and quickly exited the scene.

At home, Max found his mother, Charlotte, in the living room. Her expression was one of mild surprise, her eyes narrowing as she noticed the late hour of his return. "Where have you been?" she asked, concern lacing her voice. Max, however, wasn't in the mood for small talk. Ignoring her question entirely, he confronted her with his own. "Why didn't you tell me about my condition? Why keep this from me all this time?" His voice trembled with a mix of frustration and hurt, the words spilling out in a rush.

Charlotte blinked, visibly taken aback by the sudden intensity of his outburst. "What do you mean? I haven't kept anything from you," she replied, her tone more defensive than reassuring, as she tried to steady herself. But Max wasn't satisfied. His next words hung heavy in the air, an accusation laced with disbelief. "My condition—Artbraderial

Blood disease. It's not really a disease, is it, Mother?"

A long silence stretched between them as Charlotte watched him, her expression calm but concerned. Her gaze softened as she spoke, her voice gentle but firm. "Max, I know this isn't easy, but next week, we're going to see Dr. Rodgers." The words struck Max like a cold splash of water, and his confusion quickly morphed into anger. "For what?" he demanded, the sharpness in his tone unmistakable. His usual respect for her vanished, replaced by the raw edge of his emotions.

Charlotte, unaffected by his tone, continued. "Dr. Rodgers has developed a method to duplicate blood cells," she explained. "His work could revolutionise the way blood is used in laboratories and hospitals around the world." The anger in Max's chest began to dissipate, replaced by a growing curiosity. The revelation was monumental, but it left him with more questions than answers. With his mind a tangled mess of emotions, he muttered a half-hearted excuse about needing rest, skipped dinner, and retreated to his room, where the weight of the situation pressed on him like a heavy blanket.

The next morning, Max wasted no time. At the crack of dawn, he dialled Jocelyn's number, his voice frantic as he recounted the events of the previous night. He spoke quickly, describing how he and Siobhan had infiltrated her father's office, uncovered his personal file, and the moment of his fainting spell, which led to the startling discovery of his blood condition. Jocelyn's mind raced with the information. Her emotions were a whirlwind—anger that she hadn't been informed earlier, mixed with excitement over the ground-breaking implications of Max's revelation. But she also realised that Max might not fully understand the magnitude of the changes that were about to reshape his life.

"When do you see Dr. Rodgers?" she asked eagerly, her voice tinged with anticipation.

"One week from now," Max replied. "But honestly, I'm not sure what to expect."

Their conversation was abruptly cut short by the sound of the doorbell ringing downstairs. Max promised to call Jocelyn back, hurriedly hanging up the phone and racing downstairs to answer the door.

To his surprise, Siobhan stood on the doorstep, a look of urgency on her face. "You need to come with me," she said, her voice firm but with a trace of mystery. "There's something you need to see." Intrigued and slightly apprehensive, Max agreed to join her, eager to find out what she had to show him. "Where are we going?" he asked, his curiosity piqued.

"Just wait and see," Siobhan replied with a smirk. "Trust me, you're going to want to see this."

The walk to the park was silent, but the air between them crackled with anticipation. When they arrived, Max saw the familiar group of Renegades gathered at their usual spot. Ross, Jonas, and the twins—Anastasia and Greer—were lounging by a tree, chatting casually.

"So, you've got some special kind of blood, do you?" Ross asked, his tone light and teasing as he leaned casually against the tree. Before Max could answer, Ross moved in an instant, faster than he could react, and struck him with a shard of broken glass. The glass sliced into his skin, leaving a small but deep cut that ran from the top of his arm down to the outside of his bicep.

Max stumbled back, his mind reeling as he instinctively pushed Ross away with all his strength. "What the hell do you think you're doing?" he demanded, clutching his arm to slow the flow of blood, his heart pounding in his chest.

Ross, seemingly unfazed, shrugged coolly. "I just want to see what all the fuss is about," he said, a calculating glint in his eyes. "I want to see the window period between the incision and the regeneration... Move your hand."

Still in shock, Max stood frozen, unable to release his grip on his arm. Greer, ever the calm one, stepped forward. Without a word, she tore a strip from her clothing and gently took his hand. With surprising tenderness, she pried each of his fingers from his arm, expecting to reveal the blood-covered wound. But what she uncovered left everyone in stunned silence—Max's wound had vanished. His skin was completely healed; not even a trace of the injury remained.

Max's breath caught in his throat as he stared at his arm in disbelief. His mind raced to make sense of what had just happened. A quiet, hysterical laugh bubbled up from within him, more out of shock than anything else. Was this real? It felt like a dream—a surreal, impossible dream. He half-expected to wake up in his bed, the aroma of his mother's freshly brewed coffee from her last trip to Brazil still lingering in the air. But this wasn't a dream. This was happening to him, right now.

When the confusion of the moment began to settle, Max finally realised something else. Ross had been several meters away from him just moments before. "How did you do that?" Max asked, his voice hoarse with wonder.

"Do what?" Ross replied nonchalantly.

"Slice you with broken glass?" He added, smirking.

"No," Max interrupted, his eyes narrowing with suspicion. "Not the cut. The movement. How did you get from beside that tree to being an inch away from me without me even seeing you move?"

Ross smiled, a knowing glint in his eye. "Ah," he said, his tone almost affectionate, "intriguing, isn't it? You see, Max, you're not the only one who's special. We all have gifts, powers, if you will.

They're all different." He gestured to the twins, Anastasia and Greer, who were standing nearby. "Our twins here can read each other's minds, and they can get into other people's heads to see every thought they have. It's quite useful for... interrogation."

Max's brow furrowed. "Interrogate? Why would they need to—"

"Don't worry about that," Siobhan cut him off, her voice smooth and teasing. "What Ross meant to say is that they have fun on double dates. Isn't that right, Ross?"

Ross gave her a half-smile. "Yeah, that's what I meant dear," he said, his tone casual. Then, pointing to Siobhan, he added, "Your friend here has a rather interesting power of her own. Show Max what you can do, Siobhan."

Siobhan rolled her eyes, exasperated but amused. "First of all," she said, with mock seriousness, "I'm not your dear. Second of all— actually, there is no second. Just stop talking." She gave Ross a playful shove, then turned to Max with a grin. "Step aside, fearless leader. I wouldn't want to mess up your beautiful hair."

With a dramatic flourish, Siobhan rolled up her sleeves and snapped her fingers. The shard of broken glass that Ross had used to cut Max earlier levitated from the ground, suspended in mid-air as though controlled by an invisible force. With a careful motion, Siobhan moved her hand from one end of the glass to the other, her fingers guiding it with precision. Within moments, the jagged shard transformed into a flawless, delicate glass swan, glistening in the sunlight.

Max stood in stunned silence for a moment, his jaw slightly agape. "That's incredible, Siobhan!" he said, his voice a little breathless. A shy smile tugged at his lips. Despite his usual bravado, there was something about Siobhan that always made him feel a bit self-conscious.

"Does that only work on glass, or can you transform other materials as well?" Max inquired.

"Other materials as well," Siobhan replied. "But glass is the easiest."

"My turn, my turn," interrupted Jonas eagerly. "Allow me to demonstrate what I can do." With a grin, Jonas brandished his infamous baseball bat, the one he carried everywhere. He began to stretch his arms, legs, and torso, elongating his body until he reached the full length of the tall oak tree under which they had gathered for the past hour. He held the pose for a few seconds, revelling in the stretch, before retracting his limbs back to their normal size. However, as he shrank back to his usual proportions, Jonas inadvertently swayed his extended arm, causing the baseball bat to connect with Max's face with a resounding thump. Max, caught completely off guard, was launched backwards, propelled straight into the river where they had assembled. He hit the water with a heavy splash, his head colliding with a protruding rock, and immediately fell unconscious.

"Help him!" Siobhan shouted, her voice sharp with panic. Jonas quickly extended his elongated arm and gripped Max's limp body with both hands, pulling him from the water. "Help me pull him out," he yelled. In an instant, Ross appeared beside him, gripping Jonas's arm to assist in hauling Max back to the riverbank. Once Max was safely on dry land, Siobhan pushed past the others, her heart racing as she checked for a heartbeat. Her voice cracked with urgency. "He's not breathing!"

"Administer CPR!" came the simultaneous cry from Anastasia and Greer. Siobhan moved swiftly, positioning her hands on Max's chest. She pressed down with quick, deliberate force, delivering three powerful compressions. Then, she bent down, placing her lips against his, and breathed air into his lungs. She repeated the process, panic building as the seconds stretched on. Desperate, Siobhan continued, her focus solely on bringing Max back.

In his unconscious state, Max saw a figure standing in the distance, its shape blurred in the mist. Was it his father's silhouette? Though the figure's face remained obscured, Max felt a deep, inexplicable connection, a bond that reached across the veil of his unconsciousness. The figure was solid, commanding—a man with broad shoulders, exuding an unmistakable alpha presence. Max knew, somehow, that this was Brad, his father.

"Max," Brad's voice called out, clear and powerful, "listen to me. I know you're planning to proceed with this operation, but I must warn you of the dangers ahead. Before you continue, seek out the four ancient, long-forgotten mythical relics known as the Treasures of Gladvier. Trust me, they will be invaluable to you and your friends. Do not proceed without them. They will guide you through what is to come. The Elemental Relics hold the balance of our world. Seek them, protect them—they're more than treasures; they are the key to harmony."

Max's eyes fluttered open. The first thing he felt was Siobhan's lips pressing urgently against his, administering CPR. He coughed violently, water surging from his lungs, and sputtered, "I saw him—my father. He appeared while I was unconscious. He told me about four ancient, long-forgotten mythical relics and urged me to seek these out."

Jonas raised an eyebrow. "I've heard of that," he said thoughtfully. "My mom used to read me a story called *The Legendary Treasures of Gladvier,* a children's fantasy novel about..."

"And that's exactly what it is—a children's storybook," Siobhan interjected with a sceptical glance. "I don't like the sound of this."

"Unless you all have something better to do than lazing around under this tree all day," Ross said, his voice edged with conviction. "I say we go on an adventure. Speak up, Jonas. Tell us what you know about these legendary treasures of Gladvier."

Jonas's eyes lit up with excitement. "Legend has it that the four relics are intricately connected to the elements, each imbued with powers beyond imagination. Picture it: four ancient relics, each bound to a different element. The first one, air, waits atop Truisia Mountain. We'll scale the mountain and face its dangers to claim it."

"Then there's water, embodied in an orb that can summon rain with the twist of a hand. It's guarded by a kooky old lady who uses it to tend to her garden."

"We'll venture even deeper, confronting earth, buried in the Nasmarian Forest, where a crimson meteorite rests—guarded by creatures straight out of nightmares."

"And finally, fire. An eternal flame burns within a torch, hidden in a forgotten village. The villagers use it to light their homes deep underground."

Siobhan's voice cut through the excitement, laced with a biting sarcasm. "Well, isn't that just a thrilling bedtime story?"

Ross grinned, undeterred. "Fear not, Siobhan. We're not backing down. Prepare yourselves tonight. Tomorrow at sunrise, we set out on the adventure of a lifetime."

***

The dining room smelled of roasted vegetables and fresh bread as Max pushed his peas around his plate, stealing glances at Jocelyn and his mother. Tonight felt different—heavier somehow.

Finally, Max took a breath. "There's something I need to tell you both," he said, voice tight. "Tomorrow, I'm leaving. We're going on a quest."

Charlotte nearly dropped her fork. "What kind of quest?" Her eyes darted between Max and Jocelyn, searching for answers.

Jocelyn blinked, clearly caught off guard. "Wait, you're leaving? Where exactly?"

Max shrugged, trying to sound casual. "To find some ancient relics. It's... important."

Charlotte's face paled. "Relics? That sounds dangerous. Who else is going? How are you even planning to go? When did you decide this? Why didn't you tell me sooner?"

The questions came fast and fierce, each one heavier than the last.

Jocelyn chimed in nervously, "Are you sure it's safe? Can I come?"

Max's jaw tightened. "I don't know if it's safe, but I have to do this. And I don't think you should come. It's too dangerous."

Charlotte's voice rose, a mix of fear and frustration. "You're still just a kid, Max. Reckless and unprepared. You don't know what you're getting into. This is madness."

"I'm not reckless!" Max shot back, the frustration bubbling over. "You don't understand, none of you do!"

Jocelyn looked between them, biting her lip. The tension was thick, the room closing in.

Max stood abruptly. "I'm going whether you like it or not."

Charlotte's voice cracked with anger and heartbreak. "You can't just run off like this. You're not ready, Max."

She pushed back her chair and stormed out of the room, tears shimmering in her eyes.

Silence fell. Max let out a shaky breath and sank back into his chair.

Jocelyn reached out, her voice low. "Are you really going to do this?"

Max nodded slowly. "I don't see any other choice."

She sighed. "I'm not happy about it... but I get why you have to."

They exchanged a look — a fragile truce forged in the quiet after the storm.

CHAPTER 2

Air – The Aetherial Talisman

With the first light of dawn spilling across the sky in delicate shades of blush and molten gold, Max and his friends gathered at their designated meeting spot beneath the towering oak tree, its ancient branches stretching wide, like protective arms. Excitement crackled in the air, mingling with the cool, crisp morning breeze that whispered through the leaves, setting the stage for what lay ahead. The air felt electric with possibility as the group exchanged eager glances and nervous smiles. Today marked the beginning of their quest—a journey into the unknown in search of ancient relics that promised unimaginable power.

Jonas clutched the tattered book to his chest, the one his mother used to read him as a child—The Legendary Treasures of Gladvier. What had once seemed like bedtime nonsense had taken on new meaning in the light of everything that had happened.

Thanks to his growing obsession and long hours cross-referencing old regional maps and forgotten legends, Jonas had pieced it together. Clues hidden in the poetic prose of the story lined up with real places—forgotten landmarks, unusual weather patterns, cryptic inscriptions. He was certain the first relic was at the summit of Truisia Mountain. It was the only place in the region where the winds howled just like the tale described—constant and fierce, "like whispers from the gods."

Siobhan, her eyes shining bright with anticipation, stood at the forefront of the group. Her confident posture and fiery spirit were unmistakable. "Well, look at us, ready to take on the world," she remarked, her voice brimming with optimism, a hint of excitement underlying her words. "Let's make this day count, everyone. Our adventure begins now." With a resolute nod from Ross, the leader of their motley crew, the group set off, their footsteps stirring the quiet morning air, as they ventured out into the wilderness beyond the safety of their town, stepping boldly into the unknown.

Venturing deeper into the wilds in search of the air element, a weighty sense of purpose hung in the air, their mission a constant reminder of the stakes. They were no longer just a group of friends embarking on a simple trip; they were on a sacred quest, one that would shape the course of their lives. The ancient village—shrouded in mystery and steeped in legend—lay just beyond their reach, a distant yet beckoning beacon leading them into the depths of the forest.

Max's heart pounded with anticipation as they trekked through the thick, untamed foliage, his mind racing with images of the sacred relic awaiting them. He couldn't help but wonder about the simple folk who called this forgotten village home, their lives entwined with the very power the group was seeking. What would they find? And would it live up to the stories whispered among the elders? A pang of guilt prickled his chest as he thought of Jocelyn's wide eyes at the dinner table, the way she'd bitten her lip and asked if she could come. I hope she's not too worried, he thought, forcing his feet to move. There was no turning back now.

Beside him, Siobhan walked with a fire in her eyes, her fierce will matching his own. Her steps were sure and confident. "This is it," she murmured, her voice barely above a whisper as if the forest itself might overhear. "Our chance to unlock the mysteries of the past and harness the power of the elements." There was a sense of destiny in her words that made Max's pulse quicken.

Jonas, ever the pragmatic one, scanned their surroundings with sharp, calculating eyes, always alert, his mind working through possible strategies. "Let's not get ahead of ourselves," he said, his voice steady, even though there was a noticeable thrill in his tone, a far-off excitement for the unknown challenges ahead. "We need to stay focused and approach this with caution. The air element may be our first challenge, but it won't be our last." His words, though grounded in reason, seemed to carry an edge of excitement that none of them could deny.

With each step, they drew closer to their destination, the ancient village just over the horizon like a ghostly silhouette, waiting to reveal its secrets. The deeper they went into the heart of the forest, the stronger their will hardened, their spirit unyielding as they moved forward, preparing for the trials ahead.

With each step, Max found himself in sync with Jonas, their strides matching the steady rhythm of their journey. The two of them had fallen into an unspoken camaraderie, a quiet connection that formed through the shared silence of their footsteps. Max stole a glance at Jonas, noting the steely focus etched into his features, the quiet strength radiating from him like an unspoken beacon of confidence.

"Jonas," Max began, his voice tentative as he broke the silence that had settled between them. "I feel like I barely know you. Tell me, what's your story?" There was something in Max that longed to understand his companion better, something about Jonas's quiet reserve that intrigued him.

Jonas cast a sideways glance at Max, his expression unreadable for a moment. Then his lips curved into a wry, almost sheepish smile. "Before I answer that... I've got to say something first."

Max blinked. "Okay?"

Jonas exhaled slowly, raking a hand through his hair. "Back by the river... I'm sorry. I didn't mean to hit you. I was showing off, and I wasn't thinking. It could've gone really badly—I mean, it did go badly. I just—" he hesitated, genuine remorse darkening his tone, "—I've been feeling awful about it ever since."

Max studied him for a beat, then gave a small nod. "Yeah, it wasn't fun waking up to CPR," he said, his tone dry—but not unkind. "But... I know it was an accident. And you pulled me out."

Jonas's shoulders eased just a little. "Still. I needed to say it. I'd never forgive myself if something had happened to you."

There was a moment of quiet before Max offered a small, sincere smile. "Thanks. I appreciate you saying it."

Jonas nodded, a bit of tension melting from his posture. "Okay. Now that that's out of the way...

my story, huh? Well, where do I begin?" His voice was a bit more relaxed now, like someone finally opening a door to something long buried.

And so, as they walked, Jonas began to share bits and pieces of his past. He spoke of childhood adventures, wild and carefree, and of teenage escapades that led to lessons learned. He shared dreams chased and dreams deferred, and slowly, as he spoke, Max began to understand the layers of his companion—someone not just shaped by privilege, but by a life lived with purpose, through both triumph and struggle.

There was something about Jonas that made Max feel both inspired and humbled, as though his own struggles had been mere shadows compared to the quiet strength Jonas had cultivated in the face of his own challenges.

The longer they travelled, the more Max's curiosity about Jonas's background grew. He couldn't resist asking more.

"So, Jonas," Max continued, his voice light but curious, "tell me more about your family. What was it like growing up?"

Jonas's expression softened, a nostalgic gleam entering his eyes, and he let out a slow breath before diving into his past. "Well, Max, I come from a family that's always had everything we needed—and more. My parents are successful in their own right, but they've always emphasised the importance of hard work and humility. They taught me that success is not just about what you achieve, but about how you treat people along the way." He paused, his mind drifting back to those moments that shaped him. "We may have had wealth, but what truly enriched our lives were the moments spent together as a family, whether it was hiking in the mountains or sitting around the dinner table, sharing stories that made us laugh until we cried."

Max listened intently, absorbing every word, fascinated by Jonas's take on privilege and the value of relationships. He felt a pang of envy at the thought of such a supportive and nurturing upbringing. Yet beneath it all, there was something deeper in Jonas's character—a resilience born not from wealth, but from the depth of understanding that true strength comes from kindness, humility, and the bonds we create.

With twilight settling in, the group set up camp in a secluded spot beneath the canopy of ancient trees. The branches, gnarled and wise, stretched upwards as if seeking the last traces of sunlight. The air was crisp and cool now, tinged with the scent of pine and earth, and the atmosphere held a sense of serenity that contrasted with the adventure that lay ahead.

The others busied themselves pitching tents and gathering firewood, but Max and Siobhan slipped away from the group, eager to explore the stillness of the forest as the night began to settle around them. The world seemed to hush, as if the forest itself was holding its breath.

The air was fresh and filled with the earthy scent of the woods, the breeze carrying the promise of discovery. Their footsteps fell softly against the forest floor, the quiet sound echoing faintly in the stillness as they walked. Max and Siobhan walked side by side in a comfortable silence, their presence an unspoken reassurance. The fading light of day painted the landscape in warm hues of gold and amber, illuminating the trees with flickering patterns, as if holding onto the sun's final embrace.

Max couldn't help but steal glances at Siobhan, her features glowing in the last light of day. There was a sense of serenity in her presence, a quiet strength in her gaze that belied her youthful appearance. Max found himself captivated by the mystery that seemed to cling to her every movement, the way she navigated the world with a quiet confidence. He felt an unspoken connection, a sense of understanding between them that felt almost natural.

They walked for what seemed like hours, lost in the beauty of their surroundings and the gentle rhythm of their steps. Continuing deeper into the wilderness, their conversation drifted from dreams and aspirations to fears and uncertainties, the bond between them growing stronger with each shared word. It was in these quiet moments, far from the world they knew, that Max felt a sense of peace settling within him—knowing that, no matter the challenges ahead, he would not have to face them alone.

With night deepening and the stars shimmering like distant jewels above, Max and Siobhan found themselves standing at the edge of a tranquil lake. Its surface shimmered in the moonlight, reflecting the vast expanse of the heavens above. They sat down together on the soft, dew-laden grass of the bank, their shoulders brushing lightly, gazing out over the peaceful expanse before them. The stillness of the water mirrored the serenity that settled over them both, and for a brief moment, the weight of the world seemed to lift.

In that tranquil moment, with the world stretching out before them in all its raw, untamed beauty, Max felt a deep sense of peace wash over him. His thoughts quieted as he took in the landscape—everything felt right, as though he was exactly where he was meant to be. And as he turned his gaze to Siobhan, her eyes reflecting the starlight like pools of liquid silver, he knew, with an overwhelming certainty, that he had found a kindred spirit in this wild, unpredictable world.

The first rays of dawn crept over the horizon, washing the sky in tender shades of rose and gleaming gold. The camp stirred to life, gently waking to the promise of a new day. Max emerged from his tent, stretching his limbs with a quiet groan, savoring the crisp, cool morning air. The forest around them was alive with the sounds of birds singing their morning songs, the rustling of leaves in the gentle breeze—an enchanting symphony of nature greeting the dawn.

Jonas, ever the early riser, was already up and tending to the fire. The flames crackled and hissed as he stirred the coals, preparing a simple breakfast of trail mix and dried fruit. Max joined him by the fire, the warmth of the flames offering a welcome contrast to the lingering chill of the night. They exchanged a few words—casual greetings and small talk— while sharing the quiet morning meal. The rhythm of their conversation was easy, a reflection of their growing friendship.

Nearby, Siobhan and the others had already gathered in a loose circle, their low voices filled with purposeful conversation. Anastasia and Greer were busy checking their supplies, making sure everything was in order for the day's journey. Ross, ever the strategist, paced back and forth, his mind already occupied with the challenges that lay ahead, his eyes scanning the horizon as though he could already foresee what was to come.

With the morning fading, the group moved into action, making final preparations for their trek to Truisia Mountain. They packed up their camp, securing their gear, and shouldered their backpacks, ready to face the rugged wilderness once again. A sense of anticipation filled the air, their hearts buoyed by the promise of adventure, of discovery, and of the unknown that awaited them.

Max walked alongside Jonas, their feet crunching over the forest floor, falling into an easy rhythm. They spoke of their families, of their dreams and hopes for the future, their voices mixing with the ambient sounds of the forest around them.

Siobhan and the others walked a little ahead, their laughter and animated voices rising in the cool morning, carried on a current of conversation and jokes. Their camaraderie was undeniable, a testament to the bonds that had been formed over the course of their journey—a true sense of unity that made every step easier.

With each step forward, the towering silhouette of Truisia Mountain grew larger, dominating the horizon, standing like a silent sentinel waiting to reveal its secrets to those brave enough to seek them. With each passing moment, the group drew closer to the adventure that lay ahead, their hearts filled with a mixture of excitement and trepidation for the challenges and triumphs that awaited them.

With the sun sinking beneath the horizon, twilight cloaked the landscape in shadows, and the group quietly set up camp once again. They found a quiet, secluded spot near a small clearing and began to make their preparations for the night. They gathered around the crackling fire, its warm glow dancing over their tired faces. After a simple meal of canned beans and rice, they settled in for the night, taking turns keeping watch in the eerie silence of the forest.

The night seemed unusually still, the air thick with a sense of foreboding. The only sounds were the occasional rustle of leaves in the breeze, and the soft crackle of the fire. Max, his eyelids growing heavy from the long day, found himself drifting off to sleep. The warmth of the fire lulled him into a state of drowsy contentment, but the peace was short-lived.

Suddenly, the sound of approaching footsteps broke the stillness of the night, growing louder with every passing moment. Max's eyes snapped open, his heart pounding in his chest. Two figures emerged from the darkness, their faces obscured by shadow. Armed with crude, makeshift weapons, they moved toward the camp with threatening intent. Their eyes gleamed with malice, and their voices were low and guttural.

"Hand over your valuables," one of them snarled, brandishing a rusted blade in Max's direction. "No funny business, or else."

Fear surged through Max as he glanced around at his companions. They all seemed momentarily frozen, their faces a mixture of confusion and uncertainty. But before anyone could react, Jonas sprang into action.

With fluid grace, Jonas's body contorted and stretched, his limbs elongating unnaturally as he moved with lightning speed. In a blur of motion, he lunged at the would-be attackers, his arms and legs stretching to impossible lengths as he struck with precision. His movements were a dizzying combination of speed and agility, his elastic body bending and twisting with a fluidity that defied reason.

Within moments, the attackers were incapacitated, sprawled on the ground in defeat. Jonas stood tall, his breathing steady, his face calm and composed. "Are you all right?" he asked, his voice soft but firm as he turned to check on his friends.

The group nodded in shock, still trying to process the swift turn of events. Thanks to Jonas's quick thinking and remarkable abilities, they had emerged unscathed.

The attackers, groaning in pain, slowly picked themselves up and retreated into the shadows, their movements sluggish and uncoordinated. The group watched in tense silence until the intruders had vanished into the night. They gathered once more around the campfire, their awe was palpable. They couldn't help but marvel at the incredible display of strength and skill they had just witnessed. Despite the tension of the previous moments, the group felt a renewed sense of security, knowing they had Jonas on their side.

The first light of dawn filtered through the dense canopy, creating intricate patterns of light and dark that danced on the forest floor. The group stirred from their slumber, their bodies aching but their spirits high. They knew the day ahead would bring more challenges, but they faced it with a renewed sense of purpose.

After packing up camp and securing their gear, they set off once more along the winding forest path. The air was cool and crisp, the early morning silence broken only by the sound of their footsteps and the occasional call of a bird overhead. The dense greenery of the forest seemed to stretch on endlessly, the towering trees standing as steadfast guardians along the path.

With miles melting away beneath their feet, the group pressed on, the imposing form of Truisia Mountain growing larger with every step. The village that had eluded them for so long lay nestled in a clearing at the mountain's base, its weathered buildings bathed in the soft golden light of the morning sun. With a sense of eager anticipation filling their hearts, the group quickened their pace, eager to begin the search for the mythical relics that had drawn them here.

Little did they know, the journey was far from over, and the secrets waiting for them at the peak of Truisia Mountain would challenge them in ways they could not yet imagine.

Venturing forward, the towering peaks of Truisia Mountain loomed closer, their sheer heights draping the landscape in shifting shades of darkness. The terrain grew increasingly treacherous, with rocky outcroppings and jagged cliffs testing their endurance with each step.

At last, they arrived at the foot of Truisia Mountain, its towering slopes rising sharply into the sky, an unyielding monument to the ancient secrets of the heavens. The air grew noticeably cooler as they began their ascent, and the wind, a constant companion, whispered in soft gusts, carrying with it ancient tales of forgotten realms and untold mysteries. The scent of pine and the earth beneath their feet filled their senses, grounding them in the mountain's timeless embrace.

With each step, Max, Siobhan, Jonas, Ross, and the twins felt a deep sense of unity, drawn together by the shared thrill of adventure and the unspoken promise of discovery. Despite the uncertainty that loomed ahead, they pressed on, each heart beating faster with the anticipation of uncovering the secrets that awaited them at the summit of Truisia Mountain.

Climbing higher, the terrain grew increasingly rugged, demanding more of their physical strength and mental fortitude. Steep inclines and jagged rock outcrops challenged their progress, pushing them to their limits. At times, the path became so treacherous that they had no choice but to abandon their hiking poles and use their hands and climbing gear to continue onward.

Jonas, a seasoned climber with an instinctive understanding of the mountain's language, took the lead. His eyes scanned the terrain ahead, identifying secure handholds and footholds with practised precision. With smooth, confident movements, he uncoiled a length of sturdy rope from his pack and secured it to a boulder, creating a stable anchor point for the others to follow. His calm focus was reassuring, the others followed suit, climbing the rocky face one careful movement at a time.

Siobhan, always one to rise to a challenge, scaled the vertical face with an ease that belied the difficulty of the climb. Max watched in awe as she moved with fluidity and confidence, her every movement a testament to the bond she shared with the mountain. Beneath her, the steep drop felt both exhilarating and intimidating, but Siobhan remained undeterred, her gaze fixed firmly on the rock before her.

The rest of the group, one by one, took their turns, using the rope and Jonas's guidance to make their way up the craggy cliffs. Each handhold and foothold was a victory in itself, and the rush of adrenaline surged through their veins with every upward reach. With altitude increasing, the air grew thinner, and the wind, more biting, whipped fiercely around them, carrying with it the scent of pine and the promise of distant storms.

Despite the danger, the climb was not without its exhilaration. Every new obstacle surmounted was met with a surge of accomplishment, their spirits lifted by the challenge and the knowledge that the summit drew ever closer. Together, they climbed, drawing strength from one another, ascending toward the unknown.

At long last, the terrain began to level out, the sharp incline easing into a relatively flat stretch of land, offering a welcome respite from the grueling climb. The sun, dipping below the horizon, bathed the rugged landscape in a warm, golden light, its rays carving sharp contrasts across the mountain's jagged surface. The group paused, taking a moment to appreciate the hard-won progress they had made. It was time to set camp for the night.

They found a sheltered spot, nestled within a small grove of pines, where the branches swayed gently in the evening breeze. Stars pricked the sky, each twinkling like a promise of hope, they set about pitching their tents and gathering firewood. Max and Siobhan worked in tandem, their teamwork a smooth dance of shared laughter and occasional playful wrestling with the fabric of their tent.

Meanwhile, Jonas and Ross took on the task of starting a fire. With careful precision, they arranged the kindling, the crackling of the dry wood filling the air as they struck a match, igniting the flames. Soon, the fire blazed to life, throwing a warm, golden glow over their makeshift campsite, chasing away the shadows of the encroaching night.

The group gathered around the fire, their faces illuminated by the flickering flames. They shared stories, their voices carrying over the crackle of the fire, their laughter mingling with the chirping of distant crickets. The night sky stretched endlessly above them, a canvas of stars, while the soft, distant hoot of an owl echoed across the mountain. The night, though filled with challenges and fatigue, felt serene, a moment of quiet connection with the world around them.

Though the journey ahead was uncertain, the bond between them was undeniable, a thread woven tight by shared hardship and the promise of future discovery. The fire crackled on as they settled in for the night, wrapped in the warmth of their friendship and the comfort of the mountain's quiet majesty.

Resuming their climb the following day, the air grew even thinner, each breath more labored as they ascended further into the mountain's grasp. The winding path grew steeper, more treacherous, and they were forced to rely heavily on their climbing gear to scale the sheer cliffs and jagged outcrops.

Finally, after what felt like an eternity, they reached the peak of Truisia Mountain, where they were greeted by a breathtaking sight. Before them, a sprawling plateau lay bathed in mist, its surface dotted with ancient ruins and weathered statues that stood as silent sentinels to a time long past. The wind, now stronger, swirled around them, carrying the scent of salt and earth.

At the centre of the plateau stood a magnificent shrine, its stone walls etched with intricate carvings. Winged figures and swirling vortexes adorned the surface, their meaning lost to time but their presence undeniably powerful. The shrine seemed to hum with energy, a beacon calling them closer.

As the travellers approached, they were surrounded by a group of figures, their movements fluid and deliberate. Clad in flowing robes, their faces hidden behind elaborate masks adorned with feathers and gemstones, they were the guardians of the wind shrine—a secretive tribe of scholars and mystics who had long protected the relic within.

The leader of the tribe, a wise and venerable figure known as Elder Zephyrus, stepped forward, his presence commanding yet serene. His voice, deep and resonant, carried the weight of centuries as he welcomed the travellers to the sacred sanctuary of the wind gods. He invited them to share in the knowledge and wisdom passed down through generations, speaking of the relic they sought—a gem-encrusted pendant known as the Aetherial Talisman.

The talisman, said to hold the power to control the winds and currents of the air, had been entrusted to the tribe by the wind gods themselves, its significance fading over time, known only to the most venerable of elders. But now, with the arrival of the travellers, Elder Zephyrus saw a glimmer of hope—perhaps they were the key to unlocking the talisman's true potential and restoring balance to the winds that once shaped the land.

Speaking with Elder Zephyrus and his tribe, the travellers learned that the relic's power was far from fully understood. The key to unlocking its full potential lay in the wisdom of Sage Aeris, a revered elder who had once sought to comprehend the talisman's true nature. However, Aeris, weighed down by the trials of age and the mountain's dangers, had retreated to a secluded cavern halfway down the mountain.

Elder Zephyrus implored the travellers to find him, offering their assistance in deciphering the ancient manuscript Aeris had uncovered—a fragment of knowledge that could unlock the secrets of the Aetherial Talisman. With Aeris's insight, they might finally understand the relic's true power and fulfill their destiny as champions of the wind gods.

With gratitude and steady hearts, the travellers began their descent once more, carefully navigating the mountain slopes in search of the sage's hidden cavern.

Pressing on through the rugged, unforgiving terrain, their spirits held firm despite the mounting challenges ahead. The rugged peaks and treacherous passes stretched before them, yet their spirits remained unbroken. And then, through the mist and fog that clung to the mountain like a veil, they glimpsed it—the entrance to Sage Aeris's secluded cavern. Nestled among the jagged rocks and shrouded in an ethereal mist, it seemed like a sacred sanctuary untouched by the ravages of time.

With measured steps, they approached the cavern, feeling the weight of its ancient energy. At its entrance sat Sage Aeris, cross-legged, bathed in the flickering glow of a solitary torch. His weathered face, etched with the stories of countless years, seemed to absorb the light, and his eyes—aged yet piercingly wise—met theirs with a blend of surprise and intrigue.

"Who dares to seek counsel with an old sage such as I?" His voice rang out, deep and resonant, echoing through the cavern's cool silence. It carried the weight of countless years spent in solitude, a reminder of the wisdom—and burdens—that come with age.

"We are travellers on a quest," Ross spoke first, his voice steady, carrying an air of quiet authority. "We seek the ancient relic of the wind gods, and we have been told that you may hold the key to its whereabouts."

Sage Aeris studied them, his gaze piercing, as though seeking the truth hidden within the depths of their hearts. He seemed to weigh their words carefully, before responding with a quiet reverence.

"You seek the Aetherial Talisman," he murmured, his voice barely above a whisper, yet it held a reverent undertone. "A relic of unimaginable power, concealed deep within the heart of these sacred mountains."

Max, ever curious, stepped forward, his eyes wide with intrigue. "Do you know where we can find it?" His voice carried a mix of hope and apprehension, as though the answer might change everything.

Aeris's lips curved upward in the faintest smile, his eyes reflecting both wisdom and sorrow. "You are in luck," he said, his voice calm and resolute. "I have spent years unearthing its secrets... and now, at long last, the path is clear. But know this—the path to it is fraught with peril. Not all who seek the Talisman are worthy of wielding its power."

With a solemn nod, the sage rose from his seated position, gesturing for the travellers to follow him deeper into the cavern's mysterious depths.

The air within the cavern grew thick with an almost tangible sense of ancient power. The walls were rough-hewn, jagged, and weathered by the ages, with veins of glittering minerals winding their way through the rock, their faint reflections caught in the dim, flickering torchlight. Shafts of sunlight filtered through narrow crevices in the ceiling, etching ethereal patterns on the cavern floor like ghostly fingers of light. Moss and lichen clung to the surfaces, lending the space an air of verdant, otherworldly beauty. The sound of dripping water echoed in the distance, the steady rhythm of time's passage within these stone walls.

Venturing further, the cavern seemed to open into a grand chamber, a place so breathtaking that it felt as if they had stumbled upon a hidden sanctuary. Crystalline stalagmites, their translucent forms gleaming in the faint light, rose like frozen towers from the cavern floor. The colours of the chamber shifted as the light refracted through the crystals, bathing the space in a dazzling kaleidoscope of hues.

At the very heart of the chamber stood a pedestal, upon which rested the Aetherial Talisman—a gem-encrusted relic bathed in a soft, ethereal glow. It pulsed with a faint, otherworldly energy, projecting strange, dancing shadows upon the walls and filling the air with an aura of ancient mystery. The sight of it was so beautiful, so overwhelming, that the travellers could not help but feel a sense of awe wash over them.

Little did they know, however, that this discovery was merely the beginning. The true test lay not in finding the Talisman, but in what it would demand from them next.

As they approached the Talisman, anticipation hung heavily in the air, thick like fog. Sage Aeris stood before them, his presence commanding and enigmatic, as if he were both a part of this sacred place and beyond it. With a raised hand, he halted their advance, his gesture as ancient as the cavern itself.

The air seemed to grow still, and the travellers felt the weight of his gaze upon them, sharp and knowing. His voice reverberated through the chamber, carrying with it the solemnity of ancient rites.

"You may wonder why the Talisman rests here, hidden from the world," he began, his voice rich with history and reverence. "Long ago, wise guardians and mystical forces placed it within these sacred depths. They understood the dangers that would arise if its power fell into the wrong hands. And so, they entrusted its safekeeping to the guardianship of this cavern, far from the eyes of those who would misuse it."

The travellers absorbed this revelation, their hearts heavy with the weight of their quest. They had come in search of power, but what they had found was so much more. They had come face to face with the essence of air itself, with the very forces of nature embodied in the relic that lay before them.

Sage Aeris's voice grew solemn, his gaze sweeping over each of them. "I sense a noble purpose in your hearts," he intoned. "But before I can aid you in your quest, one among you must prove their loyalty."

A heavy silence fell over the group as the weight of the test hung in the air. The flickering torchlight danced across uncertain faces, no one daring to step forward—until Max spoke.

"I'll do it," he said, his voice steady despite the nerves tightening in his chest. "I'll take the test."

Aeris turned to him, eyes narrowing slightly in appraisal. "You step forward freely, without being chosen. That is rare." His tone carried both approval and warning. "Know this, Max—loyalty, once questioned, is not easily mended. This trial will reveal more than you expect." His gaze settled upon Max, the words heavy with prophecy. "You, Max," the sage intoned, "shall be the one to undertake the test of loyalty. If you are to wield the Talisman's power, you must first prove that your heart is true."

Max felt his heart race within his chest, yet his courage held steady. Stepping forward, he met the sage's gaze with quiet confidence. "I accept the challenge," he declared, his voice a steady affirmation of his commitment.

Sage Aeris nodded solemnly, his expression grave. "Prepare yourself, for the test will not be easy," he warned, his voice resonating in the cavern, its deep echo reverberating off the jagged walls.

With a deliberate wave of his hand, Sage Aeris conjured a shimmering portal of light, its edges rippling like a pond disturbed by a single drop. Beyond the portal, a realm of swirling mist and shadow beckoned. "Step through the portal, and face the trials that await you," he instructed, his tone both commanding and patient.

Max took a deep, steadying breath, summoning every ounce of courage within him. His heart thudded in his chest, but he didn't falter. Stepping forward, he crossed the threshold, disappearing into the swirling mists beyond.

As Max ventured deeper into the mist, a sudden shift in the atmosphere caught his attention. He stumbled upon a group of weary travellers huddled together in a dimly lit corner, their clothes torn and their faces gaunt with exhaustion and fear. These individuals were lost, their desperation palpable in the heavy air surrounding them. Seeing their plight stirred something deep within Max—an innate, unshakeable sense of compassion that urged him to act. His mind, sharp and focused on his original quest, wavered for a moment as his heart cried out to help these souls in distress.

Without a second thought, Max approached the travellers, his footsteps quiet yet steady on the moss-covered ground. He offered them a comforting smile before listening intently to their stories of hardship, loss, and an uncertain journey. Their pain mirrored his own in many ways, and Max felt a pang of empathy that ran deeper than mere sympathy.

Despite the urgency of his mission—despite the relic that called to him with its promises of power and knowledge—Max could not, in good conscience, ignore their suffering. "I can't leave them here," he murmured to himself, his voice brimming with quiet conviction. "I have to help."

His heart swelling with purpose, Max set to work immediately. He provided food and water, offered comforting words of encouragement, and used his resourcefulness to guide them along their way. His every action, no matter how small, seemed to lift their spirits, however briefly. The travellers, once fearful and uncertain, began to stand straighter, their eyes less burdened, their hope rekindled.

As hours passed, Max became completely immersed in the task at hand. The relic, his quest, the world outside—the things that once occupied his every thought—faded into the background. In that moment, the only thing that mattered was these people, lost in the vast unknown. Max had learned, in the most unexpected way, that the trial of compassion wasn't just about offering assistance—it was about embodying empathy, about giving of oneself even when faced with trials of their own.

Eventually, as the travellers finally found their way to safety, Max experienced a profound sense of fulfillment, a deep satisfaction that nothing material could replace. He may have strayed from his original path, but he had proven something far more significant—the depth of his selflessness and his unwavering loyalty to those in need. When he finally rejoined his friends, it was with a sense of peace that filled him completely. He had passed the trial, not by claiming a relic, but by choosing to protect his friends and others in need.

As Max emerged from the swirling mist, his silhouette gradually took form, becoming clearer with each step. His friends watched, their faces a mixture of hope and uncertainty, their eyes locked on him, waiting for his return. The weight of their anticipation hung heavy in the air.

With each stride, Max's confidence grew, his movements more deliberate, and a quiet strength emanated from him. The weight of his decision— the empathy he had shown—was now evident in the steady, purposeful manner in which he walked toward them. As he finally stepped into the light, his friends greeted him with open arms, their relief and admiration palpable in the air.

"You did it, Max!" Siobhan exclaimed, her voice filled with pride. Her eyes sparkled with the kind of admiration reserved for true heroes. "We knew you could."

Max, feeling the warmth of their embrace, nodded, a faint smile tugging at the corners of his lips. Despite the trials he had faced, a quiet satisfaction settled within him. He had proven something far more important than just his strength—he had proven that his heart was stronger than any trial.

"I couldn't have done it without all of you," Max said, his voice thick with gratitude. "We're in this together, no matter what."

With that, Max joined his friends, their bond strengthened by the trials they had faced and the ones still to come. As they stood together, the silent promise that they would face whatever challenges lay ahead was understood by all. Their unity was their greatest strength.

The Sage's eyes gleamed with approval as Max emerged from the mist, his friends waiting anxiously. Stepping forward, the Sage extended a hand, the ancient wisdom in his eyes betraying a depth of understanding beyond mortal years.

"Well done, young one," the Sage intoned, his voice resonating with the weight of time. "You have proven yourself worthy by passing the trial. And now, you must make a choice."

Max's heart raced as his anticipation grew. The weight of this choice was not lost on him—he knew that it would shape the course of their journey, and perhaps their very lives. He stood before the Sage, the moment of decision upon him.

"A choice, then," Aeris continued, his gaze unwavering as it locked onto Max. "The relic is yours to claim if you wish. However, if you choose to take the relic with you, you must select one companion to stay behind. The chosen companion will remain here, within these cavern walls, to live out the rest of their days wandering in solitude. The rest of you may leave together. Alternatively, you may forsake the relic, ensuring that your companions remain safe and that you depart together."

Max's breath caught in his throat, the weight of the decision heavy upon him. He turned his gaze toward his friends, their faces etched with anticipation, each of them silently asking for his decision.

The relic, the power it promised—such power could change everything. But to leave a friend behind? That went against everything Max believed. They had faced so many dangers, had trusted one another when no one else would. To sacrifice a companion for a relic would be the ultimate betrayal of the very bonds they had forged.

Max squared his shoulders, meeting the Sage's gaze with firm conviction. "I choose my friends," he declared firmly, his voice reverberating throughout the cavern, filled with warmth and compassion. "We came here together, and we will leave together. Relic or no relic."

Aeris nodded, a knowing smile curling at the edges of his lips, his approval evident. "Your choice speaks volumes, young one," he said with quiet admiration. "You understand the true meaning of friendship and selflessness. Take heart, for the true treasure lies not in material wealth, but in the bonds we forge with those we hold dear."

As Max turned to his friends, a profound sense of peace washed over him. No relic, no treasure could replace the bond they shared. Together, they had faced trials, and together, they would continue. That was the true value of their journey.

As Max and his friends began to turn away, ready to leave the cavern, Sage Aeris raised a hand, halting their departure. His gaze shifted from one face to another, his expression inscrutable, yet filled with wisdom beyond measure.

"The true trial was not one of obtaining the relic," Aeris explained solemnly, his voice carrying the weight of centuries. "It was a test of friendship and loyalty. Max, you have proven yourself worthy by choosing the bonds of friendship over the allure of the talisman."

With a graceful gesture, Aeris beckoned Max forward. A gleaming talisman, pulsating with an ethereal energy, floated before him. "Take it, young one," the Sage said, his voice rich with ancient power. "The time has come for the Talisman to fulfill its destiny once more. It has chosen you, Max, and your loyal companions, to wield its power over the winds and currents—for the greater good."

The talisman glowed brighter, its energy entwining with Max's strong intent. Aeris' keen eyes caught a flicker of unease in Max's expression. Sensing his hesitation, the Sage paused and allowed his gaze to encompass the group.

"Do not doubt yourselves, young champions," Aeris reassured them, his voice calm yet filled with the weight of ancient wisdom. "With the blessing of the Talisman comes the knowledge to wield its power."

Aeris drew the group closer, his eyes glimmering with a mixture of pride and solemnity. "Now, listen closely," he continued, his tone becoming more measured. "The Talisman is not merely an object; it is a conduit, a bridge to deeper forces. To master it is to understand its subtle intricacies."

As he spoke, his hands moved fluidly, tracing patterns in the air as if calling on the very winds themselves. Aeris began to delve into the ancient rites, explaining how each ritual and incantation was designed to unlock the hidden powers within the Talisman. His words, though cryptic, were clear in their intention—to teach them the sacred art of wielding such potent energy.

Max watched intently, his gaze fixed on Aeris's every movement. The first ritual unfolded before him with an almost hypnotic grace. Aeris performed an intricate dance, his body swaying through the motions like the wind itself, each movement both deliberate and spontaneous, fluid and controlled. Max felt a rush of excitement and nervousness bubbling within him. The air seemed charged with energy, and as he attempted to follow Aeris's lead, his eyes wandered to Siobhan. Her movements were equally graceful, but there was a fierceness in the way she danced, her expression fierce and resolute. Max's heart skipped a beat whenever their gazes met, a subtle reminder of the unspoken connection between them.

Ross, however, struggled. His limbs seemed stiff, fighting against the flow of the ritual. His movements were jagged and uncoordinated, betraying the frustration he felt. Sweat gathered on his brow as he fought to synchronise his body with the rhythm of the dance, but his steps faltered, and his frustration grew.

The twins, Anastasia and Greer, on the other hand, moved in perfect unison, their bodies in flawless harmony with one another. Their connection was undeniable; it was as if they shared a single soul between them. Each step they took was seamlessly mirrored by the other, their faces serene yet intense, as if they had been dancing together for lifetimes.

But it was Jonas who truly seemed to embody the spirit of the ritual. His body moved with an effortless fluidity, each motion a seamless extension of the air around them. His movements were as natural as breathing, every step imbued with the grace of someone who had long understood the dance of the winds. Jonas's form shimmered with an almost ethereal quality, his every motion reflecting the invisible currents of the air itself.

Max couldn't help but watch Jonas in awe. There was something magnetic about him, something more than the quiet stoicism that defined his usual demeanor. In this moment, Max saw a different side of Jonas—a side that was as powerful and untamed as the very forces they sought to control. Despite his own awkwardness, Max found himself captivated by Jonas's effortless mastery, a silent admiration blooming within him.

Ross noticed this too. After a moment's hesitation, he approached Jonas, a thoughtful expression on his face. "Hey, Jonas," he began, breaking the silence, "I've been thinking. You've got some real talent with this air stuff, don't you?"

Jonas glanced at Ross, his modest smile betraying no hint of arrogance. "I suppose so. It just feels... natural, you know?"

Ross grinned, his eyes lighting up as a thought struck him.

"I think I figured out why," he said, his voice filled with enthusiasm. "It's your build. You've got these long, flexible limbs—it's like your body was made for this." He gestured with his hands to demonstrate, his excitement growing.

"While the rest of us are all stiff and rigid, you move with a fluidity that's perfect for the air element."

Jonas's eyes widened as realisation dawned on him. He looked at Ross, a mix of surprise and intrigue in his gaze.

"You really think so?" he asked, his voice tinged with wonder.

"Absolutely," Ross replied with a grin, clapping him on the back in a friendly gesture. "You're a natural. So, what do you say? Ready to show the wind who's boss?"

Jonas chuckled, a glint of newfound confidence shining in his eyes. "You bet," he said, his focus sharp.

"Let's do this."

The group returned to their practise, the air around them humming with energy as Aeris's steady guidance led them through the intricate rituals.

As the final steps of the dance came to an end, Sage Aeris gathered them all into a circle, the glow of the cavern's crystalline formations sending soft, mystical shadows on the stone walls. The atmosphere was thick with anticipation as he took a deep breath and began chanting the ancient incantation. His voice, rich with power and wisdom, reverberated through the cavern.

"O winds of the ancients, hear my call,

Grant us passage to the realm of air. With words of old and hearts aligned,

We seek the power that lies entwined."

As Aeris spoke, the air around them seemed to shift, the energy thickening as if the very atmosphere were responding to the ancient words. Max felt a tingle of sensation run through him, a quiet hum of power thrumming beneath his skin. He focused on the chant, allowing the words to reverberate in his soul, while beside him, Siobhan closed her eyes, her lips moving in silent reverence as she echoed the chant. Ross and the twins followed suit, their voices rising in a harmonious chorus that blended perfectly with the hum of the cavern. Together, they invoked the power of the winds, their voices resonating through the air like the song of the earth itself.

But it was Jonas who truly embodied the essence of the incantation. His voice was strong, unwavering, each word filled with purpose as he uttered the chant with a depth of conviction that sent a ripple through the air. A breeze, gentle at first, began to stir around them, its whisper growing louder as the air thickened, swirling in response to their words.

Max could feel it now—the power, building within him, urging him forward. The winds howled, the magic growing more tangible with every breath. His heart pounded in his chest, and as they neared the final words of the chant, the cavern seemed to tremble in anticipation.

Finally, with a flourish of Aeris's hand, the cavern shimmered and dissolved, revealing a swirling portal of air before them. It pulsed with an eerie, otherworldly light, its edges shimmering with an energy that felt both inviting and dangerous.

"Step through, brave travellers," Aeris said, his voice rich with pride and reverence. "May the winds guide you on your journey, and may you find the answers you seek."

With a shared glance charged with purpose, Max and his companions stepped forward, crossing the threshold of the portal. As they passed through, the cavern disappeared, fading into nothingness, leaving no trace of their presence behind.

When they opened their eyes, they found themselves back in the forest, standing at the foot of the mountain, moments before their journey had begun. But this time, they carried with them the knowledge and the power of the winds—ready to face whatever trials awaited them on their quest for the ancient relics.

CHAPTER 3

Water – The Aquor Sphere

As the morning sun painted the sky in hues of pink and gold, Max and his companions stood at the edge of the forest. The air was crisp, and the warmth of the first light caressed their skin, but their minds were still reeling from their encounter with Sage Aeris. The memory of the swirling portal and the ancient incantations lingered, filling them with awe and a rekindled drive. The sage's cryptic words echoed in their minds, urging them forward on their quest.

With the guidance of the Aetherial Talisman and the wisdom imparted by Sage Aeris, they set off once more. Their eyes were firmly fixed on the next relic they sought—the orb of water. The path ahead was uncertain, but their hearts were set on their goal, and the promise of adventure fueled their every step. Together, they navigated the winding trails and rugged terrain with a sense of ease, each footfall purposeful, as if the earth itself were guiding them.

Venturing deeper into the wilderness, the dense forest slowly gave way to meadows bathed in golden sunlight. Max found himself walking alongside Anastasia and Greer, the twins whose bond seemed almost otherworldly. There was an unspoken understanding between them, a synchrony that made their connection feel as though it transcended the physical world.

Max glanced at the twins, noticing the way they moved in perfect harmony. Their steps echoed each other with an uncanny precision, as if they were two halves of the same whole. It fascinated him. He wondered what secrets lay hidden within the depths of their shared consciousness—secrets they had yet to reveal, even to him.

"Hey, Anastasia, Greer," Max began, his voice cutting through the comfortable silence between them. "I've been meaning to ask you something."

The twins turned to him, their expressions both curious and expectant. Anastasia, the quieter of the two, tilted her head slightly, her soft, melodic voice responding, "What is it, Max?"

Max hesitated, his thoughts swirling as he carefully considered how to phrase his question. "Well, we've been on this journey for a while now, and it got me thinking... What do you two plan to do once we've found all the relics?"

Anastasia and Greer exchanged a glance, a subtle but meaningful exchange, before returning their gaze to Max. The moment stretched on, the air between them thick with unspoken thoughts. Finally, Greer shrugged, breaking the silence. "To be honest, we haven't really thought about it. Our focus has always been on helping you and the others succeed in this quest."

Anastasia's gaze drifted to the horizon, her thoughts seemingly far away. "But now that you mention it..." She smiled wistfully, "We've always dreamed of exploring the world beyond our village. Maybe once this quest is over, we'll finally have the chance to see new places, meet new people, and experience life beyond the confines of our home."

Max nodded in understanding, his heart swelling with a mix of admiration and empathy. He could relate to their longing for something more. "That sounds amazing," he said, a grin spreading across his face. "I have no doubt that you two will find countless adventures waiting for you out there."

With the conversation fading into comfortable silence, they continued their journey deeper into the wilderness. But the forest around them soon grew denser and more forbidding. The air grew thick with the scent of damp earth and decaying foliage, and the sounds of unseen creatures rustling in the underbrush added a layer of tension to the atmosphere.

The path forward became increasingly difficult to navigate. Thick undergrowth tangled at their feet, while gnarled branches reached out like the hands of some unseen creature, hindering their progress with each step. The forest seemed alive, watching, waiting.

Max, stepping forward on this occasion, took the lead, his sharp eyes scanning the twisted labyrinth of trees and vines for any sign of a way forward. He knew that navigating through this dense foliage would take time and patience—a test of endurance and strategy that would challenge even the most seasoned adventurers.

Siobhan, pragmatic as always, suggested using their blades to hack at the vines blocking their path. But Ross, ever the cautious one, was quick to voice his concerns. "We don't know what kind of attention we might attract by cutting through the undergrowth. We could end up with more trouble than we bargained for."

The twins, however, offered a different solution. Their connection, honed over years of shared experiences, allowed them to sense what the others couldn't. They proposed using their combined strength to push through the tangled undergrowth, relying on their innate synchronisation to work as one. In perfect harmony, they began to clear a path, the rhythm of their movements both fluid and efficient.

Max nodded, impressed by their ingenuity. It was clear that the twins' bond was more than just emotional—it was practical, a gift that would serve them well on this journey.

With the twins now leading the way, they steadily made their way through the forest. The path, though still challenging, was now more navigable, and each member of the group contributed in their own way to overcoming this first major obstacle.

As they pressed on, the dense forest began to thin, the trees growing fewer and farther apart. Soon, they emerged into a sun-dappled glade, the air fresher and more open. The sounds of birdsong filled the air, and wildflowers dotted the landscape in vibrant splashes of colour. But their progress was halted when they reached the river—a wide, rushing torrent that blocked their path.

The water roared and churned, its surface frothing with whitecaps as it surged onward with relentless force. The river stretched endlessly before them, and Max knew there was no easy way across. Without a bridge or ford in sight, it stood as a formidable barrier between them and their goal.

Max surveyed the scene, his brow furrowed in concentration. This was a challenge they hadn't expected, but one they would have to overcome if they were to continue their journey. Turning to his companions, he called for suggestions, each of them proposing different ideas.

Siobhan suggested searching for a shallower spot where they might be able to wade across. "If we take our time and stay vigilant, we might find a safe place to cross," she reasoned.

Ross, always the builder, had a different idea. "We could construct a bridge using the trees lining the riverbank. It might take time, but with teamwork, we can make it work."

But it was Anastasia and Greer who came up with the most unconventional solution. Drawing on their knowledge of wilderness survival, they proposed constructing a raft from the fallen branches and vines scattered along the riverbank. Their suggestion was bold, but it was also pragmatic, a solution that could carry them not just across the river, but down its rushing waters to the other side.

After careful consideration, the group agreed on the twins' plan. They set to work, gathering the necessary materials, their conversation flowing freely as they worked. There was a lightness to the atmosphere, as though the challenges they faced could be overcome with camaraderie and creativity.

Max and Siobhan, working side by side, found themselves sharing stories from their pasts. Max spoke of his dream to become an explorer, his childhood filled with tales of far-off lands and the thrill of discovery. Siobhan, in turn, spoke of her love for nature, her childhood spent climbing trees and learning about the world around her.

Meanwhile, Ross and Jonas worked together, securing the branches for the raft. Their conversation was filled with lighthearted banter—sports, favourite teams, and memorable games. It was a welcome distraction, and their laughter echoed through the glade as they joked about players and strategies, reminiscing about the games that had defined their youth.

Anastasia and Greer, meanwhile, worked in quiet unison. Weaving the vines into sturdy ropes, their conversation turned inward, focused on the bond they shared. They spoke of their childhood, the challenges they had faced, and the strength they drew from each other. Their connection was undeniable, and Max couldn't help but admire it, feeling a quiet awe for the bond they shared.

The raft began to take shape under their skilled hands, the once-disjointed pieces of wood and vine gradually melding together into a sturdy vessel. With each twist of the vine and secure knot, their confidence grew, powered by a common purpose to overcome the obstacle before them. The rhythmic motion of their work created a sense of unity, each action reinforcing their joint commitment.

Anastasia, Greer, Max, Ross, and Jonas worked tirelessly side by side. Their movements were synchronised, like a well-rehearsed dance, a testament to their deep connection and unspoken understanding. Siobhan, with her sharp eye for detail, offered suggestions and adjustments, ensuring every component fit snugly into place, her focus unwavering. Her thoughtful observations, combined with the efforts of the group, guided the creation of the raft from mere fragments to a cohesive whole.

Together, they manoeuvred the heavy logs into position, binding them with tightly woven vines to form a sturdy framework. Each knot and each adjustment was made with care, resulting in a vessel that, though born from scattered debris, was now functional and robust, ready to face the treacherous currents of the river.

With the sun dipping lower on the horizon, its waning light stretched across the riverbank, creating deep pools of shade. The completed raft stood as a symbol of their ingenuity and perseverance. It was more than just a floating structure—it was the culmination of hard work and teamwork, a testament to their ability to rise above adversity.

With the daylight waning and darkness settling over the forest, the group decided to make camp for the night, agreeing it was best to rest and continue their journey in the morning light. While

Max, Ross, and Jonas ventured into the surrounding woods to forage for firewood—and perhaps a meal—Siobhan took charge of setting up their makeshift campsite. She arranged their bedding and ensured that their supplies were neatly organised, her movements efficient yet careful.

When the boys returned to camp with their catch of squirrels, they wasted no time. Working together, they quickly gathered kindling and built a fire. The crackling flames and the savory aroma of roasting meat filled the air, adding an extra layer of comfort to the night. As they sat around the fire, exchanging stories and light-hearted banter, the weight of their journey seemed to momentarily lift. The night was warm, their spirits high as they savored their meal in the company of trusted friends.

With bellies full and laughter still echoing in the air, they eventually retired to their makeshift beds. The crackling of the fire served as a lullaby, easing them into a peaceful slumber, the promise of the next day's challenges already lingering in their minds.

As dawn broke, golden rays spilled across the landscape, they stirred from their restful sleep, refreshed and ready for the day ahead. With renewed energy, they made their way down to the riverbank, where their makeshift raft awaited, ready to carry them forward on their next adventure.

With a shared nod of agreement, they carefully launched the raft into the water, watching as its sturdy frame rode the current with surprising stability. The water, smooth and unwavering, seemed to welcome their creation, a silent testament to their hard work.

As they climbed aboard, the river carried them forward, its steady current propelling them closer to their goal. Each stroke of the paddle brought them nearer to the unknown, the sound of the water and the rhythm of their paddling creating a steady beat that synchronised their movements.

As the raft glided down the river, Ross's sharp eyes caught a glimmer in the distance. Squinting against the sunlight reflecting off the water, he focused his gaze and made out a group of figures gathered on the riverbank.

"Hey, guys, look over there," Ross called out, pointing towards the distant figures. "I think there's someone waiting for us."

Max and the others turned their attention toward the shore, their faces becoming more alert as they saw the figures. Their eyes narrowed, and a quiet tension filled the air.

"Who do you think they are?" Siobhan asked, her voice laced with curiosity and a hint of apprehension.

"I'm not sure," Max replied, scanning the shoreline for any clues. "But we should approach cautiously until we know more."

With their senses heightened and their guard up, the team continued to paddle toward the shore. Each stroke of the oars seemed to carry them closer, their anticipation building. As they neared, the figures on the riverbank became clearer, revealing themselves to be a group of nomads gathered around a small campfire. Their faces were obscured by the dancing flames, their presence both intriguing and mysterious.

Max and his companions exchanged wary glances as the raft slowly drifted toward the riverbank. The nomads, dressed in weathered clothing and adorned with intricate jewelry, watched them with curious eyes. Their expressions were unreadable, the firelight flickering in their gaze.

As the raft gently bumped against the shore, Max and his companions stepped off, their feet sinking slightly into the soft, damp earth. They approached the nomads with caution, their senses alert to any sign of potential danger.

"Hello there," Max called out, his voice carrying across the water. "We mean you no harm. We're just passing through."

The nomads exchanged murmurs among themselves in a language unfamiliar to Max and his companions. One of them, an elderly woman with wise, weathered eyes, stepped forward. Her presence was calm yet authoritative, her demeanor measured as she regarded the travellers.

"Greetings, travellers," she said, her voice resonating with quiet strength. "What brings you to our lands?"

"We're on a journey to find the orb of water," Max replied, his voice steady and clear. "We seek its power to aid us in our quest."

The elderly woman nodded thoughtfully, her gaze appraising as she studied Max and his companions. Her eyes lingered on them, considering their words carefully.

"The Aquor Sphere is a sacred artifact," she said solemnly. "Few are worthy to possess its power. Tell me, travellers, why do you seek it?"

Max hesitated, choosing his words with care. "We seek the orb to restore balance to the elements," he explained. "To protect our world from those who wish to do it harm."

The nomads murmured among themselves, their expressions softening slightly. The elderly woman nodded again, her gaze meeting Max's with a newfound respect.

"You speak with conviction, young one," she said. "Perhaps there is truth in your words. But the orb is not easily obtained. It lies deep within the heart of the river, guarded by ancient spirits and powerful magic."

Max's heart sank at her words, the challenge ahead suddenly feeling much more formidable. Yet, his will did not waver. He squared his shoulders, intent on pressing on despite the obstacles in their path.

"We understand," Max said firmly. "But we will not be deterred. We will find a way to retrieve the orb, no matter the cost."

The elderly woman regarded him with a knowing smile, her eyes holding a hint of admiration. Yet, her expression remained guarded, a trace of skepticism lingering.

"The certainty in your tone is undeniable," she began, "but words alone are not enough to earn our help. We have seen many travellers come and go, all with grand promises and noble intentions. Yet, few have proven their worth."

Max glanced at his companions, understanding the weight of the challenge. He stepped forward, courage burning in his eyes.

"Please," he said earnestly, "give us a chance to prove ourselves."

The elderly woman studied him for a long moment, her eyes assessing. Then, with a slow nod, she gestured to a younger nomad. The young man approached with a small, intricately carved wooden box. He opened it to reveal a small, luminescent crystal, faintly glowing with an ethereal light.

"This is a shard of the river's heart," the elderly woman explained. "It reacts to purity of intent and strength of spirit. If you and your companions can make it glow brighter, it will prove your worthiness."

Max accepted the crystal carefully, feeling a warmth emanating from it. He turned to his friends, and each of them placed a hand on the crystal. Together, they closed their eyes, focusing their intent and sincerity into the shard.

Slowly, the crystal's light began to intensify, glowing from a soft ember to a brilliant radiance. The light grew, illuminating the entire camp in a radiant glow that seemed to mirror the group's purity and inner courage. The nomads watched in awe as the crystal pulsed with undeniable force, a symbol of their unwavering commitment.

When Max and his friends opened their eyes, they found the elderly woman smiling at them, her expression radiating a genuine warmth that was both comforting and reassuring.

"Very well," she said, her voice steady yet kind. "If you are truly committed to this quest, then we will offer you our assistance. But be warned—the journey ahead will test your strength, your courage, and your endurance. Are you prepared to face it?"

Max's gaze shifted to his companions. He saw the same fierce conviction mirrored in their eyes, a reflection of their shared purpose. He nodded, the weight of their mission settling on his shoulders, then turned back to the elderly woman, his voice calm but confident.

"We are," he replied firmly. "Lead the way."

The elderly woman nodded approvingly, a slight curve to her lips. "I am too old to accompany you on such a perilous journey, but I will send two of our most experienced nomads to guide you."

She turned to address the gathered nomads, her voice carrying across the silent group. "Liora and Kael, step forward."

From the crowd emerged two figures. Liora was tall and lithe, her sharp eyes observing everything around her with a calm, almost detached demeanor. Her dark hair was braided intricately down her back, a mark of both her strength and her care for tradition. Kael, in contrast, was a sturdy man with quiet strength emanating from him. His weathered skin, tanned and marked by years of exposure to the elements, spoke of a life lived in harmony with the harsh wilderness.

"Liora and Kael know these lands better than anyone," the elderly woman said, her voice filled with respect. "They will ensure you find your way and help you navigate the dangers that lie ahead."

Liora and Kael bowed slightly, acknowledging the trust placed in them. Liora spoke first, her voice steady and confident. "We will do our best to guide you safely to your destination."

Kael nodded, his face serious. "The journey will be challenging, but together, we can overcome any obstacle."

Max and his companions felt a renewed sense of hope as the weight of their responsibility lightened with the addition of such experienced guides. As they gathered their belongings and readied themselves to set out again, the elderly woman offered one final piece of wisdom.

"Trust in each other, and in the guidance of Liora and Kael. The path ahead will be fraught with difficulty, but your inner strength and solidarity will see you through. May the winds of fate be ever in your favor."

With those words of encouragement, the group set off, their hearts filled with a newfound strength, knowing they were not alone in their quest for the Aquor Sphere.

The group, now joined by their two trusted guides, made their way to the makeshift raft that would carry them down the river. The nomads watched from the riverbank as the group pushed off, the raft gliding smoothly over the water's surface, setting the tone for their journey.

At first, the river seemed peaceful, the gentle current guiding the raft downstream with little resistance. Liora and Kael shared stories of their past experiences, offering valuable insight into the land they knew so well. Their voices, calm and steady, blended with the soothing sounds of the river, helping to ease the tension among the group. The air felt lighter as their camaraderie grew, and with each shared story, they felt their shared purpose draw them closer together.

As the day stretched on, the golden sunlight dimmed, its fading brilliance streaking the water's surface with deepening shadows. The dense forest on either side of the riverbank darkened, its mysteries deepening with the encroaching twilight. The night's chorus of crickets and the occasional hoot of an owl added an eerie yet comforting soundtrack to their journey.

"We should find a place to camp for the night," Liora suggested, her sharp eyes scanning the riverbank for a suitable spot. "The river can be treacherous in the dark."

Kael, ever practical, nodded in agreement. "There's a clearing just ahead where we can dock the raft and set up camp. It should be safe for the night."

The group steered the raft toward the shore, landing at a small, grassy clearing nestled between the trees. They disembarked, securing the raft to a sturdy tree trunk to prevent it from drifting away during the night.

As the camp was set up, everyone worked with practised efficiency, their movements synchronised as if they had done this many times before. Siobhan and Anastasia ventured off to gather firewood, while Greer and Jonas worked together to erect makeshift tents. Max and Ross, guided by Kael, scouted the surrounding area for any potential dangers and collected fresh water from a nearby stream.

Soon, the camp was ready. A warm fire crackled in the clearing, its gentle glow lighting up the group's faces with a soft, flickering warmth. They gathered around it, sharing a simple meal of dried meat and berries. The atmosphere was relaxed, the stresses of the journey momentarily forgotten as conversations flowed easily. It was a time to bond and get to know their new guides better.

"Tell us more about the river," Ross asked, his curiosity piqued by the challenges ahead. "What's the most dangerous part of this journey?"

Liora's smile was thoughtful, almost wistful. "The river itself is unpredictable. The currents can shift without warning, and hidden rocks or submerged logs can capsize a raft in an instant. But the real challenge lies ahead—navigating through the rapids and the waterfalls."

Kael's voice was low but firm. "And there are the guardians of the relic, who will test you in ways you can't even imagine. But I believe in your strength and grit. You have what it takes to succeed."

As the fire crackled on, Max suggested that a few of them go out to hunt for additional food to ensure they were well-stocked for the morning. With a wave, they disappeared into the forest.

Meanwhile, Anastasia and Greer, the inseparable twins, settled by a tranquil stream near the camp. Their connection was more than just telepathy; it was a bond that had deepened over the years. As their journey progressed, they had begun to realise that their unique connection extended beyond thoughts alone.

Sitting cross-legged by the stream, they closed their eyes and synchronised their breathing. With each inhale and exhale, they felt a strange but powerful sensation wash over them—almost as if their minds were merging. In that moment, they experienced a heightened awareness, as if their thoughts and senses were blending into one, a shared consciousness between them.

Without a word spoken, Anastasia reached out her hand, and Greer instinctively mirrored her movement. To their astonishment, they realised they could manipulate the water in the stream, their combined willpower guiding the flow with ease.

With a gentle flick of their fingers, they sent ripples dancing across the surface of the water, shaping the liquid into intricate patterns and symbols. It felt as though they were conducting an invisible orchestra, orchestrating the water with effortless precision.

As they continued to explore their newfound abilities, Anastasia and Greer marveled at the strength of their connection. Their bond was no longer limited to mere telepathy; together, they could harness the power of water itself, manipulating it with a synergy that left them both in awe.

Soon, they returned, carrying the squirrels they had hunted, ensuring there would be enough provisions for the morning. They shared stories of their hunt and the forest before retiring to their tents, the fire flickering softly as the night embraced them in its cool, peaceful silence.

Morning arrived with the gentle embrace of dawn, its soft, golden light spreading over the campsite. The travellers awoke, stretching and blinking into the new day, feeling rested and ready to continue their journey. They moved with quiet efficiency, packing up their belongings, extinguishing the dying embers of the fire, and boarding the raft once more, the anticipation of the day's adventure filling the air.

With Liora at the helm and Kael standing close by, they resumed their journey down the river. The steady rhythm of the boat's movement against the current seemed to mirror the calm pace of their thoughts. The sound of water lapping gently against the raft became a soothing lullaby, its steady cadence grounding them as the scenery around them shifted. The dense forest that had clung to the riverbanks began to recede, making way for more open terrain—a broad, sweeping vista that opened up to reveal the wild, untamed beauty of the landscape.

The hours passed in a quiet harmony, the sun climbing steadily in the sky. By midday, the warmth of the sun on their faces was tempered by the cooling breeze that whispered through the trees. As the sun began its slow descent, its amber light spilled over the river, painting the water with a warm glow and shadows that seemed to sway with the current. The group, in high spirits, shared stories to pass the time, their laughter mingling with the sound of the river. The bonds between them had deepened in the days of travel, and the camaraderie among them was palpable.

But the peaceful calm was abruptly shattered. The gentle current ahead began to swell, the river's mood shifting as if it had sensed something. Without warning, the once tranquil waters gave way to a series of heavy rapids. The river roared, its mighty force churning as waves crashed against jagged rocks, sending spray into the air. The sight of the treacherous waters ahead filled the travellers with a mix of excitement and apprehension, their hearts racing in response to the sudden shift.

"Hold on tight!" Kael shouted, his voice rising above the noise of the water as the raft was swept toward the rapids.

The raft bucked and swayed violently, the powerful currents threatening to tear it apart. The travellers scrambled to maintain their balance, their earlier conversations forgotten as they focused solely on staying aboard. Their eyes were wide with a blend of fear and exhilaration, the raft's erratic motion throwing them off-balance with every lurch.

Anastasia and Greer exchanged a quick, determined glance, understanding without words that this was the moment to put their newly honed skills to the test. The twins moved with synchronised precision to the front of the raft, their steps sure despite the chaos around them. They positioned themselves side by side, their bodies attuned to the rhythm of the water. Eyes closing, they began to focus on the steady rise and fall of their breath, just as they had practised by the stream's edge.

With each deep, controlled inhale, they felt their connection grow stronger. It was as though their minds were merging into one, their thoughts intertwining until they became a single, unified consciousness. A powerful rush of energy surged through their veins, thrilling and overwhelming in equal measure.

Anastasia raised her hand, fingers spread wide, and Greer mirrored the gesture, their movements in perfect harmony. Together, they reached out with their minds, feeling the wild, untamed energy of the river. The waters, once chaotic and frantic, seemed to pause in response to their presence. For a fleeting moment, the river's roiling surface stilled, as though waiting for the twins to direct its next move.

With a flick of their fingers, they began to shape the water. The rapids, once wild and unpredictable, gradually softened under their will. The waves smoothed out, their crashing diminished to gentle swells, and the raft's violent rocking subsided, as though the very river was yielding to their command. The others watched in stunned awe, the tension in the air dissipating as the twins worked their magic, guiding the raft safely through the once-turbulent waters.

As they navigated the rapids, the twins continued to channel their combined willpower, their hands moving with fluid grace. They shaped the water in intricate patterns—curves, spirals, and symbols—each movement intentional, each gesture a step in an invisible dance. It was as though they were conducting an orchestra, their synchronised motions coaxing the river to follow their design.

The raft glided smoothly through the waters, carried by the gentle current that the twins had tamed. The danger passed as quickly as it had come, the river returning to its calm, steady flow. Anastasia and Greer lowered their hands, the powerful connection between them slowly fading. The air around them seemed to settle, the tension lifting as they returned to themselves, their breathing steady, their bond stronger than before.

Breathless but triumphant, the twins turned to face their companions, who were already erupting in cheers. The others clapped their hands, their faces bright with a mixture of admiration and relief, the weight of the journey momentarily lifted. A sense of victory hung in the air, as though they had collectively emerged from a storm unscathed.

"That was incredible!" Max exclaimed, his voice thick with amazement. His eyes were wide, not just with awe, but with genuine gratitude. "You guys saved us! I don't know how we would've made it without you!"

Anastasia and Greer shared a brief, proud smile between them. It wasn't just the success of their mission they celebrated—it was the discovery of their unique, unspoken bond, a connection that had proven invaluable in their most difficult moments. Their bond, strengthened by trust and their shared powers, was now more solid than ever. Together, they had not only discovered the depths of their abilities but had shown how they could overcome any challenge, no matter how insurmountable it seemed.

As the sun dipped below the distant hills, turning the river's waters in shades of deep twilight, the travellers began to see the end of their watery journey. The current, once wild and unforgiving, had given way to a much slower flow. The river widened, its rapid pace easing into a serene stretch of water that mirrored the soft hues of the evening sky. The tranquil expanse felt like a peaceful exhale after a long-held breath.

The travellers steered their raft toward the shore, where the water pooled into a calm, crystal-clear lake. The sun's final rays turned the lake into a glittering canvas, and although their muscles were sore from the day's exertions, their spirits were high, brimming with a quiet triumph.

"This looks like a good spot to disembark," Max said, his voice weary yet satisfied, pointing toward a gentle slope leading up to the shore. The group guided the raft toward the water's edge, their movements slow but deliberate, their feet sinking into the soft, damp earth as they climbed out. The cool, moist ground felt a welcome contrast to the heat of the raft, grounding them after their tumultuous journey.

Once they secured the raft, the peaceful sounds of the wilderness enveloped them—the rustling of leaves in the gentle evening breeze and the rhythmic lap of water against the shore. The air held a peculiar calm, almost enchanting, as though the world itself was holding its breath. Yet, beneath the stillness, an undercurrent of tension began to stir, a subtle unease that crept into the hearts of the travellers.

"Do you feel that?" Siobhan whispered, her eyes scanning the surrounding woods and the shimmering surface of the lake. "It's like we're not alone."

Before anyone could respond, the water began to ripple unnaturally. A collective shiver ran through the group as they instinctively drew closer together, their senses alert, their bodies tensed as one. From the depths of the lake, shimmering figures began to rise, their forms fluid and graceful, like beings made entirely of water itself—translucent, ethereal, and beautiful.

The Guardians of the Waters had appeared.

Their bodies were an iridescent cascade of water, glimmering under the fading light, and their eyes glowed with a mystical, intense blue that seemed to pierce through the very souls of those who gazed upon them. Each movement was a dance of fluid grace, their presence serene yet undeniably powerful.

Max stepped forward, his heart racing, but his voice unwavering. "We are here on a quest to find the orb of water. We mean no harm and seek your guidance. We ask for your help in our journey."

The tallest of the guardians, more radiant than the others, stepped forward with slow, deliberate grace. Its voice echoed across the surface of the lake, both melodic and commanding, reverberating in the air like the song of distant waters. "Travellers, you have shown respect for the waters, and you have proven your worth by conquering the challenges of the river. But the Aquor Sphere is sacred. It is our solemn duty to protect it."

Anastasia and Greer felt the familiar warmth of their bond, the synchronised pulse of their powers humming between them. Without a word, they moved forward together. "We are here to restore balance," Anastasia said, her voice calm and steady, "and we seek only to use the orb for the greater good."

The lead guardian's gaze was piercing, as though it could see directly into their hearts. "Your intentions are pure, but the path to the orb is not easily travelled. You must prove your harmony with the element of water. Only those who move in perfect unity with the water may claim it."

Max glanced at his companions, a quiet sense of unity passing through them. Their shared bond strengthened by their trials thus far. "What must we do?" he asked, his voice carrying the weight of their journey.

The guardian raised a hand, and the lake responded, its waters swirling into a massive, spiraling vortex that seemed to pull at the very air around it. "Enter the vortex and face the trials within. Only those who succeed will be deemed worthy of the orb."

Max took a deep breath, his pulse quickening but his spirit strong. "We accept your challenge."

With a look of silent understanding, the group stepped toward the shimmering vortex. As they approached, the Water Guardian emerged from the swirling waters. She was a figure of serene grace, her body composed of liquid that shifted like the gentle flow of streams. Her presence radiated calm power, an aura that settled over the travellers as she addressed them.

"Welcome, brave seekers," the Water Guardian intoned, her voice soft yet powerful, like the whisper of a river winding through a quiet valley. "To obtain the Aquor Sphere, you must first prove yourselves worthy by completing three trials. These trials will test your unity, resilience, and most importantly, your harmony with the element of water."

The travellers exchanged knowing glances. There was no hesitation in their hearts—no fear of failure. They had already proven their mettle, and they would see this through, no matter the cost.

"The first trial," the Guardian continued, "is the Trial of Buoyancy and Balance. You must navigate across floating platforms that will test your coordination and balance. Only by working together and utilising your unique gifts can you hope to succeed."

With a subtle gesture from the Water Guardian, the scene around them shifted. The travellers found themselves standing on the edge of a vast, open lake, its surface dotted with a series of floating platforms. Some were large and stable, while others were smaller and wobbled with every movement. The platforms ranged in size, some sturdy, others precariously rocking underfoot.

"Remember," the Guardian's voice echoed across the water, "trust in each other and in your abilities."

Max took a deep breath and stepped onto the first platform, the wood creaking beneath his feet. It swayed slightly, but he adjusted his weight, steadying himself. "Alright," he called out to the others, "let's move carefully, and help each other across."

Siobhan, agile and swift, hopped lightly onto the next platform, her movements fluid and graceful. "Follow my lead," she called back, showing them how to shift their weight to keep the platform stable.

Ross, with his strong legs and athletic build, took a bold step and jumped from platform to platform, landing firmly beside Siobhan. "I've got your back, Max," he said, offering a hand to help Max onto the next platform.

The twins, Anastasia and Greer, moved as one, stepping onto the platforms in perfect synchrony. Their telepathic bond guided them, allowing them to adjust their balance without a word. Their movements were fluid, as if they were one entity, a seamless unity of mind and body.

Jonas, watching the twins, felt inspired by their flawless coordination. He focused on his own natural flexibility, allowing his body to flow gracefully with the rhythm of the water. "We need to move as one," he said, urging the group to match their movements, each step and shift synchronised to maintain balance.

As they progressed, the platforms grew increasingly unstable and farther apart, their edges crumbling underfoot. The sheer difficulty of the challenge mounted, and Max, sensing the rising tension in the air, called out to the twins. "Anastasia, Greer, can you use your connection to guide us through this?"

The twins exchanged a brief, knowing glance, their silent communication speaking volumes. In perfect unison, they nodded, their expressions confident. They closed their eyes for a moment, synchronising their breathing and clearing their minds of distractions. A calm focus enveloped them, and, with a shared sense of purpose, they began to guide the others, their movements precise and deliberate, like dancers in perfect harmony.

"Max, shift your weight slightly to the left," Anastasia instructed, her voice calm and steady, like the steady rhythm of a metronome.

"Ross, take a longer stride on the next jump," Greer added, her tone unwavering and confident, as though she had done this a thousand times before.

The group moved with increasing synchrony, each member following the twins' guidance. Every motion was calculated, every step balanced with the utmost care. Despite the challenges of the shifting platforms beneath their feet, the coordinated effort allowed them to move with ease.

Finally, with one final collective leap, they reached the last platform and stepped onto solid ground, their bodies trembling with the exertion. Before them stood the Water Guardian, her serene face beaming with approval.

The travellers paused for a moment, breathing deeply, their hearts still racing from the exertion. A wave of accomplishment washed over them, their spirits lifted by their shared triumph. Though they knew the next trial would be just as demanding—perhaps even more so—they were ready to face whatever lay ahead, their confidence strengthened by their success.

The Water Guardian smiled gently, her approval clear in the quiet warmth of her gaze. "You have passed the first trial," she said, her voice filled with calm pride. "Your unity and balance have proven your worth. Prepare yourselves for the next trial, where your resilience and cooperation will be tested."

With a graceful wave of her hand, the scene shifted, and the group found themselves standing in a vast cavern. The walls were slick with moisture, glistening in the dim light, and the air was thick with the scent of earth and water. Before them lay a deep pool, its surface reflecting a strange, shimmering light, and suspended above it were ropes and pulleys, their intricate design promising another test of their skills and teamwork.

"The second trial is the Trial of Cooperation," the Water Guardian intoned, her voice resonating through the cavern like a gentle echo. "You must navigate this pool by working together in perfect harmony. Each task will require the combined effort of all of you. Only through cooperation will you succeed."

Max stepped forward, eyes scanning the ropes and pulleys that seemed to stretch endlessly above the pool. "Alright, team. Let's figure this out together," he said, a quiet confidence steadying his voice.

The group quickly discerned that the ropes and pulleys were part of a larger mechanism designed to lower platforms, enabling them to cross the pool. Anastasia, always sharp and analytical, stepped forward, her brow furrowing in concentration as she began to analyse the system. "If we pull these ropes in a specific sequence," she said, "it should lower a series of platforms that we can use to cross."

Siobhan, quick and agile, was the first to act. She climbed onto one of the ropes, her movements fluid and precise. "I'll start pulling on this one. Max, you take the next one. Ross, you're up after Max," she called out.

The team quickly fell into a rhythm, each member taking their position, working with unspoken understanding. Greer, joining her sister in analysing the patterns of the ropes, communicated through their telepathic bond. "Max, pull the rope to your left," she directed. "Siobhan, adjust the tension on yours."

Jonas, with his natural agility, flitted between the ropes, offering his assistance where it was most needed. "This one needs more slack," he called out, his voice steady as he adjusted a rope that was causing one of the platforms to wobble dangerously.

Ross, using his considerable strength, tackled the most stubborn rope, holding it steady with his muscles straining. "I've got this one," he grunted, his voice tight with effort as he kept the tension locked in place.

Slowly, but surely, the platforms began to lower into place, forming a precarious, yet navigable path across the water. The travellers moved with deliberate caution, each step carefully coordinated, as they communicated constantly, ensuring that every move was synchronised and safe.

Halfway across, the cavern suddenly trembled, causing the platforms to sway and creak underfoot. A collective gasp filled the air as the ground beneath them shifted. "Hold on!" Max shouted, gripping his rope tightly to steady himself.

Anastasia and Greer, their minds intertwined in a bond that surpassed words, focused all their willpower on stabilising the platforms. "We need to synchronise our movements," Anastasia urged, her voice steady despite the chaos. "On my count, everyone pull together. One, two, three!"

With synchronised precision, the group pulled on their respective ropes, the combined effort stabilising the platforms just long enough for them to cross the remaining distance. With one final, coordinated effort, they reached the other side, stepping onto solid ground once more, their hearts racing with relief.

The Water Guardian appeared before them once again, her expression one of deep respect. "You have passed the second trial," she said, her tone rich with admiration. "Your cooperation and resilience have proven your strength. Prepare yourselves for the final trial, where your true understanding of water will be tested."

As the Water Guardian spoke, the underground lake before them began to shimmer and shift. The crystalline waters of the lake seemed to come alive, swirling in a dance of liquid light, the reflections of bioluminescent fungi on the cavern walls adding an ethereal glow to the scene.

"The Trial of Harmony begins," the Guardian intoned, her voice echoing throughout the cavern. "To succeed, you must navigate the labyrinthine depths of the underground lake, facing a series of obstacles that will test your understanding of water's ever-changing nature."

With a final gesture, the scene shifted again, and the travellers found themselves standing on the shores of the expansive underground lake. The tranquil waters stretched before them like a vast, shimmering mirror, reflecting the serene sky above. Despite the peace that surrounded them, an undercurrent of anticipation pulsed through the air.

Their final challenge lay ahead—a series of tranquil pools scattered across the lake, each one reflecting a different aspect of water's essence. Some pools were serene and still, while others seemed to pulse with hidden power, their depths promising secrets to those who dared to venture into them.

Driven by fierce intent, the travellers stepped forward, Max leading the way. His steps were steady as he waded into the shallows, his companions following close behind. But as his foot landed on the submerged surface, a hidden obstacle revealed itself—Max stumbled and fell, his leg catching painfully on a submerged rock. A sharp pain shot through him as a deep cut opened on his calf, the crimson stain spreading in the water.

A collective gasp filled the air, the others frozen in shock as they watched the blood mix with the water. But to their astonishment, the wound began to heal before their eyes. The bleeding stopped almost instantly, and the flesh slowly knitted itself back together, the injury vanishing completely as though it had never existed.

The Water Guardian observed this miraculous display with rapt attention, her eyes a mixture of curiosity and intrigue, her gaze piercing the very heart of the scene unfolding before her. "A demonstration of resilience," she mused, her voice smooth and deliberate, carrying effortlessly across the shimmering expanse of the lake. "But true mastery lies beyond mere healing. Press on, and discover the very essence of harmony."

As the travellers forged ahead, navigating the winding, labyrinthine depths of the underground lake, they encountered a series of increasingly perilous challenges—each one a test that pushed the limits of their understanding of water's ever-changing nature. They braved still, tranquil pools, their surface reflecting their apprehension, and battled against furious, surging torrents, each obstacle forcing them to adapt, to bend without breaking.

Yet, despite their relentless will and every ounce of their collective strength, they eventually reached a point where the trial grew too formidable. A powerful current, merciless and relentless, swept them off their feet, pulling them helplessly into a swirling vortex of water. With every effort to regain their footing, to remain calm in the face of chaos, they found themselves unable to withstand the unyielding force of the currents.

With heavy hearts, they realised that they had failed to achieve the perfect harmony required to claim victory in this final trial. From her perch on the distant shore, the Water Guardian's gaze was filled with a complex mixture of compassion and disappointment, her eyes softening as she observed their struggle.

"It seems that the waters have spoken," she said, her voice carrying a weight of finality, her words echoing through the cavern. "Return to the surface, travellers, and reflect on what you have learned. The path to mastery is not always straightforward, but it is in facing our failures that we find the true strength to persevere."

With a collective sigh, the travellers reluctantly abandoned their attempt to complete the trial, making their way back to the shore beneath the unblinking gaze of the Water Guardian.

Once they reached the shore, the travellers paused to catch their breath, the air heavy with the silence of their defeat. The cavern's bioluminescent glow bathed their weary faces, with long shadows trailing behind them, mirroring the quiet storm of disappointment and tenacity that swirled in their hearts. The gentle light seemed to mock their fatigue, as if reminding them that they had not yet reached their final lesson.

"That was tougher than I expected," Max admitted, his voice thick with frustration, his shoulders slumped with the weight of failure.

Anastasia nodded, her brow furrowed in thought. "We did our best," she said quietly, "but maybe we're missing something crucial. We need to think about what went wrong—what we didn't see."

Greer placed a hand on her sister's shoulder, her grip warm and reassuring. "We'll figure it out," she said firmly, a soft, steadfast smile forming on her lips. "We've come this far, and we won't give up now."

Liora and Kael, the nomadic guides, approached them, their faces unreadable as ever. Liora spoke first, her voice calm but tinged with something akin to understanding. "You fought bravely," she said. "The Water Guardian is right— true mastery doesn't come from success alone. It comes from understanding our failures."

Max glanced down at his leg, the memory of its miraculous regeneration still vivid in his mind. His voice hardened with a renewed strength. "We'll have to try again," he declared, the fire of determination rekindling within him. "And next time, we'll be ready."

The Water Guardian's voice rang out again, more somber this time, as her words reverberated through the cavernous expanse. "The waters have spoken," she intoned, the finality of her statement unmistakable. "You had but one opportunity to prove your worth, and that chance has passed."

Max's gaze fell to his healed leg once more, his fingers tracing the memory of the miraculous regeneration. "We'll try again," he repeated, his voice steady, though there was a trace of uncertainty lurking behind the words. "Next time, we'll be ready."

The Water Guardian shook her head slowly, her expression filled with a pitying sorrow, yet also the weight of inevitability. "There will be no next time," she stated, her voice steady and unyielding. "The trials are unforgiving, and the chance to claim the orb is granted but once. You must leave this place."

The travellers exchanged heavy, sorrowful glances, their hearts sinking under the weight of her words. With no other choice but to accept their defeat, they began their somber ascent to the surface, their spirits dampened by the profound sense of failure that clung to them like the damp air of the cavern.

As they emerged from the depths, the cool forest air greeted them, a sharp contrast to the suffocating humidity of the underground. The sun, now setting behind the dense trees, draped long shadows that stretched across the forest floor, the fading light signaling the end of yet another chapter in their journey. They walked in silence, the sound of their footsteps the only noise to punctuate the quiet resignation that settled over them.

Their thoughts were interrupted by the rustling of leaves, the soft scent of herbs drifting through the air, and the unmistakable sense of someone—or something—approaching. Stepping into the dappled light of the forest clearing, Max was the first to see her: an old woman, bent with age, cloaked in tattered robes. Her eyes, sharp and gleaming with an unnerving intensity, watched them from beneath the shadows of her hood. Around her neck, she wore a pendant that seemed to glow with an ethereal, otherworldly light—the orb of water itself.

"Greetings, travellers," she croaked, her voice dry and creaking like the bark of an ancient tree. "I see you seek something of great value."

Max stepped forward cautiously, his gaze fixed on the glowing orb. "We are on a quest to find the elemental relics," he explained, his voice steady despite the uncertainty he still felt. "We seek the orb of water."

The old woman chuckled, a sound that seemed to reverberate through the trees, as if the forest itself were laughing along with her. "Ah, the Aquor Sphere," she mused, her voice heavy with a dark amusement. "It has many uses, you know. Not only does it control the elements, but it also holds the power to unlock the very secrets of life itself."

She gestured vaguely behind her, and the travellers followed her motion to discover a lush, overgrown garden stretching into the distance. But this was no ordinary garden. Each plant, from the smallest herb to the tallest tree, pulsed with life, glowing faintly with the same otherworldly light that emanated from the orb. The garden thrived in a way that defied the natural order, as if nourished by a force beyond the mere earth.

"I use the orb to sustain my garden," the old woman continued, her voice now tinged with pride. "These plants have properties that heal, enhance, and even prolong life. But the orb does more than just nurture the plants. It sustains me as well."

Max's eyes widened with realisation. "You use the orb to extend your life," he said, the words leaving his mouth before he could stop them.

"Indeed," the old woman replied, her lips curling into a knowing smile, revealing teeth that were remarkably white and intact for someone so ancient. "The orb's power is potent, eternal. But I have a particular need that goes beyond its typical uses. You see, I am an alchemist of sorts, and for years I've perfected potions and elixirs for various purposes. My most ambitious project has always been the Elixir of Eternal Youth. Unfortunately, I have yet to find the key ingredient to complete it."

She waved a gnarled hand, and the travellers' gazes shifted to the lush garden behind her. It wasn't just any ordinary garden—it was an enchanting space brimming with exotic plants and rare herbs, each bathed in a soft, ethereal glow that seemed to emanate from deep within. The plants pulsed with an almost sentient life, thriving in a manner that defied the natural order of things, as though touched by an otherworldly force.

"I use the orb to nurture these plants," she continued, her voice rich with a mixture of reverence and pride. "These plants are no mere foliage; they hold properties that can heal, enhance, and even prolong life. But the final component I need to complete my elixir is something far rarer."

With a deliberate motion, she pointed a crooked, weathered finger at Max's leg—the same leg that had healed fully from the deep wound he'd sustained earlier. The injury had closed so quickly, it was as though time itself had been altered. "I witnessed your wound heal on its own," she said, her tone laced with awe. "Your blood possesses regenerative properties. With your blood, I can finally finish the Elixir of Eternal Youth and achieve what I've long sought."

Max's eyes widened, his heart skipping a beat as the realisation struck him. "You want my blood to make yourself young again."

"Yes," the old woman replied, her smile stretching unnaturally wide, revealing teeth that seemed far too sharp for a human. "Your blood is the missing ingredient. A small amount, just a few drops, would be enough to complete my elixir. In exchange, I will part with the orb that has served me so well."

Max hesitated, his thoughts racing. The quest for the relics was of paramount importance, but the idea of surrendering his blood to this stranger unsettled him. What if her promises were lies?

Ross stepped forward, his face firm and his voice unwavering. "We need the orb, Max," he said, glancing warily at the woman. "But we should move carefully. We don't know what she might do with your blood once she has it."

The old woman chuckled softly, her eyes gleaming with a strange, unsettling knowing. "Fear not. I seek nothing more than to reclaim the vitality I've lost over the years. A fair exchange, don't you think?"

Max turned his gaze to his companions, seeing the concern and doubt etched into their faces. The weight of their unspoken fears settled heavily on his chest. After a long pause, he gave a reluctant nod. "Alright. I'll give you a vial of my blood. But you must swear on your life that you will give us the orb in return."

The old woman's grin widened, her eyes glinting with a mixture of greed and satisfaction. "You have my word, travellers. The orb shall be yours."

With a swift, almost practised motion, she retrieved a small vial and needle from within her cloak. She handed them to Max, her hands trembling slightly. Max accepted them with caution, his fingers brushing the cold, sterile surface of the vial. His heart beat faster as he pricked his finger, watching a few drops of blood fall into the container. The old woman eagerly took the vial, her hands shaking with anticipation.

"Here," she said, her voice barely more than a whisper, as she handed over the orb. "May it serve you well on your journey."

The moment Max grasped the orb, he felt a strange surge of energy course through him, a rush of power that both exhilarated and unsettled him. It was as though the very air around him had shifted, and a subtle, ancient presence had awoken within the orb itself. The travellers had obtained the relic, but the encounter had left them with more questions than answers. What would this mysterious woman do with his blood? What were the true consequences of this exchange?

As the travellers prepared to leave, they exchanged heartfelt farewells with Liora and Kael, their guides from the water's edge. The twins embraced each other warmly, their expressions heavy with emotion.

"We'll miss you," Anastasia said, her voice thick with sadness. "Thank you, truly, for everything."

Kael nodded, his smile bittersweet as he looked at them one last time. "It was an honour to journey alongside you. May the winds and waters guide your path forward."

With a final wave, Liora and Kael turned away, disappearing effortlessly into the dense foliage. Their figures melted into the shadows of the forest, leaving only the faintest rustle in their wake.

Max and his companions watched them go, a sense of deep gratitude swelling within their chests. They had faced countless trials together, each one testing their fortitude, but the bonds they had forged were stronger than any challenge they had overcome. Their journey had brought them together in ways that words could never fully capture.

As the sun dipped below the horizon, stretching long shadows across the landscape, the travellers readied themselves for the next chapter of their journey. Their destination now loomed before them: a forbidden forest, a place whispered about in fearful legends, rumored to be haunted by restless spirits and teeming with dangerous creatures.

That night, Max lay awake staring at the dark canopy of leaves overhead. He found himself wishing Jocelyn were there — she always knew what to say when he got tangled in his own thoughts. She'd probably scold him for getting them stuck in this mess, then laugh and find a way to make it all seem less terrible. He missed that laugh more than he wanted to admit.

With the relics of Air and Water now safely in their possession, their attention turned to the third elemental relic—Earth. Yet little did they know that darker, more formidable challenges awaited them in the heart of the forbidden forest. The mysteries within its depths were far beyond what they could imagine.

With a renewed sense of purpose and courage ignited within their hearts, Max and his companions set off into the unknown. Together, they would face whatever trials lay ahead on their perilous quest for the ancient relics.

CHAPTER 4

Earth – The Obsidian Core

The soft light of dawn filtered through the canopy, filtering dappled shadows that danced across the forest floor. The air was cool and crisp, carrying with it the promise of a new day and fresh adventures. Max and his companions stirred from their slumber, the tranquility of the morning a stark contrast to the challenges that awaited them.

Stretching their limbs and shaking off the remnants of sleep, the travellers rose from their makeshift campsite, their spirits lifted by the success of retrieving the Aquor Sphere. Though weary from their journey, there was a renewed sense of purpose that flowed through them, their focus strengthened with each passing moment.

With the relics of Air and Water safely secured, their thoughts naturally turned to the next leg of their journey—the Nasmarian forest, a place rumored to be haunted by restless spirits and teeming with dangerous creatures that could rip apart even the most seasoned adventurers. The journey ahead promised no reprieve, but it was a challenge they had already decided to face.

After freshening up and breaking their fast with a simple meal of trail rations, the companions gathered together to discuss the day ahead. Their destination was clear, though the path was uncertain. They would need to navigate the treacherous terrain of the forest, watching for signs of danger or hidden obstacles that might impede their progress.

Empowered by focus and the knowledge that they were one step closer to fulfilling their quest, the travellers set off, their footsteps muffled by the damp earth beneath them. The dense trees loomed like sentinels, their trunks rising high, blocking much of the morning light. Max couldn't shake the gnawing sense of apprehension in the pit of his stomach as they delved deeper into the unknown. The air was thick with the scent of moss and earth, and the sounds of the forest filled his ears—every rustle of leaves and snap of twigs made his heart race. But he buried his fears beneath a mask of steel, pressing forward despite the doubts within.

Siobhan walked confidently at the front, her steps sure and steady. Her sharp eyes scanned their surroundings with a predator's precision, every movement calculated. "Stay close, everyone," she called out, her voice steady despite the palpable tension in the air. "We don't know what dangers lie ahead, so let's stick together and watch each other's backs."

Jonas, ever the stoic one, nodded in agreement. His gaze swept across the shadowed forest, alert for anything out of place. "Agreed," he grunted, his hand tightening around the strap of his backpack. "We've come too far to turn back now. Let's stay focused and keep moving forward."

With each step, the air grew heavier, saturated with the scent of damp earth and decaying leaves. The path was slow and arduous, the undergrowth thickening, catching at their feet. Shadows seemed to play tricks on their eyes, darting across the forest floor, making it hard to discern what was real from what was mere illusion. Max felt his spine tingle as if the forest itself were watching them, its ancient trees holding secrets that only the bold would dare uncover.

Despite the eerie atmosphere, Max felt a rush of excitement—a surge of adrenaline. This was their chance to prove themselves, to unlock the mysteries of the ancient relics and emerge victorious. He was committed to see it through, no matter the trials that awaited them.

The deeper they went into the Nasmarian forest, the more it seemed to close in around them. The trees, gnarled and twisted, seemed to reach out with their branches, creating a dense canopy that blocked out the sunlight. The forest floor was thick with roots, undergrowth, and creeping vines that made every step feel like an obstacle. The air felt thick and oppressive, and strange sounds echoed all around—creaking branches, rustling leaves, and soft, whispering noises that seemed to come from the very earth itself.

Max couldn't shake the feeling that they were being watched. Every glance he cast toward his companions revealed the same tense expressions, their senses alert to the dangers that might be lurking in the unseen spaces of the forest. The whispers, too, grew louder as they ventured deeper, unnerving him even more.

Siobhan remained at the front. She moved with precision, her every step calculated. Her sharp eyes cut through the shadows, scanning for any sign of danger, while her instincts remained on high alert. She was the first to feel the subtle shifts in the air, to notice the slight flickers of movement that others might miss.

Jonas, with his quiet grace, matched her every move. His watchful eyes swept the surroundings, always on guard, his hand hovering near the hilt of his knife, prepared for any threat.

Anastasia and Greer, moved in perfect synchrony. Their bond was palpable in the way they moved together, exchanging whispered words, their communication a silent dance born of a deep, telepathic connection. Their bond made them a formidable pair, each anticipating the other's next move with uncanny precision.

Ross, at the rear, cast nervous glances to either side. His eyes darted between the dense undergrowth, tension simmering beneath his calm exterior. He was still proving himself, struggling to find his footing among the seasoned travellers, but his courage was growing, bolstered by the strength of his companions' camaraderie. His focus held steady even as his nerves buzzed beneath the surface.

The deeper they ventured, the more the forest seemed to shift. The undergrowth grew thicker, the path more obscure, until the travellers felt as though they were stepping into a world untouched by time. The forest seemed to hum with life, a low, constant sound beneath the rustling of leaves—a pulse, faint but undeniable.

Max glanced over at Ross, who walked beside him. His expression was intense, his brow furrowed in concentration as if he were hearing something Max couldn't. "Any idea where we're headed?" Max whispered, careful not to disturb the stillness that blanketed the forest.

Ross shook his head slowly, his lips set in a tight line. "Not yet," he murmured, his voice low. "But I can feel it. Something's buried deep beneath us. It's... calling to me."

Siobhan, who had been just ahead of them, turned around, her interest piqued. "What do you mean?" she asked, her voice a mix of curiosity and excitement.

Ross paused, his fingers lightly grazing the ground beneath him. "It's like a pulse. A vibration that grows stronger the further we go. The earth itself seems to be guiding us, pulling us toward something."

Max exchanged a glance with Siobhan, both of them caught between skepticism and intrigue. If Ross could sense something hidden beneath the earth, it might be a clue—perhaps even a sign left behind by the ancient guardians of the forest.

The travellers pressed on, their senses finely tuned to the world around them. The sound of their movements blended with the symphony of life within the forest. Each rustle of leaves seemed to speak, urging them to continue, to keep moving forward.

As the day wore on, the canopy grew denser, weaving the path ahead into deeper shadows. But amidst the darkness, Max's senses sharpened. He noticed the delicate patterns of moss on stones, the way sunlight filtered through gaps in the canopy, and the soft whispers of the forest life that hummed around them. Every small detail seemed to carry a deeper meaning, urging him to look closer.

Then, just as Ross had predicted, they stumbled upon it—a hidden grove, a sanctuary nestled deep within the heart of the forest. In the centre stood a towering oak, its branches reaching skyward like the outstretched arms of a guardian. This was no ordinary tree; it pulsed with ancient energy, as if it were the very heart of the forest itself.

Max's pulse quickened. This was it—the next step on their journey, the next puzzle to solve.

"There," Ross whispered, his voice barely audible above the gentle rustle of the leaves, which seemed to sway in time with the very pulse of the earth. "That's where we need to go."

With a shared glance, the travellers exchanged unspoken thoughts, their hearts pounding with a mixture of excitement and trepidation. Stepping into the grove, they felt the weight of something ancient and powerful settling over them, a quiet anticipation that mirrored their own.

As they approached the towering oak, its massive branches stretching high into the sky, a profound sense of reverence washed over them. The tree, gnarled and weathered by centuries of time, seemed to hum with an almost otherworldly energy. The air was thick with the crackle of magic, as if the very atmosphere was charged with possibility. They gathered around its twisted trunk, their eyes scanning the surroundings for any sign of what they were meant to do next.

"It's like the forest is alive," Siobhan murmured, her voice barely louder than the whispers of the wind. Her eyes, wide with wonder, darted from one shadowed corner to another. "As if every tree, every blade of grass, is watching us, waiting to see what we'll do."

Max nodded in agreement, his senses acutely aware of the invisible forces at play. He could feel an ancient power, lingering just beyond the veil of perception, watching them with quiet patience. "We need to be careful," he cautioned, his voice low but firm. His gaze swept over the grove, lingering on the tangled underbrush and the dark silhouettes of distant trees. "Whatever we do here, it has to be with respect and reverence—for the forest and its guardians."

Ross, his eyes alight with an intensity that matched the weight of the moment, stepped forward. "I think we need to listen," he said, his voice cutting through the stillness. It seemed to echo in the air, reverberating off the trees like a forgotten song. "To the whispers of the wind, the murmurs of the leaves... They hold the key to unlocking the secrets of this place."

With that, he closed his eyes and fell into silence, his senses reaching out beyond the physical realm. For a moment, the only sound was the soft rustling of the leaves and the distant chirping of birds. But then, something shifted—a subtle change in the air, a ripple that seemed to pass through the grove, like the faintest breath of a sleeping giant.

Max felt it too. A faint tremor beneath his feet, like the heartbeat of the earth itself. He closed his eyes, focusing, letting his mind attune to the rhythm of the forest, to the ancient ebb and flow of life pulsing through its veins. In that quiet moment, he felt both small and infinite, connected to something far greater than himself.

And then, just as suddenly as it had begun, the sensation faded, leaving behind a profound stillness, as if the world itself had paused to take a breath. Max opened his eyes, drawn to a small sapling growing at the base of the oak. Its delicate leaves shimmered in the dappled sunlight, casting a soft, ethereal glow upon the forest floor, as if the tree itself was a living beacon of light.

"It's beautiful," Siobhan breathed, her voice filled with awe, her eyes reflecting the quiet wonder of the moment.

Max nodded, his heart swelling with a deep sense of gratitude for the natural world and all its mysteries. "Yes," he agreed, his voice thick with emotion. A sense of peace settled over him, a comforting weight that soothed his restless thoughts. "And I think it's trying to tell us something."

As if in response to his words, the sapling began to glow brighter, its leaves dancing in the breeze as if animated by some unseen force, as though the very air around them was alive. Max reached out a hand, his fingers brushing against the delicate foliage. In that moment, a surge of energy coursed through him, a deep, pulsating connection that seemed to draw him closer to the heart of the forest, to the very soul of the earth.

"We're connected," he whispered, his voice barely above a breath, filled with a reverence that matched the forest around them. "To each other, to the forest... to everything."

And as they stood together in the grove, surrounded by the ancient trees and the soft hum of life that seemed to echo through the air, Max knew they were on the right path. But it was clear that this grove held secrets yet to be uncovered—clues they would need to decipher if they were to continue their journey.

Max's gaze shifted, scanning the grove for any signs, symbols, or hidden messages that might guide them forward. His eyes landed on a series of ancient carvings etched into the bark of the surrounding trees. The symbols seemed to shimmer faintly in the dappled sunlight, depicting natural elements—air, water, earth, and fire—interwoven in an intricate, timeless dance.

"These carvings," Max said, pointing to the symbols with a mixture of awe and certainty, "they must be a clue. Maybe they hold the key to unlocking the next stage of our journey."

Ross stepped forward, his brow furrowing as he studied the symbols. "I think you're right, Max. These markings seem to be connected to our journey. But there's something more to them—something I can't quite grasp."

As Ross examined the carvings more closely, he felt an unfamiliar sensation—an almost magnetic pull at the core of his being. His power, the ability to transport himself, resonated with the symbols in a way he couldn't quite explain. The symbols seemed to hum softly, as if beckoning him.

"There's something here," Ross murmured, closing his eyes and focusing on the sensation. "Something that's calling to me... Maybe I can use my power to reveal the path forward."

The others watched in silence, their breaths held in anticipation. As Ross concentrated, the air around him shimmered slightly, and then, with a sudden rush of energy, he vanished. In an instant, he reappeared, standing in the centre of the grove, a look of awe on his face.

"It's like there's another dimension here," Ross said, his voice filled with wonder and a sense of disbelief. "I saw a hidden path—one that's not visible to the naked eye. If we follow it, I think it will lead us to the next clue."

Max nodded, his trust in Ross unwavering. "Lead the way, Ross."

Ross focused once more, extending his hand toward his companions. "Everyone, take my hand. I can transport us all together."

One by one, they linked hands with Ross, their hearts racing with anticipation. The strange, tingling sensation of his power enveloped them, and in an instant, the grove around them seemed to blur, twisting and shifting as though they were being drawn into a different realm.

When the world settled once more, they found themselves standing in a different part of the forest, one bathed in an otherworldly, ethereal light. The trees here seemed to stretch higher, their branches woven together in a canopy that sparkled with the glow of unseen stars. The air was thick with magic, alive with the hum of something ancient.

Before them stood another clearing, even more mystical than the first. In the centre of the clearing stood an ancient stone pedestal, worn smooth by time, atop which rested a beautifully carved box. Its intricate design glimmered faintly in the light, and it was clear to all of them that the box held something important—another clue, or perhaps even the next relic itself.

Max approached the pedestal with caution, his every step deliberate as he scanned the surroundings for any signs of danger. The eerie quiet of the clearing made his heart race, but he steadied himself, focusing on the task at hand. "This must be it," he said, his voice a mixture of excitement and uncertainty, as he reached forward to open the intricately carved box. "Let's see what we've unlocked."

Inside the box lay a scroll, its parchment ancient and fragile, the edges curling with age. Max took a deep breath and gently unrolled the delicate parchment, careful not to tear it. The group gathered around him, their faces bathed in the soft, otherworldly glow that filtered through the trees. The stillness of the moment was palpable, as if the very air was holding its breath. The scroll was adorned with intricate symbols, their meanings foreign yet familiar, and flowing script that hinted at secrets long buried. But at the top, a riddle stood apart from the rest, written in bold, elegant letters that seemed to shimmer with a life of their own:

"I am not alive, yet I grow;
I have no lungs, yet I need air;
I have no mouth, and I can drown.
What am I?"

Max's voice broke the silence as he read the riddle aloud, his words carrying through the clearing and bouncing off the trees. The travellers exchanged knowing glances, the weight of the puzzle sinking in. Each of them pondered the riddle's cryptic clues, their minds racing to find an answer.

"It's a classic riddle," Siobhan said, her brow furrowed in concentration as she paced slowly, her eyes fixed on the words. "I've heard it before, but I can't quite remember the answer. It's right on the tip of my tongue."

The twins, Anastasia and Greer, exchanged a look that spoke volumes. They were often in sync, but this time, the answer eluded them both. "It sounds like something elemental," Anastasia ventured, her voice uncertain. "But it doesn't quite fit with what we know about the elements."

Ross, still reeling from the lingering effects of his recent transportation feat, closed his eyes and took a deep breath, focusing on the riddle's rhythm. His fingers traced the symbols etched into the scroll as he muttered the lines under his breath. "Not alive, yet it grows... Needs air, but has no lungs... And it can drown..."

Suddenly, Jonas, who had been pacing back and forth in the background, snapped his fingers. "It's fire!" he declared, his voice full of confidence. "Fire fits all the clues. It needs air to burn, it grows as it spreads, and it can be extinguished by water. It's the perfect answer."

Max nodded thoughtfully, a spark of understanding lighting up his expression. "That makes sense. The riddle is clearly about fire. But what does it mean for us? How does this guide us to the next step in our journey?"

Just as they pondered the question, the scroll began to glow faintly. The symbols and script shifted and rearranged before their eyes, as if the scroll were alive, revealing a new set of instructions beneath the riddle. The travellers leaned in, eager to read what it had to say:

"To ignite the path ahead,
Seek the flame where shadows tread.
The forest's heart will light the way,
When night turns into day."

The travellers exchanged glances, their faces lighting up with realisation. They knew what they had to do. The path ahead was hidden, but they were now certain that they needed to find a particular location deep within the forest—a place where shadows held sway, where fire could be kindled to reveal the next phase of their journey.

"It must be a place that's hidden in darkness," Siobhan said, her voice steady but fierce. "A place where we can create a light—one that will illuminate the way forward."

Max carefully rolled up the scroll and tucked it securely into his backpack, his mind already racing with possibilities. "Then we need to find this place," he said, the weight of the riddle still heavy on his shoulders. "Let's keep moving. We're bound to find some clues along the way that will guide us to the heart of the forest."

With renewed purpose, the group set off once more. The dense foliage of the forest closed in around them, the towering trees stretching long shadows that seemed to reach out with each passing step. The air grew thicker with every movement, the forest alive with hidden sounds and unseen creatures. They pressed on, eyes scanning for any sign or symbol that might point them toward the elusive heart of the forest. Though the path ahead seemed to twist and turn in impossible ways, their spirits remained high, buoyed by the knowledge that they were one step closer to unlocking the mysteries that lay hidden in the depths of the wilderness.

As the sun began to set, its golden light filtered through the dense canopy, projecting long, eerie shadows across the forest floor. The air grew cooler, tinged with the earthy scent of damp leaves and moss. Finally, after hours of trekking, they stumbled upon a secluded glade.

At the heart of the glade stood a towering, ancient tree, its gnarled branches twisting toward the sky like outstretched fingers. Its bark was thick and weathered, whispering of centuries past. Beneath the tree, the ground was strangely barren— a small, circular clearing devoid of vegetation, as if nature itself had deemed this space sacred.

"This must be the place," Ross said, his voice edged with anticipation. His eyes gleamed in the fading light. "Let's see if we can light a fire here and reveal the path."

Jonas knelt in the clearing, quickly assembling a small fire from the dry twigs and brittle leaves they had gathered. With practised ease, he struck a spark, and soon flames crackled to life. The fire flickered and danced, stretching patterns across the trees, making the surrounding darkness seem almost alive. Shadows twisted and curled, stretching into strange, elongated forms.

Then, without warning, a brilliant beam of light erupted from the centre of the fire. It shot forward, cutting through the darkness, illuminating a hidden pathway that led deeper into the forest. The travellers exchanged triumphant glances, their exhaustion momentarily forgotten. They had unlocked the next stage of their journey.

Following the glowing path, they pressed on, their footsteps barely disturbing the thick carpet of fallen leaves. With every step, the eerie sounds of the forest—whispering wind, rustling undergrowth, distant hoots and calls—grew louder, as if the trees themselves were murmuring secrets. The darkness seemed to press in around them, but the unwavering beam of light from their fire remained a steady guide.

After what felt like an eternity, the path opened into a vast, circular clearing, encircled by towering ancient trees whose massive trunks loomed like silent sentinels. At the centre of the clearing stood a massive stone altar, half-buried under moss and trailing vines. The air was thick, heavy with an almost tangible energy that made their skin tingle.

Max stepped forward cautiously, his gaze sweeping over the altar. "This must be another part of the trial," he murmured, his voice hushed with reverence.

Ross nodded, his expression unreadable. "I can feel it," he said softly, his fingers brushing against the moss-covered stone. "There's something powerful here—something connected to the earth itself."

At the base of the altar, a series of stone tablets lay arranged in a semi-circle. Their surfaces bore intricate carvings—ancient runes and symbols etched deep into the stone. In front of each tablet, small depressions were carved into the ground, waiting expectantly.

Jonas knelt beside one, tracing the worn carvings with his fingertips. "These symbols... they represent aspects of nature," he observed. "Growth, decay, stability, and change."

Anastasia pointed to the shallow indentations before each tablet. "It looks like we're supposed to place something here," she mused. "But what?"

Siobhan, who had been quietly observing their surroundings, suddenly motioned toward a tree at the clearing's edge. "Look at that one," she said. "It's different from the others. The leaves are richer, greener... and there's something glowing near its roots."

Intrigued, the group moved closer. Nestled within the tangled roots was a small, pulsating seed, radiating a soft, golden glow. Ross crouched down and picked it up, feeling warmth seep into his palm.

"I think this is what we need," he said, holding up the seed.

Max nodded. "It represents growth. Let's place it in the corresponding depression and see what happens."

Ross carefully returned to the altar and placed the seed into the space before the rune for growth. Immediately, the tablet shimmered, its runes igniting with a soft, verdant glow. Encouraged by their success, the group fanned out, searching for the remaining elements.

They found a brittle, decaying branch—its once-sturdy form now reduced to crumbling fragments—symbolising decay. A heavy, unyielding stone was chosen for stability, its weight grounding them in the moment. Finally, they gathered a cluster of dried, curled leaves that seemed to embody the inevitable passage of change.

One by one, they placed the items into their respective depressions. With each offering, the corresponding tablet flared to life, until all four glowed in unison, their radiant light piercing the twilight gloom. Shadows stretched and retreated, and an otherworldly energy surged through the air, wrapping around them like an unseen force.

"It's getting late," Max observed, glancing at the sky, now a deep indigo strewn with the first glimmers of stars. "We should find a place to camp."

Siobhan agreed. "We've made good progress today. Let's get some much-needed rest."

They carefully memorised the altar's location before setting out in search of shelter. Not far from the clearing, they found a secluded spot—a natural hollow where the ancient trees bent toward each other, forming a protective canopy overhead. The ground was blanketed in thick, soft moss, offering a surprisingly comfortable resting place.

As night fully descended, they built another small fire. Its flickering flames pushed back the encroaching darkness, its warmth a welcome reprieve from the forest's eerie chill. They sat in a loose circle, sharing a simple meal of dried meat and fruits from their packs. Though physically weary, they felt invigorated by the day's discoveries.

Ross, drawn by an inexplicable pull, wandered slightly away from the group. He leaned against the trunk of an old oak, closing his eyes. He could feel it—the quiet hum of the earth, the whisper of roots deep beneath the soil, the steady pulse of life that thrived unseen.

Max noticed him and approached, settling beside him. "You okay, Ross?"

Ross opened his eyes, a small smile playing on his lips. "Yeah... just feeling the earth," he said quietly. "It's hard to explain, but I feel more connected here. Like I belong."

Max nodded. "I get it. You've always had that connection. It's what makes you so good at what you do."

The rest of the group gradually joined them, drawn by the stillness of the moment. For a while, they sat in companionable silence, listening to the forest breathe around them.

Siobhan was the first to speak, her voice soft. "We've come so far already. I know we still have a long way to go, but I feel like we're starting to understand our abilities more and more."

Jonas nodded. "Each of us has a role to play. And the more we rely on each other, the stronger we become."

The fire crackled softly, throwing golden embers into the night sky. Above them, the stars shone down, silent witnesses to their journey.

Tomorrow, they would continue forward, deeper into the unknown. But for now, they rested—knowing that together, they were stronger than any trial ahead.

The twins, Anastasia and Greer, exchanged a knowing glance before Greer spoke, her voice steady yet filled with conviction. "We're all connected, like parts of a whole. And that connection is what's going to help us succeed."

A hush settled over the group, the only sounds being the crackling fire and the distant calls of nocturnal creatures stirring in the depths of the forest. The air was cool, thick with the scent of damp earth and pine. There was a quiet understanding among them—a bond forged through shared purpose and unspoken trust.

As the fire burned low, they prepared for sleep, knowing the trials of the coming day would demand their strength. Max took the first watch, settling beside the dim embers, his keen eyes scanning the darkened forest. The rhythmic symphony of chirping insects and rustling leaves filled the silence, a stark contrast to the weight of responsibility resting on his shoulders. Yet, despite the uncertainty ahead, a quiet confidence stirred within him. They had come this far together, and whatever awaited them in the Nasmarian forest, they would face it as one.

The trees seemed to hold their breath, as if acknowledging the presence of the travellers and the significance of their journey. And as sleep claimed them, each felt a renewed sense of purpose—a quiet strength that no trial could diminish.

The first rays of dawn pierced through the dense canopy, extending golden streaks of light across the forest floor. Birds greeted the new day with a chorus of melodic calls, their songs weaving through the crisp morning air. One by one, the travellers stirred, stretching sore muscles and shaking off the last remnants of sleep.

They wasted no time packing up their camp, their movements efficient and purposeful. The glowing tablets awaited them, and with them, the next step of their quest.

Max approached the ancient altar, his gaze fixed on the shifting, luminescent symbols. "Let's see what these clues reveal."

Gathering around, each of them placed a hand on the glowing tablets. At once, the light intensified, the markings pulsating with energy as they reconfigured into a new message. The glowing letters shimmered in the morning light as Max read aloud:

"To unlock the path, you must find the heart of the forest where the stone guardians stand. Only those who truly understand the earth will be able to reveal the hidden way."

A silence settled over the group as the weight of the words sank in. Ross took a step forward, his jaw set with steady purpose. "I think this is my test," he said, his voice steady.

Siobhan rested a reassuring hand on his shoulder. "We're all here with you, Ross. Let's do this together."

Guided by an instinct he couldn't quite explain, Ross led the group deeper into the forest. The further they walked, the more the world around them seemed to shift—the trees thickened, their roots twisting like gnarled fingers across the forest floor. The scent of damp earth and rich moss filled their lungs, the very air growing denser, heavier, as if the land itself recognised their purpose.

Hours passed before they stumbled upon a sight unlike anything they had seen before—a towering stone door, ancient and weathered, embedded into the face of a massive rock formation. Intricate carvings and runes covered its surface, each etched with precise, almost reverent craftsmanship. A beam of early morning sunlight filtered through the trees, illuminating the central symbol on the door. It pulsed faintly, as though alive.

"This must be it," Max murmured, stepping closer. He ran his fingers over the carvings, tracing their delicate patterns. "But how do we open it?"

Siobhan studied the runes, her brow furrowed. "These symbols seem familiar," she whispered, her fingers hovering over them. "I think it's a puzzle—one we have to solve."

Jonas leaned in, running a finger over the markings.

"Look here—these symbols represent the four elements: air, water, earth, and fire. I remember seeing these in a book I borrowed from the library. It was all about ancient symbols and their meanings."

Ross squinted at the smaller symbols encircling the elements.

"These look like they represent different times of the day—see how this one has rays like the sun at its peak? And this one has a crescent moon?" he said thoughtfully.

"What if the order of the elements follows the cycle of the day?"

Anastasia nodded in agreement. "If we can figure out the correct order, maybe we can unlock the door."

Jonas' eyes lit up with realisation. He pulled his tattered copy of *The Legendary Treasures of Gladvier* from his backpack and flipped it open to a page covered in faded symbols. "Of course! Look— these symbols match exactly. It all lines up. The hero had to understand the elements to solve a puzzle, just like this."

Jonas tapped the symbols thoughtfully. "Air, water, earth, fire. If this puzzle follows the same pattern, we might have a chance."

"Let's try it," Siobhan urged, her voice calm but confident.

With careful precision, Max pressed the symbols in the order they had deduced. For a moment, nothing happened. Then, a low rumbling sound echoed through the forest as the ancient stone door groaned to life. Dust cascaded from the cracks as it slowly slid open, revealing a darkened passageway beyond.

Excitement rippled through the group.

"We did it," Anastasia breathed, her eyes shining.

"Let's see what's inside," Greer added, stepping forward.

The passage was lined with glowing veins of luminescent stone, throwing an eerie blue-green light along the damp walls. Water dripped rhythmically from unseen crevices, the sound echoing in the confined space. The travellers moved cautiously, their footsteps soft against the smooth stone floor.

After several moments, the tunnel opened into a vast underground chamber. At its centre, atop a raised pedestal, rested their prize—The Obsidian Core, a red meteor rock, pulsating with an inner fire.

Ross inhaled sharply. "The Earth relic," he whispered in awe. "We've found it."

But before they could take another step, the ground trembled violently. The towering stone figures carved into the walls stirred, their eyes igniting with an eerie glow. One by one, they stepped forward, ancient guardians brought to life by the relic's presence.

"Stay back!" Jonas called, gripping his talisman of air.

Max turned to Ross, urgency in his voice. "This is your moment. Show them we are worthy."

Ross's heartbeat thundered in his ears, but he refused to let fear take hold. Taking a deep breath, he closed his eyes and reached out—not with his hands, but with his spirit. He felt the soil beneath his feet, the pulse of the earth itself. A deep warmth spread through him as he tapped into the connection, surrendering to it.

The trembling ground slowed. The advancing guardians paused.

Then, as if responding to his will, life erupted from the stone floor. Flowers bloomed in bursts of vibrant colour, their petals unfurling in delicate spirals. Vines twisted gracefully, tracing the carvings on the walls. The scent of fresh earth and wild blossoms filled the chamber. It was as if the earth itself recognised his reverence.

The guardians slowly lowered their weapons, their glowing eyes dimming to a soft ember.

Ross exhaled, his hands steady. "We're meant to be here," he said, his voice firm.

The chamber stilled. The relic's fiery glow reflected in their eyes.

And in that moment, they knew—their journey was only just beginning.

The guardians watched in silent approval as Ross continued to channel the earth's energy. He raised his arms higher, and a gentle breeze rustled the leaves of the newly formed garden. Small stones levitated from the ground, arranging themselves into a precise circle around the pedestal, as if drawn by an unseen force.

Ross's connection with the earth deepened, and for the first time, he felt the pulse of life within the soil beneath him—a steady, ancient rhythm that had existed long before him and would endure long after. The stone guardians stepped forward, their glowing eyes softening, radiating something akin to acknowledgment, perhaps even reverence.

"You have proven yourselves worthy," the lead guardian intoned, his deep, resonant voice carrying a weight that seemed to vibrate in the very air around them. "But to truly master the power of earth, you must learn its secrets."

The guardians guided Ross to the heart of the grove, where ancient runes, etched into the ground long ago, pulsed faintly with an otherworldly light. As he stepped into the centre, a strange warmth coursed through his limbs, as though the earth itself was welcoming him. The stone guardians began to chant in unison, their voices forming a solemn melody that resonated through the clearing.

The lead guardian gestured for Ross to repeat after them. Taking a steady breath, he began:

"Terra mater, anima terrae,
De profundis voco te.

Radices vitae, flores crescite,
Cum terrae vi, concordia est.
Lapides levitate, circulum formate,
Vires terrae mecum sunt.
Elementum terrae, te impero,
Omnia possibilia sunt.
Gaia, audite,
Filium vestrum.
Terra nos iungit,
Unum sumus."

The words, ancient and powerful, wove through the very fabric of reality. A tremor rippled through the ground beneath his feet, not with violence but with purpose. The earth responded to him now, bending to his will, not in servitude but in harmonious understanding. He could feel the roots extending deeper, intertwining, growing stronger. The very air felt denser, filled with an energy that hummed against his skin.

After what felt like an eternity—but was only mere moments—the guardians stepped back, their chanting fading into silence. The runes ceased their glow, leaving behind a profound sense of completion.

"You are now a keeper of the Earth Relic," the lead guardian declared. "Use this power wisely and with respect."

Ross exhaled, the weight of responsibility settling over him. He nodded, solemn and grateful.

The guardians slowly returned to their statuesque stillness, their eyes dimming until they were once again lifeless stone.

Ross approached the pedestal, his gaze fixed on the Obsidian Core. As he picked it up, its warmth seeped into his skin. He held it up, its surface glowing faintly in the dim light. "Three down, one to go," he said, a triumphant smile tugging at the corner of his lips. "Let's get out of here."

With the Earth relic in their possession, the travellers retraced their steps through the passageway and emerged into the forest. Yet, something had changed. The air still carried the familiar scent of damp soil and rotting leaves, but there was a new undercurrent of energy, subtle yet undeniable. It pulsed beneath their feet, vibrating faintly, as if the land itself was acknowledging their newfound bond.

Ross tightened his grip around the relic, feeling its steady warmth. It was more than just an object; it was a conduit, a piece of something far greater than himself. The realisation filled him with both awe and responsibility.

"That was incredible," Max said, his voice tinged with admiration. "You really connected with the Earth element back there. It was like you were one with it."

Ross smiled, though the exhaustion was evident in his posture. "It was intense," he admitted. "But I think I'm starting to understand how this power works. It's not just about controlling the earth—it's about listening to it, respecting it."

Siobhan, always perceptive, placed a reassuring hand on his shoulder. "You did great, Ross. We couldn't have done this without you."

Jonas, who had been silent until now, spoke up. "Now that we have the Earth relic, we need to be cautious. There's still so much we don't know, and we can't afford any missteps."

As night fell, they set up camp beneath the shelter of towering trees. The fire crackled, its warm glow flickering shadows across their weary faces. The atmosphere was one of quiet reflection. They shared a modest meal, exchanging stories and contemplating the path ahead.

Needing solitude, Ross stepped away from the fire and sat at the edge of their campsite. He pulled the Earth relic from his satchel, studying its surface. In the firelight, the meteor rock glowed softly, almost breathing. A pull, subtle yet insistent, coursed through him. Instinctively, he murmured the incantation under his breath. The words, once foreign, now felt as natural as his own heartbeat.

The ground stirred. Vines curled towards him, leaves rustled without wind. The earth was listening.

"Impressive," a voice remarked behind him. Ross turned to see Max watching, curiosity gleaming in his eyes. "I didn't realise you could control the earth like that already."

Ross shrugged. "I'm still figuring it out. The relic is powerful, but it's not about control—it's about understanding. And for the first time, I think I finally do."

Max nodded, clearly impressed. "We all have our roles to play in this quest. You're doing great, Ross."

As the fire burned low and the forest whispered its nocturnal song, the travellers found solace in each other's presence. The weight of their journey was immense, but so too was their strength of spirit.

Ross lay awake for some time, the relic close to his chest. The earth's song was faint but ever-present, a reminder of the power he now carried. He closed his eyes, a quiet strength rising within.

The forest, as if sensing the significance of the moment, seemed to hold its breath. Somewhere in the distance, the echoes of the earth stirred, whispering promises of trials yet to come and the strength that would be required to overcome them.

CHAPTER 5

Fire – The Eternal Torch

And so, with the weight of those whispers in their hearts, the travellers pressed on. The twilight deepened, and the Nasmarian Forest seemed to grow ever more foreboding. The once-vibrant canopy had turned into a dense shroud of shadows, stretching high above them and filtering the last rays of sunlight. As the daylight faded, an unsettling stillness began to settle, blanketing the path ahead. The forest, once alive with colour and movement, now seemed suspended in a moment of eerie calm. The air grew colder, tinged with an unnatural chill that seemed to creep into their bones, making the travellers' breath visible in the growing darkness.

Max led the group at the front, his senses heightened, every step filled with caution. The atmosphere had taken on a disquieting quality, with the slightest rustle of leaves or snap of twigs in the distance seeming to echo ominously in the silence. The weight of the forest pressed down on them, thick and oppressive. A palpable sense of foreboding seemed to seep from the earth itself, as if the land were alive and watching.

Siobhan, ever the perceptive one, cast a wary glance at the trees around them, her brow furrowed in concentration. "Something doesn't feel right," she murmured, her voice barely more than a whisper. "It's as though the forest is hiding something—something we can't see, but it's there, lurking."

Jonas, his sharp gaze scanning their surroundings, nodded slowly, his expression grim. "Stay alert. This place has a way of twisting the mind. The sights, the sounds—they may not be what they seem. Trust nothing but your instincts."

Ross, still adjusting to his newfound connection with the earth, felt a peculiar sensation deep within him. It was as if the ground beneath his boots was alive, whispering secrets just out of reach. He shook his head, trying to dispel the unease gnawing at him. "I agree," he said, his voice low and thoughtful. "The forest feels... alive. In a way that's difficult to describe. We should stay close and keep moving."

The twins, Anastasia and Greer, walked closely together, their steps synchronising despite their contrasting personalities. Anastasia, the more cautious of the two, had her hand resting lightly on the hilt of her dagger, her eyes darting back and forth with suspicion. Greer, usually carefree and full of chatter, was uncharacteristically silent. Her gaze, once full of wonder, now seemed drawn to the shadows that swirled around them, her senses fully attuned to the eerie energy in the air. They exchanged a quiet, wordless glance, their bond palpable in that brief moment of shared unease.

With the travellers pressing forward, the forest closed in around them. The trees, gnarled and twisted with age, appeared to lean inward as if observing their every move, the branches creaking in the wind. The path narrowed, and the air grew thick and heavy, each breath feeling like an effort. The shadows lengthened unnaturally, twisting and shifting with every flicker of light from their torches, adding to the disorienting sense of movement in the darkness.

They soon came upon a small, ancient bridge made of weathered stone, arching gracefully over a narrow, bubbling stream. The bridge was cloaked in moss and lichen, the surface slick with age and moisture. Below, the water churned softly, its murmur almost like a whispering voice, but there was something unsettling about it. The stillness of the scene—the bridge, the stream, the surrounding forest—felt like a frozen moment in time, suspended in a way that made the travellers feel like intruders.

Max paused, staring into the dark waters, the flickering torchlight painting strange reflections on the surface. "There's something off about this place," he said quietly, his voice heavy with suspicion. "It's as though we're being tested, as if the forest itself is waiting for us to make a move."

Siobhan shivered, her instincts on edge. She could feel the weight of the forest's gaze bearing down on them, and every sense screamed to keep moving. "Let's not linger here," she urged, her voice tense. "We don't know what's hidden in these waters—or what else this place may have in store for us."

Without another word, they crossed the bridge, their footsteps echoing softly on the timeworn stone. On the other side, the path diverged into several smaller trails, each one cloaked in darkness, the trees bending inwards as though trying to conceal the way ahead. The feeling of being watched intensified with every step.

They chose the middle path, the one that seemed to have seen the most use. The forest around them grew quieter, the oppressive atmosphere settling deeper. The only sounds now were the occasional rustle of leaves or the distant call of a nocturnal creature, but even these seemed muted, swallowed up by the dense, suffocating silence.

Then, with no warning, a cold gust of wind swept through the trees, sending a shiver down their spines. The shadows ahead seemed to ripple and congeal, twisting into a dark figure that materialised before them. It was the old woman—her piercing eyes glowing with an unsettling intensity, and an aura of dark magic that clung to her like a cloak. She stood before them, draped in flowing robes adorned with ancient symbols, her presence radiating malevolence.

"Welcome, travellers," she said, her voice soft but laden with a chilling edge. It echoed through the trees, a whisper that carried across the forest. "I've been watching you."

Max stepped forward, his posture tense, "What do you want from us?" he demanded, his voice steady but filled with strength.

A wicked smile curled at the corners of the old woman's lips, her eyes gleaming with dark amusement. "You've disturbed the balance of the elements," she said, her voice dripping with disdain. "And you intend to do so again. The relics you've found belong to the ancient powers of this world, powers that are not to be trifled with."

Siobhan's gaze hardened, her voice unwavering. "We seek to restore the balance, not upset it."

The old woman's laughter echoed like the screech of an owl in the night, sending an involuntary shudder through the group. "Balance is fragile, child. One wrong move, and it can tip into chaos. The relics are powerful, and those who seek them must be ready to face the consequences of their actions."

Jonas, his jaw clenched in frustration, spoke up, his tone tight with suspicion. "Why are you so intent on stopping us? You gave us the Orb of Water before. Why the sudden change in your decision?"

"I am a guardian of these secrets," the old woman replied, her gaze piercing, as though she could see straight through to their very souls. "I have seen the devastation power can wreak when it is wielded recklessly. You are not the first to seek the relics, nor will you be the last. But I will ensure that their power is not misused."

Anastasia, her expression fierce and focused, took a step forward, her voice unwavering. "We won't let you stop us. We are committed to restoring balance and protecting the elements."

The old woman's smile widened, dark amusement flashing in her eyes. "Then prove it," she said, her voice like velvet laced with venom. "Prove that you are worthy of the power you seek. The forest has tested you, but the real trial lies ahead. Your darkest fears await, and you must be ready to face them."

With a swift motion, she waved her hand, and in an instant, she vanished into the shadows, leaving behind nothing but the lingering sense of dread. The path ahead seemed even darker, more suffocating, and the weight of her words hung heavily in the air.

Max turned to his companions, a quiet strength shining in his eyes. "We have to keep moving," he said, his voice low but Firm. "She's right about one thing—we need to prove we're worthy. But we'll do it on our terms, not hers."

The group nodded in agreement, their purpose growing stronger. The encounter with the old woman had only fueled their determination.

As they pressed onward, the forest seemed to close in around them, the feeling of being watched never letting up. They knew that the old woman's influence stretched far beyond what they could see, and her presence would haunt them for the rest of their journey. But they were undeterred. Their mission to restore balance and protect the relics was more important than any obstacle in their path.

Their journey through the Nasmarian Forest was far from over, and the trials ahead would test their strength, courage, and unity in ways they hadn't yet imagined. With each step they took deeper into the dense wilderness, the air growing thicker with the scent of moss and damp earth, they moved closer to their ultimate goal – and to the final confrontation with the dark forces intent on derailing their mission.

As they ventured through a small, secluded clearing, the tension in the air was palpable. The encounter with the enigmatic old lady had left everyone on edge, the eerie knowledge that she had been watching them, waiting for the right moment, gnawing at their thoughts. They knew they needed to be better prepared for what lay ahead, for whatever traps she might have laid in their path.

Max, who had been silent for some time, broke the quiet with a voice that carried the weight of his thoughts. "We need to talk about what happened today. The old lady showing up means things are going to get trickier from here on out. We can't just rely on luck anymore. We need to be ready. Fully ready."

Siobhan nodded in agreement, her face etched with the same concern. "Max is right. We've come a long way, but our powers... we need to hone them, understand them better. We need to practise, strengthen them." Her eyes flicked to each of them, as if assessing their readiness.

Jonas, his expression thoughtful, looked around at the group, his brow furrowing. "We've faced a lot of challenges together, but this feels different. The stakes are higher now. We need to trust our abilities and each other completely, without hesitation. Maybe we should start training against each other, to get a better handle on our powers. See how we perform under pressure."

Ross, ever the pragmatic one, spoke up with his usual level-headedness. "We've seen what we can do individually, but we need to figure out how to work together—how to harness our strengths and combine them in unison."

Anastasia and Greer exchanged a brief but meaningful glance, a silent understanding passing between them. Anastasia, usually reserved, spoke up first. "Let's do it. We can't afford to be caught off guard again. Not by her, not by anyone."

Max stood, a fire of determination burning in his eyes. "Alright then. Let's start now. Let's see what we're really capable of." His voice was sharp, filled with purpose, and the group fell into line behind him, their unity strengthening.

They divided into pairs to test their abilities against each other, eager to push their limits and understand how best to support one another when it truly mattered.

Max paired with Siobhan. His healing powers were a recent discovery—and with them came questions he hadn't yet answered. He wasn't fully confident in their scope. So, he focused on supporting Siobhan as she demonstrated her ability to transform matter. Siobhan's concentration was unwavering as she held a nearby rock in her hands, slowly shaping it with a focused intent until it morphed into a sharp metal spear. She threw it toward Max with precision. He dodged it effortlessly, though he couldn't help but offer feedback. "Great job, Siobhan! Now, let's try transforming something a bit more complex. We need to test the limits."

Siobhan nodded, a fierce gleam in her eyes. She concentrated, her focus intensifying as she transformed the spear back into a rock, then shaped it into a wooden staff with fluid motion. "How's this?" she asked, her voice almost playful as she twirled the staff with a flourish, showing off her control.

"Perfect," Max said, a warm smile tugging at his lips. "Now, let's see if you can change its properties while it's in motion. Don't hold back."

Meanwhile, Jonas and Ross were locked in their own battle of wills. Jonas, the master of air manipulation, summoned gusts of wind that whipped through the clearing, creating powerful currents meant to knock Ross off balance. Ross, however, stood firm, using his connection to the earth to anchor himself, his feet rooted deeply into the ground as he felt the subtle vibrations in the air. "You're getting better, Ross," Jonas remarked, his voice a mix of admiration and challenge. "But try to anticipate my moves, not just react to them."

Ross closed his eyes, focusing inward. The vibrations of both the air and the earth intertwined in his senses, allowing him to perceive the world more clearly. He felt a sudden gust and reacted instinctively, teleporting just as a whirlwind formed where he had been standing. "Nice try, Jonas. But you'll have to do better than that."

Anastasia and Greer, their strengths more subtle, practised their coordination and teamwork. Anastasia, with her ability to control water, executed a series of attacks that were swift and calculated. Greer, using her telepathic link with Anastasia, was able to anticipate each move before it happened, dodging with uncanny precision. "We need to be faster," Greer remarked, her voice clipped and focused. "The old lady won't give us the luxury of time to make mistakes."

Anastasia's eyes narrowed, her concentration sharpening. "We need to be able to anticipate each other's moves instinctively. Let's go again."

The training continued well into the night, the sounds of their efforts—grunts, bursts of energy, and the crackling of the forest—echoing through the darkened trees. The group pushed themselves to their limits, each of them learning to trust their powers and the bonds that connected them. As the hours passed, they grew stronger, not just as individuals, but as a team.

Finally, after hours of intense training, they gathered around the campfire, their bodies exhausted but their spirits lifted. The firelight danced across their faces, sending wavering shadows as they settled into a comfortable silence.

"We've made good progress," Max said, his voice steady and sure, his eyes scanning the faces of his friends. "But we need to keep pushing ourselves. The final relic is still out there, and the old lady won't stop until she has what she wants."

Siobhan nodded, her gaze distant but thoughtful. "Agreed. But tonight was a good start. We're stronger together, and we're getting better."

Jonas added with a smirk, "We'll need every bit of that strength for what's coming. Let's get some rest and continue our training tomorrow. We can't afford to stop now."

The next day dawned with a crisp chill in the air, the early morning light filtering through the thick canopy of the Nasmarian Forest. The travellers awoke, the anticipation of the coming day settling in their bones like a heavy weight. They knew that every moment counted, and that their journey to find the final relic and confront the old lady was growing more urgent by the hour.

Max was the first to rise, his movements deliberate as he stoked the embers of the campfire back to life. The rest of the group gradually stirred, stretching, preparing themselves for the challenges of the day ahead. The mood was somber, but a deep-seated strength wove through their shared silence.

"Morning, everyone," Max called, passing out the rations. "We need to decide our next move. We've trained hard, but it's time to take action."

Siobhan nodded, sipping from her canteen as she thought carefully. "Agreed. We should focus on gathering more information about the final relic. We know it's a torch with an eternal flame and that it's somewhere in an ancient village. We need to find that village."

Ross, who had been meditating, opened his eyes slowly, his expression calm but sharp. "I might be able to sense the village's location if we get closer to its vicinity. The earth sometimes reveals its secrets to those who listen carefully enough."

Jonas grinned, his eyes alight with excitement. "And I can help scout ahead. The air can carry whispers of the village's presence. We should head in a direction that feels right and see if we can pick up any clues along the way."

Anastasia and Greer exchanged a quiet look, and then Anastasia spoke, her voice soft but certain. "Maybe we can use our telepathy to sense any nearby minds. If the villagers are simple folk, as we've heard, their thoughts might be easier to pick up."

Greer agreed with a nod, her expression serious. "It's worth a try. We need every advantage we can get."

Max looked around at his friends, feeling a surge of pride for their resilience. "Alright, let's pack up and get moving. We'll head northwest—it's as good a direction as any to start. Stay alert, and let's hope we can pick up some signs of the village."

The group quickly gathered their belongings and set off, each member alert and focused. As they walked through the forest, they kept their senses sharp, relying on their unique abilities to gather information from the world around them. The path ahead was uncertain, but their commitment held steady.

After several hours of travel, the forest began to change. The once thick and oppressive trees became less dense, and patches of sunlight pierced the canopy above, spilling soft beams across the uneven ground. The atmosphere lightened, and the weight of the tension they had felt earlier began to dissipate, replaced by a quiet peace that was almost tangible.

Ross paused and knelt on the earth, his hands pressing gently into the cool soil. He closed his eyes, tuning in to the vibrations beneath him. "I'm feeling something," he murmured after a moment of stillness. "The ground here feels... different. Like there's something ancient, something alive just beneath the surface."

Jonas, his senses attuned to the air around him, closed his eyes and took a deep breath, allowing the currents to guide him. "I can hear it too," he said softly, his voice barely above a whisper. "There's a faint whisper of life, not far from here. It's as if the forest itself is speaking."

Anastasia and Greer exchanged a knowing glance, their minds reaching out in unison for any sign of the villagers. Greer's eyes widened in surprise as she concentrated, her brow furrowing. "I think I'm picking up some thoughts," she said, her voice edged with intrigue. "They're faint, but they're there—calm, simple thoughts."

Max nodded, his expression focused but calm. "Let's follow those leads. Stay together and stay alert," he said, his voice firm yet reassuring.

As they pressed forward, the trees thinned even more, and the sound of a distant waterfall reached their ears, a refreshing reminder of the world outside the forest's heavy grip. The path led them to a clearing, and before them lay an ancient village, nestled at the base of a rocky hill. The villagers moved about their daily routines, unaware of the travellers' presence.

The village had an air of serenity, a stark contrast to the brooding, dense forest they had just left behind. The cobblestone paths, winding between neat cottages adorned with flowering plants and glowing lanterns, radiated a sense of calm. The gentle hum of the village, from the soft murmur of conversation to the playful laughter of children, filled the air, offering a welcome reprieve from the tension of their journey.

At the centre of the village, a cave entrance was visible, its dark mouth seemingly alive with a soft, warm glow that emanated from within. The travellers approached cautiously, their eyes drawn to the light as it bathed the surrounding landscape.

"That must be it," Siobhan whispered, her voice barely audible. "The cave where they keep the torch."

Max took a deep, steadying breath, feeling the weight of the moment. "We need to approach carefully. We don't want to alarm them. Let's find a way to talk to them and see if we can bargain for the relic."

The travellers exchanged nods of agreement, their purpose solidifying with every second. They knew the importance of diplomacy, of respecting the villagers' way of life, and they hoped to acquire the final relic without any conflict. But they were prepared for whatever challenges might arise.

As they approached the heart of the village, an elderly man emerged from the crowd, standing tall despite his age. His long silver beard caught the light, and his robe seemed to shimmer, reflecting the fading rays of the sun. His eyes, though ancient, gleamed with wisdom and kindness, and as he stepped forward, the villagers subtly parted, making way for him.

"Welcome, travellers," he said, his voice carrying a unique blend of authority and warmth. "I am Thalion, the elder of this village. We have been expecting you."

The travellers exchanged confused glances, clearly taken aback by his words. They hadn't expected anyone to know they were coming. After a brief moment of silence, one of them finally asked,

"We seek the eternal flame. Can you assist us in finding it?"

Thalion's gaze remained steady, his expression solemn yet not unkind. "The Eternal Torch is a sacred relic, one that our village has protected for generations. It holds great power, and we do not part with it lightly. Before we can grant you access to it, you must first prove yourselves worthy through a series of trials."

The travellers shared uneasy looks, their hearts steadying despite the uncertainty before them. It was clear that the path to their goal would not be simple or without cost. One of them stepped forward, asking, "What kind of trials?"

"The trials are designed to test more than your abilities," Thalion explained, his voice grave yet patient. "They are meant to test your intentions. The flame is a powerful artifact, and we must be sure that those who seek it are worthy and responsible. Each of you will be tested according to your unique abilities."

The travellers nodded in understanding. The trials would be demanding, but they had no choice but to accept them. "We are ready," Max said, his voice steady, a quiet strength radiating from him.

With the promise of trials looming, the travellers accepted the elder's invitation to stay in the village for the night. The villagers, ever gracious, welcomed them with open arms, offering warmth, comfortable lodgings, and a hearty meal.

The simple, rustic food was a welcome change from their usual fare, and the warmth of the hearths in the village homes made the night feel far more peaceful than it had in the forest.

As the evening wore on, the travellers sat together around a communal fire, the crackling flames illuminating their faces with wavering shadows. The villagers gathered nearby, sharing stories of their ancestors and the village's rich history. Despite the weight of the trials to come, the travellers found themselves at ease, comforted by the simplicity and serenity of this place.

Thalion, sensing the tension still lingering within them, approached the fire, his presence as calming as the glow from the flames. He took a seat, his eyes thoughtful as he regarded each of them in turn.

"Before we proceed further," he said, his voice carrying a gentle command, "it would be helpful to know more about those who seek the Eternal Torch."

Max stood first, his posture relaxed yet respectful. "I'm Max. My friends and I have traveled far in search of the relics that will help protect our world. I've discovered I can heal quickly from wounds and sickness, though I'm still learning how this power works."

Siobhan followed, her gaze firm and confident as she spoke. "I'm Siobhan. My gift allows me to transform matter, altering the very essence of objects. It's a skill I've been honing for some time, and I hope it will serve me well in the challenges ahead."

Jonas was next, his voice steady as he introduced himself. "I'm Jonas. I command the power of air and can manipulate winds and currents. I also have the ability to stretch my body to great lengths, which has been incredibly useful in navigating difficult terrain."

Ross, his presence grounded and calm, stepped forward. "I'm Ross. My connection to the earth allows me to sense its vibrations and even transport myself and others through the ground. It's a power I've learned to wield with precision."

The twins, Anastasia and Greer, exchanged a brief, knowing glance before stepping forward to introduce themselves. Anastasia spoke first, her voice calm but steady. "I'm Anastasia, and this is my sister, Greer. Our abilities are deeply tied to water. We can control and manipulate it at will, shaping it to our needs, and we share a unique telepathic connection—not only with each other but with others as well. It's a bond that allows us to communicate silently and work together seamlessly."

Greer nodded in agreement, her eyes glowing with conviction. "Together, we've honed our powers, learning to use them in perfect harmony. We hope to contribute to our quest with that same unity and strength."

Thalion listened intently, his gaze sharp and thoughtful as each traveller shared their abilities. His expression remained neutral but respectful as he spoke. "Thank you for introducing yourselves," he said, his voice carrying an undertone of approval. "Your powers are indeed formidable. But as you prepare for the trials ahead, remember—they are not just a test of your abilities, but also of your unity and your intentions. It is through your cooperation and understanding of each other that you will truly prove your worth."

With that, Thalion gestured toward the village's central meeting hall, its stone walls warmed by the early morning sun. The hall, bustling with activity, was where the travellers could rest and prepare for the trials that lay in wait. The night was theirs to reflect, to ready themselves for the challenges that would test their worthiness and mettle.

The night passed in quiet anticipation, the only sounds the occasional rustle of leaves in the soft breeze and the distant murmur of the village settling down. With each passing hour, the travellers felt a growing sense of readiness. They were ready to face the trials ahead, driven by the strength and courage that had carried them through their journey so far. The following day would bring new challenges, but they were united, each of them prepared to meet the unknown with courage and purpose.

As dawn broke over the tranquil village, the first rays of golden light filtered through the rustic windows of their temporary quarters, painting the walls with warmth. The sounds of nature greeted them—a gentle chorus of birds singing in the trees, the soft gurgle of a stream winding its way through the landscape. It was a serene moment, a welcome reprieve from the oppressive atmosphere of the Nasmarian Forest that they had just left behind.

The villagers went about their morning routines with a serene, almost meditative rhythm. Their movements were fluid, reflecting the peaceful life they led in this idyllic place. Thalion, ever watchful, approached the travellers as they gathered for breakfast.

"Good morning," Thalion greeted them, his tone respectful but steady. "Today marks the beginning of your trials. The Eternal Torch is more than just a symbol; it embodies balance and harmony. It is a treasure that has been guarded by our village's traditions for generations. To earn it, you must demonstrate not only your abilities but also your understanding of its true meaning."

Max, sipping a warm cup of tea, looked up and nodded. "We're ready. What do we need to do?"

Thalion's gaze was steady, his eyes reflecting the seriousness of the moment. "The trials ahead will test many different aspects of your skills and character. They are not simply physical challenges, but also tests of mental resilience, emotional strength, and teamwork. The flame represents unity, a beacon of strength forged through understanding. To earn it, you must prove that you are worthy of such a symbol."

Siobhan's curiosity piqued, she leaned forward. "What kind of trials should we expect?"

A faint, knowing smile appeared on Thalion's face. "The trials are designed to challenge you in unexpected ways. They will push you to your limits, forcing you to confront your weaknesses and recognise your strengths. The Eternal Torch is not just a relic; it is a reflection of the balance between strength and unity."

As the villagers prepared for the day's events, the travellers were led to an open area on the outskirts of the village, where several different stations were set up. Each station represented a different challenge, each one carefully crafted to test their various skills and abilities.

As the group arrived at the open space, they saw the intricate setups ahead—stations that would challenge them in unique ways. Thalion guided them toward a particular station where a large, elaborate apparatus awaited Jonas.

The station consisted of a series of elevated platforms and floating rings, all suspended in mid-air by unseen forces. The air around the station hummed with energy, a gentle but persistent breeze blowing through the space. The platforms seemed to sway ever so slightly, as if they were part of a living organism. It was a mesmerising and intimidating sight.

"This," Thalion said, gesturing toward the apparatus, "is the Trial of the Winds. For this challenge, Jonas will need to demonstrate his mastery over the element of air. The trial will test his control, precision, and ability to adapt to changing conditions."

Jonas stepped forward, his eyes scanning the intricate setup. The platforms, arranged in a complex pattern, seemed to float in mid-air with no visible support. The floating rings moved steadily in various directions, creating a chaotic yet synchronised dance. Jonas could feel the subtle currents of air that seemed to swirl around him, as though the wind itself was alive, guiding him toward the challenge.

"This looks intense," Jonas muttered, squaring his shoulders as he focused on the first set of platforms.

Thalion nodded, his expression thoughtful. "The goal is to navigate through the floating rings and across the platforms without touching them. The air currents will change unpredictably, making this a test of both skill and adaptability. You must use your abilities to manipulate the air, creating stable paths and overcoming the obstacles that arise."

Jonas took a deep breath and stepped onto the first platform, his feet light and sure. He summoned a cushion of air beneath him, softening the impact of his landing. The platform wobbled slightly but settled under his control. The breeze around him picked up, but he adjusted, guiding it with a flick of his wrist.

As he moved, the challenge grew more difficult. The air currents intensified, and the platforms began to shift more erratically. Jonas had to adjust his focus constantly, sending gusts of wind to stabilise the platforms and direct the floating rings into alignment.

Max, Siobhan, Ross, Anastasia, and Greer watched from the sidelines, their eyes wide with awe. They could see the concentration etched deeply on Jonas's face as he moved with precision, his every step calculated, every movement measured.

At one point, Jonas was faced with a wide gap between two platforms. With no time to hesitate, he summoned a powerful gust of air to propel himself across the chasm. The leap was daring, but he executed it flawlessly, landing lightly on the next platform.

The final part of the trial presented the most difficult challenge—a series of rapidly moving rings that seemed impossible to catch. Jonas, unwavering, focused his energy. He summoned a vortex of wind, a controlled tunnel of air that he could navigate through. With fluid movements, he guided himself through the shifting rings, his body moving with precision and grace.

With one final leap, Jonas landed on the last platform, his hand brushing against a glowing crystal embedded in its surface. The crystal pulsed with a warm, radiant light, signaling the completion of the trial.

Thalion approached him, his expression filled with approval. "Well done, Jonas. You have shown not only control over your element but also the ability to adapt to ever-changing conditions. This trial is more than just a test of skill; it represents the balance and harmony that the Eternal Torch embodies."

Jonas, breathing heavily but with a satisfied smile, joined his friends as they gathered around him. Their faces were filled with admiration, but they knew this was only the first of many challenges to come. The successful completion of the Trial of the Winds had bolstered their confidence and strengthened their willpower. The trials had only just begun, but they were ready.

After Jonas successfully completed his trial, the travellers gathered at the edge of the open area, anticipation hanging in the air as they awaited the next challenge. Thalion led them onward, guiding the group toward a new station, this one situated near a serene, crystal-clear lake. The water shimmered beneath the gentle touch of the morning sun, its surface glinting like polished glass.

At the lake's centre, a small, elevated platform stood surrounded by several elaborate water features, their intricate designs giving the impression of something both ancient and magical.

"Welcome to the Trial of the Waters," Thalion announced, his voice steady as he gestured toward the breathtaking setup. "In this challenge, Anastasia and Greer will need to demonstrate their mastery over the element of water. This trial will test both their creative ingenuity and their practical control over the flow of water."

Anastasia and Greer exchanged steely glances, the weight of the trial settling on their shoulders. Both had been preparing for this moment for weeks—mentally and physically attuning themselves to their abilities since their arrival.

"This trial requires both cooperation and individual skill," Thalion continued, his tone serious but encouraging. "You will navigate through a series of water-based obstacles, using your abilities to overcome them. You must work in tandem to ensure success."

Anastasia stepped forward, her gaze fixed on the central platform. It was surrounded by a sequence of rotating water spouts and geysers, their powerful arcs of water creating a dynamic and constantly shifting landscape.

"Ready?" Anastasia asked Greer, her voice firm yet filled with an undercurrent of excitement.

"Ready," Greer replied, her expression one of quiet composure.

With a deep breath, the trial commenced, triggered by the activation of the water features. Powerful jets of water erupted from the lake, shooting high into the air and then arching back down, creating intricate patterns before crashing into the water below. The jets formed temporary barriers that both hindered and challenged the travellers. Anastasia and Greer had to use their powers to manipulate the water, not only to maintain their balance but also to prevent the cascading jets from impeding their progress.

Taking the lead, Anastasia raised her arms, her focus unwavering as she harnessed the flow of the water. With a graceful wave, she summoned a stream from the lake, forming a fluid bridge that connected the platform to the shore. She continued to shape the water, conjuring several spheres that floated above the surface of the lake, their translucent forms serving as stepping stones for Greer to cross.

Greer followed closely, using her own abilities to bend and shape the water as needed. She formed a protective shield around herself, redirecting the force of the jets, and expertly manipulated the water, creating new paths and calming turbulent areas that might otherwise have thrown her off balance.

The challenge escalated as the water spouts intensified in speed and complexity. The platform itself became a moving target, with geysers and jets erupting unpredictably, forcing Anastasia and Greer to remain agile and adaptable. They adjusted their control of the water in real-time, matching the pace of the shifting obstacles.

At one point, a series of rotating water barriers formed a near-impenetrable wall, blocking their way. Anastasia and Greer combined their powers in a seamless, synchronised motion: Anastasia summoned a large protective wave that shielded them from the oncoming torrents, while Greer directed a precise, focused jet of water to create an opening large enough to pass through.

Their movements were fluid and coordinated, their partnership evident in every gesture. Thanks to their bond, they communicated telepathically, their minds in tune without the need for words.

As the trial neared its end, they faced a delicate manoeuvre. The final task required them to fill a large basin situated at the centre of the platform with a steady stream of water, carefully balancing the flow to reach the designated level.

With a collective effort, they directed the water in perfect harmony. When the basin glowed with a soft, blue light, signaling their success, Thalion approached them with a look of admiration.

"Excellent work, Anastasia and Greer," he said, his voice filled with pride. "You've displayed impressive skill, not only in manipulating the element of water but also in your ability to work as a cohesive team. This trial was a test of both your individual mastery and your collaboration."

Anastasia and Greer, drenched in lake water yet beaming with satisfaction, joined the others. Completing the trial marked another significant step in their journey. They felt a renewed sense of unity and purpose as they prepared for the next challenge that awaited them.

As the sun reached its zenith, bathing the village in a warm, golden light, the travellers took a well-deserved break for lunch. The communal dining area of the village was a welcoming space, rustic and simple, with sturdy wooden tables and benches arranged in a relaxed, informal manner. The air was rich with the enticing aroma of freshly baked bread, roasted vegetables, and simmering stews.

The group gathered around one of the long tables, still absorbing the intensity of the morning's trials. Thalion had provided a hearty meal, reflecting the village's generosity and its deep-rooted tradition of hospitality. As they sat down to eat, the group took a moment to unwind, share their thoughts, and reflect on the experiences they had just undergone.

Max, surveying his friends with a thoughtful expression, spoke up. "That was impressive, everyone. I think we're really starting to understand how to use our powers in new and creative ways."

Siobhan, still feeling the lingering effects of the water trial on her hands, nodded thoughtfully. "Anastasia and Greer really did an amazing job with the water. It's clear that mastering an element takes not only skill but also a lot of creativity."

Anastasia, wiping droplets of water from her brow, smiled. "Thanks, Siobhan. It was challenging, but it felt good to put our abilities to the test and work together. I feel like we've learned so much about ourselves and how to use our strengths more effectively."

Greer, sipping her drink, added, "It's incredible how much more we can accomplish when we combine our powers. I think today we've made real progress. But I'm curious about what's next."

Jonas, his eyes thoughtful, leaned back in his chair. "I agree. The trials are tough, but they're also a chance for us to hone our skills and learn more about each other. It's not just about proving ourselves; it's about growing stronger as a team."

Ross, glancing at the sky and nodding in agreement, spoke next. "We should enjoy this break while we can. The challenges are only going to get more difficult. We need to stay focused and continue pushing ourselves."

As they ate, the conversation shifted to lighter, more personal topics. The group shared stories of past adventures and laughed over fond memories. It was a welcome reprieve from the intensity of the trials, and a reminder of the strong camaraderie that bound them together.

With lunch finished, the group gathered their belongings and made their way back to the village square, where Thalion awaited them. The next trial loomed on the horizon, and the travellers were eager to face it with the same grit and harmony they had shown earlier.

Thalion greeted them with a knowing smile. "I trust you've had a chance to reflect and regroup. The next trial will test different aspects of your abilities and teamwork. Are you ready to continue?"

The travellers exchanged firm nods, their spirits lifted by the shared experiences of the day and the unwavering support of their friends.

Thalion led them to an area on the edge of the village, where the landscape became rugged and wild. This part of the village was starkly different from the tranquil setting they had just left. The terrain here was uneven and harsh, with large boulders and craggy outcrops scattered across the land, creating an environment that was both daunting and beautiful in its rawness.

The air was thick with the earthy scent of moss and soil, and the ground beneath their feet was solid, unwavering—firm in a way that grounded the soul. Ross felt an almost primal connection to the land beneath him, a subtle but tangible pulse that resonated deeply with his earth powers. Thalion gestured toward a large stone formation at the heart of the clearing.

"This," Thalion began, his voice imbued with reverence, "is the Trial of the Earth. It will test not only your mastery over the element but also your capacity to adapt and think strategically. The challenge before you requires more than brute force—it demands precision, foresight, and the ability to solve complex problems. It mirrors the puzzles you faced earlier, though on a much grander, more intricate scale."

Ross's eyes flared with fierce focus, the challenge igniting something within him. "I'm ready. What do I need to do?"

Thalion motioned for Ross to approach the stone formation. "Before you lies a series of natural obstacles. Your task is to create a path through them using only your earth manipulation skills. Keep in mind that the path must be navigable for your companions as well, so the practicality of your solution is just as important as its ingenuity. Consider their needs as you work."

As Ross stepped closer, he realised that the stone formation was far from a simple obstacle. It was a complex arrangement of jagged boulders, deep crevices, and uneven ground. The landscape itself seemed designed to test the limits of his control over the earth—challenging his ability to manipulate the terrain in multifaceted ways.

Thalion's voice cut through his thoughts. "Time is a factor. The trial is not just about completing the task, but doing so efficiently. Your actions will be observed, and your approach is just as critical as the result. How you solve the problem will be evaluated just as thoroughly as your success in navigating it."

Ross nodded, his mind already racing with possibilities. He closed his eyes for a moment, focusing on the vibrations beneath his feet. The earth hummed, responding to his awareness as if it were alive. When he opened his eyes again, there was a sharpness to his gaze—a clarity of purpose.

"Alright, I'll begin now," Ross said, his voice steady with purpose.

The travellers moved back, giving Ross the space he needed to work. Their eyes were fixed on him, anticipation palpable in the air as he began the challenge.

Ross approached the stone formation and placed his hands on the ground, grounding himself. He drew in a deep, centering breath, and then extended his senses deep into the earth. Beneath the surface, he could feel the layers of rock and soil, their textures, densities, and the subtle movement of the earth itself. He could feel the pulse of the land, its energy vibrating through him, guiding his every action.

With focused precision, Ross began to manipulate the earth. Large boulders rose from the ground to create stepping stones, their surfaces smooth and stable under his command. The earth shifted, forming ridges that filled in gaps and smoothed out the uneven terrain. His movements were fluid, like a dance of control, each stone obeying his will.

There was a particularly challenging section ahead—a deep, gaping crevice that threatened to block his path. Ross paused, analysing the obstacle. The solution required more than just force. With concentrated effort, he drew up large chunks of earth from nearby areas, carefully lowering them into the gap to form a sturdy bridge. The rocks settled into place with a satisfying rumble, the crevice no longer an insurmountable barrier.

Throughout the trial, Ross remained attuned to his companions, ensuring that the path he was creating was not just a personal success, but one that would serve the group as a whole. His mind worked with purpose, balancing the need for precision with an understanding of the bigger picture. His movements were methodical, each one a testament to his skill and his ability to stay composed under pressure.

As Ross neared the end of the trial, a sense of accomplishment washed over him. He had managed to navigate the obstacles, transforming the rocky formation into a network of interconnected paths. His creation was not only stable but also accessible—an intricate solution that balanced aesthetics with practicality.

When he finished, Thalion approached, his expression thoughtful but approving. "Well done, Ross. You've demonstrated impressive skill and adaptability. Your ability to manipulate the earth and create a functional path is commendable. You've completed the challenge, but more importantly, you've shown a deep understanding of the earth's power."

The travellers broke into applause, and Ross, feeling a surge of pride, joined them with a smile. The trial had been grueling, but it had reaffirmed his bond with the earth and his place within the group.

With Ross's challenge complete, the travellers gathered their things, preparing for the next trial. The sense of camaraderie was stronger than ever as they readied themselves for what lay ahead.

As the sun rose higher in the sky, the villagers began preparing for the next trial. The travellers gathered in the designated area, the stark contrast of their surroundings a sharp reminder of the challenges they had yet to face. This trial was set in a vast open space, transformed into a dramatic arena bathed in the intense, shimmering light of fire. Flames danced in carefully controlled patterns around the perimeter, projecting long, fluttering shadows. The air was thick with heat, a constant reminder of the danger and urgency that awaited.

Thalion approached them with a serious expression, his demeanor reflecting the gravity of what lay ahead. His attention to detail was evident—this trial was not just about assessing Max and Siobhan's control over fire, but also about ensuring they understood the profound duality of the element itself.

"Max, Siobhan," Thalion began, his voice carrying the weight of experience, "this trial is designed to test your mastery over fire, but more importantly, it will challenge your understanding of its nature. Fire is both a creator and a destroyer. It can bring light to the darkest places, but it can also consume everything in its path. To earn the flame, you must demonstrate that you can wield it not only with skill, but with wisdom."

Siobhan and Max exchanged firm glances, the weight of the moment pressing down on them. They had prepared for this challenge in their own unique ways, each honing their skills, and now, the time had come to see if they could wield any control over the fire element.

Thalion's voice rang out, steady and commanding. "Your task is to navigate through the fiery arena and overcome a series of obstacles. This path will test not only your ability to control and manipulate fire but also your creativity and adaptability. I will observe and assess your performance, from which I will determine who among you is most attuned to the fire element."

With those words, Thalion led Max and Siobhan to the starting point of the trial. The arena stretched out before them, divided into several sections, each presenting a distinct challenge that required precision, focus, and mastery over the fire.

The first section of the arena was a narrow passageway, its walls flanked by towering walls of flame. The fire roared with intense heat, a ferocious blaze that crackled and hissed, creating an almost impenetrable barrier of heat and light. As the flames licked at the edges of the passage, Max and Siobhan had to find a way to cross without being scorched, using their control over fire to either extinguish or divert the flames as they moved forward.

Max stepped forward first, his eyes narrowing as he focused on the searing flames. He was well aware that his ability to heal through his blood was unconventional, but he had learned to apply it in ways others might not have considered. As he neared the fiery walls, he drew on his healing power, channeling it into a barrier of protective energy that enveloped him like a shield. With each calculated step, he moved through the passage, the barrier absorbing the heat, the flames harmlessly gliding across its surface but unable to burn through.

Siobhan, her gaze fixed on Max's approach, took a different route. She closed her eyes, her breath steady and deep, and visualised the flames as a flowing current of energy, something she could bend and shape. With a slow, deliberate exhale, she extended her arms, and to her surprise, the fire seemed to respond to her mental command. She shaped the flames, directing them into flowing patterns that parted like a curtain to form a path. Her mastery over the fire was precise, each movement of her hands deliberate, transforming the destructive force of the flames into something controllable.

The second section of the arena challenged them further—a series of moving fire platforms, suspended over a vast chasm. The platforms shifted unpredictably, some plunging downward while others rose, and Max and Siobhan had to time their movements perfectly, or risk losing their footing on the narrow platform.

Max, his expression set in focused concentration, approached the floating platforms with caution. He knew that timing would be crucial. Drawing on deep, steady breaths to calm his nerves, he anticipated the movement of the platforms, moving with a calm precision. Each step was calculated, and he focused on stabilising his footing, his unwavering focus keeping him grounded as the platforms shifted beneath him.

Siobhan, however, took a more creative approach. As she moved forward, she manipulated the fire to form temporary footholds, shaping the flames into solid shapes that acted like stepping stones. Each step she took was supported by a carefully crafted flame platform, allowing her to move effortlessly across the chasm. Her ability to shape fire into functional objects showcased her creativity, turning the dangerous element into something that worked for her.

The final section of the arena was the most formidable—a massive fire dragon, summoned by an ancient mechanism hidden beneath the arena, was unleashed into the battleground. Its fiery breath shot out in powerful torrents, and its growls reverberated through the space, filling it with an overwhelming presence. Max and Siobhan knew they had to subdue or redirect the dragon's flames if they were to complete the trial.

As the fire dragon lunged at them, its scales glowing bright with intense heat, Max and Siobhan braced for the battle. The dragon's fiery breath surged toward them, and in that moment, Max instinctively stepped in front of Siobhan, his body tensing as he raised his hands, preparing to shield her from the blast.

Siobhan, her senses sharpened and focused, began manipulating the fire surrounding them. She reached out, her hands moving in intricate, flowing patterns as she attempted to redirect the dragon's searing flames away from their path. She poured all her concentration into the flames, bending them with a will that was almost effortless. The fire responded to her, swirling and reshaping itself, but the sheer might of the dragon's power was overwhelming.

The dragon roared, its fury unabated, and released another powerful surge of flames toward them. Siobhan's concentration faltered under the intensity of the heat, her brow furrowing as she struggled to maintain control. The flames pushed at her, and the heat was suffocating. Her body was being forced back by the dragon's relentless assault.

Max watched in horror as the dragon's fiery breath closed in on Siobhan. Without thinking, he acted on pure instinct, reaching out to protect her. In that moment, something extraordinary happened. A surge of energy, different from his healing power, coursed through him. His hands, now glowing with unfamiliar energy, released a powerful stream of water that collided with the dragon's flames.

The water met the fire with a hiss, a cloud of steam exploding in the air. The dragon, momentarily stunned by the unexpected element, recoiled in surprise, its fiery breath faltering. Max stared at his hands in disbelief. He had never controlled water before, and yet it had felt natural, like it had been a part of him all along.

Siobhan, equally astonished by the turn of events but quick to adapt, seized the opportunity. She manipulated the steam, bending it into a veil of mist that cloaked their movements, disorienting the dragon and making it difficult for the creature to target them.

"Max, how did you do that?" Siobhan asked, her voice a mixture of awe and confusion.

"I don't know," Max replied, his eyes wide with wonder. "It just happened. I didn't think, I just... reacted."

The fire dragon, regaining its composure, let out a deafening roar, fury evident in its every movement. It charged at them once again, its flames licking the air. But this time, Max was ready. His newfound ability now felt second nature to him, and with newfound confidence, he summoned another surge of water, directing it forcefully toward the dragon's mouth. The water collided with the fire once more, creating an explosive burst of steam that temporarily blinded the beast.

Seizing the moment, Siobhan acted quickly, shaping the remaining flames into a ring of fire that encircled the dragon, trapping it within her fiery control. The dragon roared in fury, thrashing violently, but its movements were now restricted by the impenetrable ring of fire.

Max and Siobhan worked in perfect synchrony. Siobhan's mastery over fire allowed her to divert the dragon's movements, while Max's unexpected water powers neutralised its attacks. The steam and mist enveloped the arena, creating a shifting battlefield that disoriented the dragon and gave the travellers the upper hand.

The villagers and Thalion watched in stunned silence as Max and Siobhan demonstrated their extraordinary powers. The synergy between them was undeniable, and Max's unexpected control over water hinted at something even greater, a deeper power that had yet to be fully unlocked.

Finally, after a fierce and grueling struggle, the fire dragon began to weaken. Its once deafening roars grew softer, gradually fading into faint growls, and the blazing inferno around it began to subside. Siobhan, with a final surge of willpower, called upon her mastery of the flames, transforming the remaining fire into harmless sparks that gently fluttered away into the cool evening air. Max, his own energy drained but unfaltering, directed a final torrent of water at the dragon, extinguishing the last embers of its fiery breath with a powerful, precise stream.

As the dragon's fiery aggression waned, the arena fell silent. Steam, rising from the remnants of the dragon's fire, slowly began to dissipate, unveiling the victorious figures of Max and Siobhan standing amidst the quiet aftermath. The fire dragon, now subdued and pacified, lowered its mighty head in a gesture of submission, the flames that once crackled around its form now reduced to a faint glow.

Thalion, the village elder, approached them, his expression one of profound respect and admiration. His gaze lingered on both of them, as if weighing their worth. "You have both demonstrated exceptional skill and unwavering courage," he said, his voice carrying a deep reverence. "Max, your control over water is beyond extraordinary. It seems there is far more to your power than any of us anticipated."

Max, still reeling from the unexpected revelation of his abilities, nodded slowly. His voice was thick with uncertainty. "I didn't know I could do that," he admitted, his eyes searching the ground as if grappling with the weight of his newfound strength. "But... it felt right, as though it came from somewhere deep inside me."

Siobhan, ever the steadying force, placed a reassuring hand on his shoulder. "Whatever this power is, Max, it's a part of you," she said, her voice calm yet infused with quiet confidence. "And it just might be the key to everything we need to succeed."

With the fire dragon subdued and the trial completed, the travellers had proven their worth beyond doubt. Thalion, now fully convinced of their capabilities and understanding, would make his decision on who was most attuned to the fire element. But Max's unexpected power hung in the air, a mystery that filled the group with awe and anticipation for the challenges that still lay ahead.

As the evening drew near, the tranquil village was bathed in the warm, golden glow of twilight. The day's trials were over, but the sense of accomplishment was just beginning to settle in. A palpable feeling of celebration filled the air, as the villagers, deeply grateful and thoroughly impressed by the travellers' bravery and skill, prepared a grand feast in their honour.

Long wooden tables were set up in the village square, their surfaces adorned with wildflowers and lit by flickering lanterns that bathed the scene in a soft, inviting light. The rich aroma of roasted meats, freshly baked bread, and fragrant vegetables drifted through the air, mixing with the sounds of laughter and chatter as the villagers worked diligently to prepare the feast. The travellers, still recovering from the intensity of the day's challenges, were welcomed warmly, their tired bodies comforted by the hospitality of the people.

Max, Siobhan, Jonas, Ross, Anastasia, and Greer were led to the head of the main table, a place of honour that reflected the villagers' deep respect and gratitude. Thalion, standing at the centre of the gathering, his presence commanding yet serene, addressed the crowd.

"Tonight, we celebrate not only your success in the trials," Thalion began, his voice strong and clear, carrying across the gathering, "but also the courage and unity you have shown. You have proven yourselves worthy of the Eternal Torch, and in doing so, you have demonstrated a profound understanding of the sacred relics you seek."

The villagers, moved by his words, raised their cups in a celebratory toast, their voices joining in a chorus of joy. The sound of clinking glasses reverberated through the square, filling the night air with the harmonious notes of shared triumph. The travellers exchanged grateful smiles, a deep sense of camaraderie swelling within them as they realised just how much this moment meant — not only to them but to the villagers who had come to see them as more than mere travellers, but as protectors of their world.

As the feast continued and the villagers basked in their collective joy, Thalion called for silence, and the chatter slowly subsided. Every eye turned to him in eager anticipation. "There is one final matter to address," he announced, his voice carrying weight. "The Eternal Torch is a sacred trust, a power that must be placed in the hands of one who embodies its spirit. And after bearing witness to your trials, it has become abundantly clear to me who that person is."

He turned to Siobhan, his eyes filled with wisdom and kindness, reflecting the deep respect he held for her. "Siobhan," Thalion continued, "you have shown an extraordinary ability to transform and control matter, a power that resonates with the very essence of fire itself. Your command over the flames during the trial was nothing short of exceptional. Therefore, I entrust you with the element of fire, symbolised by the eternal flame."

Thalion reached into the folds of his robe and produced the Eternal Torch a lantern crafted with intricate artistry. It was an ancient piece, its enchanted glass and metal design radiating an ethereal beauty. Inside the lantern, the eternal flame burned brightly, its steady light a beacon of hope and power. The crowd gasped in awe, the light from the flame illuminating the village square, laying long shadows as it flickered in its sacred vessel.

"This lantern," Thalion explained, "is designed to safely contain and protect the eternal flame. It will allow you to carry it on your journey without fear of it extinguishing or causing harm. The flame will guide you and bestow upon you the strength and wisdom of the element of fire itself."

Siobhan stood, her heart racing with a mixture of surprise, pride, and humility. She gazed at the flame, feeling its warmth radiate through her as she took the lantern into her hands. "Thank you, Thalion," she said, her voice steady but thick with emotion. "I will guard this relic with my life and wield its power to protect our world."

As Thalion handed her the lantern, a wave of warmth and strength flowed through Siobhan, a deep, almost spiritual connection forming between her and the flame. The crowd erupted into applause, their cheers ringing out into the night. The travellers joined in, their hearts lifted by a sense of fulfillment and purpose.

Max, watching Siobhan, felt a mixture of pride and contemplation. While he was happy for her, the revelation of his own powers still gnawed at him, leaving a lingering sense of uncertainty. The day's events had unlocked something within him, something he hadn't fully understood, and as he turned his gaze toward the horizon, he couldn't help but wonder what it all meant for the journey ahead.

The night stretched on, the stars twinkling above as the celebration continued under their vast, shimmering canopy. The travellers, now bonded more deeply than ever before, shared in the warmth of the feast, their spirits lifted by the sense of accomplishment. With the Eternal Torch safely entrusted to Siobhan, the trials behind them, and new powers awakened within them, they stood ready to face whatever awaited on their path — a path that would demand all their strength, courage, and unity in the coming days.

CHAPTER 6

Shadows of Deceit

The morning sun bathed the village in a golden glow as the travellers readied themselves for departure. Their spirits were buoyed by the hard-won success of acquiring the Eternal Torch. Villagers gathered around them, offering words of encouragement and small tokens of goodwill—a handmade charm, a pouch of dried herbs, a carved wooden talisman—each a silent prayer for their journey ahead.

Siobhan cradled the lantern containing the Eternal Flame, its flickering light a steady pulse against the morning air. She was acutely aware of the immense responsibility it carried.

Thalion approached, his expression solemn yet filled with quiet pride. "You have all shown great courage and unity. The Eternal Flame is now in worthy hands. Remember, its power lies not just in its ability to burn, but in its capacity to illuminate the darkness and restore hope."

As they prepared to leave the safety of the village, the group took a moment to say their goodbyes.

Max looked at his companions, a mixture of pride and uncertainty settling in his chest. "We'll make sure it's used for the right reasons."

Thalion gave a slow nod. "There is one more thing you should know. The path ahead will not be easy. Darkness will test you in ways you cannot yet imagine."

As they left the safety of the village, an uneasy feeling settled over the group. Though they saw nothing amiss, a sense of being watched clung to them, like unseen eyes lurking just beyond their vision. The open fields gradually gave way to the looming, twisted expanse of the Nasmarian Forest. Shadows stretched unnaturally, and the air thickened, charged with an energy that set their nerves on edge.

Siobhan walked beside Max, glancing at the lantern's warm glow. "I still can't believe what happened with the fire dragon. You saved me, Max."

Max shook his head, his brow furrowed. "I don't even know how I did it. It just... happened."

Anastasia, walking just behind them, interjected. "We need to figure out what's going on with you, Max. You've displayed abilities beyond anything we thought possible."

Greer crossed her arms. "And we need to be ready. If that old woman appears again, we should know exactly what we're capable of."

Sensing the tension rising, Ross attempted to lighten the mood. "Well, whatever it is, we'll face it together. We've handled worse."

Jonas, his sharp gaze sweeping over the dense undergrowth, remained tense. "Stay alert. This forest plays tricks on the mind. We don't know what's waiting for us."

Their journey continued, the towering trees pressing in around them, filtering the sunlight into jagged slashes across the forest floor. The rustling of leaves and the occasional snap of a twig kept them on edge. Every shadow felt heavier than it should have been, as if something unseen moved just beyond their sight.

After what felt like hours, the path opened into a clearing. At its centre stood a massive, ancient tree, its gnarled branches stretching outward like skeletal fingers clawing at the sky. The air around it was thick, suffocating, as though the forest itself was holding its breath.

Siobhan hesitated. "This place feels... wrong."

Max narrowed his eyes, his senses sharpening. A strange energy pulsed from the tree, coiling around them like an unseen force. "Be on your guard. This could be another test."

Before anyone could respond, a low, sinister laughter echoed through the clearing. From the shifting shadows, the old woman emerged, her eyes glinting with malice.

"So, you managed to acquire the Eternal Torch," she sneered. "Impressive. But your journey ends here."

The group tensed. The old woman lifted her hands, and the shadows around them writhed and twisted, congealing into dark, spectral forms. The air grew frigid, and an unnatural stillness fell over the clearing.

Max stepped forward, his voice firm. "We're not afraid of you. We'll do whatever it takes to protect the relics and complete our mission."

The old woman's smile was sharp and cruel. "You think you're strong enough to stand against me? You have no idea what true power is."

Before she could strike, Siobhan transformed a nearby rock into a polished shield, the surface gleaming in the dim light. Jonas summoned a sudden gust of wind, pushing the encroaching shadow creatures back. Ross, feeling the earth's pulse beneath him, sent a tremor through the ground, throwing the twisted forms off balance.

Max, heart steady and strong, held his ground. "We've come too far to let you stop us now."

The old woman's expression darkened. She raised her arms, chanting in a language none of them recognised. The swirling shadows intensified, their presence closing in around the travellers like a living force.

Anastasia and Greer exchanged a glance, their connection silent yet understood. Greer reached out with her mind, gently soothing her companions' nerves, while Anastasia honed in on the old woman's intent, searching for a weakness.

Ross clenched his fists, his power surging. With a focused effort, he cracked the earth beneath them, creating a fissure that trapped several of the shadow creatures. Siobhan, seizing the opportunity, transformed the imprisoned figures into harmless wisps of dust, scattering them into the wind.

Despite their efforts, the old woman remained unfazed. She lifted her chin, her voice filled with eerie certainty. "You cannot defeat me. The forest itself bends to my will."

Just as the situation seemed dire, Max felt something stir deep within him. A force, ancient and unfamiliar, welled up in his chest. Acting purely on instinct, he extended his hand—

A surge of water erupted from his palm, crashing into the shadowy figures and extinguishing them like flames doused by a storm.

The clearing fell silent. All eyes turned to Max. His breath came fast, his fingers tingling with residual energy. He stared at his hand, disbelief flickering across his face. "How...?"

The old woman's gaze sharpened. "Interesting," she murmured. "It seems you're more than you appear."

Seizing the moment, Jonas unleashed a powerful whirlwind, sweeping away the remaining shadows. Siobhan, her shield still raised, summoned a roaring blaze of fire, shaping it into a forceful blast that drove the old woman back.

Ross, summoning his strength, willed the earth to rise, forming barriers that enclosed the old woman in a ring of solid ground. Anastasia and Greer focused their mental energy, unleashing a wave of disorienting thoughts that fractured her concentration.

The old woman, now visibly struggling, narrowed her eyes in pure hatred. "You may have won this battle, but this is far from over. The darkness will consume you all."

With a final, defiant scream, she released a pulse of dark energy, shattering the earthen barriers in a violent explosion of dust and debris. When the air cleared, she was gone, leaving the travellers in stunned silence.

Siobhan lowered her shield, her expression firm. "We need to keep moving. We can't let her slow us down."

Max exhaled sharply, still processing what had just happened. "Agreed. We'll figure this out."

As they regrouped, a sobering realisation settled over them—their trials were far from over. The encounter had shaken them, but it also strengthened their commitment. They would need every ounce of courage and unity to face what lay ahead and keep the relics from falling into the wrong hands.

They pressed forward into the dense forest, tension thick in the air. Each step was accompanied by the whisper of rustling leaves and the distant calls of unseen creatures.

Siobhan broke the silence, her voice steady. "We have to be ready for whatever comes next. She won't give up easily, and we can't afford to lower our guard."

Anastasia nodded, her eyes sharp with focus. "We should find a place to camp. Somewhere defensible, away from the main path."

Jonas motioned ahead. "There's a clearing up there. It looks safe enough."

Moving swiftly, they set up camp, their movements efficient and practised. As the fire crackled to life and the stars began to pierce the darkening sky, they gathered close, drawing comfort from the warmth.

Greer turned to Max, studying him thoughtfully. "What happened back there? How did you control the water?"

Max shook his head. "I don't know. It just... happened. I felt this surge, and then the water was there."

Ross, seated cross-legged by the fire, stroked his chin in contemplation. "Maybe you have a deeper connection to the elements than we realised. It's possible you can wield more than one."

Siobhan met Max's gaze, curiosity flickering beneath her concern. "If that's true, we need to learn how to harness it. It could be the key to stopping her—and protecting the relics."

Anastasia and Greer exchanged a glance, their silent understanding evident. Anastasia spoke, her tone calm yet strong. "We'll help you, Max. No matter what it takes."

Jonas, his face illuminated by the fire's glow, added, "We're a team. We've faced impossible odds before and come out stronger. This won't be any different."

A wave of gratitude swelled in Max's chest. "Thank you. All of you. We'll get through this—together."

As the fire crackled and shadows danced against the trees, they turned their focus to planning their next move.

Morning arrived in a hush of golden light filtering through the trees, dappling the forest floor with shifting patterns. Birds stirred in the branches, their soft calls the only sound in the crisp, cool air.

Max stretched, watching his companions pack up camp with the quiet efficiency of those accustomed to life on the road. "I've been thinking," he said. "If I really can control more than one element, we need to start training now. We can't afford another surprise like yesterday."

Jonas nodded, his expression serious. "Agreed. The better prepared we are, the better our chances. Let's start with air. It's my element, and mastering it could help you stay agile and aware."

They found a secluded clearing, undisturbed by the outside world. Jonas stood in the centre, his stance relaxed but focused. Max watched him closely, ready to learn.

"Air is all about flow and movement," Jonas explained. "It's the most unpredictable element—always shifting, never still. Controlling it isn't about force, it's about guiding it. Close your eyes. Feel the air around you. Listen to it."

Max obeyed, taking slow, measured breaths. He could feel the cool breeze brush his skin, hear the whisper of wind through the leaves, sense an invisible energy swirling around him.

"Good," Jonas murmured. "Now, instead of trying to command it, become part of it. Let it carry you, like a boat drifting down a river."

Max focused, reaching outward with his mind. A faint connection flickered—a thread of something just beyond his grasp. He willed the air to move, and to his astonishment, a small gust stirred, swirling lightly around him.

Jonas grinned. "That's it! You're starting to get it. Now, try again. Make it stronger."

Max concentrated harder, channeling his energy into the air. The gusts strengthened, swirling through the clearing and sending leaves spiraling in every direction. He opened his eyes, awe flickering across his face as the wind obeyed his command.

"Excellent," Jonas praised, his voice steady with approval. "You're a natural. Remember, air can be a shield, a weapon, or a tool. Master its shape, control its speed and direction, and you'll wield a force as precise as it is powerful."

As Max continued to practise, the others watched, their expressions ranging from admiration to determination. Siobhan stepped forward, curiosity lighting up her features. "Mind if I join? I could use some pointers on refining my control over matter transformation."

Jonas nodded. "Of course. The more we train together, the stronger we become. Focus on precision, Siobhan. The more exact your intent, the more formidable your transformations will be."

Siobhan stepped into the clearing beside Max, her hands glowing faintly as she manipulated the scattered objects around her. Pebbles shifted, twigs morphed, and the air thrummed with energy as they worked side by side. For hours, they honed their abilities, learning from each other's strengths, pushing past their limits.

On the sidelines, Anastasia and Greer observed with a mix of pride and resolve. Their time would come, and when it did, they would be ready.

Ross, perched on a nearby rock, watched in silence before murmuring, "We're getting stronger, but we can't let our guard down. The old woman won't surrender easily. We have to be prepared for whatever comes next."

The morning passed in relentless training, each traveller testing the boundaries of their power. With every controlled gust of wind, every precise shift in matter, they grew not just in strength but in unity, their shared purpose binding them together.

By midday, exhaustion weighed on them, and they took a much-needed break. The relics—tokens of their hard-fought battles—lay carefully packed away, each one carrying the weight of their journey. As they gathered around a small campfire, the full gravity of their discoveries settled in.

Max stared into the flickering flames. The old woman's true nature, her veiled manipulations—it all gnawed at him. He had believed their mission was simple: find the relics. But now, doubt coiled in his gut. Had they been pawns from the start?

Siobhan broke the silence, her tone edged with unease. "We have the relics, but something still feels off. The old woman's presence—it was too deliberate, too orchestrated. It's like she wanted us to find them."

Jonas, who had been absently summoning small gusts between his fingertips, nodded. "Agreed. If she truly wanted these relics hidden, she could have made it impossible for us to get them. Instead, it's like she was guiding us. But why? What's her goal?"

Ross exhaled, his brow furrowed in thought. "I keep going over her words. If she has the power to manipulate minds, then who's to say she wasn't the one sending us those visions? Maybe Max's father appearing to him was no coincidence."

Max's grip tightened around his knees as he lifted his gaze. "My father told me to find these relics. But what if it wasn't really him? What if she used his image to lure me into gathering them for her?"

A heavy silence fell over the group, the weight of the revelation pressing down on them. If Max was right, then their mission had been tainted from the very start.

Greer, who had been listening quietly, finally spoke. "If she's been using us, then we need to rethink everything. We can't let her outmanoeuvre us again. We need to understand what she's planning and find a way to stop her."

Anastasia's expression hardened. "We should head back and regroup. We need a strategy, something concrete. If she intends to use the relics to create a weapon—or something worse—we have to be ready."

Greer glanced toward the horizon.

"Agreed. We should move quickly, but carefully. The deeper we go, the more dangerous this gets. We can't afford any missteps."

As they packed up their camp, Max's thoughts churned. Despite their victories, uncertainty clawed at him. The old woman had played them once—he wouldn't let her do it again.

Ross, sensing Max's unease, clapped him on the back. "We've got this, Max. We just need to stay focused and stick together. We've already overcome so much. Whatever comes next, we can handle it."

Max managed a small smile, appreciating his friend's support. "Thanks, Ross. I just wish I knew more about what we're up against. The old woman seemed to know a lot more than she let on."

Siobhan gathered her belongings, her mind preoccupied with the implications of their encounter. "Whatever her plan is, we need to be ready. Let's make sure the relics are securely packed and that we're prepared for any surprises along the way."

As they made their way through the forest, conversation dwindled. They moved swiftly, their focus sharpened by the unsettling knowledge that their journey was far from over. What had once been a place of adventure and discovery now felt more like a labyrinth of unseen dangers and lurking threats.

The path back stretched longer than they had anticipated. As twilight fell, the forest darkened, its once-familiar canopy twisting into an oppressive shroud. A familiar, unwelcome sensation crept over them—the distinct feeling of being watched. Every snap of a twig and rustle of leaves sent a fresh wave of tension through the group.

They stopped briefly for a meal, though their conversation remained subdued, each lost in thought. The weight of the old woman's warning—and the possibility that she could use the relics for something far worse than they had imagined—hung over them.

As night deepened, the trees became looming silhouettes against the sky, their branches clawing at the wind. The oppressive silence was only broken by the occasional distant hoot of an owl or the rustling of unseen creatures. Committed to reaching a safer location before stopping for the night, they pressed on.

After what felt like an eternity, they finally emerged from the tangled woods into a vast clearing. A silver glow bathed the field as moonlight stretched across the swaying grass, offering a brief respite from the forest's stifling grip.

The travellers set up a temporary camp, though the tension lingering between them refused to dissipate. The fire crackled, sending flickering patterns of light across their faces, their expressions shadowed with uncertainty.

Max, staring into the flames, broke the silence. "We've all been through so much. Each trial has forced us to see new sides of ourselves. It's strange, though—I thought I understood my abilities, but with the fire dragon and the way I used water... it feels like I'm still discovering what I'm truly capable of."

Siobhan glanced at Max, her brow furrowed. "You weren't the only one surprised. When I saw you use water to save me, I felt a shift—like my connection to fire wasn't as isolated as I thought. It's a reminder that our powers don't exist in a vacuum. They're intertwined, part of something larger and more complex."

Jonas, leaning back with a thoughtful expression, nodded. "And it's not just about our powers. We've all had to adapt in ways we never expected. The trials forced us to confront our limits and push beyond them."

Ross, who had been quietly observing, added, "We've learned to trust each other in ways we never did before. And it's not just about fighting—it's about understanding each other's strengths and knowing when to rely on them."

Anastasia, her gaze fixed on the stars, spoke softly. "Each of us has faced moments of doubt and fear. But we've pushed through them. That's what makes us stronger. It's not just about the relics or the battles ahead—it's about the strength we've built within ourselves and how that will guide us."

Greer, always attuned to the emotional currents between them, studied her friends. "We've all changed, and it's drawn us closer. We're not just a team anymore. We're something more—we truly understand and support each other."

As the firelight flickered and the night deepened, Max's gaze remained fixed on the flames. "I've been thinking about everything we've accomplished. It's easy to get caught up in the rush of it all, but now... the weight of what's ahead is really sinking in."

Siobhan leaned forward, poking the fire with a stick. "Yeah, and there's more at stake than just how we use the relics. We're up against someone who can manipulate minds and wield dark power. I can't shake the feeling that we're missing something—something critical."

Jonas nodded, his eyes reflecting the firelight. "The way she got into our heads, especially yours, Max, is unsettling. It means she has a deeper strategy. We need to figure out what she's planning before it's too late."

Ross, his expression grim, finally spoke. "The way she controlled the shadows and used them against us... it felt like more than just magic. It was something ancient. Something darker."

Anastasia's eyes filled with concern. "If she's capable of creating creatures or weapons with the relics, we're facing a threat bigger than anything we've ever encountered."

Greer, who had been listening intently, added, "We also need to consider how our own powers are evolving. Max, the way you used water alongside fire was unexpected. It shows that our connections to the elements aren't as rigid as we thought."

The conversation gradually shifted toward strategy—how best to use their abilities together, how to anticipate the old woman's moves, and what steps they needed to take next.

Later that night, as the travellers prepared to rest, none of them realised that the shadows around them carried secrets of their own.

Beyond their sight, in a hidden, ancient temple, the old woman stood before a grand, cracked mirror. Its surface rippled with dark energy, distorting the images reflected within. Flickering between the travellers' faces and the relics they carried, the vision pulsed with ominous intent.

Her sharp eyes, gleaming with cunning, took in every detail as whispers coiled through the air— echoes of forgotten spells, remnants of a power long buried.

She reached out, her fingers grazing the mirror's surface. The images within rippled and shifted, revealing a vast, desolate landscape—an open field beneath a storm-churned sky. It was the place she had chosen for the final confrontation. A slow, calculating smile curved her lips as she envisioned the travellers arriving, blissfully unaware of the trap laid before them.

A whisper, soft yet laced with malice, curled through the room. From the shadows, a figure emerged, cloaked in an aura of pure malevolence. The darkness clung to it like a living thing, tendrils of shadow twisting in the dim light.

"The pieces are falling into place," the figure murmured, its voice a mere breath of sound, yet heavy with command. "Soon, the power of the relics will be mine."

The old woman's expression remained unreadable, her smile grim. "Yes, but the travellers are growing stronger. We must ensure our plan proceeds without disruption. They must be drawn into a trap, one from which they cannot escape."

The figure's voice deepened, resonating with quiet menace. "The time is approaching. They will soon arrive at the point of no return. When they do, we will be ready."

The old woman inclined her head, her tone laced with deference. "Indeed, they have shown resilience, but they remain blind to the true nature of the forces they face. They believe they can wield the relics, yet they do not understand their true purpose."

The shadows around the figure deepened, thickening like a storm gathering strength. "Ensure they continue on their path. The relics must be brought to me. With their power combined, the very fabric of reality will bend to my will."

The old woman nodded, her loyalty unwavering. "It will be done. We will lull them into a false sense of security, and when the time is right, we will strike. They will never see it coming."

The figure's voice lowered to a whisper, carrying the weight of an unspoken threat. "Do not fail me. The consequences will be... severe."

The old woman bowed her head, her voice barely above a breath. "I live to serve. The relics will be yours, and with them, the power to reshape this world as you see fit."

The figure's form flickered, its presence a looming specter in the dim chamber. "The travellers are merely pieces on the board. Their strength will either serve our purpose or be crushed beneath it. They will not leave the battlefield with their innocence intact."

A faint smirk ghosted across the old woman's lips. "They are strong, but they are naive. The relics will bring about their downfall, and in the end, they will be nothing but a memory."

As the figure's presence began to wane, an oppressive silence settled over the chamber. Yet, before it faded entirely, its voice returned, cutting through the stillness like a blade.

"Do not underestimate him. The boy has already displayed an unnatural mastery over water, despite his lack of a bond. If he discovers the full extent of his abilities, it could become... problematic."

The old woman waved a dismissive hand. "It won't come to that. We will strip them of their defences, take what we need, and leave them broken. The relics' power will be yours, and with them, the means to command the very essence of reality. They are nothing more than pawns in a game they do not realise they have already lost."

The figure's gaze burned like smoldering embers. "And if they resist?"

The old woman turned back to the mirror, its surface twisting and warping beneath her gaze. Her own reflection, dark and distorted, stared back.

"Then they will fall," she murmured. "One by one. The boy, the girl, and the rest of them... They will all bow before the true power of the elements. And in the end, they will be forgotten—mere footnotes in the story of your ascension."

The air thickened, charged with a palpable malice. The figure stepped closer, its silhouette sharpening, its eyes glowing with something both ancient and insatiable.

"Remember," it hissed. "Their strength lies not only in their abilities but in their unity. Fracture that, and they will crumble. The boy—Max—he is the key. Watch him closely."

The old woman's expression darkened, her mind already working. "As you wish," she said smoothly, though her gaze flickered with something unreadable.

The figure's ambition was clear—dominion over the elements and, by extension, the world. But The old lady had ambitions of her own. Max's blood was more valuable to her than any relic, not for power, but for survival.

"Ensure the relics are delivered to me," the figure continued, its voice sharpening. "With them, my power will be absolute."

The old lady inclined her head. "Of course. The relics will be yours. But as for the boy…" She let the words trail off, her voice tinged with a quiet possessiveness.

The figure's gaze narrowed. "Your rejuvenation?"

A thin, almost imperceptible smile ghosted across her lips. "Yes," she admitted. "Max's blood holds the secret to reversing the ravages of time. With it, I can escape this wretched shell and reclaim what I lost. But that is my concern, not yours. Our arrangement stands, does it not?"

The figure studied her in silence before finally nodding. "Very well. But remember this, Jocelyn— our goals may differ, but they are bound together. Fail me, and you will learn the true meaning of suffering."

With a final, dismissive flick of her hand, Jocelyn watched as the chamber dimmed, the mirror's surface rippling like disturbed water. The shadowy figure dissipated, leaving behind a chilling silence.

Jocelyn stood still, her mind racing. The final confrontation loomed ever closer. While the figure sought dominion, she sought something far more personal—life itself. The relics were a means to an end, but Max's blood... That was the true prize.

As she gazed into the quiet mirror, memories of years spent weaving an intricate web of deception flooded her mind. To the world, she was Jocelyn Rivers—an intelligent, compassionate young girl with a heart for philanthropy. It was a flawless disguise. No one suspected that beneath the polished veneer lurked an ancient witch, her body ravaged by time, her soul consumed by an unrelenting hunger for youth and power.

Years ago, Jocelyn had uncovered the extraordinary properties of Max's bloodline. His father, Brad, had possessed the same rare regenerative abilities—a gift Jocelyn had desperately sought to exploit. She had meticulously orchestrated the circumstances surrounding Brad's death, her attempts to harvest his blood ending in failure when his unforeseen demise disrupted her plans. But Brad had been a step ahead, sacrificing himself to shield his family from her grasp.

Max, however, was her second chance. For years, Jocelyn had watched him, waiting for the opportune moment to strike. Disguised as a devoted and affectionate girlfriend, she had embedded herself within his life, earning the trust of both Max and his friends. She had subtly nudged him toward the operation, feigning concern for his health. But the procedure had been nothing more than a ruse—a carefully constructed deception to extract his blood without raising suspicion. The truth, however, was far darker: Jocelyn needed his unique blood to restore her youth and sustain her dark powers.

Max's mother, Charlotte Haywood, had long known the truth about Jocelyn. Yet fear and the knowledge of the witch's formidable strength had kept her silent. Jocelyn's magic was too powerful, her influence too vast. Any direct confrontation would have been futile. So, Charlotte had protected Max from the shadows, clinging to the fragile hope that he might somehow escape Jocelyn's grip.

But Jocelyn's patience was wearing thin. With each passing day, maintaining the illusion of an innocent, youthful teenager became more taxing. Time was slipping away, and she knew the moment to act was drawing near. The final piece of her plan rested on acquiring Max's blood, while the relics would grant her the power to solidify her dominance. She had played the long game, weaving a web of deception for years, and now, with the ambitions of the shadowy figure aligning with her own, the endgame was in sight.

A slow smile spread across her lips as she caught her reflection in the mirror—a fleeting glimpse of her true, aged form staring back at her. The years of calculated manipulation, the careful lies—all of it was about to pay off. The travellers, the relics, Max—everything was finally falling into place. She would not be denied again. This time, she would ensure that nothing and no one would stand in her way.

As the day wore on, Jocelyn steeled herself for the final confrontation. Max's power was the key, the ultimate prize. With his blood, she would defy time itself, untethering from the shackles of mortality. The stakes had never been higher, and the cost of failure was unthinkable. But Jocelyn had come too far, sacrificed too much, to allow a naive boy and his meddling friends to disrupt her plans.

CHAPTER 7

The Witch's Revelation

The campfire's flames flickered in the night, sending elongated shadows stretching across the forest floor. The travellers sat in a wary silence, the warmth of the fire unable to chase away the deep chill settling into their bones. The weight of the past weeks—both their victories and their near losses—pressed upon them, a silent burden none could shake. Despite their progress, an unshakable sense of unease lingered. Something was missing. A vital piece of the puzzle eluded them.

Dawn arrived in a soft, golden hue, bathing the clearing in gentle light where they had made their camp. The embers of their fire smoldered, sending faint wisps of smoke curling into the crisp morning air. The scent of damp earth and pine filled their lungs as birds stirred in the trees, greeting the new day with cautious melodies. One by one, the travellers roused themselves, their faces etched with quiet resilience.

Max stretched, scanning the group. Their expressions mirrored his own apprehension. The relics were in their possession, yet uncertainty gnawed at them.

Jonas, ever perceptive, broke the silence. "We're getting closer," he murmured, his voice barely above a whisper. "I can feel it. Something is… gathering around us."

Siobhan nodded, her gaze distant. "It's like we're standing on the edge of something immense. The air feels different—thicker, heavier. Whatever is coming, it's close."

Ross, usually reserved, finally spoke. "We've faced danger before, but this is different. It feels like the shadows are closing in." He exhaled slowly. "We need to stay sharp and be ready for anything."

Anastasia and Greer exchanged a glance, both sensing the shift in atmosphere. Anastasia's usual lightheartedness was subdued, replaced by a somber focus. Greer, standing slightly apart, kept her sharp eyes trained on the treeline, her body tense, as though waiting for the first sign of trouble.

As they packed up their camp, the travellers formed a small circle. Max held the lantern containing the eternal flame, his grip tightening as he met each of their eyes. "We have the relics," he said, his voice steady despite the unease creeping into his chest. "But we still don't know who—or what—we're truly up against. We need to be careful."

Greer nodded grimly. "The shadows aren't just a threat. They're aware of us. Watching. Waiting."

Ross crossed his arms. "And if they've been waiting, it means there's more to this than the relics. Something bigger. Something we're missing."

Jonas, deep in thought, hesitated before speaking. "What if... this was the plan all along? We've been so focused on gathering the relics, but what if that's exactly what they wanted? What if we're playing into their hands?"

Silence settled over them as the implication sank in.

As they set off through the dense forest, the once-familiar path now felt alien, as if the trees had subtly shifted in the night. The towering canopy choked out the morning light, leaving them in a dim world of shifting shadows. The air grew heavier with every step, thick with an unspoken tension.

They moved with cautious precision, every rustle of leaves and snap of twigs setting them on edge. The sensation of being watched became undeniable.

A cold shiver traced down Max's spine. *We're being guided,* he realised. *Herded toward something unseen.* The conversations from the night before echoed in his mind—unity, vigilance, the need to think beyond the obvious.

As the day stretched on, the feeling of unseen forces pressing in on them intensified. The forest, which had once felt like a place of refuge, now seemed a trap designed to disorient and confine. The air itself seemed to pulse with anticipation, an invisible force pushing them toward an inevitable confrontation.

By late afternoon, the forest path opened into a valley, revealing a small, secluded village at the foot of a mountain. The scent of pine and damp earth filled the air, mingling with the distant murmur of a waterfall. The village, though quiet, held an air of quiet mystery—its cobbled streets worn smooth by time, ivy creeping over the walls of old stone cottages.

As they wandered through the village, drawn by the promise of answers, they came upon a crumbling building, half-consumed by vines and moss. A faded sign, nearly lost to time, hung above the entrance:

The Arcanum: Records of the Ancients.

Curiosity and urgency propelled them inside.

The interior was thick with the scent of aged parchment and forgotten knowledge. Dust-speckled light streamed through the dirty windows, illuminating towering shelves lined with books and scrolls, their spines brittle with age. At the centre of the room stood a grand wooden desk beneath a chandelier of unlit candles, as though awaiting the return of a long-absent scholar.

Jonas ran a hand over the spines of the ancient tomes, reading their titles aloud. *"Ancient Rites and Rituals... The Elemental Guardians... The Legend of the Shadow..."* He paused, eyes narrowing as he pulled a worn, leather-bound book from the shelf. The cover, cracked and peeling, revealed faded lettering beneath the dust. Carefully, he opened it, revealing delicate, yellowed pages inked with meticulous script.

Ross leaned in, scanning the words. His breath caught. "This... this speaks of an old witch. It says she disguised herself, stealing the life force of others to sustain her youth and power." His voice was barely more than a whisper.

Max felt a cold wave wash over him. "A witch who steals life force..." He swallowed hard. A vague, unsettling familiarity stirred in the back of his mind.

Siobhan, standing beside him, paled as she turned the fragile pages. The book's illustrations depicted a woman, beautiful and young, her features sharp and striking. But as the pages progressed, her form shifted—her beauty withering, twisting into something grotesque. A crone, her face lined with malice, eyes void of humanity.

Anastasia's brows knit together as she quickly flipped through the book. "Look at this," she said, pointing to a passage. "She posed as a healer, a benefactor—gaining trust before revealing her true nature." The words sent a chill through them, conjuring memories of Jocelyn's effortless charm, her carefully placed concern for Max's well-being.

Anastasia leaned closer, her brow furrowed as she pointed at a passage inked in faded script. "Here— Junessa Ravaryn. It says she was known for taking many faces. She'd pose as a healer, a guardian, even pretending to be a friend or sweetheart—earning trust before draining her victims dry."

The words hit like a thunderclap.

Greer's fingers trembled as she traced the image—one of the earliest sketches, the youthful version of the witch. The resemblance was unmistakable. The sharp chin, the dark, knowing eyes... Jocelyn's eyes.

Max staggered back a step. "No... no, that's not possible." But even as he spoke, Jocelyn's gentle smile, her too-perfect concern, replayed in his mind—every moment now dripping with hidden malice.

Siobhan whispered, "Jocelyn Rivers never existed, Max. She was Junessa Ravaryn all along."

And they had walked straight into her trap.

Siobhan's voice trembled as she looked at him. "She wanted you from the start. That's why she pushed so hard for the operation—it wasn't just about healing. She needed your blood, your unique gifts. You were her key to staying young forever."

Max's expression hardened as the truth settled in. His thoughts spiraled back to the mysterious death of his father, Brad. It all connected—his father had likely discovered Jocelyn's true nature and tried to stop her, paying the ultimate price. His mother, Charlotte, had known the truth but had been powerless against Jocelyn's influence, leaving Max vulnerable.

Ross clenched his fists, anger simmering beneath the surface. "She played us all. But why didn't she act sooner? What's stopping her now?"

Anastasia, flipping to the final pages of the ancient text, found the answer. "It says here that the witch needed a specific celestial alignment to complete a ritual of ultimate rejuvenation. That must be what she's waiting for. And she needs the relics to amplify the ritual's power." She looked up, her expression grim. "We have to stop her before it's too late."

A heavy silence settled over the group as they absorbed the magnitude of their discovery. The carefree days of their youth seemed like a distant memory, now overshadowed by the dark reality before them. They weren't just adventurers on a quest—they were the last line of defence against an ancient evil, one that threatened not just their lives, but the very balance of their world.

Max's jaw tightened, eyes blazing with purpose. "We can't let her succeed. We have to stop her, whatever it takes." His words carried a weight that bound them all together, a solemn vow none of them would break.

As they left the ancient library, a newfound sense of purpose settled over them. Jocelyn's secret had come to light, and with it, the urgency of their mission. Time was running out. They needed to act before the celestial alignment, before Jocelyn could complete her ritual. Their journey had taken a darker turn, but their purpose had never been clearer. The final confrontation loomed on the horizon, and they would meet it head-on—united and unwavering.

The dense forest path led them deeper into rugged hills, the atmosphere growing heavier with each step. A charged silence clung to the air, thick with the promise of danger. Suddenly, a prickle of unease crawled up Max's spine. He slowed his pace, his senses sharpening.

"We're not alone," he murmured, his voice edged with warning.

Without warning, a chilling gust of wind tore through the trees, and a dense fog began to roll in, swallowing the landscape in its ghostly grip. The travellers instinctively huddled together, their senses on high alert. Then came the sound—soft at first, then growing—distant laughter, cold and mocking.

From the mist, Jocelyn emerged. Her presence was more sinister than ever, her once-youthful face now etched with malevolence. The fog curled around her like living shadows, feeding off her dark energy.

"Well, well," she drawled, her voice dripping with malice. "Look who we have here. I see you've uncovered some truths, but you still don't fully grasp the situation."

Max stared at her—no, it—the truth settling over him like a suffocating shroud.

His hands trembled at his sides, fists clenching and unclenching as if he could squeeze the memory of her smile out of existence. Jocelyn. The girl he'd trusted, the one he'd let close enough to hear his secrets—the girl he'd loved.

His voice cracked when he finally spoke. "You were never real, were you?"

The witch just tilted her head, a smile curling at the edge of her ancient mouth. The same mouth that had whispered to him in the dark, told him he was special, promised they'd always be together.

Max's chest burned. He stumbled back a step, choking on the taste of betrayal that soured his tongue. How many nights had he thought of her? Missed her? Trusted her? He felt sick.

"All this time," he rasped, "it was just my blood you wanted. Just me—a pawn."

His vision blurred—anger or tears, he couldn't tell. His fingers brushed his arm, the one she'd kissed so gently when it ached.

He'd given her everything. And she'd taken it.

Max's jaw tightened as something inside him hardened. The hurt didn't vanish, but it found shape—rage, grief, a raw edge of strength he didn't know he had.

"You don't get to have it," he hissed. "You don't get to have me."

Jocelyn's lips curled into a cruel smile. "You have no idea what you're up against. I've waited a long time for this moment. Your blood, Max, is essential to my plans. But it's not just about you— it's about your potential."

Before Max could respond, the ground shuddered violently beneath them. From the earth, shadowy tendrils erupted, writhing and reaching for the group.

Jonas reacted first, summoning a gust of wind to force back the encroaching fog. Ross slammed his hands to the ground, stabilising the shifting terrain with sheer force, but Jocelyn's power was relentless.

She raised a hand, and a sphere of dark energy crackled to life in her palm, pulsing with ominous intent. "You can't stop me," she sneered. "I will have what I need, and nothing will stand in my way."

The sphere expanded, its dark energy humming with destructive power. The earth trembled beneath them, the fog thickening, the shadowy tendrils lashing out with renewed aggression.

Anastasia and Greer sprang into action. The twins moved as one, seamlessly weaving their elemental powers together. Anastasia called forth a surge of water, sending a crashing wave toward Jocelyn, while Greer manipulated the mist, twisting it into a protective barrier against the shadowy tendrils.

Water and darkness collided in a shimmering clash of power, sending tremors through the air. The mist dampened the impact of Jocelyn's attack, but she was far from deterred.

Max, his pulse pounding, caught sight of Greer struggling against a particularly vicious tendril. Instinct took over. He stretched out his hands, a raw force surging from within him.

The earth answered.

A massive stone wall erupted between Greer and the encroaching darkness, shattering the tendril's grip. Greer stumbled back, eyes wide with disbelief.

"Max! How—?" she started, but the chaos of battle swallowed her words.

Max stared at his hands, stunned. "I don't know how I did that, but we need to keep pushing!"

Jocelyn's eyes flashed with both surprise and fury. "So, you can wield the earth as well," she murmured. "This complicates things."

Strength blossomed in Max's chest. If he had this power, he would use it. He raised his hands again, the ground rippling in response. Fissures split open, stone barriers rose, and the very earth itself seemed to fight against Jocelyn's darkness.

Anastasia and Greer redoubled their efforts. Waves surged forward, hammering against Jocelyn's growing sphere of energy. Mist swirled through the battlefield, distorting her vision and making her attacks less precise.

Despite their relentless efforts, Jocelyn remained undeterred. The dark sphere at her command pulsed with volatile energy, its sheer force threatening to shatter their defences. Her gaze locked onto Max, a predatory glint in her eyes.

"You think your newfound power can stop me?" she taunted, her voice slicing through the chaos like a blade. "You're only delaying the inevitable. The power of the elements will be mine, and you'll all fall before me."

Max, propelled by a sudden burst of purpose, tightened his control over the earth. He summoned massive boulders from beneath the surface, forging a protective barrier around his friends. The ground trembled in response, as if acknowledging his growing mastery over its power.

As the fortress of stone took shape, Ross sprang into action. With unwavering focus, he extended his hand and reinforced the structure, solidifying the earth beneath it. "We need to keep this barrier stable!" he shouted, his voice carrying over the battlefield. The ground hardened, anchoring the defence with an unyielding foundation.

Realising that defence alone wouldn't be enough, Jonas took to the air, his mastery over wind propelling him with effortless speed. From above, he unleashed a ferocious gale that ripped through the battlefield, slamming into Jocelyn with the force of a storm.

Caught off guard, Jocelyn staggered, her dark sphere wavering under the onslaught. Her expression twisted with fury as she glared up at Jonas. "You think mere wind can overpower me?" she snarled, struggling to regain control over the unstable energy.

Siobhan, watching Jocelyn's momentary lapse, saw her opportunity. Stepping forward, her sharp gaze locked onto their foe. "I'll handle this," she declared, her voice steady with calm assurance.

Channeling her power, Siobhan transformed a cluster of nearby rocks into jagged projectiles, their razor-sharp edges gleaming in the dim light. With a precise motion, she sent them hurtling toward Jocelyn. The dark sorceress managed to deflect some with a wave of energy, but others struck true, leaving shallow cuts that momentarily broke her concentration.

Still recovering from an earlier attack, Greer joined forces with Anastasia. The sisters combined their elemental strength, summoning a rushing torrent of water that surged toward Jocelyn. The crashing wave met the sphere of dark energy, colliding in a chaotic clash of opposing forces.

But even as the travellers fought with everything they had, Jocelyn's power refused to wane. The dark sphere pulsed ominously, regaining strength. "You are all so persistent," she hissed, her voice laced with frustration—and a grudging hint of admiration. "But persistence alone won't save you."

Max clenched his fists, feeling the weight of the battle pressing down on him. He dug deeper into his connection with the earth, pushing his abilities to their limit. The ground beneath Jocelyn trembled violently, fissures splitting open to destabilise her footing.

Ross, his brow slick with sweat, strengthened their defences, reinforcing the barrier as Jocelyn lashed out with retaliatory strikes. "We can't let up!" he called, refusing to let exhaustion slow him down.

Above, Jonas darted in swift, erratic patterns, summoning a vortex of wind that wrapped around Jocelyn's sphere, compressing it from all sides. The swirling pressure disrupted her grip on the dark energy, forcing her to divert focus just to keep it under control.

Siobhan seized the moment. With a sharp flick of her wrist, she transformed scattered debris into controlled explosive bursts. The shockwaves rippled outward, slamming into Jocelyn from multiple angles, breaking her concentration further.

Jocelyn roared in frustration, her dark sphere flickering as the relentless barrage of elemental attacks overwhelmed her. She struggled to maintain control, but the travellers' combined efforts were beginning to turn the tide.

Max narrowed his gaze, his focus unshakable. He summoned the earth with one final, decisive motion. The ground beneath Jocelyn surged upward in a massive upheaval, sending her crashing down into the forest floor.

Dazed, Jocelyn pushed herself up, but the battle had drained her. The flickering sphere of darkness around her sputtered, its power waning. She glanced at the travellers, her fury now tinged with desperation.

Breathing heavily, Max and the others regrouped, their energies still humming with intensity. Though the battle had been fierce, Jocelyn was finally on the defensive.

Max tightened his grip on the terrain, shifting it beneath Jocelyn's feet to keep her unsteady. Above, Jonas maintained the vortex, the winds whipping around her like a cyclone.

Siobhan, sensing the final moment had come, drew upon the fire she had only just begun to command. Flames curled around her fingers, their heat crackling in the cool night air.

Anastasia and Greer, still maintaining their water barriers, recognised Siobhan's intent. They adjusted their positions, shaping the shimmering force field around Jocelyn to keep her trapped.

Jocelyn's dark energy sputtered, her strength slipping through her grasp. She clenched her fists, glaring at them through narrowed eyes. "You won't..." she began, but her words faltered under the weight of their combined power.

Siobhan's gaze was steady. "This ends now," she declared.

With one final motion, she hurled a concentrated bolt of flame straight at Jocelyn. The fire streaked through the night, illuminating the battlefield in a searing glow.

Jocelyn's eyes widened as the bolt struck her, but instead of a violent explosion, the flames wrapped around her in a radiant inferno. The dark energy writhed and convulsed, unable to withstand the purity of the fire.

The travellers shielded their eyes as the brilliant light expanded, engulfing Jocelyn's form. Then, as suddenly as it had begun, the flames dissipated, leaving nothing behind but a gentle shimmer in the air.

Jocelyn was gone.

A hush fell over the battlefield. The last remnants of her dark energy faded into the night, leaving behind only silence—and the deep, steady breaths of the victors.

Max and the others stood together, their breaths coming fast and heavy, but the relief in their expressions was undeniable. The battle with Jocelyn was over. It had been intense, but they had emerged victorious.

"Is she...?" Max began, scanning the area, needing confirmation that Jocelyn was truly gone.

Greer, still catching her breath, nodded, her voice laced with exhaustion and certainty. "She's gone. The fire took care of her completely."

Anastasia, her sharp eyes sweeping their surroundings, added, "This is the end of Jocelyn. She won't be a threat to us again."

Max exhaled, but the breath caught in his throat. His chest tightened. He wanted to feel relief—he should have felt relief—but all he felt was the sting of what she'd done. The way she'd looked at him. The lies.

His voice was rough when he finally spoke. "She fooled me. I let her in. And the whole time— she was just using me."

He looked down at his hands, flexing them like he might squeeze the betrayal out of his skin. "I thought I mattered to her." He hated how small his voice sounded. He forced his chin up.

"But we did it," he said, louder now, finding the steel beneath the hurt. "Jocelyn is gone. And we keep moving. We don't let her win—not ever again."

Jonas, brushing dust from his clothes, gave a firm nod. "We've proven we can face whatever comes our way—together. Whatever's next, we'll be ready."

Siobhan, her usual fiery energy subdued but not extinguished, crossed her arms.

A heavy silence settled over the group as they took a moment to regroup, each lost in thought. Relief lingered in the air. They had won a battle, but the war was far from over.

Then, without warning, the air shimmered. A powerful presence filled the space, and before them appeared the four elemental mentors—Celestials of immense wisdom and power.

Zephyrus of Air. Aquael of Water. Terran of Earth. Thalion of Fire.

Each exuded an aura that resonated with their respective element, their presence commanding awe.

Zephyrus hovered slightly above the ground, a playful gust swirling around him, his laughter carrying like the whisper of the breeze.

Aquael stepped forward, emerging from a cascading veil of water, her form seamlessly blending with the flowing current. Her eyes held the wisdom of ages, her voice as soothing as a gentle stream.

Terran stood firm, his solid frame emerging from a mound of earth, embodying strength and endurance. His gaze was unwavering, a silent promise of resilience.

Thalion radiated warmth, his body encased in flames that flickered and danced without consuming him, their glow illuminating the space around him.

Aquael was the first to speak, her voice calm yet firm. "Welcome, travellers. The trials you have faced have revealed the strength within you. Now, it is time to deepen your connection with the elements."

Terran's deep, steady voice followed. "Each of you has a unique bond with your element, but your journey is far from complete. There is still much to learn. We will guide you in mastering your abilities, pushing beyond your limits, and preparing for the battles ahead."

Zephyrus twirled lightly in the air, his eyes gleaming with anticipation. "We will take you to our elemental realms, each offering its own lessons. The training will be intense, but it will shape you into the warriors you are destined to become."

Thalion's flames flickered as he nodded. "Max, your connection to multiple elements is rare and powerful. You will train with each of us, learning to balance and integrate these forces. Your friends will focus on their respective elements, and together, you will stand stronger than ever before."

Max turned to his friends, their gazes mirroring his burning resolve. The road ahead was daunting, but they knew what was at stake.

Mastering their abilities wasn't just about power—it was about survival.

Stepping forward, Max squared his shoulders. "I'm ready. Teach me how to wield the elements to their full potential."

Anastasia, Greer, Ross, and the others followed suit, nodding in agreement. They were prepared to commit to their training, to push past their limits, and to face whatever awaited them.

Their journey wasn't over. It was only just beginning.

CHAPTER 8

Training Grounds

As the group stood in the clearing, a solemn weight settled over them. The air crackled with anticipation, a silent acknowledgment of the trials ahead. Before them stood the elemental mentors—each a living embodiment of their respective forces—exuding both authority and reassurance. The moment was not lost on the travellers; they had come far, but the true test was only beginning.

Aquael, the mentor of water, stepped forward, her voice as steady and soothing as the ebb and flow of the tide. "Your journey has led you to this point, but the challenges ahead will push you beyond anything you have faced. The celestial alignment that unlocked the full potential of the relics will shift again in one month. Though different from the last, this alignment will still resonate with the elemental forces. It is during this window that you must refine your abilities and master your connection to the elements."

Beside her, Thalion, wreathed in a subtle flicker of flame, crossed his arms, his fiery aura pulsing with intensity. "For the next month, you will train under our guidance, forging a deeper bond with your elemental affinities. Time is against us, and failure is not an option. When the final battle comes, you must wield your powers with precision and strength, or all will be lost."

Zephyrus, the mentor of air, turned his gaze toward Max, his expression both knowing and encouraging. "Max, your path differs from the others. You are not tethered to one element but connected to them all. This is both a gift and a burden. Unlike your companions, who will focus solely on their natural affinities, you will train with each of us, immersing yourself in air, water, earth, and fire. This versatility will be your greatest asset—but also your greatest challenge."

Max swallowed hard, absorbing the gravity of Zephyrus's words. The responsibility weighed on him like an unseen force, yet beneath the apprehension, a flicker of excitement stirred. He had always known he was different, but now he had the opportunity to explore the full extent of his abilities.

Terran, his voice deep and resonant like the shifting earth, addressed them next. "Mastering an element is not simply about wielding power—it is about understanding its essence. Your abilities stem not just from control but from connection. You must listen, learn, and adapt. Only then will you be able to call upon your strength when it matters most."

The mentors exchanged silent glances, a mutual understanding passing between them. Aquael turned back to the group, her expression unwavering. "We will take you to places where the elemental forces are at their peak, places untouched by time, where the elements flow in their purest form. There, you will train without distraction, surrounded by the power you seek to command."

With a graceful movement of her hand, Aquael conjured a portal shimmering like liquid silver. Beyond its surface, a vast underwater world pulsed with bioluminescent life, the ocean depths calling with an undeniable pull. "Anastasia, Greer," she said, her gaze settling on the twins, "you will come with me. Our journey begins now."

Thalion stepped forward, summoning a vortex of searing flames, its heat licking at the air with a feral energy. "Siobhan, your training will be intense, pushing you to the very edge of your endurance. But fire is more than destruction—it is passion, resilience, and transformation. I expect you to rise to the challenge."

Terran placed a firm yet steady hand on Ross's shoulder, his presence as unshakable as the mountains. "You and I will journey deep beneath the earth. There, you will feel the heartbeat of the land and uncover the strength that lies within you."

Zephyrus let out a breath, a gust of wind swirling around him, playful yet powerful. Leaves danced in the currents, caught in an invisible rhythm. "Jonas, the skies are calling. The freedom and force of the air will test you in ways you do not yet understand, but I will show you how to move with the wind, rather than against it."

As the travellers prepared to step through their respective portals, Max stood rooted in place, the enormity of his task settling in. He was about to embark on a journey unlike any other, one that would push him beyond his limits and force him to evolve. Yet, as he looked at his friends—each setting out on their own paths—he took solace in the knowledge that he was not alone. They were all in this together, bound by purpose and fate.

Zephyrus extended a hand toward Max, his expression calm but expectant. "Shall we begin?"

Max exhaled, his mind clear and focused. "I'm ready," he said, stepping forward into the portal, embracing the unknown.

And so, their training began. With each passing day, the celestial alignment loomed ever closer. The final battle awaited, and by the time it arrived, they would need every ounce of strength, skill, and knowledge to stand against the darkness.

The Air Realm

As Max and Jonas stepped through the shimmering portal, an immediate shift in the atmosphere washed over them. The air was noticeably thinner, crisp with an invigorating coolness, and carried an undeniable sense of boundless freedom. They emerged onto a floating island, suspended high above an endless sea of drifting clouds. The sky stretched infinitely in all directions, a vast canvas of shifting hues—soft blues melting into deep purples, streaks of pink and gold painting the horizon as the sun descended. It felt like stepping into a world untouched by time, a place where gravity held only the faintest influence.

Beneath their feet, the ground was unlike anything they had known—springy yet firm, covered in a lush, grass-like vegetation that shimmered faintly under the twilight. Each blade seemed to sway, not just in response to the wind, but as if moved by its own quiet rhythm. Wisps of clouds drifted by at eye level, close enough to brush against their skin like gossamer silk. Looking outward, they saw other floating islands scattered across the sky, some grand and expansive, others no larger than a single boulder, all suspended as if by invisible threads. Ethereal bridges of wind connected some, while others seemed to hover independently, shifting subtly with unseen currents.

At the edge of the island stood Zephyrus, their mentor, his silhouette outlined against the boundless sky. His presence was both tranquil and commanding, his robes rippling with the air's restless energy. He exuded an effortless grace, his very essence intertwined with the wind itself. As Jonas and Max approached, he turned to them, his expression warm yet unreadable, his eyes reflecting the vast expanse around them.

"Welcome to the Air Realm," Zephyrus greeted them, his voice carrying a melodic quality, like the distant whisper of wind rushing through canyon walls. "Here, the wind is more than an element—it is your guide, your ally, and your teacher. This realm embodies movement and freedom, a place where those who listen may learn to harness the very breath of the world."

As he spoke, a playful gust of wind swirled around them, lifting Max's hair and sending ripples through Jonas's tunic. The breeze carried with it faint, harmonious murmurs, almost like a chorus of unseen voices, as if the air itself was alive with intent.

Zephyrus extended a hand toward the open sky. "The wind is not merely a force; it is a living presence. You must learn its language—understand its moods, feel its rhythms, and work with it rather than against it. It can be a gentle whisper, a roaring tempest, or an unseen hand that lifts you beyond the clouds."

To demonstrate, he lifted his arm in a subtle, practised motion. Instantly, a spiraling current of air coiled around him, responding as though it were an extension of his will. With effortless grace, he rose from the ground, hovering a few feet above the surface, his movements as fluid as the shifting sky. "This is the essence of air—weightless, unbound, ever-changing. It can shield you, guide you, or carry you where your feet cannot tread."

Max and Jonas exchanged wide-eyed glances, both enthralled and intimidated. The idea of moving with such mastery seemed impossible, yet the air around them thrummed with possibility. Zephyrus gestured for them to try, and their training began in earnest.

Max took a steadying breath, feeling the wind curling around him like invisible tendrils. He closed his eyes, attuning himself to its subtle shifts, its constant movement. As he raised his arms, mirroring Zephyrus's motion, the air responded— tentative, uncertain, but present. A gentle lift, a whisper of buoyancy beneath his feet. He wasn't soaring, not yet, but for a brief moment, he felt himself rise, if only slightly.

Jonas, ever the more instinctual of the two, embraced the moment with less hesitation. He spread his arms wide, leaning into the wind's energy. With a sudden burst of force, he propelled himself into the air—not far, just enough to experience the exhilarating weightlessness of flight before landing with a stumble. He turned to Max with a triumphant grin, exhilaration lighting up his face.

Zephyrus observed them both, his expression pleased yet measured. "Good," he acknowledged, though his tone carried a note of caution. "But remember, control is everything. The wind is not to be commanded, only guided. Respect its nature, and it will lift you. Underestimate it, and it will cast you aside."

He led them to a wide, open space where the island's edges blurred into drifting mist. Around them, smaller floating rocks hovered lazily, caught in unseen currents. The vegetation rustled with the shifting breeze, creating a constant, rhythmic whisper.

Zephyrus faced them, his gaze steady. "The wind can be as delicate as a feather's touch or as fierce as a raging storm. Today, you will learn its balance. You must manipulate air currents—not with force, but with precision and intent." He gestured to the hovering stones. "Your task is to move these without touching them. Start small— feel the air around you, direct it gently, and let it do the work."

Focused, Max and Jonas took their stances, closing their eyes to focus on the unseen forces swirling around them. Max extended his hand toward a small rock, envisioning a stream of air nudging it forward. At first, nothing happened. Then, gradually, he felt it—the wind responding, bending to his will. The rock trembled, lifted slightly, then dropped. A flicker of progress.

Jonas fared similarly, though his approach was more forceful. His rock jerked upward too quickly, then wobbled wildly before veering off course. Zephyrus's voice guided them with measured patience. "Do not force it. Let the wind flow as an extension of yourself. The more you push, the more it resists. Find harmony, not dominance."

The lesson continued, their control improving in small, steady increments. They began to understand the nuances—the way even a slight shift in focus could alter the air's behavior. Their movements became smoother, more deliberate, and soon, the rocks drifted in controlled arcs rather than chaotic bursts.

As dusk deepened, Zephyrus introduced the final challenge. Summoning orbs of soft, golden light, he set them afloat at varying heights. "Precision is as vital as power. Use the wind to strike these orbs."

Max narrowed his focus, channeling a steady current to lift a rock. He aimed carefully, guiding it forward. It wavered but stayed on course, missing the orb by inches. He exhaled sharply, frustration creeping in.

Jonas, meanwhile, took a different approach, sending a rock forward in a controlled arc. His aim struck true—the orb pulsed brightly before dissolving into mist. He grinned, raising a fist in victory.

As the sky darkened into velvety twilight, Zephyrus called for a break. They gathered around a small, glowing bonfire he conjured, its golden light flickering without smoke. The air carried a refreshing chill, but the fire's warmth was a welcome contrast.

"You both did well," Zephyrus remarked, his voice even and reflective. "The wind is a paradox—gentle yet fierce, ever-moving yet constant. To master it, you must listen, not command. Understand its rhythms, and it will move with you."

Max and Jonas nodded, absorbing his words. They realised that this was not just an exercise in control but in attunement—learning to move with the wind rather than against it.

As night fully settled, the Air Realm transformed into a dreamscape. The sky glittered with stars, impossibly bright and innumerable. The floating islands shimmered with bioluminescent flora, casting an otherworldly glow. A tranquil breeze whispered across the realm, carrying a promise of deeper lessons yet to come.

Zephyrus gestured toward a cluster of floating platforms. "Rest now. Tomorrow, we continue. The wind waits for no one."

Max and Jonas settled onto the platforms, which were as soft as clouds beneath them. As they lay beneath the star-filled sky, exhaustion mingled with exhilaration. Today had been but a beginning. Ahead lay greater challenges, greater revelations.

And as they drifted into sleep, the wind's song carried them toward the unknown.

The Water Realm

As Max and Jonas embarked on their journey through the Air Realm, it was time for Anastasia and Greer to step into the Water Realm under Aquael's guidance.

The portal shimmered before them, an undulating mirror of deep blues and greens, rippling like the surface of the ocean under a full moon. Taking a steadying breath, Anastasia and Greer exchanged a brief glance before stepping forward.

The moment they crossed the threshold, a cool mist wrapped around them like a welcoming embrace, refreshing yet unfamiliar. When the mist cleared, they found themselves standing on an extraordinary floating platform—crafted entirely of water, yet firm beneath their feet. It swayed gently, responding to their movements with a rhythmic rise and fall, mimicking the pulse of the ocean itself.

The air was thick with humidity, laced with the crisp scent of salt and fresh rain, a stark contrast to the brisk, ever-moving winds of the Air Realm. Anastasia inhaled deeply, while Greer ran her fingers through the mist, marveling at the way it curled around her skin before dissolving into the air.

Before them stretched an endless expanse of water, its surface broken only by islands formed from vibrant coral, their reefs glowing softly beneath the crystalline waves. Beneath the surface, schools of brilliantly coloured fish swirled in synchronised patterns, their scales catching the light in a breathtaking display. Towering kelp forests swayed with the current, their tendrils reaching up as if longing for the sky. Overhead, the heavens stretched vast and unbroken, painted in delicate hues of pale blue and silver, with soft, billowing clouds drifting lazily in the distance.

A disturbance rippled through the water, drawing their attention. Slowly, a figure emerged, rising with effortless grace as if the ocean itself had shaped her from its depths.

Aquael.

Her presence was as fluid as the water around her, her very essence intertwined with the realm she commanded. Her long, flowing hair cascaded down her back like a waterfall, shimmering with shifting shades of sapphire and emerald. Her attire, neither fabric nor armor, moved like liquid silk, catching the light with an ethereal glow.

"Welcome to my domain," Aquael greeted, her voice carrying the soothing cadence of a gently flowing stream. It was a sound both tranquil and commanding, filled with the wisdom of the tides. "Here, you will learn to master the element of water. It is both gentle and relentless, a force of serenity and unyielding power."

Anastasia and Greer could do nothing but stare, captivated by both Aquael and the realm around them. There was something undeniably familiar about the water's presence—as if it were already a part of them, waiting to be unlocked.

Aquael led them through the tranquil expanse until they reached a secluded lagoon, embraced by towering cliffs where waterfalls cascaded in endless streams. The water here was impossibly clear, revealing the vibrant world beneath—a city of coral, bustling with life, each creature moving in harmony with the currents.

"Before you can command water, you must understand it," Aquael instructed, kneeling at the water's edge. "Feel its rhythm, its pulse. Let it speak to you before you attempt to control it."

Anastasia stepped forward, closing her eyes as she let the cool water lap against her fingertips. A gentle current brushed against her skin, not pulling or pushing, but inviting her to move with it.

Beside her, Greer dipped her hands into the lagoon, watching in fascination as the water responded, forming ripples that expanded outward like whispered secrets.

"The water is alive," Aquael murmured, observing them closely. "It listens, it feels. If you treat it as a tool, it will resist you. But if you respect it, it will become your greatest ally."

At her guidance, they waded into the shallows, where the water was waist-deep and calm. Aquael moved her hands in a series of deliberate, flowing motions, and the water obeyed, forming waves that moved in harmony with her touch.

"Now, try," she urged, her gaze steady.

Anastasia lifted her hands, mimicking the fluid movements. At first, the water resisted, sluggish and unresponsive. But as she focused—synchronising her breath with the natural flow—something shifted. A delicate ripple formed, then another, until the water began to follow her lead.

Greer watched intently before attempting the same, her hands sweeping through the water with cautious precision. Soon, her movements aligned with Anastasia's, their energies intertwining as the water pulsed and flowed between them.

"Good," Aquael praised, a small smile tugging at her lips. "Remember, control is not about dominance. It is about harmony. Guide the water—do not force it."

As the day progressed, the twins' connection with the element deepened. Aquael introduced them to more advanced techniques, demonstrating how to summon controlled currents, direct the flow of water, and even propel themselves forward with precise bursts of energy. The water no longer felt like an unpredictable force—it was an extension of their will, responding to their intent with growing fluidity.

As the sky darkened into the soft glow of twilight, Aquael led them to a roaring waterfall at the edge of the lagoon. The sound was deafening, a symphony of power and grace.

"Now, you will learn to harness the force of moving water," she said, stepping aside so they could face the cascade directly. "Waterfalls are relentless. If you can redirect their flow, you can control even the most powerful currents."

Anastasia took a deep breath, stretching her hands toward the descending rush of water. She could feel its energy—a torrent of motion resisting her touch. But she didn't fight it. Instead, she listened, adjusting her stance and movements to work with the water, not against it. Slowly, the waterfall's descent altered, bending ever so slightly under her influence.

Beside her, Greer mirrored the process, their combined efforts creating a mesmerising split in the cascade, forcing the water to stream in two separate arcs.

Aquael's eyes gleamed with approval. "Excellent. You're beginning to understand the balance between control and surrender."

As the final traces of sunlight disappeared beyond the horizon, she guided them back toward a sheltered grotto, where the soft glow of bioluminescent plants illuminated the water's surface.

"You have done well," she said, her tone gentle but firm. "Rest now. Tomorrow, we will delve deeper into the mysteries of water. This is not just about power—it is about becoming one with the element, allowing it to shape you as much as you shape it."

Anastasia and Greer settled into the grotto, their minds alight with all they had learned. The day had tested them, pushing them past hesitation and into a world where water was no longer an obstacle, but a partner.

As they drifted into sleep, lulled by the rhythmic lapping of the waves, a quiet understanding settled within them. They were not merely students of the Water Realm.

They were becoming part of it.

The Earth Realm

As Ross stepped through the swirling portal, the world around him shifted in an instant. The gentle breezes of the Air Realm and the tranquil currents of the Water Realm dissolved behind him, giving way to a rugged and untamed expanse. The ground beneath his feet was solid, unyielding—imbued with a quiet strength that resonated deep within him.

The Earth Realm stretched before him in breathtaking majesty, a vast landscape sculpted by time itself. Towering mountains loomed in the distance, their jagged peaks crowned with a delicate veil of mist, whispering of ancient secrets. Colossal stone formations jutted from the terrain like the bones of the world, their surfaces etched with intricate carvings—stories of a civilization bound to the land, each groove a testament to an unbroken lineage of wisdom.

Lush valleys unfurled beneath the mountains, filled with thick forests where towering trees swayed in unison with the rhythm of an unseen force. The scent of damp earth and pine filled Ross's lungs as he inhaled deeply, a grounding sensation settling over him like an unspoken welcome. The air here was different—dense with life, charged with an energy that hummed beneath the surface, as if the very ground breathed along with him.

Above, the sky shifted in hues of deep green and burnished brown, a living canvas reflecting the pulse of the land. The sun hung low, its golden light stretching long shadows across the rugged terrain, painting everything in rich, warm tones. It was as if the realm itself was alive, its movements deliberate, its presence undeniable.

In the heart of this immense landscape stood Terran, the Earth Mentor. A figure of formidable presence, he seemed less a man and more an extension of the realm itself. His robes were woven from fabrics that blended seamlessly with the world around him—coarse as stone, soft as moss, and streaked with the rich, earthen hues of soil and mineral. His deep-set eyes, like polished obsidian, reflected both wisdom and the unshakable patience of the mountains.

"Welcome, Ross," Terran greeted, his voice a low rumble, like distant thunder rolling through cavernous depths. "You are about to embark on a journey that will bind you to the very essence of the earth. It is both a force of creation and destruction—unyielding yet nurturing, still yet ever-moving. To master it, you must first understand it."

Ross let his gaze sweep across the expanse before him, feeling the weight of the words settle within him. A deep-rooted connection stirred in his core, as if the very ground beneath him was calling his name. He had stepped into a realm that pulsed with energy, where strength was not just found in force but in resilience, patience, and balance.

Taking his first steps deeper into the Earth Realm, Ross felt a grounding sensation ripple up through his legs—a silent promise that this land would shape him just as he sought to shape it. Every step was more than just movement; it was a lesson, an unspoken exchange between student and teacher.

As the first rays of dawn pierced through the jagged peaks, Ross stood alongside Terran, poised at the threshold of his training. Before them, an immense rocky plateau jutted out over a sprawling valley, a vantage point carved by time and nature's unrelenting force. The terrain hummed beneath his feet—a deep, resonant energy that spoke of power lying dormant beneath the surface, waiting to be awakened.

Terran led him onto the stone platform, the morning air crisp and laced with the scent of earth after rain. Towering rock formations framed the space, their weathered surfaces bearing the silent wisdom of ages past. Verdant patches of moss and ivy clung stubbornly to their crevices, a reminder that even the unyielding could nurture life.

"Today, we begin with the fundamentals," Terran announced, his voice steady, carrying the weight of centuries of knowledge. "The earth is not something to be commanded—it is something to be understood. Feel its rhythm, its breath. Control is not the goal—harmony is."

Ross nodded, anticipation tightening in his chest. He had always admired the sheer strength of the earth—its immovable presence, its quiet endurance—but now, he was about to experience it in a way he never had before.

Terran gestured for him to stand still. "Close your eyes," he instructed. "Feel the ground beneath you—not just its weight, but its pulse. The earth speaks, Ross. You must learn to listen."

Ross obeyed, shutting his eyes and focusing on the sensation beneath his feet. At first, all he registered was the firmness of the stone, unyielding and unmoving. But as he let himself sink deeper into the moment, something shifted. A faint tremor—a pulse, rhythmic and steady. It was subtle, like the distant heartbeat of a sleeping giant.

"Good," Terran murmured, his tone approving. "Now, we move forward."

He extended a hand toward a medium-sized rock nearby, and with effortless grace, the stone lifted from the ground, hovering at chest level. His fingers moved subtly, and the rock obeyed, turning and shifting as if it were an extension of himself. A faint, golden-brown aura surrounded it, the visual manifestation of his connection to the element.

Ross inhaled sharply, his excitement growing.

"Your turn," Terran said, stepping back.

Ross approached a smaller stone, placing his hands over it as he recalled the sensation he had felt earlier. He reached for that pulse—the steady rhythm that connected him to the ground beneath him. At first, nothing happened. He clenched his jaw, frustration creeping in, but Terran's voice cut through the doubt.

"Patience," the mentor reminded him. "The earth does not yield to force. It responds to presence, to connection. Try again."

Ross exhaled slowly, grounding himself. This time, instead of forcing the stone to move, he simply allowed himself to feel it—to recognise it as part of the same force that ran through him. The earth was not separate from him; it was an extension of his own energy.

A shift.

The rock trembled, then lifted just slightly, hovering a fraction above the ground. The sensation sent a thrill up Ross's spine.

"Excellent," Terran said with a satisfied nod. "Now, we advance."

The training continued, moving from lifting to shaping—learning to mold the earth, to summon barriers, to carve pathways where none existed. With each attempt, Ross felt his connection deepen. The weight of the training was exhausting, but the satisfaction of progress outweighed it.

By midday, sweat clung to his skin, his muscles ached, yet he felt invigorated. The Earth Realm was unlike any place he had ever known— alive, powerful, unrelenting. Every grain of soil, every boulder, every towering peak seemed to whisper of strength and endurance, of lessons learned through time and trial.

As the sun dipped lower, draping golden light across the valley, Terran led Ross to the plateau's edge. The vastness of the land stretched before them, untouched and eternal.

"You've done well today," Terran said, his voice carrying the quiet pride of a mentor who had seen a seed take root. "But remember—the earth is not mastered in a day. It will teach you as much as you are willing to learn."

Ross gazed out over the horizon, the weight of the day settling into something deeper—a sense of belonging, of purpose. He had only scratched the surface of what the Earth Realm had to offer, but already, he knew this journey would shape him in ways he had yet to understand.

With a final glance at the vast expanse before him, he turned, ready for what lay ahead.

The Fire Realm

As Siobhan stepped through the portal, an intense wave of heat surged against her skin, wrapping around her like a living force. The air shimmered with scorching energy, crackling with unseen embers that danced in the realm's oppressive warmth. She had entered a world ablaze with fiery splendour—the Fire Realm.

Before her stretched an infernal landscape where rivers of molten lava coursed like liquid gold, their surfaces rippling with the heat of the earth's fury. Jagged volcanic peaks loomed against the horizon, their summits wreathed in plumes of smoke and searing embers. The ground beneath her boots was a mosaic of obsidian rock and scorched terrain, its surface faintly glowing as if breathing with the realm's inner fire.

Above, the sky churned with a tempest of deep reds, smouldering oranges, and molten golds, an endless, turbulent canvas where flame and shadow intertwined. Occasional geysers of fire erupted from fissures in the ground, spewing arcs of molten light that briefly illuminated the realm with bursts of blinding brilliance.

Siobhan's breath caught as she absorbed the breathtaking, yet formidable, world around her. The very air was thick with the acrid scent of sulphur and charred earth, a potent reminder of the realm's untamed power. Despite the oppressive heat, a distinct energy pulsed through the environment—one that was both intoxicating and intimidating, alive with an undeniable sense of primal force.

And at the heart of this blazing expanse stood Thalion, the Fire Mentor.

He was an imposing figure, his very presence exuding the raw essence of fire. His eyes burned with a golden intensity, molten and piercing, as if they could see straight into the soul. His attire moved like living flames—robes that shimmered with hues of ember and gold, shifting fluidly with each motion. The cloak draped over his shoulders appeared to be woven from fire itself, its edges crackling softly as embers danced from its fabric.

"Welcome to the Fire Realm," Thalion declared, his voice a deep, commanding resonance, carrying both warmth and authority. "Here, you will learn to command the element of fire—a force of immense power, capable of both creation and destruction. Embrace its energy, but never allow it to consume you."

Siobhan's heart pounded with anticipation. The Fire Realm was as exhilarating as it was perilous, and she was eager to uncover its secrets. Every flickering flame, every flowing ember, seemed to whisper of knowledge waiting to be unlocked.

Thalion's gaze held a steady intensity as he studied her. "Let us begin." He gestured toward the sprawling expanse of molten rivers and jagged rock. "To master fire, you must first attune yourself to its essence. Feel its heat, listen to its rhythm, and learn to wield its power."

Siobhan inhaled deeply, feeling the heat coil around her like an invisible presence. It wasn't just overwhelming—it was alive, responding to her very breath. This realm was a test of endurance, but it was also a gateway to power. With a steady heart, she stepped forward, ready to embrace the challenge ahead.

The morning sun had barely risen over the searing landscape when Siobhan's training began under Thalion's watchful eye. The heat was relentless, pressing down on her like an unseen force, but she refused to falter. She stepped forward with quiet strength, her boots sinking slightly into the pliable ground, which pulsed with the realm's molten energy.

Thalion stood before her, his form shimmering in the heat waves. "Fire is not merely destruction," he began, his voice steady and rich with wisdom. "It is energy in its purest form. It can be as gentle as a flickering candle or as merciless as a wildfire. Control is not about suppression—it is about understanding."

With a fluid motion of his hand, Thalion reached toward a bubbling pool of molten rock. From its depths, a flame rose, curling into the air like a living creature. The fire swayed and shimmered at his command, its warm glow bathing the scorched earth in trembling shadows.

"The key to wielding fire lies in intent and precision," he explained. "Your will must guide its energy, shaping it with purpose rather than impulse."

Siobhan watched closely, mesmerised by the effortless grace with which he commanded the flame. Then, it was her turn.

Stepping toward a fire pit where several small flames crackled, she extended her hands, feeling the residual warmth curl around her fingers. She closed her eyes, tuning into the flickering rhythm of the fire. She didn't force it—she listened to it.

At first, nothing happened. Then, as she focused, she felt it—the flame responding, its energy subtly shifting under her intent. Slowly, the fire stretched outward, its glow intensifying in a controlled arc.

Thalion nodded in approval. "Good. Fire is a reflection of your inner strength. It will respond to your emotions, so remain steady."

Encouraged, Siobhan continued practicing, guiding the flame in slow, deliberate movements.

For the next exercise, Thalion led her to a wider expanse where molten rivers flowed like liquid sunlight. "Observe the movement of the lava," he instructed. "Understanding its rhythm will teach you how to shape and channel greater forces of fire."

Siobhan exhaled slowly and stretched out her hands. She focused on the lava's relentless flow, envisioning it bending to her will. As she concentrated, the stream of molten rock slowed, shifting into a more controlled path, curling and bending in deliberate motion.

A flicker of satisfaction crossed Thalion's face. "Well done."

As the day wore on, she practised tirelessly, shaping fire, channeling its intensity, and honing her newfound abilities. The exercises were grueling, the heat unrelenting, but with each lesson, she felt herself growing more attuned to the element's volatile beauty.

By evening, the sky blazed with deep crimson and molten gold, the entire realm bathed in an ethereal glow. Exhausted but exhilarated, Siobhan lowered herself onto a warm rock, letting the comforting heat seep into her skin.

Thalion approached, his form radiant against the smouldering horizon. "You've made a promising start," he remarked, a rare smile playing at his lips. "But mastery requires patience and perseverance. Fire does not yield easily—it must be earned."

Siobhan met his gaze, a fire kindling deep in her eyes. She knew the road ahead would be long, but today had ignited something within her—a connection to the fire, to its unyielding spirit.

As the embers of the evening flickered in the air around her, she closed her eyes, feeling the warmth settle into her bones. The Fire Realm was both a challenge and a sanctuary, and tonight, wrapped in its relentless heat, she knew she was exactly where she needed to be.

CHAPTER 9

The Shadowy Figure Unveiled

In the farthest reaches of existence—where reality begins to blur with the unknowable, and the air itself pulses with ancient, forgotten energy—there lies a realm long concealed from mortal perception. This is a place where the laws of nature are pliable, where time meanders without pattern, and where long-dormant powers lie slumbering, waiting to be stirred once more.

Malachor was not birthed in darkness, but forged within it.

Eons ago, before the world coalesced into its present form, there existed a sacred council of primordial beings known as the Celestials. Tasked with safeguarding the universe's delicate harmony, each Celestial embodied a fundamental element— air, water, earth, and fire. Together, they maintained the balance of natural forces. But among them stood a fifth, unique and solitary. His purpose was not to control a single element but to mediate between opposing forces. He was the sentinel of equilibrium between light and shadow.

This fifth Celestial was known as Umbros, the *Guardian of Twilight*.

Neither wholly of light nor wholly of darkness, Umbros existed in the liminal space between the two—a being of dusk and dawn, whose essence represented balance itself. His role was paramount: to ensure that neither side would ever overwhelm the other, preserving cosmic stability.

Yet balance, while noble, proved a heavy burden.

Over countless ages, Umbros bore witness to an unending cycle of conflict. Civilisations blossomed only to crumble. Wars erupted as light and darkness vied for dominance. With every new rise came a fall, and with every peace, the seeds of the next discord were already sown. The ceaseless struggle began to erode Umbros' faith in his mission. Doubt crept into his heart like a slow-spreading rot.

Haunted by futility, he sought a way to end the chaos forever.

In desperation, he sought out the Well of Echoes, a forbidden font of primordial power, buried deep within the fabric of existence. It was whispered to contain the raw echoes of creation itself—unshaped and untamed. Umbros believed that by harnessing this forbidden energy, he could impose a new order: a realm ruled not by fragile balance but by one supreme force—his own.

But the Well did not bring enlightenment. It brought corruption.

The chaotic energies within twisted Umbros' essence, distorting his purpose and warping his soul. What emerged from the Well was no longer the serene Celestial of Twilight, but a being reborn in darkness and ambition. From that moment forward, he became Malachor—not a keeper of balance, but a force of absolute control.

Where Umbros had once mediated, Malachor now sought to subjugate. The harmony he once defended was now a lie in his eyes—a temporary illusion. Only by extinguishing both light and shadow could he create a new dominion of singular darkness. Power became his obsession, domination his creed.

The Celestials, horrified by the transformation, united to confront their fallen brother. But Malachor, emboldened by the Well's power, fought with a wrath that cracked the very foundation of their realms. His strength was unmatched—raw, unrelenting, and steeped in the void. The battle was cataclysmic.

Ultimately, it took the combined force of all four elemental Celestials to subdue him. Together, they forged a prison beyond time—a pocket of the void so deep and remote that no light or thought could reach it. There, Malachor was sealed away, cut off from the world he once sought to rule.

Yet even in exile, Malachor endured.

His will did not wane; it sharpened. Isolated from the physical plane, he became something else entirely—a disembodied presence capable of slipping through the cracks of reality. Within this exile, he became a master of subtlety, planting whispers in the minds of those vulnerable to ambition, grief, or rage.

From his prison, Malachor nurtured chaos.

He became the invisible spark behind countless wars, the echo that stoked betrayal in the hearts of rulers, the shadow guiding assassins' blades. Each act of madness, each moment of fear, each surge of despair—these were the offerings that nourished him. He no longer needed form to exert influence. He was a phantom force, infecting history with quiet precision.

Still, his prison held.

That is, until now.

The elemental relics—ancient artifacts once guarded by the Celestials themselves—had been scattered and hidden to prevent any one force from becoming too powerful. Over the centuries, their purpose faded into legend, their protectors grew distant, and their wards weakened. Sensing the shift, Malachor's reach extended further.

Through his forbidden knowledge, he uncovered a devastating truth: these relics were more than symbols of power. They were keys—anchors tied to the fabric of his prison. With all of them gathered, he could dismantle the bindings that restrained him and restore his physical form.

His return would not merely mark a resurgence; it would herald a new era of shadow, unopposed and unchallenged.

And so, the Travellers—brave, curious, and unaware of their part in a much larger game—began to draw closer to the relics. In their hands, Malachor saw both the instruments of his liberation and the seeds of their downfall. Their strength made them dangerous, but also malleable. All he needed was time—to divide them, to exploit their fears, and to strike when they were at their weakest.

Malachor wove his web with meticulous care.

He whispered to old cults that worshipped forgotten gods, to sorcerers who thirsted for forbidden rites, and to spirits trapped in bitterness and vengeance. Each was offered a glimpse of power, a taste of revenge, a promise of fulfillment. These agents became the eyes and hands of Malachor across the world, setting his plans in motion.

He knew better than to reveal himself. Not yet. A full reveal would risk resistance. Instead, he continued to manipulate from the margins, letting paranoia and doubt erode the unity of the Travellers. Every decision they made, every battle they fought, brought them closer to the edge—closer to the moment he could strike.

In the forgotten ruins of civilisations, beneath the roots of ancient forests, and deep within crumbling temples, his presence grew bolder. His whispers louder. The world, though unaware, was teetering on the brink of his return.

Malachor was not idle in his prison. He was preparing.

And now, the time of shadows was drawing near.

And then, as the Travellers unknowingly drew closer to their fate, Malachor began to channel his influence into a more substantial form. No longer content to murmur from the abyss, he moved with precision, summoning the strength to manifest a shadow of his former self into the physical realm—a wraith-like apparition, elusive and half-formed, able to traverse the material world and exert limited influence upon it.

This spectral figure marked the beginning of his resurgence, a tangible expression of his rising power. Through this dark proxy, Malachor could observe the Travellers more intimately, steer their path with subtle manipulations, and quietly set the stage for his return.

Yet Malachor understood the peril of haste. His adversaries remained formidable, and the Celestials—though diminished—still retained the potential to disrupt his plans. For now, he would wait, gnawing at the ancient seals that bound him while guiding the Travellers ever closer, step by unwitting step.

His grand design neared completion, and with every passing day, the darkness he commanded grew more potent, more insistent. The world, blissfully unaware, marched toward a precipice, its people blind to the calamity looming just beyond their horizon. But Malachor saw clearly. He had waited millennia. Soon, his time would come.

Far beyond the known world, past the final edges of creation, sprawled Malachor's domain—a realm untouched by even the faintest light, where time held no sway and reality bent beneath the weight of despair. This was no mere land of shadows; it was a void given shape, a place where darkness had mass and will.

Here, the air hung heavy—not with mist, but with the sorrow of lost souls, a suffocating atmosphere woven from centuries of torment. The ground beneath was no soil or stone, but an endless obsidian expanse, sleek and cold, stretching outward in all directions. The polished surface mirrored warped reflections of those who dared walk it, each step echoing like glass beneath footfalls, laced with the murmurs of the damned.

Overhead, the sky was a seething tempest of blackened clouds, forever locked in violent churn. Crimson lightning split the gloom at random intervals, revealing ghastly silhouettes in momentary flashes. Each bolt ripped through the silence with a thunderous crack, reverberating through bone and spirit alike, as though the very fabric of the world groaned under the strain.

At the heart of this cursed realm loomed Malachor's fortress—a titanic bastion of stone and metal, twisted as if forged by the void itself. Spires clawed skyward in defiance of heaven, each jagged peak an affront to light and hope. The citadel pulsed with ancient malevolence, a magnet for the grotesque and damned that prowled its shadowy outskirts.

Within its walls, ancient runes glowed faintly, etched into the stone like forgotten scars, still thrumming with forgotten power. The corridors twisted and shifted like a living maze, confounding all who entered. At its centre sprawled Malachor's throne room—vast, echoing, and paradoxically claustrophobic, thick with the weight of centuries-old power.

Malachor sat upon a throne hewn from the same obsidian as the plains beyond, its angles cruel and unwelcoming. He was not a figure of flesh, but an embodiment of darkness itself—a shifting, inconstant presence whose shape flickered like smoke. Only his eyes, pale and cold, remained fixed—twin beacons of malice in a sea of shadows.

Silence reigned in the chamber, broken only by the occasional hum of dark energy rippling through the air. But this was no tranquil quiet—it was the tension of a bowstring drawn tight, of ruin held barely in check. Malachor's thoughts swirled with schemes, each more sinister than the last.

This realm was no prison—it was a monument. Every spire, every echoing hall, every tortured whisper bore witness to his power, his rage, his unrelenting will. He had forged it as a mirror of himself: vast, consuming, merciless. And yet, beneath the suffocating dominion he commanded, there lingered a craving—a hunger to escape, to extend his reach beyond this shattered domain and reclaim the world that had once cast him out.

His gaze shifted to the relics hovering before him—not in the physical realm, but in a vision woven from shadow and memory. These artifacts were the final keys, the instruments of his liberation. Their energies pulsed in rhythmic defiance, alive with the very forces that once bound him. He could feel them resonating with his essence, yet they remained agonisingly distant, restrained by ancient wards still holding strong.

The Travellers, oblivious to their role, were drawing them closer with every step they took.

The fortress groaned under the weight of his frustration, the very walls quivering. Rising from his throne, the darkness around him thickened, swirling with heightened intensity. His voice, low and resonant like the tolling of a gravebell, echoed across the chamber.

"The time is near," he intoned, each word heavy with impending doom. "Soon, the relics will be mine—and with them, the world shall drown in endless night."

Outside, the storm surged with renewed fury. A jagged bolt of lightning struck the tallest spire, unleashing a shockwave of energy that rippled across the obsidian plain. In the distant shadows, twisted creatures shrieked in response, their cries echoing across the void in a haunting chorus.

Yet Malachor's ambition stretched beyond mere possession. The relics were only a means to an end. What he sought was total dominion—a world reshaped in his image, bent beneath the weight of his will. And to achieve that, he had to extinguish the one force that had always defied him: the light.

His thoughts returned to the Travellers. They were evolving, growing in strength, yes—but that only made their inevitable downfall more delicious. He would break them, not with brute force, but with despair. He would unravel their bonds, crush their spirit, and leave them husks of who they once were.

And when they stood before him, broken and spent, he would take what he was owed.

The storm howled, echoing the fury within. The world remained ignorant of the horror that loomed just beyond its veil. But not for much longer. Soon, they would learn the name Malachor—and tremble.

Deep within the fortress, as the tempest raged above, another disturbance stirred. In the winding corridors of that accursed place, a figure emerged— cloaked in torn robes, shrouded in darkness. A servant, bound by ancient oaths, approached with nervous purpose, clutching a message of urgency too important to delay.

Its footsteps faltered as it neared the heart of the citadel. The walls pulsed with the oppressive force of their master's dominion, each step a battle against the instinct to flee. Shadows pressed close, and the air thickened with foreboding.

Halting outside the throne room, the servant trembled. Drawing a rattling breath, it gathered what little courage remained, and stepped inside. The oppressive stillness consumed it instantly, the weight of Malachor's presence pressing like an avalanche. It had entered the lion's den—and whatever message it bore had better be worth the risk.

Malachor did not stir as the servant entered, but the shifting shadows that composed his form deepened, coiling tighter, as if reacting to the intrusion of something foreign. The servant, shrouded in trembling deference, dared not lift its gaze, keeping its eyes fixed on the cold, unforgiving stone beneath its feet.

"My lord," the servant whispered, its voice barely audible, "the preparations are complete. The elemental realms have accepted the Travellers... and their training under the Celestials progresses as expected."

The air around Malachor crackled with barely restrained force as his form subtly shifted. Faint, eerie lights flared where his eyes should have been, locking onto the servant with piercing intensity, as though the darkness itself were appraising the messenger.

"And the relics?" His voice was a low, ominous rumble—each word weighted with ancient power and quiet fury.

"They remain with the Travellers, my lord," the servant replied, voice quivering like a leaf in a storm. "They remain beyond our reach... but not forever. Soon, they will be within your reach."

For a long, suffocating moment, Malachor was silent. The shadows around him thickened, becoming a living pressure in the room. Then, he spoke—his tone measured, but laced with menace.

"Do not fail me," he hissed, each syllable sinking into the servant's soul like a blade. "The relics are the key to my release. I have waited centuries... I will not wait much longer."

The servant bowed low, terror emanating from every motion. "Yes, my lord. We will ensure the Travellers do not falter. The relics will be yours."

Malachor's form eased slightly, the shadows around him loosening like coils released. "Good," he murmured, more to himself than to the servant. "Very good."

Without daring another glance, the servant turned and retreated swiftly from the throne room. Its heart thundered with each step as it passed through the dim corridors of the fortress, which now seemed to breathe with silent hostility—as if the very walls were listening, sensing, waiting for the slightest misstep.

Back within the chamber, Malachor turned his attention to the storm raging beyond the darkened, rune-framed windows. The relics were close—so close he could almost feel their ancient energy humming in the air. Soon, they would be his. And when that moment came, the world would kneel, and the last remnants of light would be extinguished.

Malachor's Past Encounters with the Celestials

Centuries ago—long before the relics were forged—the world was a battleground where light and darkness clashed in titanic struggle. Malachor had not always been bound to the shadowy realm he now inhabits. Once, he roamed freely, his influence spreading across the lands like a creeping blight, corrupting everything it touched.

In that ancient age, the Celestial Guardians were more than protectors; they were elemental warriors, each charged with maintaining the balance of creation itself. These divine beings stood as sentinels over air, water, earth, and fire—the four pillars upon which the natural world rested.

Malachor's first fateful clash with the Celestials came during a rare celestial convergence—a moment when the veil between realms thinned, allowing beings of immense power to cross into the mortal plane. Drawn by this weakening of the boundaries, Malachor emerged with a singular purpose: to absorb the elemental essence and ascend to a higher state of being—one beyond even the gods.

The Celestials—Zephyrus of Air, Aquael of Water, Terran of Earth, and Thalion of Fire—joined forces for the first time in eons to confront the threat. What followed was a cataclysmic war that tore through oceans, split mountains, scorched plains, and blackened skies. Each Guardian unleashed the full, unbridled force of their element, their wrath echoing with the primal fury of nature itself.

Aquael, serene but unrelenting, conjured tidal waves that towered over mountains and icebergs that crashed like celestial blades against Malachor's darkness, striving to drown his corruption in endless waters.

Zephyrus, ever-moving and unpredictable, wielded the winds as weapons—summoning hurricanes and cyclones to rip at Malachor's form, scattering his shadow across the sky like ash in a tempest.

Terran, the immovable sentinel, commanded the earth to fracture and upheave. Chasms yawned wide beneath Malachor's feet, threatening to entomb him beneath crushing stone and molten depths.

Thalion, fierce and untamed, brought forth firestorms and blinding gouts of flame, intent on searing away the taint of Malachor's darkness with cleansing infernos.

Yet Malachor endured.

He was not of the same order as the Celestials. He was a being born from absence—from shadow and void. Their attacks, though devastating, only fueled his adaptability. He fed on the chaos, twisted it, learned from it.

It was then the Celestials understood: Malachor could not be destroyed by power alone. His essence was tethered to the fractures of reality—to the forgotten spaces where light dared not tread. As long as he had even the smallest tether to the world, he would return, stronger and more wrathful.

In desperation, the Celestials pooled the last of their strength to forge four relics—each one a vessel for their elemental essence. These were not just weapons; they were seals, crafted to both suppress and contain Malachor's presence.

In a final act of sacrifice, the Celestials succeeded in banishing Malachor to the shadow realm, sealing him within a prison forged from elemental harmony. The relics were hidden in secret, each protected by powerful wards and concealed from mortal reach. It was not a permanent solution—but it was the only hope they had to prevent a world ruled by darkness.

Though imprisoned, Malachor's will still seeped into the fabric of reality. His fury and hunger echoed through the walls of his realm, pressing against the barriers, always searching for a crack. The Celestials, their strength spent, faded into myth, watching over the world from afar, their duty now passed to time and fate.

But time, as always, erodes.

Within his prison, Malachor has spent the ages studying the fault lines of his containment, unraveling the secrets of the relics, and deciphering the nature of the elements themselves. His battles with the Celestials had not been in vain. He remembered the blistering fire of Thalion, the inexorable tides of Aquael, the steadfast might of Terran, and the ever-changing currents of

Zephyrus. Each one was a key. Together, they formed the lock—and the path to his return.

And so, Malachor waits, his hatred a seething storm. He dreams of a world subdued, where elemental forces no longer resist but obey, where the brilliance of the Celestials is extinguished beneath his shadow, and where his name is spoken in reverence and fear.

All he needs are the relics—and the will to seize them.

*The Gathering of
Malachor's Forces*

In the cold, oppressive darkness of his shadowy realm, Malachor's power had swelled steadily over the centuries. Yet he knew that raw strength alone would not be enough to shatter the prison forged by the Celestials. He required more than brute force— he needed allies. Beings steeped in darkness, driven by hunger for chaos, dominion, and vengeance. Thus began his quiet summoning, a call that slipped through the veil of worlds to reach those willing to serve a higher, darker purpose.

The Dark Call:
Malachor's influence seeped like black tendrils through the fractured seams between realities. His essence became a whisper in the ears of the wicked, a cold pulse in the hearts of the ambitious and the corrupt. Those dwelling in the forgotten corners of

existence—creatures that feared the light and feasted on despair—felt his beckoning.

His first response came from the Umbrals, ancient shadow wraiths born from the same primeval darkness that fed Malachor's essence. Long believed to be vanquished or lost to time, they slipped back into the world like nightmares half-remembered. Without form or face, they drifted between planes like streaks of midnight, their motives singular: to obey the one who controlled the void. As spies and messengers, they carried Malachor's will across realms, marking the first tremors of a rising storm.

The Fallen:

Next came the Fallen—once-noble beings now hollowed by their thirst for vengeance and seduced by the corrupting promise of dark power. They were warriors and sorcerers, heroes twisted into shadows of their former selves by betrayal, loss, and ambition.

Among them was Erevan, once a fabled defender of the realms. Betrayed by those he had sworn to protect and left to die on a battlefield steeped in blood, Erevan had been consumed by rage. In his lowest hour, Malachor found him—offering not just survival, but resurrection. Clad now in scorched-black armor and bound by unholy oath, Erevan served as one of Malachor's most ruthless captains. His soul, once a beacon of hope, now pulsed with the darkness that had remade him.

The Beasts of the Abyss:
From the deepest trenches of the world, Malachor summoned the Abyssal Behemoths—colossal monsters cast out long ago for their mindless savagery. These abominations were remnants of an earlier age, forged in primal fear and banished to the underworld where they gnawed at the roots of the earth.

Towering and grotesque, with claws that tore mountains asunder and jaws that crushed ancient stone, their wrath was primal and relentless. Though their minds were blunt and instinctual, under Malachor's sway they became weapons of sheer devastation. Sent forth in limited numbers, they served as shock troops—testing the strength of the realms, unearthing their weaknesses, and sowing terror that spread like wildfire.

The Cult of Shadows:
Even among mortals, Malachor's whisper did not go unheard. In cities and villages, his dark vision gave rise to the Cult of Shadows—a clandestine order of followers who worshipped the void and yearned for the return of their shadowed master.

Ordinary people—disillusioned scholars, forsaken nobles, outcasts—became his agents. Drawn by promises of power, immortality, and revenge, they spread silently through society, corroding it from within. At the helm of the cult stood Lyria, a sorceress of formidable talent and ambition. Once denied recognition by the elder magical orders, she had turned to forbidden rites. In her dreams, Malachor showed her a world reborn in darkness, where she would rule at his side as Queen of Shadows. Her devotion was unshakable, her leadership merciless, and under her, the cult became an invisible knife poised at the heart of the realms.

With his forces steadily gathering, Malachor's reach extended further into the mortal realm. He knew that the sacred relics held by the Travellers were the keys to his liberation—but seizing them by brute strength alone would be folly. Malachor was not only a warlord but a master strategist, skilled in deceit and misdirection.

He unleashed the Umbrals to sow seeds of paranoia—spreading rumors, twisting truths, and turning allies into adversaries. The Fallen struck at critical outposts, disrupting communication and destabilising defences. The Behemoths were sent to ravage lands, their destructive path diverting attention from Malachor's deeper game.

And all the while, the Cult of Shadows worked from within—tracking the relics' locations, gathering intelligence, and positioning themselves to strike. Hidden by potent wards and illusion, they remained ghosts in the fabric of civilisation, manipulating events under Lyria's command with surgical precision.

Malachor's transformation was almost complete. No longer a forgotten entity bound in darkness, he had become the orchestrator of a rising empire—an unseen general marshalling an army of nightmares. The Travellers and the Celestials sensed the shifting tide, but the scale of his resurgence remained obscured, like the calm before a cataclysm.

The Celestial Alignment neared, a rare cosmic event that would thin the veil separating dimensions—and with it came Malachor's best chance to shatter his prison once and for all. But he would not act hastily. A single premature strike could unravel centuries of preparation.

So he waited.

Patient. Calculated. Unrelenting.

And while the world slept, Malachor watched. His fingers reached further into the minds of the weak and the hearts of the proud. His army swelled. His influence deepened.

The darkness was no longer coming—it was already here, and the world stood oblivious on the edge of its unraveling.

It was during the night of a partial lunar eclipse—a rare event when the veil between worlds thins—that Malachor made his presence known to the Travellers. Separated by realms and immersed in their elemental training, each of them was visited by a haunting vision: a dark, foreboding glimpse of the future should Malachor's plans come to fruition.

Jonas, deep in the Air Realm, had collapsed into sleep after a grueling day of practise. His dreams took a sudden, vivid turn. He found himself on the edge of a jagged cliff, gazing down at what was once a thriving landscape. Now, it was reduced to a scorched wasteland. The sky churned with soot and swirling shadows, a suffocating dome of despair. In the distance, cities burned, their fires flickering feebly against the oppressive gloom that cloaked the world.

At the heart of this devastation stood a solitary figure—Malachor. His very presence seemed to twist the atmosphere around him. As he extended a hand, the cliff beneath Jonas began to crumble, breaking away into the abyss. The once-familiar winds Jonas had learned to command now turned feral, howling with violent force that mirrored Malachor's power. The relic Jonas carried grew impossibly heavy, tugged by an unseen force as if yearning to join the darkness. In that moment, he understood: this was no ordinary dream. It was a warning. A vision of what would unfold if Malachor seized the relics.

In the Water Realm, Anastasia and Greer were met with a similarly harrowing experience. Their vision began beneath the surface of Aquael's once-pristine waters, now tainted and impenetrable. The ocean, once a sanctuary teeming with colour and life, had transformed into a dark, claustrophobic tomb. Coral reefs that once dazzled with vibrancy now lay broken and grey, lifeless skeletons of what once was.

As they navigated the oppressive depths, ominous silhouettes drifted around them—twisted sea creatures, warped by corruption, their glowing eyes filled with menace. At the core of this abyssal nightmare stood Malachor, massive and commanding, surrounded by violently churning currents that spiraled into whirlpools. The relic in their possession pulsed with an eerie, urgent light, seemingly aware of his nearness. It trembled with something like fear. Anastasia and Greer understood instinctively: if Malachor took the relic, the oceans would no longer nurture—they would consume.

In the Earth Realm, Ross's vision was equally dire. He wandered through a forest that had once been lush with life, now grotesque and unfamiliar. The trees, once tall and verdant, were contorted and blackened, their bark cracked and weeping sap like blood. The soil beneath his boots split with every step, rejecting life as though cursed.

The path led him to a clearing torn apart by violent upheaval, where the ground had been ripped open into a vast, bottomless chasm. From within that abyss came Malachor's dark energy, rising like a foul mist. The earth trembled in resonance with his presence, and the relic Ross carried vibrated with mounting intensity, as if echoing the deep imbalance. Ross, who had always drawn strength from the soil, now felt alienated from it—as though even the land itself had been seduced by Malachor's darkness.

Siobhan's vision, in the Fire Realm, was perhaps the most terrifying. She stood amid a hellscape of ceaseless flame. Yet the fire brought no comfort, no vitality—only unbearable, searing heat that burned without warmth. The volcanoes that had once been sacred and alive now spewed endless plumes of black smoke, cloaking the sky in ash and cutting off the light.

At the centre of the inferno stood Malachor, towering like a god of ruin. The flames writhed in obedience to his will, contorting into grotesque forms that danced at his feet. The relic Siobhan bore turned ice-cold against her skin, a chilling reminder that the elemental fire she once trusted had been warped. It no longer created; it only destroyed. She realised then that should Malachor triumph, fire itself would be redefined—becoming a force of annihilation rather than transformation.

Each Traveller awoke with a jolt, drenched in sweat, their hearts pounding. The visions had pierced deeper than dreams. The despair, the dread, the sense of helplessness—it was too real to dismiss. They understood, with unwavering certainty, that Malachor had reached across the realms to send them a message. This was not just a prophecy. It was a threat.

Yet within the terror lay purpose. These visions were not merely a display of power, but a call to arms. A sobering reminder of what was at stake. Their quest was no longer just a path toward mastery of their elements—it was a battle for the fate of the world itself. The relics were not simple artifacts; they were the last safeguard against the encroaching shadow.

With their return to training, the weight of destiny pressed upon them more heavily than ever before. They were no longer apprentices. They were guardians of balance, defenders of a fragile world teetering on the brink. And far away, hidden in the folds of the void, Malachor watched with cruel satisfaction.

His warning had been delivered.

The game had begun.

And the stakes had never been higher.

CHAPTER 10

Mastering the Air

The days in the Air Realm passed both swiftly and with a sense of timelessness, as though the very wind played tricks on the fabric of time itself, making the week feel simultaneously fleeting and eternal. Under the stern yet patient guidance of Zephyrus, Max and Jonas immersed themselves in the deeper mysteries of air. They were no longer merely learning how to control the element—they were beginning to understand its essence, its nature, and its spirit.

On the second day, Zephyrus introduced them to the *Dance of the Winds*, an ancient elemental technique that demanded more than just command over air currents. It required surrender—to move not against the wind, but in harmony with it, allowing the element to flow *through* them, not just around them.

He led them to a vast, open plateau high above the clouds, where the wind howled with unpredictable fury. Towering columns of vapor encircled the plateau, pulsing with a gentle inner light that bathed the landscape in a silvery, dreamlike glow.

"Feel the wind—don't resist it," Zephyrus instructed, his voice carried effortlessly by the breeze, as if the wind itself was speaking through him. "Let it guide you. Let it carry you."

Max closed his eyes, grounding himself in the moment. At first, the wind felt chaotic—sharp gusts tugged at his limbs as if trying to unbalance him. But as he stilled his thoughts and tuned in to the rhythm of the air, a pattern began to emerge. He sensed a pulse—subtle, like a heartbeat buried in the breeze. He allowed his body to sway, turning gently, responding to that hidden rhythm. The more he surrendered to the flow, the more the wind seemed to welcome him, lifting him slowly from the earth, cradling him in its invisible arms.

Jonas watched with a mixture of awe and focused intent, then stepped forward to join. His movements were more tentative, unsure at first, but Zephyrus's quiet presence and guidance helped him attune to the current. Gradually, Jonas too found his balance. His feet skimmed the ground as the wind lifted him, steady and sure.

As the two moved in tandem, the air around them responded. Small whirlwinds formed at their feet, swirling like playful spirits, weaving around their legs as if dancing with them. The moment was breathtaking—less a performance and more a communion with the element. For the first time, Max felt the air not as a force to wield but as a living presence—dynamic, responsive, and deeply alive.

Evening settled in as Max collapsed onto a bed of cloud-soft moss, every muscle in his body aching in protest, singing with exhaustion. The day's trials had left him hollowed and humming, but in a way that felt earned. Jonas dropped beside him with a theatrical groan, the two of them still vibrating with the aftershocks of what they'd just experienced. Below them, the plateau where they'd courted the wind now lay still and reverent, the vapor columns pulsing faintly like slumbering giants.

"That," Jonas panted, wiping sweat from his brow, "was the most terrifying ballet lesson I've ever had."

Max barked a laugh—sharp and sudden—which startled a flock of silver-feathered birds from a nearby tree canopy. "You call that ballet? I watched you nearly faceplant into a cloud when that gust spun you sideways."

"Strategic repositioning," Jonas retorted, eyes twinkling with mock pride, though his grin betrayed him. He reached into his pack and produced two crescent-shaped fruits, their skin glistening in the dimming light. With a flick of his wrist, he tossed one to Max. "Cloudberries. The more grounded cousin of whatever they spiked that skybrew with."

The fruit burst open against Max's teeth, tart and sweet in equal measure, its juice fizzing on his tongue like a spark finally set free. He glanced at Jonas. "You think Zephyrus is going to make us dance again tomorrow?"

Jonas tilted his head back, studying the sky as ribbons of auroral light began to unfurl and shimmer across the heavens. "Nah," he said after a moment, "tomorrow he'll probably have us juggle tornadoes or something equally insane." His voice softened as his fingers absently traced idle patterns in the moss. "But seriously... you felt it today, didn't you? That sense of... aliveness?"

Max's thoughts drifted back to that moment high above the earth, when the wind had cupped him gently—not like a weapon or a wild force to command, but like a partner in some ancient ritual. "Yeah," he murmured. "At first, it felt like it was testing me. Measuring who I was. But then... it chose to trust me. Like I was worth the effort."

A breeze curled around them, cool and electric, carrying the sharp scent of distant storms—ozone and wild promise. Jonas exhaled, long and slow. "I used to think air was just about freedom. But today... it felt more like a dialogue. Like it was asking us questions."

They slipped into a companionable silence, each turning inward as the sky above them shifted. The constellations realigned themselves in slow motion, stars waltzing into new formations. Amid the celestial rearrangement, Max thought he saw the outline of a figure mid-step—dancing across the heavens. Whether it was an optical illusion or a cosmic joke, he couldn't say. But when he looked over at Jonas, he saw the quiet awe in his friend's eyes and knew he wasn't the only one who had seen it.

The following day brought a stark contrast. Zephyrus guided them to a secluded valley nestled deep in the heart of the realm, where the wind fell still and the atmosphere felt thick, charged with a silence that prickled against their skin.

Here, they would learn the *Breath of Life*—a technique rooted not in force or defence, but in restoration. It focused on the nurturing side of air: the ability to heal, to give life rather than take it.

"This is not about strength or dominance," Zephyrus said as they stood amid the quiet. "Air is not solely the breath of storms. It is also the breath that sustains. Creation begins here."

They sat cross-legged on the cool earth, hands resting gently on their knees, palms turned skyward. Zephyrus led them through a series of controlled breathing exercises—deep inhalations, careful pauses, slow exhalations. Each breath drew in the surrounding air, cleansing it, then releasing it with intentional gentleness.

Max struggled at first. His instinct was to control, to harness and direct. But the breath required the opposite. It wasn't about power—it was about offering. When he finally allowed himself to exhale with purpose rather than force, something shifted. He focused on the patch of wilted grass before him. With each breath out, he envisioned the air nourishing the soil, caressing the blades of grass with quiet vitality.

Gradually, the faded green brightened. The grass straightened, vibrant once more. A simple act, yet it filled Max with a profound sense of accomplishment—this was power of a different kind: subtle, generous, and quietly awe-inspiring.

Jonas, too, was moved by the experience. He had always viewed air as a weapon—useful in defence, formidable in attack. But now he saw its gentler face, the silent sustainer of life. In that still valley, surrounded by silence, he began to reimagine the purpose of his gift.

The valley remained unnervingly silent as night fell, the kind of silence that pressed in from all sides. The air was so still that Max could hear the slow, steady rhythm of his own heartbeat, each pulse echoing like a drumbeat in the vast quiet. He and Jonas sat shoulder to shoulder on a smooth outcropping of stone, their backs resting against the sun-warmed rock, eyes turned upward toward a sky spangled with stars—brighter here than anywhere else in the realm, untouched by wind, cloud, or the flicker of torchlight.

Jonas let out a sharp breath, the sound slicing through the hush. "I don't get it."

Max turned to look at him. "Get what?"

"This whole... healing thing." Jonas flexed his fingers, staring at them with narrowed eyes, as if they'd just failed him in some fundamental way. "Air isn't supposed to fix things. It's meant to move. To slice. To *cut*."

Max thought back to the moment the grass had straightened under his breath, to how colour and life had returned to it—as if responding to something unseen, something remembered. "Maybe it's not about fixing," he said slowly. "Maybe it's more like... giving back what was already there."

Jonas shot him a sideways look. "Since when are you the poetic one?"

"Since I watched a patch of dead grass wake up just because I breathed on it."

Jonas snorted, but the sound lacked its usual edge. He reached down and picked up a withered leaf, dry and curled at the edges, and turned it absently between his fingers. "I tried it," he muttered after a pause. "After you left. On this." He nodded toward the leaf. "Didn't do a damn thing."

Max frowned. "You sure you were doing it right?"

"Oh, excuse me, Master of Breath, I didn't realise there's a correct way to exhale."

Max rolled his eyes but didn't take the bait. Instead, he gently took the leaf from Jonas's fingers and laid it flat across his own palm. "It's not just about breathing," he said. "It's about *believing* the air can do it. You have to mean it. Like it's a gift."

He closed his eyes, steadying his thoughts, and focused on the quiet rhythm of his lungs, the rise and fall that Zephyrus had taught them to listen for. When he exhaled, it wasn't just a release—it was a surrender. A giving.

The leaf trembled.

Slowly, the brittle edges began to soften, the delicate veins threading through it darkening, pulsing with a muted shimmer of green.

Jonas stared, eyes wide. "...Okay. That's creepy."

Max grinned. "Admit it—you're impressed."

"I'm *concerned*." But Jonas's gaze lingered on the leaf longer than he needed to, his expression clouded with something unspoken, something fragile. "You really think this works on people?"

Max's smile faltered. He thought of Siobhan, of the way fire danced in her hands—beautiful and volatile, as though she herself were a candle always moments from burning out. "I hope so."

Jonas was quiet for a while, the silence between them returning—but this time, it felt less heavy, less final. Then he stood abruptly and brushed the dust from his trousers. "Well. If you start glowing and levitating, I'm tossing you into the nearest river."

Max laughed, shaking his head. As the sound faded into the stillness, he noticed something shift in Jonas beside him - the tension in his frame easing slightly, his breathing no longer quite so measured. And when the wind finally stirred again, just before dawn, it brought with it the faintest trace of green—earthy, new, and full of life.

On the fourth day, Zephyrus revealed yet another dimension of air's potential—communication. The *Whispering Winds*, he called it, a method of sending thoughts and messages across vast distances through the currents of the air itself.

He led them to the realm's highest peak, where the sky opened in every direction. The wind here was thin, sharp, and clear—untainted by the turbulence found below. From this summit, the Air Realm unfolded in all its ever-changing beauty: roiling clouds, flickering light, the endless dance of currents weaving patterns across the sky.

"Air is the world's great messenger," Zephyrus said, his voice light yet steady. "It listens. It carries.

It remembers. No other element can match its reach."

They stood apart, testing their connection. Max tried to push his thoughts into the wind, shaping them into words and intentions. At first, they scattered—lost among the eddies and crosswinds. But with patience and clarity of mind, the message began to carry. He heard Jonas's voice drift back to him, soft but unmistakable, spoken not through sound, but through the wind itself.

It was like eavesdropping on the world. Max's mind spun with the possibilities—not just communication, but intelligence gathering. Secrets, warnings, truths—all could ride the currents. The wind was more than breath, more than motion. It was information. It was memory. It was a web that connected every corner of the earth.

As the lesson ended and the sun dipped beneath the cloud line, Max stood in quiet reflection. He was beginning to see that mastery of air was not about domination. It was about attunement—about listening, feeling, breathing with the world. And in learning to do so, he was not only becoming stronger—he was becoming *connected.*

The scent of roasting cloudberries and spiced tea drifted through the cool evening air as Max and Jonas settled around the small fire just outside their shelter. After hours spent straining to catch the whispers of the wind, the familiar crackle of flames and the shared comfort of a warm meal brought a welcome sense of ease.

Jonas passed Max a carved wooden bowl filled with steaming broth. "Think the others are eating this well?"

Max grinned, blowing on a spoonful. "Doubt it. Siobhan once burned water trying to make soup."

Jonas chuckled. "And Ross? I'd bet good silver he's got a perfectly organised camp, with rations measured down to the last grain."

"Probably," Max agreed, shaking his head as he pictured their meticulous, ever-prepared friend. "The twins, though—they're definitely sneaking second helpings whenever Aquael isn't paying attention."

The fire popped, sending a flurry of glowing embers into the air. They rose like tiny fireflies, dancing upward toward the darkening sky. For a moment, neither spoke. The weight of the day's training—of learning to listen rather than command—settled around them like a second cloak.

Jonas stretched, wincing as his shoulders cracked. "Miss them?"

Max didn't answer right away. He watched the smoke rise and dissolve into the starlit sky, his thoughts drifting to Siobhan's infectious laughter, the twins' perfectly synchronised eye-rolls, Ross's dry, pointed commentary. "Yeah," he said at last, his voice quiet. "Even Ross's lectures."

Jonas smirked. "Careful. That's dangerously close to sentimental."

"Shut up." Max lobbed a cloudberry at him. "You're the one who tried to send a wind-message to Greer earlier."

Jonas raised his hands in mock surrender. "Guilty. But to be fair, I need to know if she's finally beaten Anastasia at sparring."

Max laughed, the sound bright and unguarded. The wind picked it up and carried it into the night—not transformed by magic, not cloaked in meaning, but simply as it was: easy, warm, and alive with friendship.

The fifth day proved to be the most intense and demanding of all. Zephyrus led them to a remote and volatile stretch of the realm, where massive thunderheads churned above like a living wall of shadow. Forks of lightning split the sky, each crack echoing through the atmosphere like the lash of a celestial whip. The wind carried the scent of ozone and the distant rumble of something ancient awakening.

"Today," Zephyrus said, his voice solemn and heavy with purpose, "you will witness the true essence of air. You will not just endure the storm—you will command it."

Max's pulse quickened as he stared into the heart of the approaching tempest. The sky grew darker by the second, and the wind howled like a restless spirit, tugging at his clothes and lashing his hair across his face. Yet, amid the chaos, he felt no fear. Instead, adrenaline surged through him—this was the moment he had been craving. A true test of will, strength, and connection to the element.

Under Zephyrus's guidance, they were told to extend their senses—to feel the storm's rhythm, to become one with its wild pulse. Max closed his eyes and let himself sink into the moment. He could feel it then—the immense and unyielding power that charged the air around him. It wasn't just a storm. It was alive.

With deliberate focus, Max reached for that energy, summoning the wind and calling the lightning with his intent. The storm resisted at first, wild and unbridled, but he held fast, shaping the chaos with the force of his will.

Jonas struggled beside him, his concentration faltering under the storm's pressure. He battled to hold control, sweat streaking his brow as his body braced against the wind. But together—anchored by Zephyrus's steady presence—they gradually bent the storm's fury to their command. What had started as a brutal onslaught became something else entirely: a raw, controlled surge of elemental might.

By the end of the trial, they were utterly spent—bodies trembling, minds awash in awe. But within that exhaustion was a newfound reverence.

Air was no longer just a concept or an ability—it was a force of nature, majestic in both its fury and grace.

The storm had left them shaken—but exhilarated.

Max and Jonas sat on the leeward side of a massive boulder, their backs pressed against its sun-warmed surface. It radiated lingering heat from the afternoon sun, grounding them after the chaos of the tempest. Between them lay a modest meal—dried fruit and thick slices of nutbread, slightly crumbled from the journey but still welcome. The air was electric, still buzzing with the remnants of nature's fury; each breath tasted of ozone and rain-washed earth.

Jonas exhaled deeply, a long, satisfied sigh as he stretched his arms high above his head. "Never thought I'd say this," he muttered, "but I missed solid ground."

Max chuckled, low and dry, flexing his fingers as tiny arcs of static flickered between them—residual sparks from the storm still playing on his skin. "You think the others are dealing with anything remotely like this?"

"Siobhan's probably setting half a forest ablaze just for the hell of it," Jonas said, casually tossing a chunk of nutbread into the air and catching it with a quick snap of his teeth. "And the twins? I'd put money on them stirring up tidal waves just to see who can make the bigger one."

Max laughed softly, the image vivid in his mind. "Ross is definitely somewhere giving a detailed lecture to some poor earth elemental about correct sediment layering and structural integrity."

Jonas snorted. "While jotting it all down in that weatherproof notebook of his, no doubt."

They drifted into an easy silence, one born of exhaustion and familiarity. Overhead, the last shreds of storm clouds unraveled across a darkening sky, their edges kissed by the gold and lavender hues of twilight. The wind had calmed, now little more than a whisper that carried the scent of damp pine from the lower slopes.

After a while, Jonas broke the quiet. "You know," he said, voice softer now, "I used to hate storms."

Max turned to him, brows raised. "You? Mister 'I'll-fight-anything-that-moves'?"

Jonas shrugged, unusually serious. "Where I grew up, storms weren't just noise and spectacle. They were roofs ripped clean off and fields flattened overnight. I never saw them as anything but destruction." He glanced down, idly picking at the hard edge of his bread. "But today... it didn't feel like that."

Max remembered the exact moment the lightning had responded to his call—not with hostility, but with a strange sense of recognition, almost like an answer rather than a reaction. "It wasn't just chaos," he said slowly. "It was... alive. Like it knew us."

Jonas nodded, a contemplative look settling over his face—so rare, it made Max pause. "Makes you wonder what else we've been wrong about," he said quietly.

Above them, the sky deepened into velvet, and the first stars emerged—sharp, brilliant pinpricks of light against the clean slate left behind by the storm. In the distance, a breeze stirred, lifting the edge of Max's cloak. It carried something new, something gentle and familiar—not a threat or a warning, but a whisper of what lay ahead.

A promise.

The sixth day unfolded in stark contrast to the chaos of the one before. Zephyrus brought them to a tranquil meadow, where the tall grasses swayed gently under a peaceful, steady breeze. The air was light, almost playful, and the sun filtered through wisps of clouds in soft golden hues. Here, amid the quiet, they were invited to reflect.

Max spent the day in thoughtful silence, seated beneath a towering tree with leaves that rustled like whispers. He revisited every lesson, every challenge. It became clear to him that the element of air was not just about speed or destruction—it was layered, alive, and deeply nuanced. It could be soft and nurturing, or sudden and merciless. He understood now that the real mastery lay in restraint and timing. Knowing when to summon power, and when to let stillness speak.

Across the field, Jonas sat in similar contemplation. His usual confidence had given way to something more grounded. The realm had challenged not only his strength but his perspective. He had once viewed air merely as a weapon—fast, sharp, relentless. But in its gentler moments, he discovered its power to heal, to guide, to soothe. His understanding of the element—and himself—had changed.

The twin moons of the Air Realm hung low that night, their silvery glow flooding the floating meadow in a dreamlike luminescence. Max lay on his back in the soft grass, arms folded behind his head, eyes tracing the constellations that pulsed overhead like distant watchfires. The breeze carried with it the scent of rain-soaked earth, a lingering gift from the storm that had rolled through hours earlier. The atmosphere thrummed with residual energy—restless, vibrant, and full of whispers for those attuned enough to hear them.

A shadow passed over him.

Jonas stood nearby, a waterskin dangling from one hand, a familiar half-smirk playing on his face.

"You look like you're trying to memorise the sky," he remarked, tossing the waterskin toward Max's chest.

Max caught it with a grunt. "Maybe I am." He took a swig—the liquid inside was crisp and slightly sweet, like morning dew concentrated into something bold and alive.

"What is this?"

"Zephyrus called it 'skybrew,' remember? Made from cloudberries—or some other poetic nonsense. Still tastes better than it sounds." Jonas sank into the grass beside him with a sigh, stretching out his legs.

"You're leaving tomorrow."

It wasn't a question.

Max nodded, absently rolling the waterskin between his palms. "Water Realm's next."

Jonas let out a snort. "Hope you like being soggy."

A comfortable silence settled over them, broken only by the rustling of grass stirred by the breeze. For days, they'd trained shoulder to shoulder—pushing their limits, trading blows, laughing whenever one of them got knocked flat by an errant gust. But now, with Max's departure looming, the unspoken weight of change pressed down on them both.

"You ever wonder why it's us?" Max asked, his voice barely above the wind. "Out of everyone in the world, why are we the ones doing this?"

Jonas tilted his head, considering. "You asking if I believe in destiny?"

"I'm asking if you ever feel like you're not enough." The words slipped out before Max could reel them back.

Jonas was silent for a moment. Then, to Max's surprise, he laughed—not mocking, but genuine and warm.

"Every damn day." He plucked a blade of grass and began to twirl it between his fingers. "When Zephyrus first brought us here, I was sure I'd mess up so bad he'd personally toss me off the edge of the realm."

Max raised an eyebrow. "You? Mr. 'I-can-outfly-a-hurricane'?"

"Shut up," Jonas said, grinning despite himself. "The point is, it's not about feeling like you're enough. It's about showing up anyway. It's about getting back up every time you fall. And you?" He flicked the grass at Max. "You don't quit. Even when you probably should."

Max smirked. "Was that a compliment?"

"Call it an observation." Jonas's expression grew more thoughtful. "Just... don't forget what you learned here. Air's not just about speed or power. It's about listening—to everything. Especially the quiet things."

At that moment, the wind curled gently around them, carrying the ghost of a distant storm in its currents. Max closed his eyes, letting the air move across his skin. And for the first time, he noticed something new—he could feel Jonas in the breeze too. The steady rhythm of his breath, the way the air bent around his presence, like he belonged to it.

"You'll keep training with Zephyrus?" Max asked, eyes still closed.

Jonas shrugged. "Someone has to keep him from dying of boredom." He paused, then added more softly, "And when we face Malachor, someone's going to need to know how to hold the skies."

Max felt a knot form in his chest. No grand declarations. No tearful goodbyes. Just quiet certainty. A promise that didn't need to be spoken.

He raised the waterskin. "To not quitting."

Jonas clinked his against it. "Even when we should."

They drank, and the wind carried their laughter far across the meadow, into the moonlit night.

As the final day arrived, Max prepared to leave the Air Realm. The week had altered him in ways he hadn't anticipated. With each lesson, each trial, he had peeled back layers of himself he didn't know existed. Zephyrus had not only taught him how to command air but had helped him understand its soul—and, in turn, his own.

At the edge of the realm, the portal shimmered like liquid glass, sending flickers of light across the wind-swept plain. Zephyrus stood beside Max, his gaze firm but filled with an unspoken pride.

"You have done well, Max," he said, his voice measured, bearing both encouragement and warning. "But the path ahead will not be easy. The challenges will grow harder. Your power alone is not enough—you must evolve, stay open, and stay grounded. The relics are important, yes, but it is your connection to the elements that will shape the outcome of what's to come."

Max nodded, the weight of Zephyrus's words pressing into him like the wind at his back. "Thank you," he said earnestly. "For everything. I won't forget."

With a final nod, Zephyrus raised his hand, and the portal flared in welcome.

The portal's luminous surface rippled like disturbed mercury, its edges unraveling into fine threads of silver energy. Max adjusted the straps of his pack, the weight of the week's lessons carved deep into his muscles—his bones still thrummed with the memory of the wind's rhythm, as if the air had rewritten him from within.

As he turned to say farewell, he found Zephyrus watching him with an intensity that felt ancient—storm-gray eyes brimming with something that hovered between pride and warning.

"You've learned to listen to the wind," the Celestial said, his voice carrying the patience of centuries and the gravity of storms. "But now you must hear what the air remembers."

A sudden gust swept around them, charged with the metallic scent of lightning and something more primal—the ozone tang of a magic older than names. Above, the sky dimmed unnaturally. Clouds curled into spirals, folding in on themselves as if trying to remember a shape long forgotten.

"Malachor's shadow grows longer with each dawn," Zephyrus continued, his gaze scanning the horizon. "And your path now crosses with dangers more ancient than your civilisation."

Max's heart thudded harder in his chest. "You've fought him before."

The space between them shimmered as Zephyrus lifted his hands. The wind responded like a loyal scribe, conjuring images in currents of mist and light—memories inscribed in the air itself.

The Air Realm unfolded before Max's eyes as it once had been: a boundless sky scattered with floating archipelagos, crystalline spires rising like songs into the atmosphere, each island resonating with the harmony of the wind. But then— corruption. The colours dulled. The sky turned a bruised violet as monstrous storms unfurled from the edges of the world.

At their centre stood Malachor. His form twisted between flesh and shadow, smoke and something worse. Where he passed, the air turned foul. Birds dropped from the sky mid-flight, their wings calcified into stone. Even the clouds collapsed in on themselves like lungs starved of breath.

"During the Celestial Sundering," Zephyrus's voice echoed through the vision, "he didn't seek power—he sought to claim the breath from the world itself."

The scene shifted again—this time to the Celestials. Towering beings of radiant energy, their bodies shimmered and transformed, fluctuating between humanoid figures and raw elemental force. They floated not with wings but on currents of pure will, moving like thoughts made visible.

"The Celestials did not come as conquerors," Zephyrus said, his tone reverent. "We came as surgeons. Our purpose was not to fight Malachor, but to excise him—cut him out like a sickness. The act nearly tore this realm apart."

Max watched in awe as the Celestials wove strands of golden light into the heart of the storm. Their movements were precise, deliberate—terrifying in their grace. The vision ended in a searing flash of light, followed by the faint image of four objects plummeting toward the earth like falling stars.

The memory dissolved. Max staggered slightly, his ears ringing, lungs burning as if he'd held his breath for too long.

Zephyrus's voice softened to a whisper. "What you carry are not mere tools, Max. They are echoes of that battle. Fragments of something far greater."

Max's thoughts leapt to the relics his companions carried. "You're saying... they were weapons?"

"I'm saying they are pieces of a story we don't fully understand." The Celestial's expression darkened. "But Malachor fears them. That alone should tell you something."

The wind surged once more, threading around them like a living thing. In its wail, Max caught fleeting cries—stormbirds far off in the distance, and beneath that, whispers. A language he didn't know but somehow felt deep in his skin, tingling along his spine.

Zephyrus straightened, the weight of responsibility settling into his stance. "The Celestials have stepped back from this war. The burden of balance now lies with the Guardians... and with those like you."

Max swallowed, his throat dry. "Why show me this?"

"Because air remembers what earth forgets." Zephyrus placed a steady hand on Max's shoulder. "And when you find yourself before Malachor, remember—he is not invincible. He *was* stopped. He *can* be stopped again."

The portal behind them pulsed, its glow intensifying until it painted their faces in molten silver.

"One last lesson," Zephyrus said, his form beginning to blur at the edges as the wind began to reclaim him. "The greatest storms are born from the smallest disturbances. Remember that, when you doubt your role in what's coming."

With the Celestial's words still ringing in his ears, Max took a deep breath, savoring the crispness of the Air Realm one last time before stepping forward. As he crossed the threshold into the unknown, a swirl of emotions swept through him—excitement, determination, and a quiet current of unease.

He emerged into the Water Realm, its cool mist settling over him like a veil. Behind him, Jonas remained, continuing his training under Zephyrus's watchful eye. Ahead, an entirely new element waited to be understood. The road would be long, and the trials unforgiving—but Max felt ready.

He carried the wind within him now—not as a weapon, but as a companion.

CHAPTER 11

Beneath the Surface

Max stepped out of the portal and into the Water Realm, and at once, everything shifted. The air was heavy with moisture, wrapping around him like a damp cloak, and the gentle, melodic sound of trickling streams and distant cascades filled the silence. He stood at the edge of a vast lagoon, its surface shimmering like glass beneath a soft turquoise sky. The scenery couldn't have been more different from the airy, open expanse of the previous realm. Gone were the high winds and boundless skies—in their place rose mist-veiled waterfalls, glistening stones, quiet streams winding through mossy banks, and the deep, endless ocean stretching far beyond the horizon.

He took in the serene, almost surreal beauty before him, his gaze soon settling on two familiar figures waiting at the water's edge—Anastasia and Greer. The twins were already clothed in garments that appeared woven from the very element they now trained in. Their robes of pale blue rippled and shimmered, flowing like liquid silk around their forms, as if moved by an unseen current.

"Welcome to the Water Realm, Max," Anastasia said with a warm smile, her voice blending naturally with the sounds around them.

"We've been expecting you."

Greer nodded, her expression more reserved but not unkind. "Aquael is ready to begin your training. This realm holds vast knowledge, but it asks for humility and patience in return."

A familiar mixture of anticipation and unease stirred in Max's chest. His time in the Air Realm had tested him, yet it had helped him begin to understand his abilities. Now, he stood on the threshold of another domain—one that was both nurturing and potentially destructive, fluid yet forceful. He would need to surrender his expectations and attune himself quickly if he hoped to learn from it.

The first morning in the Water Realm began with a meeting that Max would never forget.

Aquael, the Elemental Mentor of water, emerged slowly from the heart of the lagoon. Her form rose with the elegance of a tide unfurling, water cascading off her figure as though she was born of the element itself. Her long hair flowed behind her like strands of quicksilver, and her eyes—an impossibly deep blue—held a calm intensity, the kind forged by centuries of wisdom and experience.

She offered Max a graceful nod. "Max, the water is a mirror," she said, her voice as soft and steady as waves lapping at a shore. "It reflects all that lies within—your strengths, your fears, your hidden truths. To command the water, you must first come to know yourself."

She guided him to the edge of the lagoon with slow, deliberate steps. "Your first task is simple," she said. "Connect with it. Feel its energy. Listen."

Max lowered himself to the water's edge and extended a hand into the cool, clear depths. At once, he felt a subtle shift, a gentle pull—not physical, but something deeper, like the water was calling to his inner self. It wasn't just an element to be bent to his will; it was a force with a voice of its own.

He closed his eyes, focused on the sensation. The water slid between his fingers, not cold but alive, shifting and responding. It was soothing, yes, but beneath its calm surface was an undertone of mystery—a sense of power held in reserve.

From nearby, Anastasia and Greer observed silently. They'd already taken their first steps in mastering water, and they understood what this moment meant. It wasn't just about ability—it was about beginning to open oneself fully to something larger, something elemental.

The sun hung low over the Water Realm, scattering a warm amber glow across the gently rippling lagoon. Max sat on the smooth stones at the water's edge, the coolness of the surface grounding him after a long day of training. The lesson still lingered in his fingertips—that strange, weightless moment when the water had acknowledged him. It was a connection unlike anything he'd felt with the wild, unpredictable air he had spent the past week learning to control.

He trailed his fingers through the shallows, watching the ripples distort his reflection until it no longer looked entirely like his own. It was as if the water held a mirror not only to his face, but to something deeper he hadn't yet uncovered.

A soft splash broke the stillness beside him. Anastasia eased onto the rocks with quiet grace, her bare feet sliding into the lagoon until the water reached her ankles.

"It's different from air, isn't it?" she asked, her voice barely above the lapping tide.

Max exhaled slowly, the memory of the wind answering his call flashing in his mind—how it had come to him in a rush, full of life and eager to move.

"Air is all movement and chaos. But this…" He lifted his hand, letting a few droplets slip through his fingers. They fell back into the lagoon like threads of silver, vanishing into the larger whole. "It's like trying to have a conversation with someone who never breaks eye contact."

Greer appeared on his other side, her arrival marked by the soft crunch of pebbles. She picked up a smooth stone and flicked it across the water; it skipped four times before disappearing beneath the surface.

"At least Water listens," she said, nudging a ripple with her toe. "Earth's like shouting at a mountain."

The twins exchanged one of their silent glances—those wordless moments that Max was still learning to interpret. There was a whole world of understanding between them that didn't need to be spoken aloud.

"Air came naturally to you, didn't it?" Anastasia asked, turning back to him.

Max nodded slowly, remembering how the wind had embraced him as if it already knew him. It had carried his joy, his frustration, even his doubts. "It felt… familiar. Like something I'd known all my life, but only just remembered."

Greer snorted, nudging him with her shoulder. "Of course it did. You're all reckless energy and impulsive ideas."

Max raised an eyebrow. "And water? What does that make me?"

"Patient," Anastasia answered without hesitation.

"Stubborn," Greer added with a grin.

"Deep," they said in unison, their matching smiles caught in the reflection of the still lagoon.

As the last light of day melted into twilight, the water around them began to shimmer faintly. Bioluminescent algae stirred to life in the shallows, illuminating the lagoon with a soft, ethereal glow. It was as though the realm itself was breathing—slow and deliberate, in a rhythm as old as the world.

Max closed his eyes and listened—not the way he listened to the wind, eager and alert, but the way the water asked him to: with stillness. With presence. With patience.

And for the first time since arriving, the Water Realm no longer felt like a puzzle to solve or a force to conquer. It felt like a teacher—ancient, silent, and waiting for him to understand the language it spoke beneath the surface.

On the second day, Aquael led them away from the lagoon to a still lake cradled between high, jagged cliffs. The surface was motionless, undisturbed—a perfect reflection of the sky and stone above. It felt sacred, like a place that had waited centuries for their arrival.

"Water flows, adapts, reshapes itself in response to its environment," Aquael said. "Today, you'll learn to move as water does—without force, without resistance."

The twins stepped forward first. Together, they walked into the lake, stopping when the water reached their waists. In perfect unison, they lifted their hands. The water responded instantly, swirling up around them in fluid ribbons that danced across their arms and shoulders. Their movements were precise, yet effortless, like a ritual learned through instinct and trust.

Max watched with quiet awe. There was something deeper than talent at work—it was their bond, the synchronicity of shared experience, years of understanding one another without words. The water seemed to sense that and responded with grace.

Then came his turn.

He stepped into the lake, feeling the cool embrace of the water wrap around his legs. He closed his eyes again, focusing on what he'd felt at the lagoon. Slowly, he raised his hands and reached out—not to control, but to connect.

At first, nothing. The surface remained still. Doubt crept in.

Then, faintly, he felt it—the water stirred, a soft swirl brushing against his legs like a sigh. It was subtle, but it was there.

"Good," Aquael said, her tone gentle and encouraging.

Anastasia offered him a smile of quiet support. "It takes time. But you're finding your rhythm."

As the day wore on, Max began to feel more at ease. He still fumbled occasionally, the water slipping through his fingers when his concentration wavered, but something was changing. He could sense the water beginning to respond—not just to movement, but to emotion, to intent.

The twins remained close by, offering guidance when needed and patiently demonstrating new forms. Max noticed how the water answered differently for each of them, shaped by their distinct personalities. Greer moved with precision, her energy contained. Anastasia flowed more freely, intuitive and light. She, however, was still discovering what her own rhythm felt like.

That evening, they gathered by the lakeshore. The night was quiet, lit by the soft glow of aquatic fireflies that drifted above the surface.

They spoke as friends, no longer just students of the elements. Anastasia shared the frustrations of her early days—how difficult it had been to let go and trust the process. Greer spoke of how water had challenged her to release the need for control, to surrender to the unknown. Their words weren't just stories—they were reminders that growth was often slow, that mastery required vulnerability.

Max listened closely, feeling their bond deepen with each shared reflection. For the first time, he saw his journey not just as an individual quest, but a shared experience. He began to understand that the Water Realm didn't just teach skill—it asked for connection, collaboration, and above all, trust. Trust in the element, in those around him, and in himself.

The fire crackled gently between them, sending tiny sparks swirling into the twilight as Max plopped down between the twins on the smooth, river-washed stones. Water dripped from his hair as he shook his head like a drenched dog, spraying both girls with a light mist.

"I think my fingers are permanently pruned," he groaned, holding up his hands to examine the deep wrinkles etched into his fingertips.

Greer tossed him a towel without looking. "Wait until day five when we do the deep dives. You'll be sprouting gills by then."

Anastasia stretched her arms overhead, her joints popping faintly in the quiet. "Remember your first week here, Greer? You refused to get in the water for three whole days because you thought the fish were staring at you."

Greer's cheeks turned a shade pinker in the firelight. "They were! That huge striped one wouldn't stop following me. I swear it had a vendetta."

Max chuckled, the image of the normally unshakable Greer being haunted by a curious fish brightening his mood. "At least you didn't almost drown trying to skip stones like I did today."

"True," Anastasia conceded, flashing him a grin. "That was a first—even for this place."

They fell into a companionable silence, the kind that only came from shared exhaustion and mutual trust. The lake's surface rippled softly, stirred by the evening breeze, its shifting reflections carving shadows across their faces. Max absently traced swirling patterns into the damp stone beneath him, grounding himself in the moment.

"Wonder how Jonas is doing back in the Air Realm," he mused, his voice low.

Greer let out a short laugh. "Probably driving Zephyrus insane with nonstop questions. That boy could talk the ears off a stone guardian."

Max smirked at the thought. "I still can't believe he tried to ride a tornado on day three."

"'Advanced aerial reconnaissance,'" Anastasia quoted, using air quotes.

"More like 'advanced face-planting,'" Greer shot back, and they all burst into laughter.

Above them, the first fireflies flickered to life, drifting lazily over the water like glowing embers broken free from the flames. In that moment, with the scent of smoke in the air and laughter still fading into the night, Max realised this—*this*—was exactly what he needed after a long, grueling day of training. Not more drills or lectures. Just the steady rhythm of friendship, and the unspoken comfort of being understood.

The third day of training introduced a formidable challenge. Aquael led them to a powerful river that surged through the heart of the realm, its current wild and relentless, as though daring them to stand against it.

"Today," Aquael said, her voice rising above the roar of the water, "you will confront the full force of water's power. But you will not do it alone."

Max glanced over at Anastasia and Greer. The silent exchange between them spoke volumes—they would have to rely on each other to succeed.

As they neared the riverbank, Aquael outlined the task: they were to construct a barrier strong enough to divert the current without allowing it to shatter their control. Max's confidence wavered; the idea of managing such a feat alone was overwhelming. But before doubt could root itself too deeply, Anastasia stepped closer, her fingers brushing against his arm in quiet reassurance.

"Don't worry," she said, her eyes steady. "We've got this. Together."

Greer, ever the tactician, gave a short nod. "We'll build the foundation. You focus on reinforcing it. Let the current pass through you, not against you."

Together, they waded into the river. The water pulled at their limbs with increasing strength, threatening to break their footing. Anastasia and Greer raised their hands in unison, and Max mirrored them. At first, the effort was disjointed. The river surged and crashed, seeking any weakness. But gradually, as their rhythm aligned, they became a single force—steady, resilient.

The river began to yield, its fury bending around the invisible shield they formed. Max could feel the energy coursing through him—not as an adversary to be overpowered, but as a powerful ally, one he could guide with the unwavering support of his friends.

By the session's end, they were drenched and drained—but victorious. They had redirected the river's path through unified effort, and for the first time, Max felt what it truly meant to be part of something greater than himself. Their strengths didn't just complement one another—they amplified each other.

The river had finally released them at dusk, depositing all three of them on the muddy bank like shipwreck survivors washed ashore. Max groaned as he peeled a strand of slimy riverweed from his shoulder. "I think there's a fish in my boot."

Greer didn't bother moving. "If it is, give it my condolences for being trapped with you." Anastasia sat cross-legged nearby, wringing what felt like gallons of water from her sleeves. "Remember when we thought water training would be the peaceful element?"

Max snorted, recalling the serene blue lagoon from their first day—the deceptive calm before the chaos. "Aquael lied to us."

"Technically," came a melodic voice from behind them, "I said water adapts." Aquael stepped lightly over a fallen log, somehow looking as flawless as she had that morning, untouched by the day's chaos. "I never claimed it was gentle." She dropped three honey-glazed buns into their laps with a faint smile. "Eat. Tomorrow, we begin tidal wave theory."

As she vanished into the deepening twilight, Greer muttered into the grass, "I really hate it when she does her mysterious fade-out thing."

Anastasia took a giant bite of her bun, cheeks already sticky with syrup. "You're just bitter you can't dissolve into mist on command."

Max watched as Aquael skimmed across the surface of the now-glasslike river, the water so tranquil it betrayed no hint of the earlier storm.

Greer nudged him with a muddy elbow.

"Do you think Jonas is getting better food in the Air Realm?"

Max perked up at that. "Zephyrus once served us cloud vapor. Said it was 'atmospheric essence.' Tasted like wet socks," he confirmed through a mouthful of pastry.

Greer laughed, stretching her sore arms behind her head as the stars blinked awake above them—each one reflected perfectly in the calm river below, as though the water had forgotten its rage entirely. Somewhere upstream, a frog let out a proud, echoing belch.

"See?" Anastasia said, flicking her last crumb to a duck waiting nearby. "Perfectly calm element."

That evening, the bond between them deepened. They shared stories under the stars, laughed until their sides ached, and playfully sparred in the shallows. It became clear that mastering water wasn't only about skill—it was about trust, connection, and discovering strength through unity.

On the fourth day, Aquael guided them deeper into the Water Realm, to a secluded lagoon encircled by steep cliffs. The water here sparkled with a soft, ethereal glow, and a hush blanketed the space, as if the very air revered it.

"Today," Aquael said gently, "you will connect with the heart of water. This place holds its essence. Here, you will not merely move water—you will learn to become one with it."

Max felt a ripple of awe as he stepped into the lagoon. The water welcomed him like a familiar friend, reacting to his presence with a gentle pulse. It wasn't just fluid—it was aware.

The twins slipped into the water first, submerging briefly before rising to let only their faces break the glassy surface, eyes closed in quiet communion. Max followed, submerging into the cool, glassy depths. Something shifted the moment he let go—the element didn't just surround him; it entered him, filling the spaces between heartbeats, coursing through every fiber of his being.

For hours, they remained there, moving in silence, exploring the boundaries of their control. But more importantly, they listened. Max began to sense the language of water—the way it responded to intent, emotion, rhythm. With each breath, his control grew more instinctual, more fluid.

Anastasia and Greer remained close, lending strength when his focus wavered, celebrating each breakthrough with quiet encouragement.

The freshwater lagoon still hummed with latent energy as they trudged back to camp, their clothes soaked through and clinging to their skin, hair plastered messily to their foreheads. Max ran a hand through his dripping hair, flicking a cascade of droplets into the fading light.

"I think I absorbed half this spring today," he muttered.

Greer wrung out the sleeve of her tunic, producing a steady stream of water that splashed onto the sand.

"Congratulations," she said dryly. "You're officially part fish."

Anastasia stretched her arms overhead, her muscles relaxing with a deep, satisfied sigh.

"Told you you'd get the hang of it."

Max collapsed onto a sun-warmed rock near the edge of camp, letting the last rays of sunlight bake some warmth back into his chilled limbs.

"Yeah—right up until that weird pulse thing happened. What was that?"

"The lagoon laughing at you," Greer replied without missing a beat, already rummaging through their supply pack. She pulled out a tightly wrapped parcel—seaweed folded around a piece of roasted fish—and tossed it his way.

"Eat. You'll need your strength for tomorrow."

Anastasia lowered herself beside him, her damp curls catching the evening glow as she unwrapped her own meal.

"It wasn't laughing," she said, voice soft. "That's just how water talks when it's happy."

Max raised a skeptical brow.

"Water has moods now?"

"Obviously." Greer took a hearty bite, gesturing with her half-eaten parcel. "Rivers are chatty. Lakes are sleepy. Oceans—complete drama queens."

Anastasia nodded solemnly.

"And ponds? Absolute gossips."

Max snorted mid-bite, nearly choking on his fish.

"So what does that make our grumpy river from yesterday?"

"A toddler throwing a tantrum," the girls said in perfect unison.

As twilight deepened, the shore came alive with the soft glow of bioluminescent algae. The water shimmered in pulses of ethereal blue, washing a gentle light across the sand and reflecting in their wide, tired eyes. Max watched in silence, suddenly aware that the rhythm of the glow mirrored the beat of his own heart—calm, steady, strong.

Greer flopped onto her back with a theatrical groan.

"Ugh. Romantic water tomorrow. Just what I needed."

Anastasia nudged her with her foot.

"Hush. It's beautiful."

Max leaned back, hands laced behind his head, and gazed up at the sky streaked with stars. For the first time since arriving in the Water Realm, it didn't feel alien or overwhelming. It felt... familiar. Not just a place to pass through, but one worth remembering. One that tugged at something deeper.

Somewhere, he realised with a quiet start, that had begun to feel like home.

By the day's end, Max had not only honed his abilities—he had formed a bond with water that went beyond command. It was no longer an external force to manipulate. It was a part of him now, as natural and vital as breath.

The fifth day introduced a test of seamless collaboration. Aquael assembled them at the lake's edge, her expression unreadable.

"Today," she said, "you must prove your ability to work in harmony. Your task is to raise a large sphere of water from the lake, maintain its integrity, and guide it through an obstacle course without allowing it to collapse."

It was a delicate task—requiring precision, balance, and a shared focus. Max's nerves buzzed with anticipation, but so did his excitement.

Anastasia took initiative, assigning roles and keeping their energy in sync. Greer offered quiet insights, adjusting their formation and maintaining balance, while Max concentrated on control and stability, channeling all he had learned.

They moved as one—an elegant triad of purpose and trust. The sphere hovered above the lake's surface, shimmering with internal light, as they guided it through a path of floating hoops, narrow passages, and shifting platforms.

When they reached the end with the sphere still intact, laughter erupted from all three of them. The celebration was not just for the success—it was for what the success represented. Max looked at his companions and saw not just allies, but family.

The golden hour light shimmered across the lake's surface, glinting like liquid gold as the three of them lounged on the sun-warmed stones by the shore. Nearby, their successful water sphere bobbed gently, almost like a loyal pet waiting for further instruction. Max reached out and tapped it absentmindedly, sending prismatic ripples cascading across its translucent surface.

"Stop poking our accomplishment," Greer chided, flicking a lazy splash of water in his direction.

"It's undignified."

Anastasia stretched out, lacing her fingers behind her head with a smirk. "Says the one who had it doing loop-the-loops mid-challenge."

"That was tactical," Greer countered, sitting up indignantly. "Aquael said, 'guide it through obstacles.' She didn't specify how."

Max chuckled as the orb shimmered in response to his mood, its surface quivering with mirrored laughter. "Pretty sure she didn't expect us to make it pirouette through the final hoop like a ballerina on water."

As if conjured by their antics, Aquael emerged at the water's edge, her expression caught between amusement and restraint. "I'll admit, that was... imaginative," she said, one brow arched. With a fluid gesture, she dissolved the sphere into the lake with a gentle *plop*, like it was exhaling its last task.

"Though perhaps tomorrow, we'll aim for precision rather than performance."

"Tomorrow?" all three groaned in unison, the harmony of their dismay echoing faintly off the cliffs.

Aquael's laughter rippled outward like a song carried on the tide. From seemingly nowhere, she revealed a floating platter of vibrant fruit—berries, peaches, and slices of melon glistening with dew. "Eat. You'll need the energy for—"

"If you say 'tidal waves,' I'm defecting to the Earth Realm," Greer interrupted, already reaching for a fistful of berries.

Max plucked a sun-warmed peach and leaned back, its sweetness perfuming the air as he gazed at the first stars kindling in the dusky sky. The lake mirrored the constellations, winking back as if still remembering the touch of their joined will. Somewhere beyond the distant ridgeline, he imagined Jonas probably attempting to persuade Zephyrus to let him surf a hurricane.

The thought made him grin. They were improving—steadily, unmistakably. Maybe even enough to handle whatever was waiting on the horizon.

The sixth day carried them to the deepest part of the realm—an underwater cavern shrouded in mystery and darkness. The descent alone tested their endurance.

"This," Aquael said, her voice echoing against the cave walls, "is where water reveals its most potent form. Here, beneath the surface, under pressure and in silence, you will face your final trial."

They dove together, their bodies cutting through the still water in synchronised motion. The deeper they swam, the heavier the pressure became, compressing around them like an invisible weight.

At the cavern's lowest point, they were challenged to create a protective sphere around themselves, shielding their bodies from the crushing depths. Max took point this time, calling on the quiet strength he'd cultivated. The twins flanked him, reinforcing his barrier with calm precision.

The task was grueling. The water here was unforgiving, twisting and coiling like a creature defending its domain. But together, they endured. Their barrier held.

When they finally ascended, breaking through the surface with gasping breaths and wide grins, Max felt something shift inside him. It wasn't just about control anymore—it was about resilience, trust, and the unshakable bond forged in the depths.

The cavern's chill still clung to their skin as they lounged on the moonlit shore, swaddled in thick, handwoven blankets Aquael had produced from seemingly nowhere. A pot of something savory simmered over a low fire, its aroma—rich with herbs and spices—cutting through the crisp night air and stirring their appetites.

Greer flexed her fingers, watching droplets of water drip from her knuckles and sparkle like tiny gems in the firelight. "I take back every bad thing I said about the lake. That cave was an absolute menace."

Anastasia chuckled as she passed around steaming bowls. "You said the same thing about the river. And the whirlpools. And that one particularly judgmental tidepool—"

"Okay, fine," Greer admitted with a roll of her eyes, "maybe water in general is a menace."

Max accepted his bowl with a grateful grin, the warmth seeping into his chilled palms. "At least it's an honest menace. That cave didn't pretend to be anything but terrifying."

Without a sound, Aquael appeared at the edge of the firelight, adding a plate of honey-glazed rolls to their humble feast. "The deepest waters always speak truth," she said, her voice soft but certain, her eyes catching the flames like polished obsidian. "Just as you three did today."

They ate for a while in easy silence, the fire crackling gently as the events of the dive replayed in Max's mind—the suffocating pressure of the deep, the moment their protective barriers had merged instinctively, and the quiet, unspoken trust that had bound them together in the darkest reaches.

Anastasia was the first to speak again. "Remember when we could barely make a ripple together?"

Greer snorted. "Now look at us. Professional menace-tamers."

Max stared into the surface of his untouched tea, its stillness a quiet contrast to the chaos they'd braved. It reflected his face—calm now, but shadowed with memory. "Think we're ready for whatever's next?"

The twins shared one of their familiar, silent glances, a whole conversation passing between them in the space of a heartbeat. Then, in perfect harmony, they replied, "No."

Aquael's laughter rose like music, dancing with the crackling of the flames as the first stars emerged in the indigo sky above. "Good," she said with quiet approval. "That means you're learning."

Out on the glassy expanse of dark water, a fish broke the surface, its leap sending ripples outward. The splash echoed through the stillness like a round of applause.

On the seventh and final day, Max, Anastasia, and Greer returned to the lake where their journey had begun. The water was calm, reflecting the pastel hues of dawn. Aquael awaited them, pride glowing in her eyes.

"You have each grown beyond what I could have imagined," she said, her voice imbued with warmth. "Water no longer flows around you—it flows through you. You have not only mastered the element... you have become part of it."

Max felt a surge of emotion rise in his chest. These days had shaped him—not only as an elemental, but as a person. The trials had forged him in more ways than one. And the friendships he had built? They were unbreakable.

Max turned to Aquael, the water shimmering around her like a living veil. For a moment, he simply looked at her, trying to find words vast enough to contain his gratitude.

"Thank you," he said finally, his voice low but steady. "For everything. You didn't just teach me control—you reminded me who I am."

Aquael stepped forward, her expression calm but warm, like a still lake reflecting the dawn. "The water remembers, Max. And now, so do you. What you've learned here will never leave you."

She raised her hands, drawing the moisture from the air, the river, the very space between them. The water obeyed her will, swirling and folding in on itself, forming a rippling archway that shimmered with light. A portal—fluid, living, and full of promise.

"Go with clarity," Aquael said. "And do not forget to listen."

He turned to Anastasia and Greer, his voice thick with gratitude. "Thank you. I couldn't have done any of this without you."

Anastasia's smile was soft but radiant. "We're a team, Max. That's never going to change."

Greer gave a rare, genuine grin. "This isn't goodbye. Just a pause."

With one final glance at the serene waters—the place where he'd discovered not just his power, but his purpose—Max stepped through the portal, ready to embrace whatever the Earth Realm had in store.

CHAPTER 12

The Strength of Stone

The transition from the watery, ethereal world of Aquael to the Earth Realm was immediate and jarring. Max felt it the moment he stepped through the portal—an abrupt shift that replaced weightlessness with gravity. The air was thick, the ground unyielding beneath his boots. It was like being pulled from a dream and dropped into something ancient and real.

What struck him first wasn't the landscape, but the scent—dense and organic, like wet moss, fresh clay, and tree bark soaked after a summer storm. It was the aroma of roots and rain-soaked stone, a scent that grounded him in the present.

Ahead, Ross waited beside a towering figure—Terran, the Earth Elemental mentor. Ross's face lit up the second he spotted Max, his hand shooting up in a wave brimming with energy Max hadn't seen since the early days of their journey.

"Max! Welcome to the Earth Realm!" Ross's voice thundered, echoing across the rocks like a boulder rolling downhill.

Max grinned and jogged forward, closing the gap between them. "Good to see you, man. How's it been?"

"Hard work," Ross said, rubbing dirt from his cheek with the back of his hand, his grin betraying how much he'd come to enjoy it. "But I've learned more than I expected. Terran's no joke—he pushes you in ways you didn't know you needed."

Beside him, Terran exuded a calm, immense strength. He looked less like a man and more like a sentient monolith carved by time itself. His presence was a force—steady, unshakable, and ancient. His eyes, dark and deep-set, held the quiet power of mountains and the weight of centuries. Every motion he made seemed attuned to the rhythm of the earth, each gesture slow and purposeful.

"Welcome, Max," Terran said, his voice low and resonant, like bedrock cracking beneath pressure. "The Earth Realm embodies stability, resilience, and endurance. These are not merely traits—they are necessities. You will come to rely on them in the days ahead."

Max nodded, already feeling the realm press into him—not unkindly, but with a firm hand. He turned to take in the world around him.

The Earth Realm was nothing short of majestic. Towering cliffs loomed in the distance, their sheer faces etched with veins of quartz and moss. Dense forests sprawled beneath the cliffs like ancient tapestries, and caves yawned wide and dark beneath overhangs of stone. Giant tree roots twisted through the ground like veins, creating natural paths and tangled thresholds. Far off, a jagged mountain range rose to pierce the sky, their icy caps glinting in the sunlight.

There was no wind to dance through the trees, no tide to churn—only stillness. Heavy, rooted, and sacred. It wasn't lifeless; it was eternal.

Ross clapped him on the shoulder with a familiar grin. "Terran's got a full training schedule lined up for us. Hope you're ready to work."

Max chuckled. "After a week of being tossed around like driftwood, I'm ready for some solid ground."

Terran didn't believe in easing into things. Without delay, he led them through a thick grove to a wide clearing surrounded by jagged boulders that stood like ancient guardians. Vines draped their faces, and lichen clung to their crevices. Max could feel something beneath him—a subtle thrum in the earth, almost like it was breathing.

"Before you can shape the earth," Terran began, his tone firm and instructive, "you must respect its nature. Earth is patient. It neither hurries nor yields. It is the foundation of all things—and when it moves, it does so with intention."

He gestured to Ross. "Show him."

Ross stepped forward confidently. His hands brushed the soil as he lowered himself to his knees. Closing his eyes, he steadied his breath. Max could feel it then—a faint tremble underfoot. Ross exhaled slowly, and the earth began to rise. A thick column of stone pushed its way from the ground, the sound of grinding rock echoing in the stillness. The pillar was crude yet solid, evidence of control through practised will.

"Not bad," Max said, his voice tinged with real admiration.

Ross shrugged, wiping his palms on his trousers. "It's all about listening to the earth, not controlling it. You learn to move with it."

Terran gave a small nod. "The earth speaks to those who wait. Max, your turn."

Max knelt down, the soil cool beneath his hands. For a moment, he felt nothing but dirt and silence. Then, just beneath the surface—something. A rhythm, slow and powerful, like a distant drumbeat.

"Feel its strength," Terran instructed. "Don't command. Invite."

Max exhaled, letting go of tension as he concentrated. He visualised the ground shifting, lifting. At first, it resisted. Then, gradually, a tremor stirred the dirt. A small mound began to form. It was rough and uneven, far from elegant—but it moved because he had asked it to.

It was a beginning.

Terran's expression didn't change, but there was approval in his silence. "The connection is there. You must nurture it."

The rest of the day unfolded in laborious, meditative practise. Terran guided them through the fundamental principles—how to raise earth, shape barriers, lift heavy stones, and mold the ground beneath their feet. The work was physical and demanding. Unlike water, which responded with fluid grace, or air, which moved in quick bursts, earth required intent—stillness before movement, and strength behind every gesture.

Ross, already well into his training, demonstrated more advanced techniques. He showed Max how to anchor his stance, distribute energy, and channel focus without rushing. They practised side by side, sweating under the weight of the tasks but growing more attuned to the realm's rhythm.

As twilight bled into night, Terran called a halt. The light faded behind the cliffs, spilling darkness across the training field. Max's arms ached, and his legs felt leaden, but there was a quiet satisfaction humming inside him. He had done more than learn; he had connected.

They settled around a small campfire, its flames reflecting in the glossy sheen of nearby stones. The Earth Realm's silence wrapped around them like a heavy blanket—comforting in its permanence.

Max turned to Ross, his voice low. "You've really grown since we split up."

Ross gave a modest shrug, though the pride in his eyes betrayed him. "I've had a good teacher. But there's still a long road ahead."

Max nodded, looking toward the distant mountains, their jagged outlines stark against the deepening sky. He had no idea what trials awaited in the days to come. But here, under the watch of the stone and stars, with earth beneath his back and courage building in his chest, he felt ready to meet them.

The campfire crackled between them, its golden light flickering across the polished faces of the nearby standing stones. Shadows danced in the grooves of the ancient rock, shifting like memories stirred by flame. Max flexed his stiff fingers, the echo of exertion still clinging to his knuckles—he could almost feel the phantom weight of the earth he had shaped and moved throughout the day.

Ross jabbed at the fire with a charred stick, sending a burst of sparks spiraling upward. "So. How's it compare?"

Max exhaled slowly, the breath slipping between his teeth like steam from cooling stone. "After water? It's like trading a dance partner for a boulder."

A low chuckle rolled from Terran's spot by the fire, deep and steady as bedrock. "Boulders," he said, "have their own rhythm." He raised his palm, steady and open, and a small stone lifted from his hand, rotating slowly. Tiny flecks of mica shimmered as they caught the firelight, glinting like stars in orbit.

Ross grinned, his eyes reflecting the orange glow. With a practised flick of his fingers, a pebble rose from the dirt and began to circle Terran's stone in perfect harmony. "Took me three days to get that right."

Max watched, transfixed, as the stones spun in the air—so deliberate, so fluid, despite their weight and form. "Okay, that's cheating," he muttered. "Earth shouldn't be able to move like that."

Terran closed his fist, and the stones dropped neatly into his palm. "Everything moves, Max. Even mountains." He tossed one of the stones to him. "The difference is patience."

The rock was still warm from Terran's grip. Max turned it over slowly in his hand, studying the smoothness of its surface—edges softened by time, pressure, and the quiet passage of countless years. He traced a shallow groove with his thumb, feeling the history etched into its skin.

Somewhere beyond the firelight, an owl called out, its voice long and low. The sound echoed off the cliffs, rebounding as if the land itself were replying. Max lay back, sinking into the firmness of the earth beneath him. It was solid, immovable—and yet, not without motion. The ground offered both comfort and challenge, as if daring him to listen more closely, to feel its slow rhythm in his bones.

They drifted off to sleep beneath the open sky, embraced by the strength of stone and the quiet promise of what was to come.

The second day of training was focused more on the deeper, more spiritual aspects of earth's energy. Terran guided them beyond the surface-level understanding of soil and stone, unveiling the Earth as a living, breathing entity—an ancient force that cradled memory, power, and life itself.

"The earth isn't just solid ground," he said, his voice steady and resonant. "It's a force that connects everything. It remembers the footsteps of the past, carries the weight of the mountains, and nourishes life from beneath."

Max and Ross spent the morning barefoot in the forest, each step a lesson in mindfulness. They tuned their senses to the world below—feeling the tremble of roots, the pulse of underground springs, the hidden currents of energy threading through soil and stone. Each moment brought new awareness, as if the earth whispered in rhythms only the attentive could hear.

By midday, Terran introduced more advanced techniques. They began learning how to influence the ground's density—softening earth into sand or compacting it until it was firm as granite. Max struggled at first, trying to force the changes, but Ross stepped in with a reminder grounded in patience.

"It's not about brute strength," Ross told him. "You've got to harmonise with it. Move with the earth, not against it."

Taking those words to heart, Max shifted his approach. He let go of control and started listening, sensing the earth's response. By evening, he could subtly shift the consistency beneath his feet—creating a soft sinkhole or forming a pathway stable enough to run across without resistance.

The rest of the week grew increasingly complex. Each task tested their coordination and deepened their elemental connection. Max's bond with the earth evolved from tentative curiosity into something steadier, more instinctive. Ross, fully immersed in his training, had become not just a companion, but a reliable ally—someone who challenged Max to push beyond his limits.

Terran had retired early, leaving Max and Ross alone beneath a sky dusted with stars—brighter and more numerous than any Max had ever seen.

Ross tossed another log onto the fire, sending a spray of sparks spiraling upward. "So," he said, brushing dirt from his hands, "how are the others really doing?"

Max stretched his legs, muscles still aching from a long day spent navigating unpredictable terrain. "Jonas is probably driving Zephyrus insane by now. Last I saw him, he was arguing that 'extreme windsurfing' qualified as elemental training."

Ross chuckled, shaking his head. "That sounds like him. And the twins?"

"Anastasia's been threatening to drown Greer at least twice a day," Max said, grinning at the memory. "But you should've seen them when they worked together. It was like their minds synced the moment they touched water."

"Still trying to outdo each other, I bet."

"Worse," Max laughed. "They made bets on how long it'd take me to stop flailing like a drowning cat."

Ross raised an eyebrow, amused. "And how long did it take?"

"Three days. Maybe four." Max scratched the back of his neck, then gave a sheepish shrug. "Okay, five. But in my defence, water's a slippery little thing."

The fire cracked and popped, sending glowing embers into the air. Ross prodded it with a stick, his expression growing distant. "You ever wonder how Siobhan's doing in the Fire Realm?"

Max's smile faltered. He stared into the flames, watching them dance and shift, catching fleeting glimpses of her fierce grin in the flicker. "Every day," he said quietly—quieter than he meant to.

Ross, always perceptive, didn't push. Instead, he reached into his pack and pulled out two uneven clay cups. "Made these last week. The glaze is terrible, but they hold liquid."

Max took one, examining the rough surface. It was imperfect, pocked with tiny dents and still bearing the fingerprints of its maker. "Since when do you do pottery?"

"Since Terran decided that 'true earth mastery involves creation, not just manipulation,'" Ross replied, mimicking their mentor's gravelly voice with uncanny accuracy. He poured tea from a small iron kettle nestled beside the fire. "Turns out I'm better at cracking bedrock than shaping mugs."

The tea had a rich, mineral taste with an earthy sweetness Max couldn't quite place. He took a slow sip, letting the warmth settle through him. "You've changed, you know."

Ross arched a brow. "Have I?"

"Not in a bad way," Max added quickly. "Just... steadier. More anchored."

To Max's surprise, Ross laughed. "That might be the most obvious thing you've ever said. We are literally in the Earth Realm."

"Yeah, well," Max said with a shrug, "maybe some of it's rubbing off on me too."

They fell into an easy silence, the kind that didn't need to be filled. The fire crackled, shadows danced across their faces, and somewhere in the distance, the chorus of night creatures hummed softly. Overhead, the stars blazed as if suspended just beyond reach, their brilliance unfiltered by clouds or wind.

Eventually, Ross spoke again. "Think we're ready for what's coming?"

Max stared into the depths of his cup, watching tiny flecks of sediment swirl and settle. "No," he said honestly. "But I think we're getting there."

And then, somewhere just beyond the perimeter of the firelight, the ground shifted—a low, almost imperceptible groan, as though the very earth had exhaled. Neither of them said a word, but both felt it. The realm was listening.

By the third day, Max's awareness of the earth had sharpened. He could sense the latent strength in the rocks beneath him—the silent, immovable essence that had endured the pressure of ages. Terran now introduced a new phase of training: mastering the manipulation of stone.

The session began in a wide clearing bordered by towering cliffs, their rugged surfaces bearing the marks of time. Terran stood at the edge of the training field, his arms folded, eyes steady.

"Stone is different," he said. "It doesn't yield. It endures. To work with it, you need more than will—you need resilience. Master this, and you'll command the earth's most formidable power."

Ross stepped forward confidently. He had already spent two weeks in the realm, and his control was impressive. With a focused breath and a clenched fist, he raised several boulders from the earth with fluid motion. With a forceful gesture, he launched them toward a cliff face. They hovered for a breath, then smashed into the rock wall, bursting into clouds of dust and rubble.

Max stared, wide-eyed. "I'm supposed to do that?"

Terran chuckled under his breath. "Eventually. But first, feel the stone. Connect with it."

Closing his eyes, Max grounded himself. He reached inward, letting his awareness drop down into the bedrock below. The stones felt dense and unmoving, their presence ancient and unmalleable. But slowly, Max coaxed their energy upward. His fingers tingled, and a small rock at his feet began to tremble. With considerable effort, it lifted off the ground—only a few inches, but enough to stir the air.

Ross gave him a nod of approval. "Not bad at all for your third day."

Before Max could respond, the stone plummeted back with a heavy thud. His arms ached, and sweat trickled down his back. Still, Terran offered a rare nod.

"Good. Now again."

The fading light drenched the cliffs in molten gold, pulling shadows into sharp relief against the jagged terrain. Max collapsed onto a flat boulder, his chest heaving and arms trembling from the relentless training. Nearby, Ross methodically stacked stones into a precarious tower, each movement deliberate and steady, a testament to his control even after a grueling day.

"You made progress today," Ross remarked, just as a pebble rose smoothly into the air and settled neatly atop the stack.

Max groaned, stretching out his stiff fingers. "If by progress you mean giving myself a headache trying to convince rocks to defy gravity..."

Ross chuckled, the corners of his mouth twitching upward. "Better than my first attempt. I launched a boulder straight up—" he pointed toward the dimming sky, "—and nearly got flattened when it came back down."

A sharp laugh escaped Max. "Let me guess. Terran wasn't exactly thrilled?"

"Actually," came a deep, rumbling voice from behind, "it demonstrated a solid grasp of kinetic principles." Terran emerged from the cliffside shadows, arms full of firewood. "Just... poor judgment."

Max and Ross exchanged glances—Terran rarely handed out compliments. When he did, they tended to arrive like aftershocks: unexpected and forceful.

As their mentor knelt to build the fire, Max examined the fresh blisters blooming across his palms. "How long did it take you to move boulders like that?" he asked Ross.

"Eight days before I could lift one without it crushing my foot." Ross tossed him a waterskin. "But you've got a head start—you already understand the energy patterns in air and water. That's more than I had."

Max took a deep drink, the coolness rushing down his throat like a mountain stream. "Yeah, except earth doesn't flow. It resists. It's like arguing with a very stubborn wall."

Terran sparked the fire to life with a subtle motion. Flames bloomed between the stones, their glow licking the nearby rock faces. "Walls," he said, glancing at Max, "can be walked through—if you know where the door is."

The cryptic remark settled over them like a puzzle wrapped in smoke. As the fire gained strength, its light flickered against the mineral veins threading through the stone, revealing subtle patterns and glimmers—reminders of the earth's ancient memory.

Max picked up a nearby rock, turning it thoughtfully in his hand. The granite was rough and cold on the surface, but as he held it, he sensed a latent warmth, a slow-burning energy that seemed to whisper of lava flows and timeworn mountains—of the earth's molten beginnings.

"You think the others are struggling this much?" Max asked, his voice quieter now.

Ross snorted. "Jonas? Absolutely. Last time we trained together, he kept trying to cheat at rock climbing by calling the wind."

"And the twins?"

Ross hesitated, then exhaled in reluctant acknowledgment. "Probably showing off already. Anastasia always had a way of making the impossible look effortless."

The fire popped, sending a spray of glowing embers upward. They danced into the sky like tiny stars trying to return home. Max watched them vanish into the dark, his mind wandering to Siobhan—her laughter like firelight, wild and warm. He wondered if she ever stared into flames and thought of him.

Without warning, Terran rose. "Tomorrow we shift to metamorphic stone. Its memory runs deeper." With that, he turned and disappeared into the night, footsteps silent on the stone.

Ross let out a weary sigh and stretched out on his bedroll. "Translation: prepare to have your backside handed to you by rocks that remember when continents formed."

Max lay back, the solid ground pressing firm against his spine, the fatigue settling deep in his bones. Above them, the stars wheeled across the sky—ancient, unhurried, and eternal. Somewhere beyond the distant peaks, their friends faced their own challenges. But here, with the fire's warmth brushing his skin and the earth's quiet strength beneath him, Max felt something unexpected take root.

For the first time in a long while, he felt exactly where he belonged.

On the fourth day, the training took a sharper turn. Terran introduced the concept of using the earth offensively—shifting from defence and connection to assertive, tactical application.

"The earth is not always passive," Terran explained, motioning toward several towering stone spires around them. "It has force. It has fury. Today, you'll learn to command that strength—not just to protect, but to strike."

The stone pillars looked immovable, their bases thick and weathered as if rooted in the earth for centuries. Ross stepped forward first. Without hesitation, he summoned a deep rumble from the ground. Cracks split the base of one spire, and with a groaning roar, it toppled over, crashing with thunderous finality.

Max felt a knot in his stomach as Terran signaled for him to try.

He approached one of the pillars, placing a hand on the ground. He breathed deeply, pulling in the grounded stillness beneath him. Then he exhaled sharply, pushing his will through his arms and into the earth. The ground shook faintly—but the spire stood firm.

"Don't ask," Terran reminded him. "Command it."

Max steadied himself, this time taking a slower breath and letting go of his doubt. He envisioned the energy surging up from the depths into his body, building behind his hands. He moved decisively—and with a crack like thunder, the base of the pillar split. The spire groaned, then collapsed to the side, sending a plume of dust skyward.

Ross gave him a wide grin. "Now you're getting it."

Max wiped the sweat from his brow, grinning despite the exhaustion. Each success—no matter how hard-earned—was a sign of growth.

The scent of crushed stone still clung to them as they sat around the fire, the day's destruction now reduced to jagged silhouettes etched against the softening twilight. Max flexed his aching fingers, watching the blisters on his palms glow an angry red in the firelight—fresh badges from the grueling work behind them.

Ross tossed him a cloth-wrapped bundle with a casual flick. "Terran's miracle salve. Smells like a troll's armpit, but it works."

Max peeled back the cloth and recoiled immediately, gagging. "Ugh, that's foul." Still, he dabbed the thick paste onto his hands, wincing as it met raw skin. "Worth it if it means I can move my fingers tomorrow."

Across the fire, Terran was already focused on his next task—methodically repairing one of the toppled spires. His broad hands moved with surprising care, coaxing fractured stone back into place like a potter reshaping soft clay. The contrast between his size and his precision lent the moment a quiet serenity, a rare calm after the brute force of demolition.

"You hesitated at first," Ross said, poking the embers with a charred stick. His voice was easy, but watchful. "What changed?"

Max stared into the flames, replaying the moment the pillar had finally crumbled beneath his will. "I kept thinking about water—how you have to flow with it. But stone..." He clenched his salve-slicked fist, heat curling in his voice. "Stone needs to know you're serious."

A low, approving chuckle came from Terran's side of the fire. "Well said." The Celestial brushed dust from his palms as the last of the fractures sealed behind him. "Earth doesn't yield easily. It tests your character before it offers respect."

Ross stretched his arms overhead, joints cracking audibly. "Wait till you get a taste of lava flows. Then you'll really—"

"Lava flows?" Max choked, eyes wide.

Ross grinned, unbothered. "Kidding. Mostly."

The fire crackled between them as a silence settled in—comfortable, shared. Max tilted his head to the stars above. The constellations here were unfamiliar, slower in their drift, somehow heavier in their stillness than those that adorned the skies of the Air Realm.

"You think the others are learning combat too?" Max asked, his tone casual, but laced with curiosity.

Ross snorted. "Jonas? He's probably weaponizing tornadoes by now. And the twins?" He mimed a tidal wave crashing with an exaggerated swoop of his arms.

Max smiled, but it faded as quickly as it came. "Siobhan won't need much training to turn fire into a weapon."

The logs shifted, sending up a shower of glowing sparks. They danced above the flames like flickering fireflies before fading into the night sky, brief and beautiful.

Terran rose abruptly, his shadow stretching long and angular across the stone ring. "Tomorrow, we train in earth's most essential purpose—defence. Rest well."

His heavy footsteps echoed softly as he walked away.

Ross leaned closer, lowering his voice to a conspiratorial murmur. "Translation: he's going to try to crush us with boulders and see who screams first."

Max groaned, flopping onto his back. The ground beneath him felt steadier now—not just solid, but responsive. He was starting to sense its presence, quiet and watchful. If strength was the Earth Realm's promise, then protection was its silent vow.

On the fifth day, Terran introduced one of the earth element's most vital functions: its ability to protect. This training was relentless, involving mock combat scenarios that tested both reaction time and trust in the element's ability to shield.

Terran raised towering stone walls, shaping them into a labyrinth of narrow paths. The terrain twisted in every direction, forcing Max and Ross to remain alert.

"In battle," Terran said, "the earth becomes your armor. Learn to summon its strength the moment you need it. Hesitate, and you'll leave yourself exposed."

Without delay, Terran hurled a volley of sharp projectiles—small but fast-moving shards of rock and dirt. Ross responded effortlessly, raising a seamless wall that absorbed the blow. Max, less prepared, scrambled to shield himself. His first barrier was thin and shaky, and the impact sent a jolt through his arms.

"Faster!" Ross called out, deflecting another wave.

Max grounded himself again. This time, as the next attack came, he moved with more confidence. A solid wall of earth surged upward in front of him, absorbing most of the impact. Dust exploded around him, but he stood firm.

Terran's voice cut through the haze. "You must trust the earth. Let your need speak louder than your fear. The earth will rise to meet it."

By sunset, Max was raising shields with more instinct and speed. While still a step behind Ross, he had gained something more valuable than technique—faith in the earth's power to endure and defend. He now understood that true mastery meant more than aggression. Sometimes, strength lay in being unbreakable.

The firelight flickered against the freshly carved stone walls encircling their camp—silent monuments to the labor and sweat of the day's efforts. Max rolled his shoulders, grimacing as dull aches radiated through the muscle, each throb a stubborn reminder of Terran's punishing training sessions. Though the sparring had ended hours ago, he still felt the ghost of every blow.

Ross approached and handed him a steaming cup of herbal brew, the steam curling in the chill evening air. "Drink up. Tomorrow's going to be worse."

Max raised the cup and took a tentative sip, only to recoil with a sharp grimace. "Did you steep this in dirt?"

"Close enough," Ross replied with a crooked grin as he settled onto a nearby slab of rock smoothed by weather and time. "It's ground shale and mountain herbs. Terran swears by it for sore muscles."

Suppressing a groan, Max forced down another mouthful, the bitterness clinging to his tongue like damp moss. As he swallowed, he paused. There—beneath him—was a subtle, rhythmic vibration. A faint but steady pulse that travelled upward through the rock, familiar in a way that was hard to explain. It was the same cadence he'd come to recognise during their shield drills, when the ground itself seemed to move in sync with their breathing.

Ross followed his gaze, eyes narrowing with recognition. "You feel it too, huh?" He pressed his palm flat to the earth. "Like the ground's humming."

Max mirrored the motion. The steady vibration thrummed up through his hand, lodging itself deep within his bones like an echo he hadn't noticed until now. "It's different from yesterday," he murmured. "Less... aggressive."

"That's because you're finally listening," came Terran's voice, low and steady, emerging from the shadows beyond the firelight. The earth guardian stepped into view, arms full of twisted roots, their surfaces gnarled and slick with mineral sheen. "Defence isn't about force. It's about harmony. You don't overpower the ground—you attune to it."

He dropped the roots beside the fire, where they immediately stirred, unfurling toward the heat as if waking from slumber.

Ross nudged one with the toe of his boot. "Please tell me we're not eating these."

Terran's lips curled into something that hovered between a smile and a smirk. "They're for grounding. Tomorrow, you'll learn to ride the tremors."

Max sat bolt upright, nearly sloshing his tea into the dirt.

"Wait—earthquakes?"

As if in response, the roots began to tremble faintly, weaving intricate patterns into the soil—lines and loops that pulsed with subtle energy. Protective geometry carved by nature itself. Ross eyed them warily. "You're joking."

"Earth never jokes," Terran replied, kneeling beside one of the vibrating tendrils. He ran a weathered hand along its surface, and the root responded instantly, stilling beneath his touch.

Energy rippled outward from his palm, shimmering faintly as it passed across the rough texture of his stony skin. "It only reminds. If you want to move mountains, you must first understand how they shake."

Max watched, transfixed, as the roots continued to etch fractal designs into the ground—symmetrical, organic patterns that seemed to hum with purpose. Nature's shock absorbers, alive and reactive. He lowered his hand again, this time with more reverence, and felt it—that deep, dormant energy churning just beneath the surface, patient and potent, waiting to be called upon.

A pebble bounced off his head. He turned to see Ross grinning. "Stop looking so enchanted. This is exactly how caves collapse."

For once, even Terran allowed himself a rare expression of amusement. "Which is why we train in open fields," he said, before rising and disappearing once more into the darkness beyond the firelight.

The fire crackled, roots whispered against the soil, and overhead, the first stars emerged—pinpricks of silver in an endless black sky. Max stared into the night, his senses sharper than they had been hours earlier. Something had shifted. The ground no longer felt like a passive tool or even a loyal ally. It was alive—brimming with silent strength, pulsing with intention. And for the first time, its vibrations felt less like noise and more like a language he was finally learning how to hear.

The penultimate day in the Earth Realm was devoted to one of the most formidable techniques: channeling the force of an earthquake. It was a perilous and demanding skill, one few dared to attempt. Yet Terran, ever the resolute teacher, insisted that Max and Ross be introduced to it.

They stood at the edge of a jagged cliff, overlooking a vast, desolate canyon bathed in morning light. The air was heavy with anticipation, and the only sound was the whisper of wind curling through stone crevices.

Terran's voice broke the silence. "Today, you will summon the raw force of the earth. Beneath your feet lies ancient energy—steady, relentless, and waiting to be called upon. But remember this: earthquakes are not weapons to be unleashed without care. Misguided power causes destruction beyond control."

Ross, grounded in confidence after weeks of intense training, stepped forward first. He squared his stance, eyes narrowing in concentration as he pressed his palms downward. A quiet hum seemed to rise from the ground as if responding to his call. Moments later, the earth trembled beneath them. Tiny rocks skittered down the canyon walls as vibrations pulsed outward in rhythmic waves. Then, with one precise motion, Ross halted the tremors. The silence that followed was almost reverent.

Max watched, both inspired and daunted. Now it was his turn.

He stepped forward, closed his eyes, and stretched his awareness into the soil. Beneath the surface, he could feel a deep rumble—a pulse of ancient strength. Tentatively, he reached for it, coaxing it upward. The ground beneath him began to quiver. Encouraged, he pushed harder, but the power surged beyond his grasp. The tremors intensified, turning wild and erratic. Cracks began to form along the cliff edge.

"Max!" Ross shouted, sensing the danger.

Terran acted instantly. With a sweep of his arm, he steadied the ground, extinguishing the quakes with practised precision. Max stumbled back, breath ragged, shame flickering in his eyes.

Terran's tone was firm but not harsh. "Power without focus is chaos. Earthquakes are ancient fury, Max. You must learn to guide, not just summon."

Max nodded solemnly, absorbing the gravity of the lesson. Though he wasn't yet ready, the veil had been lifted. He now understood what was possible—and what was at stake.

The canyon lay silent now, its once-violent tremors reduced to a breathless stillness. Jagged edges that had splintered moments before were now softened, the raw upheaval tempered by

Terran's intervention. Dust hung in the cooling air, glittering faintly in the dying light.

Max sat apart from Ross, his back to a leaning boulder, absently running his fingers over the new cracks lining his palm—tiny fissures where the earth's raw energy had surged through him like fire in stone.

Ross wandered over, tossing a waterskin with casual precision. "Drink. Earthquake hangovers are brutal."

Max caught it, wincing at the dull ache in his shoulder. "Did I nearly kill us?"

"Nah," Ross replied, dropping down beside him with a grunt. "That cliff was stable. Mostly." At Max's narrowed eyes, he lifted a hand in mock surrender. "Okay—maybe 60% stable. Tops."

A long shadow stretched across them as Terran approached, his boots silent against the dust. In his hands, he held three flat stones, each etched with delicate spiral grooves and softly humming with energy.

"These will help," he said, handing one to each of them, keeping the third for himself. The stone in Max's palm was warm—surprisingly so—and vibrated faintly, like it held a heartbeat of its own.

Max frowned, turning his stone between his fingers. "What—"

"Listen," Terran said, cutting him off.

The stone pulsed once. Then again, in a deliberate, steady rhythm. The sound wasn't audible, but Max felt it resonate through his bones, grounding him. It wasn't random—it was controlled, intentional. A rhythm shaped by something ancient and vast.

"The Earth's heartbeat," Terran explained, voice low. "Memorise it. Let it guide your resonance."

Almost immediately, Ross's stone matched the rhythm, syncing smoothly. Max's wavered—jittering like a bird startled mid-flight—before slowly aligning with the beat, thudding in time with the earth itself.

Terran gave a curt nod. "Tomorrow, we refine."

Without another word, he turned and disappeared into the shadows, his silhouette swallowed by the canyon's depths.

Ross let out a long breath. "That's new. He's never shown me those stones before."

Max rolled the smooth surface of his stone against his palm, watching the grooves shimmer faintly with each pulse. "Guess we're not completely hopeless."

Ross snorted. "Speak for yourself."

Night pressed in around them, thick with dust and starlight. Overhead, the constellations swam behind a veil of sediment, distorted but still watchful. From deep within the canyon, a small rock shifted, tumbling into unseen depths—a quiet echo of the forces they'd stirred today.

Max closed his fingers around the stone, its steady pulse now a part of him. Not quite an apology from the earth. But maybe... an acknowledgment. A fragile truce between power and intent.

The final day arrived with a shift in tone. Terran led Max and Ross to a secluded, tranquil glade nestled within the heart of the Earth Realm. Here, the soil was dark and fertile, vibrant with life. Moss carpeted the rocks, and a quiet breeze carried the scent of wild herbs and damp earth.

"This is where we end," Terran said, his voice low and calm. "Today is not about power, but about presence. Grounding is the soul of earth manipulation. Without it, your strength will fracture under pressure. The earth is not just fierce—it is enduring, patient, and still."

Max and Ross lowered themselves to the ground, sitting cross-legged beneath the shade of an ancient tree. They pressed their hands to the cool soil. The pulse Max had felt before—chaotic and roaring—was now gentle, like the steady beat of a heart at rest.

As Max breathed deeply, a profound calm enveloped him. He felt rooted, anchored—not just to the ground, but to himself. The earth wasn't merely an element to wield; it was a teacher, a guardian, a constant presence.

Moments passed in silence until Terran finally spoke.

"You've done well. Remember this peace. Remember this connection. Wherever you are, the earth remains beneath your feet—quiet, patient, and strong. Call on it when you need to return to yourself."

Max and Ross rose slowly, exchanging a glance filled with mutual respect. They had walked through storms together, literally and figuratively. And though their training here was complete, something within them had only just begun.

Max stood at the edge of the portal, the glow of the Earth Realm sending its final light behind him. A week ago, he had arrived unsure and uncertain. Now, he carried within him a deeper stillness, a bond forged through dust and stone.

He turned to face Terran and Ross one last time, heart full of quiet gratitude.

"Thank you," he said, bowing his head to Terran. "I've learned more than I imagined was possible."

Terran inclined his head, the hard lines of his face softening. "The earth has accepted you, Max. Carry its wisdom with you—patience, endurance, and balance."

Ross stepped forward, clapping Max on the shoulder with a grin that masked a trace of emotion. "Don't forget your rock-throwing moves when you're dealing with fire," he said with a wink. "You're going to need them."

Max laughed, though nerves tugged at the edges of his smile. "I won't. And thanks—for everything. I'll see you soon."

With a final nod, Max stepped through the portal. Light and energy swirled around him, lifting him from the ground and carrying him forward. The Earth Realm faded behind him, and ahead—blazing and untamed—the Fire Realm awaited.

CHAPTER 13

A World of Heat and Flame

As Max emerged on the other side, the air slammed into him like a furnace blast. The Fire Realm was everything he'd imagined—and far more. The sky glowed with hues of orange and deep crimson, streaked with ribbons of smoke that twisted like serpents across the horizon. Towering black rock formations jutted from the scorched earth, their jagged peaks glowing faintly with the heat of distant lava flows. Molten rivers slithered through the cracked terrain, pulsing like veins beneath the skin of a living world. The air was thick with the acrid scent of scorched stone, sulfur, and smoldering embers.

Just a few feet ahead stood Siobhan, her silhouette outlined by the ever-shifting glow of nearby flame geysers. Her fiery red hair seemed almost alive here—gleaming brighter under the realm's infernal light, as if the environment itself responded to her presence. When her gaze met Max's, she smiled. Her expression radiated warmth that contrasted with the harshness around them.

"Max," she said, stepping closer, her voice gentle despite the crackle of flames in the air. "You made it."

He offered her a crooked smile, a nervous flutter rising in his chest that had nothing to do with the sweltering heat. "Barely," he replied, trying to keep his tone light. But already, he felt the oppressive weight of this realm pressing in on him. "This place is... a lot."

Siobhan chuckled, her eyes glinting. "It's overwhelming at first. But you'll adjust. You always do."

A presence loomed behind them. Thalion, the Fire Elemental mentor, stepped forward. He was imposing—tall and broad-shouldered, with eyes like twin embers and hair that shimmered like burning coal. Every movement radiated strength and purpose, as if fire itself answered to him.

"Max," he said, his voice low and resonant, like distant thunder. "Welcome to the Fire Realm. Here, you will face your most demanding trial yet—

not just learning to wield fire, but to master the fire within yourself."

Max's throat tightened. He had weathered air, embraced water, and endured the weight of earth. But fire—fire was unpredictable. He could feel it now, seething in the air around him, unruly and alive. And for the first time, doubt crept in. What if he couldn't control it?

Max's initiation into the Fire Realm proved as grueling as he had feared. Thalion wasted no time. He led Max and Siobhan to a rocky plateau where the heat shimmered visibly in the air, warping the ground in waves. In the distance, firestorms crackled and howled across the sky, a constant reminder of the realm's volatility.

"Summon your fire," Thalion instructed, his voice unwavering.

Siobhan stepped forward first. Her focus was immediate. She raised her hand, her eyes narrowing slightly—and a small flame flickered to life above her palm, steady and bright. She turned to Max, offering a quiet nod of encouragement.

"You have to feel it," she said. "Fire isn't just power—it's emotion. Anger, passion, the will to protect. You can't force it. You have to *become* it."

Max closed his eyes and reached inward, searching for the spark she described. But there was nothing. No warmth. No flicker. Just emptiness.

Frustration gnawed at him as he tried again, harder. Still, nothing.

Thalion crossed his arms, watching. "You're resisting," he said. "Fire isn't like the other elements. It doesn't wait. It doesn't yield. It demands your truth—raw, unfiltered. Let go of control, or it will never answer you."

Max opened his eyes, jaw clenched. That was the problem. He wasn't angry. He wasn't filled with rage or fierce passion. How was he supposed to conjure fire when he had spent most of his life trying *not* to burn?

Siobhan moved closer, her voice quieter now. "It doesn't have to be rage," she said. "It can be the fire that warms a home, the spark that drives you to protect someone you love. Find what stirs your soul—that's where the flame begins."

Her words stayed with him, even as doubt continued to gnaw at the edges of his conviction.

The sun had long since vanished behind the smoldering horizon when Max finally collapsed onto the jagged obsidian outcropping that marked their makeshift camp. His hands trembled—not from exhaustion, but from the slow-burning frustration of a day spent chasing a spark that refused to ignite.

Siobhan settled beside him, her presence steady and grounding, and pressed a warm clay cup into his palms. "Drink. It'll help with the heat sickness."

Max took a cautious sip, bracing for the realm's usual punishing intensity. Instead, a startling coolness unfurled through his chest—like mint cultivated in volcanic soil, refreshing yet with an undercurrent of heat. "How is this cold?"

"Fire and ice aren't so different," came Thalion's deep voice from across the firepit. The mentor sat cross-legged, feeding flickers of flame into their campfire with casual flicks of his wrist. "Both are extremes. Both consume."

Ross would have loved that paradox, Max thought. He missed his friend's steady presence—the way the earth's solid certainty had always grounded him. Out here, in this volatile terrain of flame and ash, everything felt unstable. Even himself.

Siobhan's knee brushed gently against his as she leaned in. "You're thinking too hard."

"I'm not thinking hard enough, apparently," Max muttered, staring at his unresponsive palms, fingers curled like unopened buds.

Thalion's shadow stretched long and wavering as he stood. "Fire isn't summoned through thought," he said, his tone more riddle than instruction. Then he turned and disappeared into the ember-lit haze, his silhouette swallowed by the swirling darkness.

The silence that followed was broken only by the pops and cracks of pitch bubbling in the nearby lava flows. After a while, Siobhan began to hum—a lilting, half-forgotten melody that rose and fell like cooling waves on scorched stone. Max recognised it instantly.

"You remember that?" he asked, eyebrows lifting in quiet surprise.

She smiled, her expression soft as the flames painted molten gold across her cheeks. "You whistle it when you're nervous. Which is always."

The familiar tune seemed to loosen something knotted deep in his chest. Without thinking, Max reached for her hand—then paused, suddenly aware of how much the gesture meant. But Siobhan didn't pull away. Her fingers were calloused and warm, her grip unflinching, a tether to something solid.

"Tomorrow," she said gently, "stop trying to *create* fire. Just remember what it feels like to stand up when every part of you wants to fall. That's all flame really is."

Above them, the smoke-streaked sky shimmered with heat distortions, warping the stars into mirages—like rivers of molten light drifting across a canvas of ash. And in that surreal glow, Max finally understood: fire wasn't something to conquer. It wasn't an element to command. It was the part of himself he'd buried, feared, and tried to snuff out for years.

When he finally drifted to sleep, his dreams didn't flicker—they burned.

Thalion was relentless. On the second day, training intensified. The task was simple in theory: call the flame. But for Max, it remained elusive.

Siobhan performed with ease, conjuring flickers of fire that danced across her fingers like tame lightning. Max, however, could only summon a weak glow—an ember that died before it ever truly lived.

The pressure was crushing. *He* was supposed to be the one to bring balance, to stand against Malachor. And yet, he couldn't even light a spark.

"I don't understand," he muttered after another failed attempt. His hands trembled with a mix of fatigue and shame. "Why won't it come?"

Siobhan approached, her tone calm and compassionate. "You're forcing it," she said, touching his arm gently. "Fire doesn't bend to reason. It rises from the heart." She tapped his chest lightly. "You need to stop thinking—and start *feeling*."

He met her gaze and, for a moment, the fear receded. She believed in him—even when he didn't. He managed a small nod, but inside, the storm still churned. *What if fire wasn't meant for him at all?*

The obsidian training ground radiated lingering warmth into the cooling evening air as daylight slowly drained from the sky. It didn't so much darken as deepen—shifting from a furious scarlet to the smoldering violet of a dying ember.

Max slumped against a basalt column, absently rubbing his raw palms together as if friction alone might coax heat back into his body.

Siobhan plopped down beside him, her boots sending up tiny embers that twirled in the gathering dusk. "You're sulking," she said, nudging his shoulder with hers.

"I'm strategising," Max muttered, though the faint twitch of his mouth betrayed him.

"Uh-huh." She pulled two charred sweetroots from her coat pocket and handed him one. "Eat. You'll need energy for tomorrow's spectacular disasters."

The sweetroot's caramelised crust cracked under Max's bite, releasing a burst of cinnamon heat that raced through his sinuses and cleared his head. "Wow," he gasped, blinking against involuntary tears. "That's..." He took another bite, the shock giving way to a warmth that bloomed in his chest. "...actually incredible."

Siobhan grinned, licking spicy residue from her fingers. "Thalion's recipe. He buries them in lava vents until the sugars crystallise."

Despite the burn still tingling on his tongue, Max found his hand reaching for more. The heat was oddly comforting—gradual, building— reminding him of the flames he'd yet to command. "Think he'd teach me how to make these?"

"Only one way to find out." Her eyes sparkled with mischief. "Survive tomorrow's training, and maybe he'll consider it."

They sat in companionable silence, watching distant fire geysers sketch streaks of light across the smoky sky. After a while, Siobhan stretched out her legs and sighed. "Think Jonas has annoyed Zephyrus into summoning another hurricane yet?"

Max snorted. "At this point? He's probably chained to a cumulonimbus cloud doing penance."

Siobhan's laugh sent sparks leaping from the firepit—until they suddenly froze midair. Max, without thinking, had shaped a drifting wisp of smoke into a miniature tornado. The vortex spun in perfect symmetry for three seconds before vanishing, its precision unmistakable.

Siobhan's brows lifted. "That," she said slowly, "wasn't just air." The lingering smoke shimmered faintly at the edges—an orange glow warping the air like rising heat. "You've been holding out on me."

Max stared at his fingertips, which still tingled with warmth. He hadn't meant to summon fire—but somehow, the realm had responded.

"What about the twins?" she asked, curiosity sharpened.

"They've mastered synchronised tidal manipulation," Max replied, tracing a watery spiral in the air. It evaporated instantly in the heat. "When I left, Anastasia was teaching Greer how to spin whirlpools in opposite directions. Nearly flooded an entire plateau."

Siobhan gave a low whistle. "Let me guess—Aquael pretended to scold them while secretly taking notes?"

"Exactly." Max chuckled. "Though she made them rebuild the terrain stone by stone afterward."

"And Ross?" Siobhan asked, brushing glowing cinders off her sleeves.

Max's smile softened. "He rebuilt an entire canyon wall. Terran actually called it 'acceptable work'—which, coming from him, is practically glowing praise." He mimicked Ross's rigid bow, making Siobhan snort. "Though he *did* get reprimanded for apologising to the boulders."

Their laughter stirred the firepit again, flames leaping in delight. Siobhan twirled a finger, shaping a figure from the fire—an unmistakable caricature of Jonas being flung in a cyclone.

Max watched her creation intently, drawn in by her fluid control. "How do you make it look so effortless?"

The figure crumbled back into ash. Her expression turned thoughtful. "It's not." She extended her palm, where a small flame flickered to life. "This took me weeks. I scorched half my wardrobe before I could hold it steady."

He watched the firelight dance in her eyes. "What changed?"

She closed her hand, extinguishing the flame. "I stopped trying to dominate it." Reaching over, she pressed his palm against the warm stone beneath them. "Feel that? The realm's heartbeat. The fire's already in you, Max. You just have to stop fearing what happens when you let it surface."

Above them, stars emerged—burning steadily through the haze, not twinkling like in gentler realms but holding their light with unwavering intensity. Max felt it then: the truth that he hadn't feared failure—but what success might ignite.

Siobhan bumped his shoulder. "Tomorrow, we try something different."

"Oh?" He arched a brow. "Like what?"

Her grin returned, all trouble and promise. "You'll see."

As night deepened, distant lava flows splashed restless shadows across their faces. In the darkness beyond the training grounds, Max could've sworn he heard Thalion's low chuckle—whether it was mockery or approval, he wasn't sure.

By the third day, exhaustion weighed on Max like lead. The constant blaze, the emotional toll, the mounting frustration—it was almost too much. And yet, Siobhan never left his side. She was patient, supportive, a quiet force of nature in her own right.

Each evening, after the relentless trials, they sat together near the slow-moving lava flows. The molten rivers pulsed with deep orange light, etching writhing shapes into the faces of the scorched cliffs. It was during these twilight moments that Max began to open up—about his fears, his doubts, his past.

Siobhan listened without interruption, her presence comforting. She didn't try to fix him. She simply *saw* him.

One evening, as they sat in silence, Siobhan turned to him, her face aglow in the lava's shimmer. "You're harder on yourself than anyone else ever could be," she said softly. "But you don't have to carry it all alone. You're stronger than you think."

Max gave a weary smile. "Doesn't feel like it. I can't even summon a flame."

"Strength," she said, "isn't never failing. It's refusing to give up—even when everything inside you wants to."

Her words lit something inside him—small, but real. He turned to her, and in that quiet space, their eyes met and held. There was a charge between them, subtle but undeniable, as if the fire around them recognised what was forming.

His heart pounded. Slowly, he leaned in. Siobhan met him halfway. Their lips met in a soft, lingering kiss—gentle, unspoken, but filled with the fire of mutual understanding. Around them, the flames seemed to respond, growing warmer, not wilder. Embracing.

When they finally parted, Max's heart raced— not from anxiety, but from something deeper.

"We'll figure this out together," Siobhan said, her fingers entwining with his.

And for the first time since stepping into the Fire Realm, Max truly believed they would.

The kiss had shifted something fundamental between them—deepening their connection and giving Max a renewed sense of direction. When training resumed the next day under Thalion's watchful eye, Max noticed a subtle but undeniable change stirring within him. He wasn't angry—not exactly—but something else had taken root: a surge of purpose, desire, and the fierce need to protect those he loved.

He thought of Siobhan, of the others who were depending on him, and for the first time, a flicker of warmth sparked deep in his chest.

He reached inward, focused on that feeling, and when he opened his hand, a small flame shimmered into existence. It wasn't large, but it burned steadily, its glow dancing softly in the air.

Thalion raised a brow, his expression approving. "There it is," he said with a nod. "Now hold onto it."

Max focused harder, trying to feed the flame, but the moment he forced it, the fire stuttered and vanished. Frustration clenched at his chest, but Siobhan was there, her fingers tightening around his.

"You're getting closer," she whispered, her voice steady and encouraging.

Max managed a smile, but uncertainty lingered beneath the surface. He was improving—but too slowly. What if he didn't master the fire in time? What if, when the moment of truth came, he wasn't enough?

The next morning brought fresh tension. Day five began with more grueling training. Thalion pushed both Max and Siobhan relentlessly, demanding more precision, more power.

Siobhan's progress was undeniable—her command over fire was fluid, almost effortless. She wove flames through the air like threads, shaping blazing walls or hurling ribbons of fire across the practise field with grace.

Max, by contrast, remained trapped in his struggle. No matter how deeply he reached or how fiercely he focused, his flames remained weak, flickering out before they could take form—or flaring wild, beyond control.

"You're still trying to force it," Thalion snapped, as Max stood breathless and drained. "Fire must flow from within. Let it emerge, don't drag it out."

Max clenched his fists, his frustration boiling. "But I'm not like you—or Siobhan," he muttered. "I don't have that kind of fire inside me."

Thalion's gaze sharpened, his ember-bright eyes narrowing. "Maybe you're looking for the wrong flame. It's not always the loudest or fiercest that burns brightest, Max. Find the spark."

Max's eyes drifted toward Siobhan. She stood nearby, silent, her expression full of concern. Her presence steadied him, and he could feel her unwavering belief in him—but something inside still refused to release. Thalion might be right. Maybe Max lacked the raw emotion that fire demanded.

The rest of the day was a blur of disappointment. He managed to summon flickers, but none lasted. The more he tried to focus, the more the flames slipped from his control. By nightfall, he was exhausted—both in body and spirit.

But Siobhan wouldn't let him sink into despair. That evening, they sat beside the lava horizon, its molten currents weaving a reddish glow over their faces.

"You're trying too hard to be someone you're not," she said softly. "Maybe your fire isn't born from fury. Maybe it comes from your need to protect the ones you love."

Max turned to her, her words resonating. His affection for her had deepened into something fierce, something real. Could this quiet, steady feeling be the spark he'd been missing all along?

On the sixth day, Max arrived at training with a strengthened will. Siobhan's words echoed in his mind like a steady drumbeat. He wouldn't search for anger anymore. He would draw strength from something stronger: his devotion to those he cared about.

The Fire Realm sweltered around him, but Max barely noticed. He closed his eyes and concentrated on the people who needed him—on Siobhan, his friends, and the innocent lives that would suffer if he failed. He didn't force anything. He simply *felt*.

Warmth surged through him, not scorching, but steady and purposeful.

When he opened his eyes, a small flame floated in his palm. It was modest, yes—but it held. It didn't flicker away or lash out of control. For the first time, Max wasn't chasing the fire. It had come to him.

Siobhan beamed with joy. "You did it!" she said, rushing to his side.

He grinned back, breathless and relieved. "It's not much—but it's something."

Thalion remained quiet, his expression unreadable. Then he gave a short nod. "You've found the spark. But don't get comfortable. Fire is more than warmth—it is power, and you'll need to master it completely. There's still much to learn."

Max nodded, feeling both lifted and challenged. He was finally on the path, but he knew it was only the beginning.

That night, the lava's glow lit the sky in shifting waves. Sitting together on a ridge, Siobhan leaned into Max, their shoulders pressed close.

"You're getting there," she said, her voice a balm to his tired soul. "You're figuring it out."

Max glanced down at her, heart swelling. Somewhere along this journey, his feelings had evolved into something undeniable. Siobhan had become his anchor, his light in the inferno.

He turned toward her, and in a moment of quiet certainty, he kissed her. It was gentle, tentative—yet full of unspoken emotion. Her hand slipped into his, returning the kiss, and for a heartbeat, the world seemed to vanish, leaving only the heat between them.

When they finally pulled apart, Max smiled, his heart still racing. "Thank you," he whispered.

Siobhan met his gaze, eyes luminous. "We're in this together, Max. Always."

The seventh day dawned with an ominous heat, signaling Max's final test in the Fire Realm. Thalion summoned both Max and Siobhan to the summit of a jagged cliff, where molten rivers pulsed below, sending plumes of steam into the sky and bathing the rocks in a fierce crimson glow. The air shimmered with intensity, thick with heat, tension, and the weight of what was to come.

"Today, you will face the true essence of fire," Thalion declared, his tone as unyielding as the stone beneath their feet. "You've learned to summon it—but now, you must prove you can wield it under pressure. Fire is alive, chaotic. It does not obey until you earn its respect."

Max inhaled deeply, bracing himself. He had come so far over the past six days, but the flame still eluded complete control. Some part of him remained hesitant—guarded—uncertain of what would happen if he surrendered fully to the fire's power.

Without further warning, Thalion raised his arms and unleashed a storm of flame across the craggy terrain. The inferno surged like a wave, licking at the stone and splitting the air with a roar. Max and Siobhan sprang into action. She moved with practised grace, weaving shimmering walls of heat to repel the blasts. Max tried to mirror her, but his flames sputtered, flaring and fading like a candle in a storm.

"You're faltering, Max!" Thalion's voice rang out like thunder. "You're letting the fire control you!"

Teeth clenched, Max fought to steady himself. Sweat drenched his brow, but it wasn't just the heat—it was frustration, fear, and self-doubt clawing at him. He wanted to protect Siobhan, to stand strong beside her, but the fire wouldn't respond. It danced around him erratically, slipping through his fingers like wind-blown ash.

Siobhan edged closer, her eyes steady despite the surrounding chaos. "Max," she called out, her voice clear and grounded, "don't try to cage the fire. Let it move through you. You don't have to fight it—feel it. Trust yourself."

Her words struck something deep within him. For a moment, everything fell away—the roar of the flames, the weight of the trial, even Thalion's piercing gaze. Max closed his eyes and reached inward, not toward force or domination, but toward emotion. He thought of his friends, of Siobhan, of every moment that had brought him here. His heart burned with the drive to protect, not just survive.

A pulse of heat surged through him—not destructive, but steady, focused. With a cry that echoed across the cliffs, Max extended his hands, and the fire responded. It swirled out in a ring of brilliant orange and gold, forming a barrier that curved protectively around him and Siobhan. It trembled under Thalion's continued barrage, but it held firm.

For the first time, Max wasn't forcing the fire. He was harmonising with it—moving as one.

When the flames died down, Thalion approached, his face inscrutable. He studied Max in silence before speaking. "You've taken a step few ever reach," he said finally, his voice rough but tinged with respect. "But mastery isn't granted in a single day. The fire is with you now, and in time, you may command it fully. Today, you learned to listen to it."

Max gave a short nod, torn between pride and the knowledge that his journey was far from over. Still, he'd broken through a wall he hadn't even known existed—and he hadn't done it alone.

That evening, as twilight crept across the scorched landscape like smoke, Max and Siobhan stood together at the edge of the lava flows. The molten river glowed like a sleeping beast, but it no longer intimidated him. The heat pressed against his skin like a familiar hand—intense, but no longer threatening. It was a part of him now.

Siobhan laced her fingers through his. "You're stronger than you know," she said quietly, her gaze reflecting the firelight. "And when the moment truly comes, you won't hesitate."

Max turned to her, warmth blooming in his chest that had nothing to do with the heat around them. "As long as you're with me," he murmured, voice low and steady, "I'll be ready for whatever comes next."

Max turned slightly to look at Thalion, who stood nearby, watching them with quiet patience, his silhouette framed by the glowing light. The weight of the training, the harshness of the trials, all came rushing back. They had learned so much—more than just physical strength, but the kind of endurance that came from facing the fire and surviving.

"Thalion," Max began, his voice steady but full of gratitude, "thank you. For everything. For pushing us when we thought we couldn't go any further."

Siobhan stepped forward, her tone equally sincere. "You saw something in us we didn't see ourselves. We wouldn't be here without you."

Thalion's expression softened, the usual stoic mask momentarily lifting. He gave them a slight nod. "The path was always yours to walk," he said, his voice gruff but proud. "I only pointed the way."

Max smiled, the heat of the moment not just from the lava surrounding them, but from the bond they shared. "Still. We owe you. And we won't forget it."

Siobhan's gaze was unwavering. "We'll carry your lessons with us, always."

Thalion's eyes glinted in the firelight. "Then go," he said, a rare warmth in his voice. "Show the world what you're capable of."

Together, they stepped through the shimmering portal, leaving the Fire Realm behind. But Max knew the fire wasn't gone—it had found a home within him, and its journey had only just begun.

CHAPTER 14

The Gathering Storm

Max and Siobhan stepped through the fiery portal, emerging into the cool hush of the forest. The crisp breeze brushing against their skin was a welcome contrast to the blistering heat of the Fire Realm. Birds called from the treetops, leaves rustled softly overhead—familiar sounds that once would have brought comfort. But everything felt different now. They had changed. All of them had.

Over the past month, each of the Travellers had been shaped by the elemental realms they had trained in—bent, broken, and rebuilt by air, water, earth and fire. Their time apart had left marks deeper than scars; it had forged them into something more.

As Max and Siobhan stepped into the clearing, the ancient stone circle came into view—weathered and quiet, the same place where they had once stood before parting ways. The others were already gathered.

Anastasia and Greer sat side by side, their usually immaculate attire still damp with the lingering moisture of the Water Realm. Jonas stood nearby, the ever-present breeze tugging playfully at his dark hair. Ross leaned against a tree, arms crossed, his body taut with strength, his posture so rooted it felt as if the earth itself held him steady.

A wave of emotion surged in Max's chest—warmth, relief, something like pride. These weren't just fellow travellers anymore. They were his people. His family.

"Max! Siobhan!" Anastasia's voice rang out as she leapt to her feet, her face breaking into a wide, genuine smile. She rushed over, her arms flung open in greeting. "It's so good to see you both!"

Greer gave a small nod, her typically composed demeanor brightened by a rare, playful grin. "You made it through Fire, huh? What's it like walking out of an inferno?"

Max chuckled, running a hand through his sweat-dampened hair. "Let's just say I walked out a little crispier than I went in."

Siobhan looked at him fondly, her eyes glowing with quiet pride. "He's being modest. He did more than understand it—he stood in the heart of it."

Ross pushed off the tree and strode toward them, clasping Max's hand with a solid grip. His eyes narrowed slightly, a smirk playing on his lips. "You look different, mate. There's a bit more heat behind those eyes." His gaze flicked subtly to Siobhan, the smirk deepening. "And I'm not just talking about the flames."

Max's cheeks flushed as Ross's implication struck home. The Fire Realm hadn't only changed his abilities—it had changed his heart. That moment between him and Siobhan—the kiss, the closeness—it hadn't faded. If anything, it had settled deeper inside him. He glanced at her. She met his eyes, cheeks tinged with the same unspoken truth. The others clearly hadn't missed the shift between them.

Anastasia raised a teasing eyebrow. "So... besides harnessing fire, anything *else* ignite over there?"

Before Max could muster a reply, Jonas broke in, cutting through the laughter with a more serious tone. "Alright, alright—save the romance for later. We've all been to hell and back. Let's hear it—what were the other realms like?"

They sat together in a loose circle on the grass, the afternoon sun spilling through the trees in fractured light as each of them began to speak.

Jonas shared first—his experience in the Air Realm had been grueling, requiring delicate control and relentless focus. Winds could be wild, playful, even violent, and learning to ride their rhythms had pushed him to his limits.

Anastasia and Greer described the depth and unpredictability of the Water Realm, how they had learned not to fight the currents but to become part of them, to move in harmony with the tides and let go of control in order to find power.

Ross spoke last before Max, recounting how the Earth Realm had grounded him, taught him patience and persistence. He'd come back physically stronger, yes, but his real transformation had been inward—a deeper connection to the land, to something ancient and unshakable.

When Max's turn came, he spoke of fire—its rage, its beauty, the razor-thin edge between destruction and rebirth. He spoke of learning to channel its chaos without being consumed. But he held back the deeper truth. He didn't tell them about the quiet hum still lingering beneath his skin, a fire that hadn't settled. Something unfinished. Something waiting.

Eventually, their stories dwindled into silence. It wasn't awkward—it was shared. A moment of stillness after the storm of experiences.

They were stronger, yes, but with that strength came the growing shadow of what lay ahead.

Ross finally broke the quiet, his voice low and thoughtful. "It's good to be back, but... something's coming. I feel it. Like the air before lightning strikes."

Max nodded slowly, his eyes fixed on the forest's edge. "I've felt it too. The quiet before everything changes."

***

Far from the peace of the forest, deep in the blackened lands of Malachor's domain, a different energy stirred—colder, crueler.

Malachor sat perched upon his jagged obsidian throne, his cloak draped like shadows over his form, eyes gleaming with calculated malice. Before him, his forces amassed—monstrous, unwavering. The Travellers, once insignificant, had now become necessary pieces in his grand design. They had survived the elemental realms, grown stronger. Perfect.

Now the final game could begin.

Within the towering, bone-forged walls of his citadel, his most trusted generals arrived one by one—summoned from across the fractured realms, each as deadly as the next, relentless in their pursuit.

Nekros was the first—his long, black robes trailing behind him like smoke. The necromancer bowed low, his voice dry as dust. "My lord, the legions of the dead await. Their souls hunger for release... or revenge."

Karos followed, his armor darkened with soot, eyes glowing with bloodlust. "My battalions stand ready, sharpened and ruthless. We await only your command, and the mortal realms will fall."

Then, barely visible even as she moved, came Talia—cloak wrapped tight around her, face hidden in a veil of shadow. "They will not hide from me," she whispered. "I will find them. I always do."

Last came Zarn—massive and hulking, a behemoth of stone twisted by Malachor's corruption. His voice rumbled like splitting bedrock. "Walls will crumble. No stronghold can defy me."

Malachor rose slowly, his presence suffocating the air around him. He stepped forward, each motion deliberate, a predator closing in. His voice was quiet but cut like a dagger. "The relics the Travellers carry... they are the key. They think they've grown strong. But they only bring me closer to what I desire. They cannot hide. We will find them. I will take what is mine."

Miles away, in the heart of the forest clearing, the Travellers remained unaware. But they were being watched.

Talia, concealed within a magical projection conjured by Nekros, observed them from afar—eyes scanning every detail, every gesture. Their strengths. Their weaknesses. Their bonds.

"They're still together," she murmured, her voice floating through the projection. "Just as you said. But not for long."

Malachor's reply echoed across the dark realm like thunder. "Tell the others to prepare. The hunt begins."

Across the broken land, his army stirred. Zarn's footsteps shook the ground. Karos's soldiers raised their blades. Nekros whispered to the dead. And Talia vanished into darkness.

The war had begun.

***

That night, beneath a canopy of stars, the Travellers sat in quiet companionship around a modest fire. The orange glow flickered across their faces, but the usual sense of peace that accompanied warmth was missing. An invisible weight pressed in on all of them.

Max sat close to Siobhan, their fingers brushing now and then, each touch lingering a little longer than it needed to. Across from them, Ross stared into the fire as if trying to read the future in the dance of its flames. Jonas lay stretched out on the grass, eyes to the heavens, seeking strength from the very skies he had come to command. Anastasia and Greer leaned close together, their calm presence a soft echo of the water they'd come from.

Eventually, Ross spoke, his voice heavy with reflection. "We've all changed. When we first came here, we were lost—clueless. Now... it's like we're carrying something inside. Something we didn't have before."

Jonas turned his head, propping himself up on one elbow. "Yeah. I feel it too. But there's something else. I swear... I keep thinking we're not alone."

Anastasia shivered, though the night was warm. "Like there's a shadow always just behind us. Watching. Waiting."

Greer's voice was almost a whisper. "It's him, isn't it? Malachor. He's not just coming. He's already here."

Max's mind drifted to the relics they had acquired—mystical artifacts brimming with ancient energy, each uniquely attuned to an elemental force they had come to understand, if not yet master. These relics weren't just powerful tools; they were lifelines, each one a bond forged between wielder and element.

Around him, the others clutched their relics close, their expressions solemn with the unspoken knowledge that what they carried wasn't simply magical—it was essential. Without these relics, they might not survive what was coming.

"Whatever it is," Siobhan said, her voice steady but edged with purpose, "we need to be ready. We didn't endure all this training for nothing."

A stillness followed her words. The fire crackled softly, its amber glow dancing across their faces as each of them wrestled with the same unspoken question: *Had they grown enough?* And if not, would it matter?

***

While the Travellers tried to shake the uneasy tension clinging to them like a second skin, far across the realms in the obsidian corridors of Malachor's citadel, a different kind of stillness settled—one born of brooding power.

Nekros, the necromancer, knelt before the throne, his skeletal fingers curled in reverence as he awaited his master's word. The chamber was thick with shadow, the air charged with something ancient and malevolent.

"The Travellers are gaining strength," Nekros rasped, his voice scraping the silence like bone on stone.

"Their powers have evolved since entering the elemental realms. They are no longer as naive as when they first arrived."

Malachor's voice, low and commanding, reverberated off the cold stone walls. "Their strength means nothing if they lack the wisdom to wield it. They are still children, grasping at forces they barely comprehend. But even fools may become dangerous if left unchecked."

He rose from his throne in a swirl of ink-dark robes, his every movement like smoke taking shape. "Mobilise our forces. We strike when the time is right—not a moment sooner. I want them shattered before they even understand they've been defeated."

A twisted grin curled Nekros's lips. "As you wish, my lord. They will not escape what's coming."

Malachor turned toward the vortex of shadows that churned at the far end of the hall, his gaze hard and unyielding. His eyes burned with ambition, not for conquest alone—but for possession.

"The relics will be mine. And when they are," he said, voice a whisper laced with thunder, "this world will kneel."

***

Back in the clearing, under a blanket of starlight, the Travellers made a quiet pact to rest. Though the road ahead was steeped in uncertainty, they understood that their strength—both magical and emotional—would need time to restore.

The campfire burned low, throwing long, flickering shadows into the forest beyond. Max and Siobhan wandered away from the circle, drawn by the hush of the surrounding trees and the rare stillness that came in the aftermath of chaos.

They walked in silence for a while, the cool air from the Fire Realm's edge brushing against their skin like a whispered promise. Moonlight filtered through the canopy above, casting soft silver patterns over the path ahead.

Max stole a glance at Siobhan. Her face, touched by the moon's glow, bore a quiet strength. She had changed—grown sharper, more confident. There was fire in her now, not just in the element she controlled, but in the way she carried herself. Still, beneath that flame, he saw something softer—something new.

"I've been thinking," Max said quietly, breaking the silence, "about what's coming. I don't know what Malachor's planning, but I can feel it... like a storm just beyond the horizon. Worse than anything we've faced."

Siobhan turned toward him, her eyes reflective. "You're probably right. But we're not who we used to be. We've trained, we've fought... and we'll face whatever's next the same way we always have. Together."

Max nodded slowly, though unease lingered. "Don't you find it strange?" he asked. "That I can channel fire... but it doesn't always feel like it's mine? Like I'm borrowing it, not commanding it."

Siobhan gently placed a hand on his arm. Her touch was grounding, warm in a way that went beyond elemental affinity. "Fire is unlike the other elements. It doesn't just answer to willpower—it answers to emotion. Passion. Fury. Love. It's raw, unpredictable. To command it, you need to connect with something deeper than strength."

Max exhaled, a soft sigh of frustration. "That's what worries me. I don't have that kind of fire. Not the kind that sets fire to the world. What if I never find it?"

She stepped closer, her gaze unwavering. "What if it's not about finding it, but about trusting it when it comes. Maybe it's something else—something you haven't discovered yet."

He looked at her, eyes searching. In that moment, the world quieted. The looming threat of Malachor, the relics, the journey—they all faded. There was only Siobhan, her hand still on his arm, her presence a steady flame in the dark.

Without another word, Max leaned in. His lips met hers—tentative at first, then certain. The kiss was gentle, but it carried the weight of everything unspoken between them. In that fleeting embrace, the storm held off.

When they parted, Siobhan smiled, the firelight catching the curve of her lips. "See?" she whispered.

"There's more fire in you than you think."

Max laughed softly, the tension in his chest loosening. "Maybe I just needed the right kind of spark."

***

As night deepened, the Travellers lingered close to one another, taking comfort in their shared silence. It wasn't safety—but it was something close. Yet far beyond their camp, past the veil of trees and realms, Malachor's preparations neared completion.

In the citadel's inner sanctum, Nekros stood before a tall, obsidian mirror, its surface rippling like disturbed water. Within its reflection, he could see the Travellers huddled around their dwindling fire, unaware of the encroaching danger.

"They still believe they are hidden," he murmured, his voice low with contempt. "Fools."

Behind him, Karos and Talia waited in silence, their armies—one of shadows, the other of corrupted nature—primed for deployment. Beside them, Zarn, the Earth Elemental General, let out a low growl, eager for battle.

Malachor's voice broke the stillness like a thunderclap. "It is time. Begin the hunt. Let them know the shadows are no longer distant. Let them *feel* our presence. And when their guard is broken, we will strike."

Nekros bowed deeply. "As you command."

The mirror's surface darkened until the Travellers' image vanished completely, leaving only a void where light had once flickered.

***

Back in the forest, as Max and Siobhan returned to the camp, the gentle hush of the woods shifted. A subtle sound—barely more than a whisper—brushed through the branches above. Leaves rustled, and the hairs on Max's neck stood on edge.

He stopped in his tracks. "Did you hear that?" he whispered, scanning the shadows between the trees.

Siobhan nodded, her instincts sharp. Her hand moved swiftly to her relic, fingers closing around it like a reflex. "Something's wrong."

They reached the edge of camp just as the air thickened—no longer peaceful, but heavy with a presence that hadn't been there before. The fire still glowed, but its warmth felt distant now, as though something unseen had drawn a curtain between them and the comfort they had briefly known.

The silence that followed was no longer restful. It was the silence before something breaks.

The first strike came without warning.

A shadowy figure shot from the trees, moving with a speed that defied the limits of human perception. Max barely had a chance to react before a dark, swirling force collided with him, sending him crashing to the ground. The impact knocked the air from his lungs, leaving him momentarily stunned.

"Max!" Siobhan shouted, her voice sharp with panic. Her hands were already glowing, flames crackling at her fingertips as she summoned her magic.

From the shadows, more figures manifested—draped in cloaks of darkness, their eyes glowing with a malevolent light. Malachor's forces had found them.

The Travellers stood in a loose formation at the heart of the clearing, each one clutching a sacred relic. Though Max held no relic of his own, he felt the gravity of responsibility settle heavily on his shoulders. Over the past month, they had trained relentlessly, learning to master the elemental forces tied to their relics. But tonight, something felt different. The air was thick with unease—like the quiet before a storm breaks.

Jonas stood beside Max, the air relic gripped tightly in his hand. The wind stirred violently around him, mirroring the tension etched into his features.

"Do you feel that?" Siobhan asked quietly. Her fiery red hair shimmered in the low light, her expression taut with concern. She hovered protectively near the fire relic, alert to every shift in the atmosphere.

Max nodded, his eyes scanning the tree line. He could feel it too—a looming pressure. The twins, Anastasia and Greer, stood side by side, their water relic pulsing faintly with energy between them. Ross stood nearby, grounded and tense, his stance wide, hands clenched around the earth relic like it was the last thing tethering him to calm.

"Something's coming," Ross said, his voice low and grim. His gaze swept across the darkening landscape, jaw tight.

Before they could brace for it, the earth shuddered beneath their feet. A pulse of dark energy rippled through the air, and then the figures emerged fully—dozens of them, faces obscured, their presence chilling. At their head strode Nekros, Malachor's trusted lieutenant. His pale, angular face twisted into a smirk that made Max's blood run cold.

"Well, well," Nekros said, voice slick with mockery. "The brave little heroes, gathered around their shiny relics. How charming."

The Travellers instinctively tightened their formation, forming a defensive circle. Max stepped between Jonas and Siobhan, inhaling deeply to steady himself. He had no relic, but he would fight alongside them until the end.

"We knew they'd come," Jonas muttered, his fingers white-knuckled around the air relic. "Just didn't think it would be tonight."

"We're ready," Anastasia said firmly, though fear shimmered beneath the surface of her voice.

Max could feel the tension building like a rising tide. Then Nekros raised his hand—and all at once, chaos descended.

Dark forces surged forward, and the clearing exploded into battle. Jonas called on the winds with sweeping gestures, sending powerful gusts into the front lines, scattering enemies like leaves. Ross summoned jagged walls of earth, slamming them into the advancing soldiers to slow their charge. The twins moved with fluid synchronicity, summoning crashing waves to drown their foes in torrents of icy water.

Siobhan, flames roaring from her palms, held her ground beside Max. She moved like a dancer, each motion laced with precision and fire. Max fought at her side, relying on his agility and the elemental training he had acquired.

But the wave of enemies kept coming— relentless, without end.

At the edge of the chaos, Nekros stood still, watching with detached amusement. His pale eyes never left the fight, calculating, waiting for the perfect moment.

"Max! I can't hold them much longer!" Jonas shouted, his voice strained as he struggled to keep the swirling winds in check.

Max's frustration mounted. They were fighting with everything they had, but the darkness just kept pushing.

Then he saw it. A flash of dark energy streaking toward the twins.

"Anastasia! Greer!" he yelled, but the warning came a heartbeat too late.

The blast hit them squarely, knocking both to the ground. Their relic tumbled free, sliding across the battlefield until it came to a stop—just in front of Nekros.

"No!" Anastasia cried, scrambling forward, but a shadowy soldier snatched the relic before she could reach it. With practised efficiency, the soldier handed it off to Nekros.

He held the water relic aloft, his sneer triumphant.

The sight sent a jolt of dread through the Travellers. One relic lost.

Max's heart pounded. *They can't take another.*

With a single nod from Nekros, the tide of the battle shifted. From the edges of the field came Malachor's generals—dark, monstrous beings forged from magic and hatred. Their power dwarfed the others.

One of them—a hulking brute formed of stone and shadow—charged Ross with terrifying speed. Ross called upon the earth again, raising a wall to block the advance, but the creature smashed through it like paper. With a bone-jarring blow, it tore the relic from Ross's hands.

"Ross!" Max yelled, leaping forward, but another blast of dark magic struck him, halting his advance.

Two relics gone.

Nearby, Siobhan was surrounded, her flames raging in every direction. She fought like a wildfire, refusing to give an inch—but her magic was faltering, her strength taxed.

Nekros began his slow, deliberate approach toward Jonas. Shadows curled around him like smoke, thick with menace.

Jonas stood his ground, wind whipping around his body like armor. With a fierce cry, he summoned a vortex to keep Nekros at bay—but the lieutenant cut through it effortlessly.

"You're strong," Nekros said, voice low and smug, "but not strong enough. Hand over the relic."

Jonas clenched his jaw. "Never."

Max tried to reach him, but the battlefield had devolved into pure chaos. Shadow soldiers were everywhere. For every one they took down, two more rose to take their place.

Then came the blow—Nekros struck with dark energy, and Jonas staggered, the relic slipping in his grip. Nekros lunged, and in a flash, he tore it free.

"No!" Max roared, watching helplessly as Jonas collapsed, clutching his side where the energy had struck him.

Three down.

Only Siobhan remained, her back to the fire, her body trembling with exhaustion. Enemies circled her, tightening their noose.

Max fought with everything he had to reach her, but the shadows formed an impenetrable wall.

Nekros approached her slowly, savoring the moment. Siobhan summoned a final burst of fire, flinging it toward him in defiance. He blocked it effortlessly with a wave of his hand.

"It's over," he said, his voice like ice, reaching out for the fire relic.

With a cry of defiance, Siobhan lunged forward, desperate to stop him—but Nekros was too fast. In a blur of motion, he tore the fire relic from her grasp, raising it high as the chaotic clash around them fell eerily silent.

Max's heart plummeted as Nekros stood tall, now clutching the fire relic alongside the others. The battle was lost. Their last hope extinguished.

Nekros examined the artifacts in his hands, his expression gleaming with cruel satisfaction. Around him, the dark forces began to withdraw, their mission complete. The relics—sacred emblems of the elements and the Travellers' final line of defence — were now in enemy hands. Moments later, Nekros vanished into the shadows with his battalion, leaving only silence and ruin in their wake.

Max collapsed to his knees, his breaths short and uneven, as the crushing weight of failure bore down on him. The relics were gone. He had failed—not just to protect them, but to shield his friends from this devastating outcome.

Siobhan stumbled to his side, her face drained of colour, exhaustion written in every line. "Max…" she whispered, her voice shaking. "They took them all."

Max's fists curled into the dirt, his body trembling with rage and disbelief. "We were supposed to stop them," he muttered, voice raw. "We were supposed to *protect* the relics."

Ross approached, limping, his face bruised and streaked with blood. Anastasia and Greer followed, their expressions solemn, bearing the scars of a battle bravely fought but ultimately lost.

"We'll get them back," Jonas said, though the doubt in his voice betrayed his words.

Max turned toward him, urgency flaring anew. "We have to. If Malachor harnesses the power of those relics—"

A sudden blast of wind cut him off, unnatural and cold, laced with something sinister. The air thickened, suffused with the choking taint of dark magic. Before any of them could react, the ground beneath their feet cracked open, and a surge of shadow burst upward like a tidal wave of corruption.

Everything happened in an instant. Jonas reached for the wind, Ross for the earth, and the twins moved to channel their water magic—but it was too late. The shadows struck first, coiling around their limbs, binding them in chains formed from raw, malevolent energy.

"No!" Siobhan screamed, her palms igniting in a desperate blaze of fire—only for the flames to sputter out, smothered by the encroaching darkness.

From within the blackness, shapes emerged—Talia, Karos, Zarn, and Nekros. They had never retreated. They had staged the withdrawal, luring the Travellers into a false sense of hope before striking with brutal precision.

The Travellers fought against their restraints, but the darkness was relentless, pulsing with ancient magic that fed on fear and despair.

Nekros stepped forward, eyes glowing with an otherworldly light, his grin as sharp as a blade. "Fools," he sneered. "Did you truly believe you could win? Malachor *will* rise—and you will be there to witness his return."

One by one, the generals sealed the bindings tighter, locking each of the Travellers in chains steeped in shadow. The relics, now in the enemy's possession, pulsed with corrupted energy, already aligning themselves with Malachor's will.

Jonas glared at them, his jaw tight. "You won't get away with this. We *will* stop you."

Talia chuckled darkly, her voice laced with venom. "Oh, you'll have your chance. But first, you'll watch the world fall—ashes and ruin, born of your failure."

And with a final surge of darkness, the Travellers were consumed by shadow, torn from the battlefield and hurled into Malachor's lair—powerless, bound, and unable to stop the storm now gathering on the horizon.

CHAPTER 15

Malachor's Ascension

The Travellers found themselves bound in chains forged from dark magic, their elemental powers smothered beneath the oppressive force of Malachor's sinister energy. Dragged through a bleak and hostile landscape by his merciless generals, they were led deeper into the cursed heart of Malachor's realm—a place that felt more like a living nightmare than any physical plane.

Jagged rock formations jutted from the cracked earth like broken teeth. Blackened clouds churned above, blotting out any trace of light. The very air was thick with corruption, toxic and suffocating. Even the Travellers—so deeply attuned to the elemental forces—could feel their strength draining with every breath, the shadows closing in with cruel intent.

Their captors—Nekros, Karos, Zarn, and Talia—marched ahead with grim satisfaction etched across their faces. These four generals of Malachor had long waited for this moment. Max, Jonas, Siobhan, Ross, and the twins had fought with everything they had, but now, with the relics lost and Malachor's resurgence imminent, hope felt like a dying ember.

As the group approached Malachor's ritual chamber, a heavy silence fell over them. Every step toward the obsidian gates felt like a descent deeper into despair. The Travellers were not just prisoners—they were witnesses to the rebirth of a dark god.

The chamber was colossal and ancient, built from black stone that pulsed with malevolent energy. At its centre stood Malachor himself— towering, draped in shadows, and exuding a presence so powerful the air itself seemed to quiver. Before him hovered the relics they had once sworn to protect, now suspended in midair, each one vibrating with elemental force twisted by the dark magic that surrounded them.

Malachor's voice—low, gravelly, and filled with wicked joy—echoed through the chamber.

"For centuries, I have waited... and now the moment is at hand. The relics, once my prison, shall now unlock my return to dominion."

The Travellers strained against their bindings, but the magic that held them was ironclad. Max's heart pounded in his chest as he looked to his companions. Siobhan, Jonas, Ross, Anastasia, and Greer—all wore the same expression: fear mingled with defiance. They had to act. But how? They were stripped of power, and Malachor stood poised to unleash ruin on the world.

With a sweeping motion of his arm, Malachor began the ritual. Dark tendrils of energy slithered from his form and wrapped around the relics, intertwining with their core essence. The chamber trembled as ancient seals began to crack, the force of centuries-old magic beginning to unravel.

The generals stood guard, unmoving, their eyes cold and vigilant. But Max, even in his weakened state, refused to surrender. He shut his eyes, reaching inward—searching for the bond he had cultivated with the elements over the past month. Air, water, earth, fire—he summoned them all in his mind, trying to grasp even the faintest thread of connection.

A sudden gust stirred within him.

Air.

The element responded first.

With a surge of will, Max summoned a razor-sharp wind that sliced through the chamber. It howled like a banshee, disorienting the generals and forcing them to shield their eyes.

"Now!" Max shouted, seizing the fleeting moment.

Ross and Jonas moved immediately. Ross, still tethered to the earth despite his restraints, sent a pulse of energy through the floor. Their chains cracked. Jonas called on the wind, sending a concentrated burst that knocked Karos and Talia back a step.

"Let's go!" Anastasia cried, joining her twin Greer as they summoned torrents of water to extinguish the dark flames that had coiled around them.

Freed, the Travellers scrambled to form a defensive line—but their enemies were swift to recover. The generals surged forward, blocking their path with unrelenting force.

"You will not leave here alive," Nekros snarled, his tone thick with malice.

The Travellers knew this confrontation was inevitable. Each one now stood face-to-face with a shadow from their past—Malachor's chosen generals, driven by dark purpose and thirst for vengeance.

Jonas squared off against Talia, the elusive assassin shrouded in the veil of night. Her twin daggers danced through the air with deadly precision, each strike a blur. Jonas used wind to amplify his agility, narrowly dodging as she weaved in and out of his reach.

"You cannot defeat the dark," Talia whispered before vanishing into the shadows once more.

Jonas tightened his stance and drew a deep breath, then unleashed a swirling vortex that tore through the room. It forced her from hiding, her cloak of shadows ripped away by the current. They clashed again and again—his wind against her darkness—neither gaining the upper hand.

Meanwhile, the twins faced the brute force of Karos, the armored juggernaut whose every step sent tremors through the floor. Their streams of water collided with his blade and bounced harmlessly off his enchanted armor.

"Your tricks are meaningless," Karos growled, swinging his axe with devastating power.

But Anastasia and Greer fought in seamless unison. Their attacks flowed like a symphony, weaving currents around his legs and aiming for the cracks in his armor. Still, Karos advanced with relentless force, shrugging off their tactics with grim tenacity.

Ross faced Zarn, once a noble guardian of the Earth Realm—now corrupted into a behemoth of stone and wrath.

"You've forgotten what the earth truly is," Ross said through gritted teeth as Zarn hurled a boulder the size of a cart toward him.

Ross answered with a surge of power, raising a wall of stone that shattered the projectile in midair. Their battle was raw and primal—earth clashing with corrupted earth. Every strike echoed like thunder, but Zarn's tainted strength slowly wore Ross down.

Siobhan stood alone against Nekros, the necromancer whose presence seemed to suck the warmth from the room. Her flames sputtered in his aura, struggling to burn through the dampening shroud of death he brought with him.

"Life always yields to death," Nekros whispered, summoning skeletal warriors from the floor.

Siobhan's fire surged in defiance, but her strength waned. Nekros's power smothered her element, each wave of undead draining her vitality. She fell to one knee, her breath ragged, flames flickering weakly around her hands.

"You burn brightly," Nekros said coldly, "but even the fiercest fire dies in time."

From across the chamber, Max's chest tightened as he watched her fall. Rage and desperation coursed through him. He had always struggled with fire—the raw emotion it required, the fury it fed on. But now, something inside him ignited.

Siobhan—his partner, his flame—was fading before his eyes.

"No!" Max roared, the sound tearing through the clamor like a thunderclap. Heat surged within him, building like a storm.

Nekros turned toward him, his dead eyes narrowing.

"You're weak, boy. You lack the hatred. That's why the fire eludes you."

But Max didn't need hatred.

He had something stronger.

His fists clenched. The walls around his heart cracked open, and in their place roared a fire born not from anger—but from love, from loyalty, from everything he had refused to give up.

His eyes burned.

His skin glowed.

And fire—true, untamed, elemental fire— answered his call.

Max's thoughts flashed back to his training. Siobhan had urged him to find the fire within, to harness it not through control, but through surrender. But to do so, he had to strip away everything—his fear of losing control, the calm mask he wore, and the instinct to hold back.

Now, that moment had come.

His eyes burned with renewed ferocity. The fear that had long shackled him disintegrated, replaced by a tidal wave of anger and desperation. The fire within him ignited, no longer a flicker but a roaring inferno that surged through his core, threatening to devour him whole. This time, he didn't resist.

As Nekros lifted a skeletal hand to deliver the final blow to Siobhan, Max's body erupted in flames.

"No more!" Max's voice thundered, rippling through the battlefield like a shockwave, infused with the full magnitude of his unleashed strength.

Fire exploded from him—a chaotic torrent of searing heat and blinding light. The air around him quivered, and the earth beneath his feet cracked and scorched under the weight of his awakening. The flames roared through him, unbound and primal, but he no longer feared the power. He embraced it.

Nekros stumbled backward, his bone-thin frame recoiling in disbelief. "Impossible!" he rasped, his necromantic energy unraveling before the blaze.

Max's gaze locked onto him, molten fire swirling in his eyes. "You underestimated me," he said, his voice low but weighted with the gravity of what he had become. "You underestimated the fire within."

With a guttural cry, Max thrust his hands forward. A searing inferno burst from his palms, engulfing Nekros in its path. The necromancer howled in agony, his dark sorcery unraveling as the flames tore through him. The battlefield was overtaken by the crackling roar of fire and Nekros's dying screams.

His twisted body—once a towering monument of death magic—was reduced to nothing more than charred bone and ash. The scorched earth beneath him smoked and hissed, the last traces of his malevolence vanishing in the heat.

When the flames subsided, Max stood at the heart of the devastation, chest heaving, his body glowing with the lingering embers of power. His hands trembled—not from weakness, but from the intensity of what he had just unleashed. The fire had nearly consumed him... but somehow, he'd held on.

Siobhan lay nearby, wounded but alive. Her wide eyes met his. The exhaustion etched into her face gave way to something else—wonder. Awe.

"Max..." she whispered, voice fragile and raw.

He dropped to his knees beside her, the fire flickering out as he took her hand gently. "Siobhan," he said, his tone soft and trembling with concern. "Are you alright?"

She nodded faintly, colour returning to her cheeks as the necromantic curse that had weighed on her began to dissolve. "You... you did it," she breathed, her gaze locked on his. "You found the fire."

Max exhaled shakily, the adrenaline still coursing through him. "I didn't think I could," he admitted. "I've always been afraid of what might happen if I let go. But when I saw you—when I thought I might lose you—I couldn't hold it back."

Siobhan reached up, her hand brushing his cheek with delicate familiarity. "I always knew you had it in you. You just needed the right reason."

For a moment, silence stretched between them, heavy with everything unsaid. Their hands remained clasped, the world falling away as the connection between them deepened. The chaos, the fire, the danger—all of it melted into the background. All that remained was them. Alive. Together.

But peace was fleeting.

In the distance, the clashing of steel and cries of war reminded them the battle had not ended. Max helped Siobhan to her feet, and they both knew this was only the beginning. Malachor still lived—and the true fight was yet to come.

Max turned to the scorched ruins where Nekros had stood and tightened his grip on her hand. A fierce fire ignited in his eyes.

"We end this," he said firmly. "Together."

Siobhan nodded, her strength rekindled. "Together."

For a heartbeat, despite the wreckage around them, a sliver of hope broke through. Weeks of relentless training, elemental awakening, and near-death struggles had led to this moment. Now, shoulder to shoulder, they were ready to face Malachor and his deadly generals. But something darker stirred in the air—something ancient and overwhelming.

Atop the blackened altar, Malachor stood at the centre of his dark ritual. The stolen relics, each a fragment of elemental power once protected by the Travellers, pulsed with an ominous glow. His voice was low, speaking in a language long buried by time. The four relics hovered above him, their protective enchantments unraveling, siphoned into his body like fuel.

The sky above them dimmed unnaturally. A weight pressed down on the battlefield. The ground trembled underfoot. Ross gripped his staff tightly. Jonas's fists clenched. The twins stood shoulder to shoulder, eyes locked on the ritual with hardened focus.

Max glanced at Siobhan, his chest tight with urgency. "We have to stop him before it's too late."

But as he stepped forward, an unseen force hurled him back. A barrier, invisible but impenetrable, now surrounded Malachor—shielding him from any interference.

Malachor's voice rose, booming across the chamber. "For centuries, I have waited. Bound in shadow. Forgotten. But now..." His eyes burned with ancient, terrible power. "Now I rise."

The relics, drained of all energy, fell to the ground with hollow clinks. From the heart of the altar, power exploded outward. The air warped. Malachor's form began to shift, expanding with the stolen strength of the elements. Air, water, earth and fire—he controlled them all now. The very forces the Travellers had fought to master flowed through him effortlessly.

Jonas, eyes blazing, shouted, "We can't let him finish the transformation!"

He charged, summoning the wind with a powerful gesture, but a wall of stone surged from the earth, cutting him off. Ross followed, manipulating the terrain in an attempt to counter, but Malachor's strength overpowered him with ease.

"He's too strong!" Anastasia shouted. She and Greer combined their water abilities, trying to douse the inferno Malachor conjured with a simple motion. But it was futile. His command of the elements was absolute.

Then, the chamber itself seemed to pause.

A brilliant light split the darkness overhead. The battlefield hushed. From the radiance descended four figures, each cloaked in a presence so immense that even the trembling earth seemed to bow.

Zephyrus, Guardian of Air, arrived first. Wreathed in swirling currents, his silver robes danced in a wind only he could command. His chiseled features bore the stoic calm of countless storms. With each step, the atmosphere shifted, as though the sky itself obeyed him. His eyes crackled with energy, and the air around him seemed to hum with anticipation.

Then came Aquael, Guardian of Water. She moved with fluid grace, her gown rippling like the surface of a moonlit lake. Her presence was serene but unwavering, a current of immense strength hidden beneath calm waters. Her hair flowed like waves in a tidepool, and droplets hovered around her like gems suspended in midair. Her deep blue gaze swept the chamber, seeking the heart of the corruption with piercing clarity.

The ground trembled beneath their feet as Terran, Guardian of Earth, emerged from the shadows. Towering and formidable, his presence carried the weight of ancient continents. His armor, forged from living stone, was entwined with gnarled roots and vines that coiled across his broad chest and muscular arms. His face bore the weathered marks of time, etched with lines that mirrored the stoic grandeur of ancient mountain ranges—unyielding and eternal. As he stepped forward, the earth responded, shifting and reshaping itself around him as if welcoming a long-lost master.

Then came Thalion, the Fire Guardian, arriving in an explosive burst of flame that scorched the air. His blazing aura crackled with intense heat, and the crimson armor he wore shimmered like molten rock pulled from the heart of a volcano. His face was a portrait of fierce resolve, eyes glowing with the intensity of a thousand suns. Every movement left searing trails of fire in his wake, yet within that inferno burned a discipline forged by countless battles—a commander of chaos, not its servant. His presence exuded both searing warmth and imminent peril, as though a single misstep could ignite the very air around him.

Side by side, they stood before the Travellers, embodiments of the raw elemental forces they were sworn to protect. Their presence shifted the very atmosphere of the chamber. Shadows that once clung to the walls recoiled, and the space itself seemed to widen, struggling to contain the immense energy their arrival summoned.

Malachor, standing defiantly at the chamber's centre, hissed through clenched teeth but betrayed no fear. "So," he sneered, his voice laced with contempt, "the Celestial Guardians finally show themselves. You're too late. This world already belongs to me."

Zephyrus stepped forward, the sound of his voice like distant thunder rolling across storm-tossed skies. "You have desecrated these lands for long enough, Malachor. The balance you've upended—we will restore it."

Thalion raised his hand, flames roaring higher around him. "Your darkness ends here. Your reign of terror is finished."

Aquael and Terran flanked them, forming a united front. Streams of water coiled gracefully through the air, the ground trembled beneath their feet, and the air crackled with kinetic energy. Their elemental forces swirled together, a harmonious storm of Air, Water, Earth, and Fire that surged with impossible force. The very fabric of the chamber trembled under their united presence—a breathtaking display of primal power fused with purpose.

For a heartbeat, it looked as though Malachor would be crushed under the sheer might of their combined strength. Blinding light poured from the Celestials, their elemental energies an overwhelming tide of natural power. But Malachor was no ordinary adversary.

With a sinister grin twisting his features, he raised the relics high above his head. Each pulsed with dark energy, the room filling with a dreadful vibration. "You think you can stop me?" he mocked, his voice reverberating with malevolent glee. "These relics are more than symbols of your past glory—they are the instruments of my ascension. With them, I transcend the laws of this world!"

Dark energy erupted from his form, coiling like black smoke infused with raw magic. It struck outward, pushing back the Celestials' elemental power. The relics—each representing Air, water, earth and fire—glowed with corrupted intensity, their twisted light forming a grotesque mirror of the forces the Celestials once controlled.

The Celestials groaned in unison, straining as the darkness bore down upon them. Aquael's serene waters turned volatile, hissing and steaming under the dark heat. Zephyrus's winds faltered, buffeted by the tainted air. Terran's grounding strength cracked as the floor betrayed his command. Even Thalion's flames sputtered, dulled by the consuming shadow.

"You cannot win," Malachor thundered, his voice amplified by the relics pulsing in rhythm with his fury.

"The elements now answer to me. Your sacred powers are nothing compared to what I've become."

The Travellers watched in stunned horror as the Celestials —once their shield, their last hope— began to weaken. Aquael's calm countenance twisted with strain as her control over the currents slipped, water lashing chaotically around her. Terran's unshakable form faltered as fissures split the ground at his feet. Zephyrus's once-mighty gales dwindled to dying whispers, lost in the chaos. Thalion gritted his teeth, flames flickering as if a storm threatened to snuff them out.

Malachor laughed, manic and triumphant, basking in the power that now surged through his veins. "You were stewards of the relics," he spat. "Now they serve me. How poetic. How pathetic. Does it burn, knowing your legacy now fuels my rise?"

With a final burst of malevolent energy, Malachor unleashed a cataclysmic blast. The chamber quaked violently as the Celestials were hurled backward, slamming into the walls like fallen titans. Their luminous forms dimmed, armor fractured, and elemental auras faltered—once brilliant, now flickering like dying embers.

A terrible silence descended.

The Celestials, paragons of elemental might, lay motionless. The Travellers stood paralysed by fear, hearts pounding as they took in the devastation. What had moments before seemed a hopeful stand now looked like the remnants of defeat.

Malachor's voice slithered through the silence, thick with mockery. "Is this all the Celestials can offer?" He turned slowly, eyes narrowing as they locked onto Max. "You and your little band don't know the meaning of true power. But don't worry... you will. Soon."

Max clenched his fists, his breath shallow, rage swirling just beneath the surface. His gaze swept over the fallen Celestials —protectors reduced to ruins. This was their final line of defence, and it had shattered. His friends stood beside him, their faces pale with fear, eyes wide with disbelief that mirrored his own.

CHAPTER 16

All Things Broken

Malachor's eyes gleamed with malevolent delight as he turned to face Max and Siobhan. A cruel smile curled his lips as he stepped over the fallen Celestials, his dark aura pulsating with raw, oppressive power.

"You," he hissed, his voice venomous and slow. "You believe you can defy me? How pitiful."

Max's heart pounded in his chest, his thoughts spinning as he reached for a plan. The elements churned around him, wild and unbound, slipping through his grasp like water through open fingers. Malachor's dominance—his command over the relics, his overwhelming force—was stifling.

Beside him, Siobhan remained standing, though her skin had lost its colour and her breathing came in short, labored gasps. Yet the fire within her hadn't gone out. It flickered—diminished, yes—but fiercely alive. She turned to Max, her emerald eyes bright with defiance.

"We can't give up," she whispered, her voice quiet but unyielding. "Together, we still stand a chance."

Max gave a shaky nod, even as dread twisted inside him. They had to fight—but how? The Celestials—their mentors, their protectors—lay broken and motionless across the chamber floor. What power could they possibly wield against a being like Malachor?

The sorcerer raised his hand, dark energy curling around his fingers like serpents.

"Enough of this." His voice echoed with cold finality. "Your part in this tale ends now. Watch as I shape this world into what it was always meant to be—mine."

With a sharp motion, he unleashed a bolt of black lightning toward Siobhan. She had only a heartbeat to react, summoning a barrier of flame. But the darkness ripped through it as though it were nothing. The impact hurled her backward, slamming her into the ground with devastating force.

"Siobhan!" Max screamed, sprinting to her side.

She groaned, trying to rise, her limbs trembling. Blood stained the corner of her lips, and the blaze that once enveloped her was now little more than an ember.

"Stay with me," Max pleaded, voice cracking under the weight of panic. He reached for her hand—but Malachor was already there, looming over them like death itself.

"Such wasted potential," Malachor sneered, his gaze fixed on Siobhan. "You could have been something greater—if only you'd embraced the darkness. Now? You're nothing."

Without warning, he drove a spear of shadowy energy through her chest.

Time fractured.

Max's breath caught. He watched in horror as Siobhan's eyes widened. Her body convulsed, a final gasp escaping her lips. The fire surrounding her blinked out.

"No..." Max whispered, the word torn from him.

Siobhan's trembling hand reached for him, her fingertips brushing his cheek.

"Max..." she whispered, her voice barely audible. "I... love... you."

Her hand fell. Her body went still.

Max stared at her lifeless form, unable to accept the truth that screamed before him. Siobhan—his comrade, his anchor, the girl who had become his heart—was gone.

A hollow void cracked open inside him. Grief, unfiltered and searing, collided with a rising tide of fury. He gathered her limp body in his arms, tears pouring freely as the sound of Malachor's laughter echoed like a distant, cruel drumbeat.

And then—something shifted.

The long-dormant fire within him stirred. First a spark, then a flame, and then a blaze that surged upward like a phoenix reborn. His pain, his anguish, his fury—they fused into a force too powerful to contain.

The air pulsed around him. The ground quivered beneath his feet. Energy crackled in the air, responding not to thought, but to feeling. His fists clenched, and the elements surged.

The fire ignited, brighter than it ever had. Wind roared, lifting dust and ash into the air. Earth groaned, splitting beneath him. Water swirled and condensed, droplets hanging in the charged silence.

"Malachor," Max growled, voice low and dangerous, filled with unbearable grief and unyielding strength.

The energy surrounding him intensified—fire coursing through his veins, grounded by the earth, sharpened by the wind, and fluid as the sea. Power shimmered around him, rippling with such intensity that even the Celestials—injured and dazed—lifted their heads in wonder.

Zephyrus's breath caught in his throat. "Impossible," he murmured. "The elements... all of them? At once?"

Terran, his aura fractured and flickering, shook his head slowly. "No one—not even the Celestials—was capable of that."

But Max heard none of it. All he could see was Malachor—the destroyer, the thief of everything he held dear. The relics still glowed in Malachor's grasp, but now Max could *feel* them—he could sense their ancient threads tethered to the elements, and to him.

He knew—without doubt—he could command them.

"You took her from me," he whispered, voice vibrating with fury. "You took everything."

Malachor's smug expression faltered. The air around Max shimmered with power, and his eyes burned with the force of elemental fury.

"What are you—"

Before the words left Malachor's lips, Max unleashed his fury.

A torrent of fire erupted from his hands, a searing wave so intense that the very air sizzled. It struck Malachor head-on, engulfing him in relentless flames. But Max was only beginning.

He raised his other hand, and the earth responded—jagged pillars of stone shot upward, slamming into Malachor with crushing force. Wind screamed through the chamber like a cyclone, and vapor in the air twisted into a tidal current, encasing the sorcerer in a whirlpool of elemental wrath.

Malachor screamed. He fought, clawing against the power engulfing him. But Max—driven by grief and guided by purpose—was unrelenting.

With a roar, Max summoned the full might of the elements, fusing them into a single, blinding surge of power. Flame, stone, air, and water converged in a cyclone of unstoppable energy and struck Malachor with the weight of a thousand tempests.

The relics shattered in his hands, their stolen magic dissolving into nothing. Malachor—once untouchable—was now a fading figure caught in a maelstrom he couldn't escape.

"You will never hurt anyone again!" Max bellowed, pouring every last ounce of strength into his final strike.

The chamber shook violently. Walls split and crumbled, the floor cracking beneath their feet. The air boomed with the deafening scream of power unleashed. Malachor, still consumed by the storm, was swallowed by the earth as it split wide, vanishing into the abyss.

Silence fell. The light dimmed. The energy dissipated.

Max stood motionless in the heart of the wreckage, his body trembling, his breath ragged.

Around him, elemental sparks drifted like ash, slowly fading.

Malachor was gone.

The Travellers—bruised, bloodied, exhausted—staggered to their feet, their eyes fixed on Max. Even the Celestials, who had lived through centuries of war, stared at him with wordless awe.

Max collapsed to his knees. His strength was gone. His heart felt hollow.

He reached for the place where Siobhan had fallen. But she didn't rise. Not with flame, not with fury. Siobhan was still—motionless—and the world was colder for it.

Tears welled in his eyes, spilling freely as the weight of the battle—and the cost—settled on him. Malachor was vanquished. But what did it matter? Siobhan was gone.

He knelt beside her body, his tears soaking into the fabric of her clothing. Grief overtook him. The fire that had blazed so fiercely now smoldered low, dimmed by sorrow too heavy to carry.

The chamber stood eerily still. The trembling earth quieted, the surging wind calmed, and the harsh brilliance of battle faded into silence.

But the war wasn't over.

From the shadows emerged three figures—Karos, Talia, and Zarn—Malachor's most loyal generals. Their expressions were unreadable, but their eyes gleamed with cold purpose. Despite their master's defeat, they remained steadfast, their allegiance unwavering.

Ross, Anastasia, Greer, and Jonas pushed themselves to their feet, bruised but not broken. Their weapons trembled in their hands, but their eyes burned with relentless fire. The Celestials—though still recovering—stood tall once more. Their presence alone was a declaration: the fight was not yet done.

Karos, his armor cracked and scorched from the battle's fury, sneered at Max with unrelenting malice. "You think this is over, boy? Malachor may have fallen, but we are not so easily undone."

Max's vision blurred with exhaustion. The searing grief of Siobhan's death and the volatile power he had unleashed still clouded his mind. But at the sound of Karos' voice, a familiar fury surged back—raw, untamed, and blistering. He clenched his fists, ready to summon the elements once more. And yet...something rooted him. Not fear. Not fatigue. A presence—foreign yet unmistakably powerful—stirred within him, stilling his rage.

His gaze returned to Siobhan's lifeless form, lying still amidst the rubble. A desperate, reckless thought ignited in his mind.

His Artbradaerial blood.

It had always set him apart—unnaturally fast, impossibly potent, more curse than blessing. And yet, time and time again, it had saved his life. Could it do the impossible one more time? Could it bring her back?

Max looked down at his arms. Veins pulsed with elemental energy, residual from the storm he had conjured. His blood was no longer just his own—it had fused air, water, earth, and fire. A living conduit of nature's might. His heart pounded as an idea rooted itself deeper.

Could this force revive Siobhan?

Movement ahead snapped his attention. The enemy generals were advancing, weapons drawn, their eyes filled with cruel purpose.

Ross stepped forward, his body Weathered and worn but his will unbroken. He positioned himself protectively in front of Max. "We'll hold them off," he said, his voice hoarse but unwavering. His eyes flicked briefly to Siobhan, then back to Max. "Do what you need to do."

Max's throat tightened. He wasn't sure if this would work—wasn't even sure what *this* was—but he couldn't let her go. Not after everything. Not after how fiercely she had fought beside him.

He dropped to his knees beside her, pulling a dagger from his belt. His hands trembled as he sliced a shallow wound across his palm. Bright crimson blood welled up instantly, glowing faintly from within. As the first drop fell onto Siobhan's chest, it sizzled, a delicate glow spreading from the contact point.

Something was happening.

The elemental force still surging inside him was reacting—merging with his blood, awakening something ancient and unknown. Max could feel it coursing outward, wild and luminous.

"Please," he whispered, voice raw with grief and hope. "Please come back to me."

He pressed his bleeding hand against the wound on her chest, focusing every ounce of energy on the connection. The blood, now fused with elemental power, seeped into her. For a heartbeat, there was only silence.

Then—her fingers twitched.

"Siobhan?" Max breathed, hope crashing over him like a wave.

Her back arched violently, as though struck by lightning. Max recoiled, startled, but the link had been made. His blood—his life—had found hers.

Siobhan gasped, lungs straining as if drawing her first breath all over again. Her chest rose and fell, weak but steady.

"Max?" she whispered. Her voice trembled, fragile but unmistakably alive.

A sob of relief tore from Max as he pulled her into his arms, tears streaking down his face. Her warmth, her breath, her presence—it was all real. She was alive. Against all odds, she was here.

But danger still pressed in.

The generals had closed the gap.

Siobhan, though pale and weakened, sat up with grit burning in her eyes. A faint glow pulsed beneath her skin—fire rekindled. "We finish this together," she said, more command than suggestion.

Max nodded, the storm within him coalescing into a burning conviction. This time, his power surged not from grief, but from love—and purpose.

He helped Siobhan to her feet as the other Travellers squared off with the approaching enemies.

Ross stood tall, fists glowing with the steady might of the earth. "We've fought too hard to fall now," he growled.

Anastasia and Greer, side by side, summoned a tidal wall, water churning with vengeance, ready to crash upon the foe.

Jonas raised his staff toward the ceiling. The wind howled in answer, swirling around him. His gaze locked on Talia, the assassin who had once bested him. "I won't let you hurt anyone else." he snarled.

The generals hesitated. Even they could feel the shift. The Travellers stood battered, but no longer broken. A unity of purpose bound them tighter than steel.

"You've lost," Talia spat, blades gleaming. "Malachor may have fallen, but we will finish what he started."

Max stepped forward, his voice steady, rich with newfound certainty. "No. You won't."

The elements rallied around him. Fire and wind danced at his fingertips. Siobhan mirrored him, flames rippling in her eyes. Together, they unleashed a cataclysm—flames spiraling with gales, a tempest of light and power that shattered the chamber's silence.

Ross slammed his fists into the floor, calling forth pillars of stone that crushed Karos beneath their weight. Anastasia and Greer's torrent surged forward, drowning Zarn in a maelstrom of water. Jonas summoned a cyclone that engulfed Talia, her scream vanishing into the vortex.

One by one, the generals fell.

As the dust settled, silence crept into the chamber. The Travellers stood shoulder to shoulder, bruised, bloodied, but victorious. The Celestials emerged from the shadows, their expressions solemn and proud.

Zephyrus approached Max, awe shining in his eyes. "You've accomplished what even the Celestials once feared," he said. "You've channeled the full force of the elements—and survived."

Terran's voice, low and grave, followed. "But remember: power exacts a toll. You've done the unthinkable today, but the future is uncertain. Be vigilant."

Max's hand found Siobhan's, her fingers lacing with his. Her presence reminded him why he fought—not for glory, but for the people he loved.

Together, they had defied darkness. Together, they would face what came next.

***

The aftermath was a surreal blend of ash, silence, and flickering light. Elemental energy still shimmered in the air, clinging to the chamber like morning mist. Max stood amidst the wreckage, the battle with Malachor lingering in his bones.

From the far side of the chamber, the Celestials stepped forward once more.

Aquael, serene as the sea, approached. "You've achieved what many believed impossible," she said, her voice echoing with ancient calm. "But the relics... their destruction has consequences. We must speak of their true purpose."

Terran, steady as bedrock, stepped up beside her. "They were never our source of strength," he said. "They were seals—keys that confined Malachor. With them broken, his prison lies in ruins. Yet this is not the end of your world."

Max stiffened. "Then what is it?" he asked, sensing a deeper truth.

Thalion, the flame-hearted Guardian, met Max's gaze. "The source of your strength isn't found in artifacts. It lives within you. You proved that today. You wield the elements as no one has before."

Zephyrus smiled, the wind stirring faintly at his side. "The darkness will return, in new forms and faces. But your bond—the connection you share—is what will preserve balance. Never forget that."

The moment turned quiet, heavy with finality. As the Celestials began to retreat into the fading glow of their essence, Max turned to his friends—his family.

"I'm grateful," he said, voice thick with emotion. "Not just for the fight, but for the heart you all gave. We didn't do this alone. We never will."

Ross clapped a hand on his shoulder. "We're bound now. Distance doesn't change that."

Anastasia and Greer exchanged a soft glance before chiming in, "We'll keep the balance. No relics required."

The Celestials shimmered like heat mirages, their forms dissolving into the ether.

"Goodbye, Celestials," Max called. "Thank you."

Zephyrus' final words carried on the wind. "The true power lies within you."

A portal shimmered into being, its energy humming with promise. Max and his companions stepped forward. Behind them, the chamber faded—once a place of darkness, now a beacon of transformation.

Max looked back one last time. "Together," he whispered, his voice steady.

Ahead lay uncertainty. But whatever the future held, they would face it side by side. And that was a force greater than any relic ever forged.

ABOUT THE AUTHOR

Craig van den Heever is a South African-born author now based in the UK, where he lives with his wife and two children. By day, he works as a Financial Controller; by night, he dives headfirst into the vivid worlds of fantasy storytelling. Drawing inspiration from his lifelong love of anime and the mystique of elemental magic, Craig creates immersive tales that ignite the imagination—especially for young adult readers.

His debut novel, *Elemental Relics*, and its thrilling sequel, *Elemental Relics: Stormforged*, explores the timeless connection between nature, personal identity, and the forces that shape destiny. With every page, Craig invites readers into a universe where the elements—air, water, earth, and fire— dance in a delicate balance, revealing the strength of the human spirit in the face of chaos.

When he's not writing, Craig enjoys staying active at the gym and drawing inspiration from the world around him. *Elemental Relics* is only the beginning of what promises to be an extraordinary creative journey.

Connect with Craig on Instagram: @elemental.relics